CW00494911

Penguin Books

CAROLE KING IS AN ALIEN

Yasmin Boland started tapping out short stories and love poems in her early teens, when her mum got a new electric typewriter. She became a full-time writer at twenty and has contributed to publications including *Playboy*, *She*, *B*, *New Woman*, *black+white*, the *London Evening Standard* and the *Sydney Morning Herald*. Yasmin lived in London for most of the nineties, freelance writing and television producing. She currently lives mostly in Bondi Beach, Sydney. This is her first novel.

CAROLE KING IS AN ALIEN

YASMIN BOLAND

PENGUIN BOOKS

Penguin Books Australia Ltd
487 Maroondah Highway, PO Box 257
Ringwood, Victoria 3134, Australia
Penguin Books Ltd
Harmondsworth, Middlesex, England
Penguin Putnam Inc.
375 Hudson Street, New York, New York 10014, USA
Penguin Books Canada Limited
10 Alcorn Avenue, Toronto, Ontario, Canada M4V 3B2
Penguin Books (N.Z.) Ltd
Cnr Rosedale and Airborne Roads, Albany, Auckland, New Zealand
Penguin Books (South Africa) (Pty) Ltd
5 Watkins Street, Denver Ext 4, 2094, South Africa
Penguin Books India (P) Ltd
11, Community Centre, Panchsheel Park, New Delhi 110 017, India

First published by Penguin Books Australia Ltd 2000

1 3 5 7 9 10 8 6 4 2

Copyright © Yasmin Boland, 2000

All rights reserved. Without limiting the rights under copyright reserved above,
no part of this publication may be reproduced, stored in or introduced into a retrieval
system, or transmitted, in any form or by any means (electronic, mechanical, photocopying,
recording or otherwise), without the prior written permission of both the copyright owner
and the above publisher of this book.

Designed by Marina Messiha, Penguin Design Studio
Cover photograph courtesy of IPL Image Group
Author photograph by Piritz Mierovitch
Typeset in 11.5/14 pt Perpetua by Post Pre-press Group, Brisbane, Queensland
Printed and bound in Australia by Australian Print Group, Maryborough, Victoria

National Library of Australia
Cataloguing-in-Publication data:

Boland, Yasmin.
Carole King is an alien.

ISBN 0 14 028964 X.

I. Title.

A823.3

This project has been assisted by the Commonwealth Government
through the Australia Council, its arts funding and advisory body.

To Claudia, Lisa and Melissa
the real deal

with love and thanks . . .

. . . to my beautiful sister, Claudia, for your guidance, laughs and patience in the face of another obsessor, to the lovely and gifted Lisa for your two-way inspiration, endless support and patience in the face of seventy-two manuscripts, to Melissa for your enthusiasm, belief, giggles and wayward thoughts, to Robbie for your Mercurial moments and belief, to Anna M for being so loyal and true (fingers crossed for Malta!), to Cliff and Moira – the best rock and proofer, Jane P for your insightful via-Darwin critique and more, to PMcQ, in whose Palace I began, to Joyy for manifesting, Nadine for printing, distributing and our pre-airport chat, to Jascha for being a smasher (and supporting Lisa, who supported me), to Big Bertha and Max, Jessica A for your generosity and chats and inspiration, Anne-Marie L and Luke D for your encouragement and time, to Philippe et Françoise, Van and Carole, Gita and Dr Thom K, Werner at the Clapham Common Buddhist Centre and Oonagh O'M (for TCP), to Sandra B and Sheryn G (AWF), Yesterfive-hundy, John P, Jenni G (GM), Dr Keith and Karen, Chris and Andrea, Fi C, MEV, Becky M, Thea, Tonia W, Annika, Gaby N, Cate P and Greg J for reading but not laughing too hard at various early drafts, to the unearthly vibes at 152 & 158 BBBB, to Toni No Baloney for our Queen Street wish, Carolyne G for 'lovely' explanations, to La Leigh for Bolly belief, Fi Mc, Vicki, Robbo, Daveena, Dawn B, Anita N and Vici McC, Scottie, Monty, Rufus, Fergle, Hamish and Hugo for those wondrous, heavenly Earlsfield years, Sir Martin Brofman (http://www.healer.ch) for teaching me how to clear a blue chakra, Judy C for her warped Tapestry *album and vision, to Pete for top photo skills, to Madonna Duffy for brilliant de-sludging and expert guidance, to Fiona Daniels for closing the deal with perfect Libran care and attention, and to Julie Gibbs for making it real . . . and to everyone else who believed that Carole King could possibly be an alien.* Thank you!

http://www.yasminboland.com

It's not good enough to ignore the mystery,
just because it can't be explained . . .
Graham Hancock, author of *Fingerprints of the Gods*

One doesn't discover new lands without consenting
to lose sight of the shore . . .
André Gide, 1869–1951

sailing out to sea

There was a tall, dark and really rather handsome man gently running his fingers around my navel.

'Take a deep breath in, Cara,' he commanded.

I inhaled.

'Okay, now breathe out, through your nose.'

I exhaled.

'Good. Now, keeping your lips together, breathe faster. In and out. In. Out. In. Out.'

What kind of way was this to make a living?

I admit it. There are times when I feel unusual. I love artichokes more than chocolate; I'd rather stick pins in my eyes than squeeze a lover's zits; I sometimes sympathise with Ally McBeal; I think many penises are *objets d'art*.

All slightly weird, I gather.

Moreover, I can't see why anyone'd go for George Clooney, Leonardo DiCaprio or Keanu Reeves over Ewan McGregor, Edward Norton or Ben Mendlesohn. Even now, I sometimes still miss Princess Diana. And Michael Hutchence. I think Monica Lewinsky should (probably) cash in to her heart's content and – *quelle horreur* – I have almost no interest in shoes.

But, hallelujah, today was different.

As I listened to a statuesque, olive-skinned and sensuous-looking 'alternative therapies healer' applying something resembling chaos theory to my breathing patterns, I felt very 'normal', in comparison. If slightly over-oxygenated.

Shanti Deva worked by appointment in Central London, with various minor royals and major celebrities. I, on the other hand, was a lowly journalist, reclined in his lavish Mayfair rooms with my tape recorder and a list of standard questions. I was to interview him for an article I'd been commissioned to write for the *Sunday News*.

'Through your nose, Cara, not your mouth. In and out quickly,' he said in a soothing, Italian-sounding accent. He placed his fingers lightly over my lips to stop me 'cheating'.

Shanti's main treatment room was certainly ideal for this kind of carry-on. The ceiling was draped with violet voile, the walls painted deep red, and luxuriant velvet curtains all but masked the afternoon sunlight outside the open windows. Dozens of flickering candles created an ambience as seductive as Aphrodite's boudoir, while Hindu sitar music wafted into my ears like a brainwashing, primordial sound. The table I lay on was swathed with green silk, and surrounded by pink quartz crystals and the billowing scent of ylang-ylang essential oil.

'Good, Cara,' he soothed. 'Breathe out slowly now, breathe out your ego . . .'

Easier said than done, my friend.

In one hand, Shanti waved three long incense sticks above my stomach, while in the other, he wielded a large pink crystal.

'Okay. Let the fast breath subside. Start to breathe naturally, Cara,' he repeated, looking at me intensely. 'As in nature, after chaos comes peace. Float. Floooooooat. Forget why you are here, Cara. Take this chance to better yourself. Your aura is very scattered.'

Shanti Deva had reportedly enjoyed great success in treating Fergie for depression, with his own special mixture of herbs and colonic irrigation. Gwyneth Paltrow and Jerry Hall had apparently both seen him for eternal blonde beauty enhancement; he was allegedly treating Posh Spice for higher consciousness and Peter André for feeling *démodé*. I, meanwhile, was trying hard to keep a straight face.

'This is Nagchampa incense, queen of all aromas,' he told me, brandishing the fudge-coloured sticks above my eyebrows like a magician's wand. I resisted an urge to sneeze through their smoky clouds.

'Breathe down through to your solar plexus, Cara. It is your power centre. It can set you free. Your powers are restricted now . . . Breathe out your fear, breathe in the good of the universe, breathe out all that is Cara . . .'

He squinted down at me as he touched the pink crystal lightly and quickly to various parts of my (fully clothed) anatomy.

'Don't be afraid of your powers,' he implored, rolling the quartz under his palm and around my navel.

I confess that I felt a shock of energy move through my body as his hands touched me. It zapped from the tip of my head down through to my toes.

'For someone called Shanti Deva, you look very Italian,' I wanted to say. With his stunning green eyes, thick black hair, Roman nose and strong chin, he looked far more Mediterranean than Eastern. Quite where he'd picked up his strange Hindu-sounding name, I had no idea. I presumed it was in southern India, where fifty rupees bought you a more spiritual personality, a Bindi spot and an instant knowledge of karma and Tantra.

Now didn't seem the right time to start firing probing questions, though, despite the fact that I was growing desperate to talk about something other than my 'powers'.

'Don't be afraid,' he repeated, as if this should mean something to me now. 'I am using the crystal to work through your aura, Cara. Pink quartz has long symbolised love.' He clicked his fingers in an arc around my head. 'Your fear of your powers means you are restricting them, Cara. Just relax.'

I was honestly trying not to be afraid of my 'powers', whatever they were. Out of this little incense-waving session I was supposed to get a one-page article for the *Sunday News*; any 'healer' possibly in contact with Gwyneth Paltrow's solar plexus was good enough to warrant at least a one-page feature. Throw in a few crystals – and a heavy hint of Posh Spice – and you could easily stretch it to a double-page spread.

As it transpired, Shanti Deva was happy to treat me for the article, and to wax lyrical about my power centre, but he steadfastly refused to confirm or deny having celebrity clients. This wasn't surprising; it was a well-known fact in metaphysical circles that the quickest way for a 'healer' to lose a famous patient was to do more than hint they might be on your books.

Setting down the incense and crystal, Shanti started applying a sweet-smelling oil into a point between my eyebrows.

'This is a mixture of mint and neroli for your third eye,' he intoned. His finger rubbed lightly, in a circular motion. 'It dissolves blockages and sharpens the senses. Your third eye sees beyond this third dimension, but yours has been asleep for twenty-three lifetimes. It is opening up. I can see it blinking into the daylight –'

'What do you mean lifetimes?' I interrupted, wondering if third eyes wore mascara.

'Lifetimes, past lives, reincarnations, Cara.' He then ran his fingers in a light, spidery motion from my navel, over my stomach, between my breasts, over my throat, neck, forehead and to the top of my head.

'This clears your meridians and connects you with your past lives,' he said. 'So you won't be afraid of your powers any more . . .'

'How many past lives have I had, Mr Deva?'

'Eighty-seven. You and I have known each other in three of them.'

Lord.

His hand came to a sudden halt above my stomach.

'Power cut?' I asked, grinning.

'You've had an upset stomach.'

'Oh. I have, yes,' I admitted. 'I think I ate a dodgy curry the other night –'

'It's nothing to do with what you've eaten, Cara. The upset was a medium for the message. There is something in your life now that you can't stomach. What is it?'

'I'm not sure, Mr Deva.'

'Think about it.'

Could it be that I am sent to write articles about people like you?

'You are on a mission. Learn by your dreams, Cara,' he insisted. 'Promise me you will keep a dream diary, at least for a month.'

'What do you mean?'

'When you wake up, write down your dreams. Or even better, keep a tape recorder by your bed and speak into it when you awake . . .'

'Okay.' Anything for some peace.

'Good. Rest a while now.'

By the time I got home from Shanti's late session, it was well past dinner-time. Neither of my flatmates, Monique or Lucy, was to be found, so I took a cup of decaf to my room and prepared to settle in for the night. I loved my room; I loved that when the curtains were open I could lie in bed and see out onto our leafy, usually overgrown garden below. Back when I was in love and in bed with my ex, Jonathan, or even these days, single and with just our adopted stray cat, Mouser, for company (and the *Sunday Times* or the *Guardian*, and toast and tea and Radio One), I felt I could be happy here for the rest of my life.

Shanti's session had exhausted me, so I hit the hay around 10.30 p.m. – only to wake up during the night in a very weird dream state. As I gazed into the dark, I could see my bed, but somehow it looked foreign. The bed, all the bedroom furniture, even the walls of my room, now seemed to be made out of three-dimensional perspex. I was lying on top of a slab-like perspex bed.

As panic rose, I reassured myself I was a normal person having a strange dream. Shanti Deva would surely have an explanation for this. Stress? Exhaustion? Third eye thrombosis?

I saw a man.

Just gorgeous. Amazing. With deep brown eyes. Almost black. He had something like love or harmony emanating from him, his eyes and his cheeky grin. When I say I 'saw' him, what I mean is that I imagined that I could see him, I could feel his presence, his warmth. His brown eyes radiated beauty and loving. They loved me. He had a sort of naughty half-smile on his lips, too. A sexy smile. His skin was olive. He was beautiful.

My imagination wandered further. In my hallucinogenic haze I said goodbye to the man in my vision and felt as though I was floating up to the ceiling of my bedroom, able to look down at myself.

I could see myself tucked up in bed under my duvet cover with the pink, blue and white clouds on it. Attaching 'me' up on the ceiling to my body below was a long, shimmering silver cord. My body was like an anchor to the me floating about. I could control my movements up here above myself. I drifted left and right.

'Hey, you!' the me-on-the-ceiling said to the me-in-bed.

'Yeah?'

'Do yourself a favour.'

'What?'

'Go to Cameron Street.'

'What? Where's Cameron Street?'

'Good question.'

Weird.

Maybe I could fly around my room. Or even around the house. Moni and Lucy had to be home by now, and tucked up in their beds. I was sure they wouldn't mind an intrusion made in the name of metaphysics.

Feeling a little like Tinkerbell on acid, I floated through the crack between the wall and my bedroom door and up the corridor, onto the first landing and into Lucy's room. Blonde and doll-like, she was snuggled up in bed with her duvet up to her chin. Her bobbed strawberry-blonde hair was spread out in a messy fan behind her, lit up by moonlight which poured in through the windows. She looked so beautiful as she lay there asleep, I wished I had a camera. It was a shame she would never know how she looked tonight.

I thought of Monique and, in an instant, I was in her room. This time, no travelling was needed. What a dream. This was like magic.

Omigod.

Oh, shit.

Monique was . . . she was bonking someone. She was on top of him. Astride. Puffing and panting, her auburn hair flying as she gyrated on him. Shit. It was Rufus. Rufus! Moni was shagging our friend Rufus.

I whizzed out of her room and back to my own.

This was incredible. What a cool way to travel.

I stole a peek at myself below. There I was, asleep on my side, cuddling my pillow. My room was dark, but I could see myself. My dark brown hair, longish and straight, had fallen across my face. My eyes were closed. And I was, of course, bloody alone as usual. Even Mouser had deserted me, out through his series of cat flaps. I was just glad to look down and see I didn't have two chins. And at least I wasn't snoring.

I followed the silver cord towards my body, resumed my position inside it, stared at the ceiling and thought, 'Wow!'

The next day, as I wrote up the Shanti Deva article from home, I decided against mentioning the weird dream. Instead, I wrote the piece very straight, figuring that readers would interpret Shanti's aura-speak for themselves. In many ways, Shanti Deva was an easy target for a newspaper journalist like me – a rich millennium hippy in a white 'healer's' coat, a champagne New Age mystic who allegedly charged his celebrity patients hundreds of pounds per session. But he was right about one thing. I definitely should start keeping a dream diary.

just say 'om'

Whatever Shanti Deva did with those crystals and joss sticks left me light-headed for days afterwards. I felt vaguely disorientated, and some very strange events occurred.

On the day that my article appeared, in fact as a direct result of it, I was contacted by a spook mystic woman named Gaelle Carrington-Keane. If Shanti Deva was a garden variety New Age hippy, Gaelle Carrington-Keane was the deluxe, prize-winning glasshouse version.

When the phone rang, I was at home alone, sitting at the kitchen table with fresh air and sunshine pouring in through the open windows, sipping coffee and staring at a pile of very nasty bills, set out in front of me in order of urgency of payment.

My main dilemma was how I was going to be able to afford the rent, credit card and electricity bills without committing myself to writing a six-page Before/During/After horror feature on liposuction, focussing on one of Hollywood's cosmetic-surgeons-to-the-stars. I wasn't even going to get to go to Hollywood to write the piece. Chance would be a fine thing. The magazine I'd be writing for would send me the gory pictures, then I'd interview US liposuctioner and liposuctionee over the phone. I was queasy at the best of times and the idea made me feel bilious. I did, however, need the money, as I'd been slacking off lately, waiting for some interesting work to come up. Before Shanti Deva, it had been women's mag classics such as 'My Boyfriend Left Me for Another Man' and the like.

I picked up the ringing phone.

'Cara?' an older female voice asked, sounding as if she knew me, but otherwise unfamiliar.

'Yes?'

'Hello, Cara. My name is Mrs Gaelle Carrington-Keane — that's G-a-e-l-l-e Carrington-Keane — K-e-a-n-e. Like you, I'm a legal alien.'

'I beg your pardon?'

'An alien, a foreigner. I'm also an Australian in London.'

'I see.'

'But I work as a mystic, Cara.'

'A-ha.' Gordy lordy. These New Agers were everywhere these days.

Gaelle then showed astounding perspicacity if not psychic ability by stating the blindingly obvious in her high-pitched voice. 'So, ah, you're probably wondering why I'm ringing you, aren't you, dear?' Like so many Australians who stay in London too long, her accent had been flattened into a trans-equatorial drawl.

'Mmm. I am, actually.'

'Well, you see, I read your article about Shanti Deva in the *Sunday News*. And I love the way you write.'

She paused, so I thanked her, doodling her name on the

electricity bill. Gaelle Carrington-Keane. Gaelle Carrington-Keane. Gaelle Carrington-Keane.

'And I'd very much like to meet you.'

'A-ha.'

'Don't you want to know what for?'

'Well, I guess you want me to write a story for you?' I ventured, feeling jaded. The longer I worked as a freelance journo, the more I became used to strangers calling me to 'let me know' they had a tale to tell, which they thought would fit 'just perfectly into the *Sunday Times* colour magazine', or whatever. I presumed this Gaelle Carrington-Keane also had something she wanted to promote. Perhaps she was going to use her psychic ability to change the world.

'I do want you to write for me, but it's a bit more interesting than that,' she replied.

'Yes?'

'Well, I want you to do the research on my forthcoming autobiography.'

'Mmmm . . .'

'And to write it.'

'Oh.' This was a new one. I was flummoxed. No questions, no nothing.

'Right,' I said. 'So you want me to write your book because you liked my Shanti Deva story?'

Ommmm. I am tuning into my psychic mind and I feel sure that this woman is a loony.

'Yes,' she said.

'I see. Well, that's wonderful. But don't you think we should meet first?' I was trained and paid to be slightly suspicious. Plus it was congenital.

'You're very suspicious. But I'm going on faith. You might think it's impulsive of me to call you. But I call it intuitive. I'm a very intuitive person. I know we could have great success working together.' She paused before adding, 'Do you believe me?'

I looked at my pile of bills and I wanted to believe her. 'Excuse me for asking, but what would I be paid for the book, Mrs Carrington-Keane?' Might as well cut to the chase.

'A rate of 120 pounds for every day you spend with me, whether or not the book is published. After that, if it does go ahead and go to print, you will receive fifty per cent of the royalties.'

A pretty amazing offer, by anyone's standards. 'So, ah, have you got a book deal?'

'Of course,' she replied. 'But does that make any difference to you? If you are being paid, do you mind if it leads to a book or not?'

'Um, I guess not.'

'Good. The time has come to tell my story. I'm willing to agree to payment terms in writing before we meet,' she went on, 'if for no other reason than to show you how important it is to me that you are the person to do the job.'

'I see.'

'Well, that's settled, then,' she said, sounding like one of those telephone salespeople trained to close a deal before the customer even realises he or she has signed up. 'My only stipulation is that for the first month, I won't be doing any straight interviews with you. We'll just chat and get to know each other. I want to be sure how the book is going to unfold before proceeding. You'll be paid to listen to me and my ramblings, and to get to know me. And vice versa, of course.'

'Of course. Mmm. It sounds good,' I said, rapidly calculating that three days of this work would get me out of the immediate rent and electricity bill crisis. 'But you really don't think we should meet first?'

'Not at all. We don't need to meet. You are the journalist I've been looking for. I know it.'

Wow. This was wonderful, if weird. If nothing else, this Gaelle Carrington-Keane gig would be intriguing – and decently paid. And I wouldn't mind a foray into the book world.

'Cara, give me your bank details and I will have your first five days paid in for you in advance.'

Twist my rubber arm.

'So does that suit you?'

'Sure.' This was just fine. 'But . . .'

'Yes?'

'Well . . .'

'Yes?'

'Well, no buts, I guess.' I gave her my bank account details before I could change my mind.

'Wonderful,' she said happily. 'I'll have Cam, my assistant, put the money in your account first thing tomorrow. Can you start tomorrow? We can have our initial meeting. How does that fit with your schedule?'

I told her I had nothing to prevent a meeting the following morning.

'Lovely. It's 16 Eaton Square.'

Eaton Square – a locale strictly for the rich, well-coiffed, buffed and manicured. 'Okay,' I said, wondering what I was getting myself into.

'Superb,' she concluded. 'I'll see you tomorrow then.'

As soon as I'd agreed to Gaelle's terms, I knew a drink or three was in order. Lucy and Monique were already down at the Lord Alvery, our local drinking hole, so I went to find them. It was a balmy evening, just right for a drop of ale. London residents always came out to play in droves as soon as the capital's temperature rose to something above chilly, and the Lord Alvery had a drinking garden which made it a top spot for a bit of evening carousing.

By the time I arrived, Moni and Lucy had set up camp at a table near the river. I spotted them almost silhouetted by the glare of the smoggy sunset, which was fast turning pink above the Thames. As I approached, I could hear Moni laughing at something Lucy was saying. Moni was the older of the two and dressed like the über-career girl she was. Her wardrobe boasted Nicole Farhi and Joseph ensembles and she had an auburn bob sharp enough to cut coke. I loved her. She worked as a producer on a morning programme on Sky One called 'The Matt and Melissa Show' and she hated it with a passion. She'd summarised the reasons for me once – 'One, I've got the world's biggest pain of a boss, Dale the Dickhead, who makes my skin crawl; two, I've got an assistant called Lillian who's forever looking for ways to undermine me; and three, the hours are longer than any sane person would put up with. I'm surprised they didn't give us quills dipped in blood when we signed our contracts.' But Moni always had one eye on her next gig, and this job was a stepping stone.

As I neared them, I could hear her protesting at something Lu was saying.

'You've got to be kidding, Lucy!' she was squealing. 'Tell me you're kidding.'

They hadn't seen me.

'. . . and not only that,' Lu continued, 'but he thinks we should do astro moon-cycle contraception.' They cackled even louder, as if Lu had just delivered the punch line to a very funny joke.

While Moni had been imbued with Girl Power long before it was invented, Lu was gentle, with pale skin, light blue eyes, a wide grin and a raspy voice which perfectly completed the convincing facade of innocence. But she was no fool. Not usually. I listened to her tinkling laugh.

'Hello?' I said, waving to get their attention.

'You know, Moni,' Lu said, still highly amused. 'Astro moon-cycle contraception.' She said it as if Moni should have read about it in *Cosmo*. 'It's where you judge your fertile periods by the moon. It's, ah, like –'

'– like a great way to get pregnant?' The two of them exploded into fits of laughter. I watched the scene, absorbed.

'Hello?' I said, again, for good measure, once they'd settled.

'Hey, C,' Lu said, sounding slightly choked.

'Hi, Cara,' said Moni. Her skin was shiny with laughter. They were miles away. I decided to save my news. I wanted centre stage for my 'Shag the Cat, I've Got a New Job' announcement.

I sat down next to Lu. 'What are you two talking about?'

'Niall's latest plan,' Moni said.

I snuck a sip of Moni's Pils. 'So what's astro moon-cycle contraception?'

'Okay, Cara. Listen.' Lu pushed a wisp of hair behind her ear as if she meant business, reminding me of a five-year-old who'd walked into a grown woman's body. 'Now,' she began. 'Niall says that if we learn to really follow the moon cycles, and if I get in touch with my ovulation and menstrual rhythms, then I'll be able to figure out how my body follows the moon . . .'

'Huh?' I asked. Even seated at a beer-soaked table, surrounded by empty pint glasses and dirty ashtrays and talking nonsense, Lu looked beautiful. Tonight she wore a cream rough-silk top with a pair of torn Levis that she was forever promising herself she'd bin. But even her most expensive clothes were usually unironed and floppy on her. She couldn't go anywhere near linen and owned none. She was also very much New Age inclined these days. In fact, if it wasn't for the fact that I was certain most of the hocus-pocus stuff Lucy got into – like aromatherapy and cranio-sacral-something – was a passing phase, I'd have been having serious words with her. I thought the whole New Age malarky self-indulgent at best and a crutch at worst. As far as I could see, these people spent a lot of time navel-gazing and less time doing something that might actually effect some change in their lives. Perhaps unfairly, I blamed Lu's boyfriend, Niall, a sweet but nevertheless lentil-eating hippy, for her own recent interest in alternative realities and frequencies. Niall was always telling me that in order to become self-aware I had to be less aware of myself, and other such contradictory stuff.

'So what I'm saying,' Lu went on, 'is if I really start to follow the moon's cycle and get in touch with my own, we'll be able to dispense with the Pill and condoms and –'

'– get pregnant!' Moni burst out again. They both laughed until Moni snorted. Moni, it must be said, was like a dog with a bone when it came to risky contraceptive measures, after what she described as 'a run-in with a backyard abortionist as an angst-ridden and pregnant seventeen-year-old'. She'd told me the story once, when I'd ribbed her during one of her sanctimonious 'Use Condoms' tirades. Moni grew up on a farm out in the middle of nowhere, New South Wales. The nearest town was a place called Birrunga (population 3000), where mod cons such as guilt-free abortions on Medicare weren't easily available to teens. She had boarded at Ascham, a posh Sydney girls' school where a lot of her rural corners had been rubbed off at an early age. But one summer back home, she did the Rural Girl Thing and fell in love with, and then fell pregnant to, one of her dad's temporary jackeroos.

Moni's always said that she'd use 'condoms *and* the Pill and whatever else' she could get her hands on to avoid the same thing ever happening again.

She turned to me. 'I've already told Lucy that if she really plans on not using condoms with Niall, there are about 300 vile STDs he'll have to be tested for before we'll even let him back in the house.'

'Moni, don't be ridiculous. *I'm not going to stop using condoms!*' That silenced the gaggle of Pimms-drinking Sloanes to our left. We did that a lot – stunned the locals into amazed silence, bless them.

'I'm not going to stop using condoms,' Lu said again more quietly, still smirking.

'Okay, okay,' I said, clapping my hands demandingly. I couldn't wait any longer. 'Hey, girls, girls, listen. Listen!'

'What? What's happening? Why are you so late?' This was Moni.

Finally, some attention. 'Send in the regular pay packets, girlies.' They looked blankly at me. 'I'm employed,' I said.

'What?' Moni raised one perfectly plucked eyebrow. She knew I experienced fear and loathing when it came to full-time jobs. But this was no ordinary job.

16

'I'm going to write a book for a psychic woman I've never met, called Gaelle Carrington-Keane. She saw my Shanti Deva story in the *Sunday News* and she wants me to write her book. I'm going to make millions.'

'Woo.' Lucy smiled.

'God, C, that's great. Who's Gaelle Carrington-Keane?' said Moni.

'Well, all I know is that she says she's a psycho – sorry, psychic – and that she lives in Eaton Square, so she must have a fair bit of dosh, and she wants me to go around to her house tomorrow morning to meet her and get started.' There was general merriment and beery laughter as they absorbed my news. They knew this job was a much-needed financial bonus.

'Well done, C. Excellent. It calls for celebrating,' Moni said, raising her half-full pint to me.

'I know.'

'Champagne, darling, yah?' she asked, affecting the Sloaney lingo.

'Nah,' I replied. I stood up, ready to go to the bar. 'One thousand beers!'

We drank a lot that night at the Lord Alvery. By closing time at eleven, we were all near legless. As the bar staff started wandering amid the punters collecting empty glasses and yelling, 'Tiiiiiiiiiii-ime', we gathered our belongings.

'So, Cara, tell me something,' said Moni, draining her last lager.

'Mmm?'

'Does the fact that you now have a sort of permanent job mean that you'll have some money?'

'Ha, ha, Moni,' I said dryly.

To be fair, Moni had reason to be a little sick and tired of Lu and me forever living on the breadline. Of the three of us, Moni had definitely taken most to the English lifestyle. She had a full-on career and a growing number of high-powered connections; she'd been to a few very smart balls, courtesy of various lovers and ex-lovers, and she knew how to beat on a pheasant shoot. ('You beat the trees with a branch to scare the birds into the air. It made me cry,' she'd explained to us, distressed after a weekend in the 'kun-tray'.) Lu and I lived a less high-powered existence, especially work-wise. Lu was a graphic designer, but didn't have to work too hard at it – she had wealthy parents, and her rich dowager grand-mother, who'd ruled Sydney's Vaucluse in the thirties, had left her an enormous trust fund. But Lu still lived frugally, trying her best to pay her own way and planning to do something bigger and bet-ter with her inheritance.

I, in the meantime, had high ideals about what I should and shouldn't be writing, which sadly didn't always cover my bills. Fleet Street was a jungle, and if I wasn't careful, I ended up knee-deep in its sludge. I'd recently been commissioned to write an article about methamphetamine, the drug known as Ice, which was supposed to (a) make you feel very sexy and (b) quite possibly kill you if you took too much. The dismal detail to be hinted at in the cover line: many men felt so horny, they wanked until they bled.

The article was for a British men's magazine, but when I spoke to Scotland Yard and Narcotics Anonymous about it, both insisted that there was no real methamphetamine problem in London and that 'writing about it will only create a demand which creates a supply'. I told the editor of the mag, thinking he might have a conscience and kill the story. His response was a blank, 'So?' He didn't get where he was by considering the karmic ramifications of his actions.

With Gaelle Carrington-Keane up my sleeve, though, not only would I have a regular income, but I could also tell the likes of that editor to stick some Ice up his double-page spread.

'Yes, Moni, I might actually have some dosh. But not tonight.' I spilled my leftover pennies onto the beery table. 'In fact, this 75p fortune you see before you is my total savings until my first pay goes in tomorrow morning.'

Moni tut-tutted and pulled a tenner from her wallet, like a kind aunt lending her errant niece money.

We swerved out of the pub and started towards home. We lived in a terrace in Battersea's Lavender Sweep, just south of the Thames, handy to Clapham Junction British Rail and fifteen minutes by black cab from Trafalgar Square if there was no traffic. The large front room, which I could see lit up now as we staggered to the front door, was painted pale apricot and furnished with fine, sturdy big-cushioned sofas and armchairs bought by someone with more money and taste than me.

There was a large, airy kitchen where we ate breakfasts and most dinners, a dining room used for the odd legendary dinner party, a tiny bathroom upstairs and four spacious bedrooms, one of which Lucy and I used as our home office. Then there was the garden, where we hung out as soon as the sun deigned to show its face.

'I am sooooooo knackered,' Lu moaned as we crashed past the big navy front door.

'Oh, God, me, too,' Moni replied.

'You deserve to be knackered, Moni,' Lu said sympathetically, giving her a slap on the back.

I went straight to the kitchen for water, while Moni and Lu took the sofa option in the living room. What on earth had I been thinking? I had a new job to start in the morning and I needed to be on my toes. This was no time to be out getting so pissed. I meandered to the living room and plopped onto the sofa.

'I can't believe I have to wake up early tomorrow.' Lying back against the comfy cushions, I drained my glass of water in the desperate hope of avoiding a hangover.

'Oh, poor diddums,' Moni said, sounding unsympathetic. 'What time? Eight? Nine? Do you think you'll manage it?'

'Ha,' I replied, for want of a better response. She had a right to sound at least a little sarky. While Lu and I had easy lives as freelancers, waking whenever we wanted most days, Moni's hectic producer's job meant early starts every weekday. So while Lu and I often spent mornings lazing and late afternoons sipping tea and watching 'Through the Keyhole' if work was slow, Moni would be hard at it at least ten hours a day at her smart warehouse offices in the Docklands. She usually rocked home to find Lu and me collapsed on the sofa in the living room or in the garden chatting about life and the universe. We forever told her she was working too hard and she forever agreed, but seemed unwilling or unable to break the cycle.

'I'm not used to getting up at sparrow's fart,' I pleaded. 'Peak hour on public transport is a nightmare.' I usually exercised my freelancer's privileges and avoided the morning crush by booking afternoon appointments. Somehow Gaelle Carrington-Keane had convinced me to see her at 10 a.m.

'So, you start tomorrow?' Lu asked, plumping the large cushion behind her.

'Mmmhmmm.'

'So, what's going to happen next?' Moni asked, sipping her water.

'I meet her, I interview her, I write the book, I guess,' I replied, feeling far too comfy on the sofa to explain in more detail. I knew I should have been in a better state when I was about to face Gaelle Carrington-Keane. New Age Nice or not, she probably wouldn't appreciate a hung-over biographer landing on her doorstep.

'You should have heard her as she explained why she'd chosen me on the phone,' I went on. 'She sort of lowered her voice and said, "*You are the one*", or something like that. I asked her why she didn't want to interview me first before signing me up, but she was insistent that she wanted to "go on faith". She's already paid me for five days.'

'She's supposed to be psychic, isn't she?' asked Lu, who was always rushing off for tarot, crystal and palm readings. 'Maybe she knows psychically that you're the one for the job.'

'Maybe. But if she doesn't like me, or if she goes off the idea of going public, she can pull the plug. She told me if we part company, I get a minimum one month's pay and no more is said about it. We won't start the actual interviews for at least a month, anyway, even if we do go ahead.'

'What a jammy job,' Moni commented enviously. 'Are you sure she's for real?'

'I don't know, but I do need the money, so I'm willing to find out.'

'Ooh. It's so exciting,' Lu sighed. She knew a guaranteed income was a rare thing in this freelance lifestyle. Both of us lived from cheque to cheque. I spent my money on comestibles and CDs, while Lu spent hers on aromatherapy massages and weekend herbal courses with lover-boy Niall.

'Anyway,' I said, 'I can't wait to meet her. I think I've got a serious fruit loop on my hands. She said she'd been planning this book for years, but avoided the media because she knew she'd be ridiculed. She said it in this kind of spooky voice. "*Now the time has come to tell my story.*"'

I realised I was mimicking her, so I guiltily added, 'I really should be upstairs sleeping or reading clippings about the cosmic realms or something.'

'Hmmm,' Moni said. 'I should be upstairs bonking some hunk.'

'Ha. Well, I will be upstairs bonking some hunk soon enough. Niall said he might come around tonight after he finishes his shift with City Mission,' Lu said.

'So you call Niall a hunk, do you?' Moni teased. 'Niall the lentil eater?'

'Moni. How can you say that?' Lu squeaked with a pouting bottom lip, pleading with me to intervene. Moni loved goading Lucy.

'I don't see how his lentil eating can be denied,' Moni said.

'I thought you liked him.'

'I do. But you can't deny he eats lentils, can you?'

'Listen,' she grinned cheekily, 'he might be a lentil-eating hippy, but he's into Tantric sex.'

'Say no more.' I smiled.

'Yeah,' Moni admitted. 'You should consider yourself lucky to have a Good Bloke.'

And that was the bottom line as far as I was concerned. Whether or not Niall was a lentil eater wasn't the real point. I might not have gone out with him in a pink fit, but Lu liked him a lot and that was a very good thing.

I would also have very much liked to have had a boyfriend I thought was a Good Bloke. Moni and I were both long-term single, and while her career meant she rarely had time for anything beyond a few one-month wonders, I, meanwhile, was getting very bored with dating and going-nowhere relationships. Not to mention sleeping alone.

'Lu, for all the ribbing about his weirdness, I like Niall,' I said. I really hoped things went well for them. Life had been tough, and I mean extremely tough, on Lu in the heart department recently. She told me it was so bad she felt there was a rent in her heart chakra.

'And, hey, if it doesn't work out for me and him, I can always pass him on to one of you,' Lu joked. 'You're always salivating over his body.' This was also true. The sight of Niall in a towel after his early morning bath was rather refreshing. But I wasn't frantic for a lover. Even bored with singleness, I couldn't be dealing with the chinless lads I'd been meeting of late. At least now I had something interesting happening on the work front to think about, plus the comfort of a foreseeable future.

After more chat and an impromptu bowl of chocolate chip Häagen-Dazs each, we all collapsed. The ever-wise Moni drank three more glasses of water and went to bed, twirling all the way up the stairs — something which I seem to remember was a reference to an earlier conversation we'd had that evening regarding whirling dervishes and Sufiism. Lucy, meanwhile, threw up in the kitchen sink. Like the wafer-thin biscuit that exploded the fat bloke in the Monty Python sketch, that last spoonful of Double Choc Chip And Bits O' Biscuit was her demise. Niall finally arrived, cleaned up and led her upstairs. At that point, I decided that not moving was the best course of action, so I closed my eyes and spent a wired-up night on the sofa.

3

half human, half star trek

The next morning I took myself off to Gaelle's house by taxi — I was too late and too frail for public transport   and quickly found her red front door. I tugged nervously at my ponytail before buzzing her bell. After the talk of the past twenty-four hours, she was beginning to loom large in my imagination. I ran my hand over the smooth columns on either side of her elegant porch as I waited for a reply; pure marble. Gaelle's apartment building was tall, white and stately, in a row of Georgian townhouses which had been converted into plush flats. The rarefied air of Eaton Square seemed cleaner than in South London (Sarf Lundarn), and they had patches of lawn here, which were hard to come by south of the river, unless you counted the commons. There were no tower blocks in view, no skips, and no rubbish in the gutters. And probably no good, cheap curry houses, either.

It was Gaelle herself who finally answered the door. Nothing she'd said to me prepared me for the vision of womanhood I found standing before me. Her figure was what you might politely call well rounded. She looked like she hadn't worn make-up since the seventies and her hair was coiffed in a fetching blonde perm. She wore a pair of pale blue cord trousers and a multicoloured homey-looking jumper. Despite the much-loved granny facade, she struck me as a tough old bird. Not someone to mess around with.

'Cara. I'm Gaelle. Please come in,' was all she said to me as she stood in the doorway. Her eyes were watery, but sharp. Her bottom, I couldn't help noticing as she turned to lead the way up the stairs, was enormous.

She led me to her front room, a huge, burgundy-coloured space, lined with shelves stacked with pot plants, lamps and hundreds of books. Star, moon and sun mobiles, wind chimes and incense holders littered the room. Sort of Mayfair-meets-Hippy-Chick Chic. It looked like someone else had expertly decorated the place in period style and then Gaelle and her junk had moved in afterwards.

Before we sat down, she buzzed on an intercom.

'Amanda, Cara is here. Will you bring us some tea, please?'

'No problem, Gaelle,' replied a Lundarn-sounding voice.

She gestured for me to sit in one of the velvet-covered Georgian armchairs placed elegantly amid the rubble of the room. We sat in silence. I was about to say something banal, like, 'Hi, how are you, nice to meet you at last,' when she put her hand up as if to silence me. Cocking her head to one side and squinting, as if she was listening out for something, she spoke.

'Cara,' she said.

'Yes?'

'Cara, you've been drinking, haven't you?' The way she said 'drinking', she might as well have said 'slaughtering newborn babies and eating them for lunch'.

Before I had time to wonder whether it was the previous night's beer, Stoli or Jim Beam seeping through my pores, Gaelle continued.

'You know, Cara, no-one ever solved their problems through drinking. Or drugs for that matter. Well, not through most drugs, not through the sort of highly toxic drugs they're taking these days . . .'

I sat there with my mouth wide open, not sure what to say. Of course it should have occurred to me. Gaelle Carrington-Keane was a mystic. And mystics like to make profound statements and surprise you with their insight. But how did she know we'd been hitting the bottle last night?

'Last night, during my meditation, I focussed on your energies,' she said. 'I felt you drinking, with friends. You were laughing, but there was sadness, too, wasn't there? One of your friends, the blonde one, she was talking about her life. Her lover. But she wasn't talking about her sadness, was she? She is sad, isn't she? Deep down, underneath the laughter, she's sad about the past and confused about the present. About men. About her previous lover?'

'Umm.' Gaelle was right, but I knew not how.

'So, you all drank until she felt better and threw up. She had a lot to let go of – she processed a lot last night. But how about you? How are you feeling now?'

Mercifully, before I could answer, the door from the living room opened and a pretty, round girl with rosy cheeks and curly hair walked in carrying a tray of tea things.

At the same moment, a tall man came in through the door which led to the street. He was exotic, erotic and the weirdest-looking guy I'd seen in a long time, in his own delicious way. Dark blond, longish hair. Kind of scruffy looking, like he had no-one to iron his clothes for him. He was wearing Levis and a blue cotton shirt with a white starburst pattern on it. The shirt was unbuttoned at the bottom, so as well as chest hair up top, I could see a tanned stomach with golden down where the shirt missed his jeans.

Hmmm. His thick locks were tied back in a little ponytail at the nape of his neck, and his puppy dog brown eyes were staring right into mine. His smile was gorgeous. Transfixing. He looked at me and I felt as if we were sharing a private joke, but one we'd made up thousands of years ago and I'd since forgotten. His eyes had deeply engraved lines around them, as if he'd spent a lot of his life laughing. He was staring at me with them as if they were missiles.

Omigod. Omigod. It hit me. This was the man from the tripped-out dream I'd had after my session at Shanti Deva's. What had happened in it? All I could remember was his face. But hang on, why was I even thinking such nonsense? It was all too much for a Monday. I was hung-over, dazed and seriously confused. I decided there and then to commit to starting a diary of my more unusual dreams.

'Cara.' Gaelle turned to the girl holding the tray. 'This is Amanda.'

Amanda put down the tray and sort of bobbed her head at me a bit.

'And this,' Gaelle gestured expansively at the man near the stairs, 'is my assistant, Cameron Street, who'll be overseeing all our research and interviews, won't you, Cam? Cam, this is Cara Kerr, who's doing the research and the writing.'

'Hey, good to meet you,' Cam said amiably in an accent that was softly London. I liked him – even more – straight away. God. He was English and I fancied him. That hadn't happened in what could only be described as a very long time. He had shoulders and a chin and a drop-dead gorgeous face. His body radiated some kind of energy that made me want to draw nearer to him.

Hang on. 'I'm sorry?' I said. 'Cam will be "overseeing" which interviews?' From what I had gathered so far, Cam was her assistant, which meant that his job was to set up the research and interviews, not to sit in on them.

'He'll be sitting in on the interviews for my book,' Gaelle replied slowly, as if speaking to a subnormal child.

'I see. Right.' Why did they need someone to oversee the research? Didn't she trust me? He might have been gorgeous, but I didn't want him watching over my shoulder. It would make me nervous, quite apart from piss me off. 'I didn't know someone would be sitting in,' I finished lamely.

He smiled a lovely smile. 'Look, I'll be hanging around more than sitting in,' he said. 'Gaelle wants you to get to know her, rather than just basing the story on interviews and old clippings. I really won't be in your way.' Pause. 'It's nice to meet you, anyway.' He was more polite than he looked.

'Oh, I'm sorry, no, that's fine, nice to meet you, too,' I said. I'd have to think about this later.

I turned back to Gaelle Carrington-Keane to see if she had anything to add. She was reclining in her chair, saying zilch, but paying close attention. She smiled, shrugged her shoulders, waved her hand around in the air a bit like the Queen saying hello, and asked, 'Do you want me to continue to tell you about your friend who was drinking with you last night, Cara?'

Not that again. Did I really want Amanda and Cam to hear this? I regretted being hung-over. Mr B-b-berocca hadn't done his job this morning. My head was spinning.

Gaelle didn't wait for an answer. 'In any case,' she went on, 'your blonde friend will be fine. She'll find love within six months. It's just around the corner for her. She'll have to sort more wheat from chaff yet before she really makes room in her life for Mr Right. Timing is hard with prediction, as time isn't linear, but at a wild guess I'd say within the next year to eighteen months, she'll be married with kids in the offing, just as she wants. But not in this country.'

I thought she'd finished, when she added, 'As for you and your relationships, Cara, you need to learn that making love with Kundalini energy can transform you. Kundalini is creative sexual energy which makes physical loving transcendent. That's what you should be looking for.'

Lord.

With that, she leaned over and lit an incense stick. As the blue smoke swirled, she stood up.

'So, now that we're all here, let's get busy. I want my book to be part autobiography and part esoteric self-help, for people who want to expand their psychic abilities. I will supply all the information you need.'

I nodded.

'So I take it you're 100 per cent committed in your agreement to join me in this venture?' she asked, hands on hips.

Why the heck not? I mean, what else was there? Liposuction articles?

'I would love to,' I told her. I could practically hear the verbal contract being drawn up.

'Good,' she said. 'As you'll know if you've checked your bank account, you've already been paid for five days. So, Cara, let's start with an initial working period of four weeks, then we'll see if we want to proceed. You won't need to come in every day, though, most likely.'

'Fine,' I said, and hoped she was right. Every day was a little more than I'd had in mind.

'We'll let the tea draw for a while longer,' she said. 'Would you like to see the room where I do my work, C? Can I call you C?'

'Yes, of course,' I said. And can I call you Gaelle? I wondered.

'And you *can* call me Gaelle,' she replied. 'So, shall we have a look at where my work goes on, then?'

'Umm . . . yes, please,' was the best I could muster. Maaan. I was already surrounded by spooks and mystics, what with Shanti Deva, Lucy and her spook lover Niall. Now I was going to be working with one.

Gaelle led us from the living room into a corridor lined with windows on one side, which overlooked a lush garden, and deep wooden panelling on the other. She opened a door from the corridor.

'This is my work room,' she said reverently.

I stood next to Cam, planning to follow any lead he offered. I figured that of those here and present, aside from myself, he had to be closest to sane.

Gaelle's work room was large and windowless, softly lit by spotlights in the ceiling and on the walls. A veritable vortex of images, you could say. Dotted along one wall on wooden shelving were half a dozen vibrantly healthy, evidently hydroponically grown maidenhair fern pot plants. There were at least twenty different types of crystals in there, either hanging suspended from the ceiling and refracting the fairy lights lining the cornices, or sitting on tables, in giant clumps of purple, white and silvery quartz. Sweet-smelling sticks of incense burned around them, filling the room with a scent Lu had taught me to recognise as that hippy stalwart, patchouli.

Running the length of one wall was what looked like a sort of makeshift non-religious mini altar. Set on a long, low table covered with a black and red mirrored Indian cloth sat a smorgasbord of New Age pictures, prints, models and diagrams.

Amid the clutter were a miniature plastic statue of the Virgin Mary and a jade carving of Buddha. Pictures of Christ sat in hand-painted frames near diagrams of pyramids, inverted pyramids, three-dimensional drawings of the Star of David and, most compellingly, several hand-drawn pictures of faces that were half human, half Star Trek. Incongruously, there were also framed photos of Calvin Klein, Carole King, and British TV presenter Caron Keating. Strange.

All this was bordered by what must have been three dozen candles set on a shelf that ran at waist height around the room. The thought 'Where's the fire exit?' occurred to me briefly.

Gaelle paused ceremoniously at the entrance of her work room and took off her shoes, motioning for me to do the same. I did, hoping my feet didn't smell. Taking the weight equally on her bare feet as though she might topple if she rushed, Gaelle padded to the bookshelves, which carried hundreds of tomes with such names as *The Pleiadian Handbook*, *Miracle Meditation for Beginners*, *Conversation With God* and — I squinted just to be sure — *Are Dolphins Aliens?*. The rest of the large living space was taken up with a deep red, three-piece velvet suite, a nest of three tables with a reading lamp on top, and one more low table, this one piled high with new and old magazines.

She picked up an old black-and-white photo in a frame. Smiling out from a period that could only have been the sixties was a small, blonde woman.

'I was a debutante, you know,' she said, glancing from me back to the picture. 'I was a Sydney girl, an Eastern Suburbs debutante, and I threw it all away to follow my soul path.'

A-ha.

'You should do some research, C,' she said. 'Go to the library. I was married to a man named Brian Carrington-Keane. I left him to follow my soul path. You'll find out more. I'll tell you more.'

'I'll courier you over some notes,' Cam added.

Intriguing.

Setting down the photo, she allowed me to soak up the vibes of her work room. There was no art adorning the walls, just one framed poster. It showed a picture of Stonehenge taken at sunset, with the image of a classic cigar-shaped UFO superimposed (I could only assume) hovering above it. At the bottom of the poster, printed in a large, pink and rounded seventies-style font were the words 'I BELIEVE'.

She turned to glare at me and Cam. She was standing under an overhead lighting fixture that wasn't doing a very flattering job. The roots of her curly blonde perm showed up black against the back lighting, the bags under her eyes were unbecomingly highlighted and her chin looked tripled. Bizarrely, the waistband of her Calvin Klein knickers was visible above the top of her cords, cutting into her white and flabby flesh.

Obviously unaware of any of this, she spoke to me in a very low, stern voice.

'Cara, I hope you won't be drinking too heavily when you're working with me,' she began ominously. 'You are about to take a quantum leap.'

I looked around me. At the candles, the fairy lights, the mock-altar and poster. I think the words that occurred to me at that moment were something to the effect of: 'She's off her trolley.'

4

happiness and jack daniel's

'She's off her firkin trolley!' I said to Lucy, Monique and Niall, who were gathered around our garden table. It was 4 p.m. and I was back home. Moni had returned uncharacteristically early from work, as hung-over as me after the previous night's efforts at the Lord Alvery. Lucy reported that her working day had 'never really started'. Niall had popped over with a cardboard box full of herbal teas to help us all recover. Instead, we'd opted for G&Ts in the late afternoon sun.

The last of the daylight lingered over our small patch of garden, weak rays of sunshine sliding through the grey air, which smelled surprisingly clean. Mouser, so called because of his monstrously sized mouse-like ears, lay sprawled on the damp, recently rained-upon grass, his furry ginger stomach turned upwards, the better for us to stroke.

I had by now totally convinced myself that Cam was in fact not the man in my dream. That would be too weird. I hadn't even mentioned it to the girls. It was too silly to talk about. But that didn't stop me thinking about it.

'So, how did it go?' asked Moni after I plopped myself down on the grass. 'How's the famous Gaelle Carrington-Keane? What's she like?'

'Well, not to put too fine a point on it, she's a full-on loony psycho psychic type,' I replied. I told them about her work room, her weird manner, the UFO poster. 'It was all very chi-chi, in a really non-chi-chi kind of way.' There were so many trendy hippies about these days, living in Eaton Square and chanting mantras to clear themselves of the negative ions caused by their filthy lucre a-go-go. Gaelle was different, though. She didn't wear Armani; more like Oxfam op shop stuff, except for the Calvin Klein knickers.

'Is she really psychic, do you think, Cara?' asked Lucy, obviously impressed. 'I love mystic types. Can I come and see her? Will she tell me when I'm going to find love and go back to Australia?'

I laughed, but was still very confused by one thing – Gaelle may have seemed nuttier than a pecan pie, but she'd spoken with amazing accuracy about us all getting pissed the night before. I still couldn't work it out.

'Hey, Niall,' I asked, remembering one of her more tangential comments. 'Do I smell of alcohol?' Niall leaned down from his wicker garden chair to sniff my proffered arm.

'No, more like perfume,' he said in his slow hippy drawl, sounding bemused, even for him. 'Why?'

'Gaelle said she knew I'd been drinking. I wondered if I was smelly or something.'

Niall laughed. He was a high-cheekboned, chisel-chinned and seriously short-haired hipster who seemed to have taken one trip too many during his days on the modelling scene in Tokyo, and had gone a bit hippy dippy. His main aim, he said now, was to open a healing centre. And, apparently, do something called astro moon-cycle contraception, if last night's conversation was anything to go by.

A few weeks earlier, at Lucy's relentless insistence, Niall had brought around his modelling portfolio to show us. He'd been genuinely coy as we flicked through it, drooling. Staring out from pages torn from *Vogue*, *Maxim*, *GQ* and the like were pictures of him unshaven and rugged in woolly jumpers on a rainy hill, dark and brooding in a café, looking hot and vulnerable between satin sheets, and, our favourite, wet with nipples on high beam, his bronzed pecs and abs glistening with something that looked like morning dew, but which he told us was ironing aid, sprayed on him by a stylist. As we flicked through his portfolio, Niall entranced us with tales of the obscene amounts of money he'd earned, of the New York apartments he'd lived in and the unlimited drugs he'd had access to. And then he told us how he'd left it all behind.

'You just turned your back on it all?' Moni had asked, uncomprehendingly. It was hard to see him in that world now, but it was hard to imagine just farewelling it, either.

'Yep,' he'd drawled. 'I was sick of the anorexic girls, the bitching, the coked-up egos and paranoid photographers.' He'd slammed the smart, grey book shut with a bang, long before we'd had our thrill fill. 'I just want to help people now. Use the money I earned in New York to open a healing centre or something.'

We'd sat for ten seconds in silent homage to Niall's morals. At that point, with gas, rent and Mastercard bills mounting, I'd have sold my body to New York's elite photographers in a second, had I enough discipline to beat it into shape. The most exercise I took was the odd walk around Clapham Common. I had to thank my mother's good genes for the fact that I was slim, despite my high chicken green curry and lager intake.

'Come on, C,' Lu was insisting now, her G&T almost finished. 'What else did Gaelle say?'

'She actually said something like, "You were out drinking with your flatmates and one was blonde," or something.'

Wow. Hushed silence. Lu was captivated. Her eyes were very wide.

'And then there was the matter of her amazing predictions for you,' I said to her as enticingly as I could, enjoying the moment. Lucy's eyes widened to frog-like.

'Was it good?' she asked in the baby voice she reserved for mornings, shock and hangovers.

'Absolutely,' I replied. 'Can you take it?'

'Sure.'

'Well, she said you would discover soon enough that happiness is found in true love and not in the bottom of a bottle of Jack Daniel's. Or words to that effect.' We laughed.

'And what about a bottle of Jim Beam?' Moni asked, smiling.

'Hang on a minute,' Niall interjected, as his chiselled cheekbones caught the sun's rays. 'Does this mean she's going to go off with someone else?'

'Nooo, not at all,' I said, not having a clue if it were true.

'Right.' He blinked, a little nervously, as he stroked Lu's knee with the palm of his hand.

'What else did she say?' Moni asked.

I hesitated because I didn't want to upset Niall further.

'I'll tell you the details later,' I said, 'but suffice to say that love is just around the corner for one of us. Actually, I wouldn't mind a bit of love in the corner with her assistant, Cam. He's quite sexy.'

'AND GOD KNOWS WE NEED SOME HOT SEX AROUND HERE!' Moni and Lucy shrieked. It was our private joke and battle call. Niall shuddered and pretended to be fascinated by a little speck of nothing in the bottom of his teacup. Perhaps he was looking for happiness in there, too.

'Speaking of sex,' I remembered, 'she told me that I should be looking for transcendent sex in my relationships.'

'As opposed to . . . ?'

'I don't know. Banal bonking?'

'Well, transcendent sex sounds good to me,' said Moni.

'Yeah,' said Lucy.

'So, ah, anyway, what's for dinner?' I asked, changing the subject, before we got Niall onto the topic of hippy sex.

'How about chicken with almonds?' asked Moni. 'We've got all the ingredients.'

I'd mastered cooking chicken with almonds (as well as beef wellington and kedgeree) a year earlier when I was commissioned to write an article about a ritzy live-in cooking school in Edinburgh – an intense, three-day affair attended by the well-heeled daughters of the landed gentry. As well as teaching me how to lay a formal/casual/country/romantic-style table, arrange flowers, not to mention how to seat a duke in relation to an earl or a duchess, I'd learned how to cook chicken with almonds. It was an apparently infallible recipe and Moni and Lucy's undisputed favourite.

'If you cook, I'll wash up,' Moni bargained.

'No problem. Niall, do you want to stay for dinner?' I asked, half hoping he'd say no, so I could recount more of the day's events to the girls uncensored.

'Ah, thanks, but I'm meeting my brother,' he replied. 'We're going to a showing of *Powder* at the Clapham Picture House. I've been wanting to see it for ages. They say it's a true story about a guy who was a walk-in.'

'Pardon?'

'You know, a walk-in. When an alien walks into a human's body by prearranged agreement. Apparently, this movie reveals the truth about walk-ins.'

'Right,' I said, staring blankly at him, which was probably my most common response to Niall when he went into deep hippy mode. If I had asked him to explain himself it could have taken light years. His hippiness extended to a belief in aliens with pointed heads, Ascended Masters who channelled 'higher information' to mere mortals and the indelible power of crystals.

'Maybe next time,' he finished.

'Absolutely, Niall. Our backyard is your backyard,' I said.

'My mull bowl is your mull bowl,' said Moni, smiling.

'My sheets are your sheets,' said Lucy. 'But please let's use a condom.'

Oops.

He did a double take as he realised, in one horrid moment, that his worst nightmare was a reality and that we did indeed talk about him and his sex life with Lu behind his back. I could just hear him thinking, 'I bet they know the size of my knob, too,' as he prepared to depart.

'Okay, well, thanks for the dinner invitation,' he said, standing his ground with dignity.

'Sure, Niall.'

'Bye, then,' he said, picking up his overcoat and giving Lu a kiss on the lips.

'Byeeee,' we chorused.

For a moment after the front door slammed there was silence, then Moni and Lucy were all over me for info about Gaelle.

'Tell us more, C.'

'Did she really say I was going to fall in love?'

'What does she look like? Does she do private readings?'

I told Moni and Lu the almost-full story so far, including that Cam would be sitting in on the interviews, which was a major downer as I might be paranoid and he might be a pain. I added details about his amazing good looks, which was a bright spot on the job scene, but no real help on the paranoia front. This was an important job and I didn't want to mess up my first book-related opportunity because I couldn't hang on to my hormones. And then I told the girls what Gaelle had said about Lucy and her amazing performing love life and about Gaelle's strange, strange work room.

'Wow,' said Lu.

'Did she say anything about me?' asked Moni.

'Um, I'm not sure. She was pretty fixated on Lucy. But I think that was because she said she knew she was pissed last night. It was all very strange.'

'Wow,' Lucy said again. 'She sounds amazing. Please can I come and meet her?'

'Well . . .'

'Why not?'

'Well, I didn't say you couldn't, I just need to get to know her a bit better . . .'

'Tell me what she said again, C.'

'Lu!'

'Oh, tell me.'

'She said you'd find love within a year or two and that you'd get what you want, but it wouldn't be in this country.'

'I want a proper reading,' Lu squealed.

'Are you sure you didn't give her any hints that might have made her realise we'd all been pissed last night?' asked Moni, ever the voice of reason.

'No, definitely not,' I said. 'I walked in the door, she took me to her living room, sat me down and asked me why we drank so much. Unless she was at the Lord Alvery or around here spying through the window last night, I have to say it's quite weird that she guessed.' God, I hope she can't read my mind, I thought. Imagine trying to work with someone who could do that.

'Well, let's just hope she's not a mind reader or you'll really be in trouble. Imagine trying to work with someone who could do that,' Moni laughed.

I looked at her with alarm.

I set about cooking, while Moni washed up last night's dishes. Lucy laid the table, turned on the stereo, poured us each a glass of white and flicked through the evening newspaper, reading us snippets, ignoring the front-page debate about the Millennium Dome and skipping to page three where Tony Blair's latest schmooze with a popstar was reported.

'Oh, God, I forgot to tell you,' Lucy announced suddenly. 'I've got this great new job on, too . . .'

'What's that?' I asked, measuring basmati rice into a huge pan of boiling water.

'Here, look.' She went to her leather satchel on the floor and pulled out something swathed in blood-red silk.

'What have you got there?' Moni asked, her face sudsy with washing-up foam.

'It's wonderful. I got it through Jessica, the American woman I met at the Crystal Healing Workshop where I met Niall . . .'

From under the silk she pulled out what looked like a deck of cards. 'They're called Nirvana Cards. They're for fortune telling. These are the US version,' she said, spreading them out face down in a fan-shape on the table. 'They're sort of like tarot cards but without the scary bits. I'm designing the UK version.'

'Excellent. Top job.'

'Firstly, I have to decide if I'm going for a traditional or original design. Then I'll think about what the cards mean to me.'

'Sounds like a good excuse to play around with tarot cards and ask lots of questions about your love life, if you ask me,' Moni said.

'They're not tarot cards. They're really different.' Lu made a face and asked us if we wanted to pick a card.

'In a minute,' said Moni.

'Mmmm. Later,' I said, chopping the chicken into bite-size pieces.

'Okay, just for me then,' said Lu. She closed her eyes and held her hand out flat, letting it hover backwards and forwards over the spread.

'Lu, you look like a human Geiger counter.'

'The first thing I have to do is get a fix on the present,' she replied before chanting: 'What's going on for me now, cards? What's going on for me now?'

'What's a fix on the present?'

'If the cards accurately describe the present, I know they're working and I can ask another question.' She chose a card and turned it over. '*Letting Go . . .*' She picked up the accompanying interpretations book. 'Okay. *Letting Go . . .* It says, "*Letting go of past failures and disappointments. Bringing your mind to the here and now. Opening your heart and mind to the future. Moving through the detri . . . detri . . .*"'

'Detritus?'

'Mmmm. What does that mean?'

'Rubbish.'

'Thanks. "*Moving through the detritus will take you to a brand new clearing . . .*"'

'Oooo-er,' I said from the kitchen counter.

'Watch that detritus, it'll get you every time,' added Moni, who had no time for impracticalities such as not moving forward.

'It's true. I should let go of the past.' Lu nodded, as she put the card back in the pack. 'Okay, now for the future.' She shuffled furiously, then spread the cards out on the table again. 'Okay. What should I be doing for my best possible future, cards? What should I be doing for my best possible future?' Lu waved her hand above the cards again.

Moni paused and I stopped my chopping and mincing and dicing and slicing to watch. Lu turned the card over. Her eyes widened.

She held up the card. 'Omigod. *Letting Go.* I got the same card. Spooky.'

'It's rigged,' Moni laughed. 'Pour me another glass of wine will you, and stop with your New Age nonsense.'

Shaking her head, Lu put the cards away and did as she was asked, looking distracted. She passed us both some wine, muttering about how weird it was that she'd got the same card twice.

It was always comforting to sit down and eat a proper meal together. We were like three Aussie girls adrift in an English ocean sometimes, especially when things were getting hairy, as they had been lately. It was still very exciting and challenging and new being in London, even after three years, but sometimes it was also good to have each other to come home to. Moni had been working so hard lately, and we hadn't had much time to chat. Lucy needed some togetherness and support. And I just liked being at home en masse.

London was a good place to be an Australian. For my money, we came into fashion in the late eighties, when Kylie was smiling from the cover of nearly every magazine, and when my backpacking predecessors earned us all a good reputation for straight talk and hard work, whether pulling pints in London or working as part of the so-called 'Australian media mafia', as I now did. The Poms still liked to pigeonhole us as Returnees From The Colonies and in turn I think we sometimes played at shocking them, simply to live up to our reputation as good-time marauders. Although there were more differences below the surface than above, we liked the Poms and usually felt very welcome. Moni, Lu and I were fairly inseparable, but we had some good English mates.

We'd known each other since high school in Sydney. In fact, I knew Moni, who knew Lucy. During uni we rented a house together in Newtown. It was a battered terrace with an enormous backyard where we had many an all-weekend house party. Mental As Anything's classic 'Too Many Times' was our theme song. After three years of larking about ninety-nine per cent of the time – though Moni did more work than Lucy and I put together – we somehow fluked our degrees.

Post graduation, Lucy, who'd studied graphic design, was taken on at a Balmain design studio run by a friend of her mother's. I graduated with a major in English and wriggled my way into freelance writing, doing a lot of film reviewing and interviewing actors for *Cinema Papers* and the *Sydney Morning Herald*, as well as for a few street mags that paid peanuts but provided fun gigs. Moni's career ended up being the most illustrious of all. She went straight into TV, initially working as a coffee-maker-cum-researcher. Then she did a current affairs show (until a story about a former priest marrying a former stripper did her in) and even part-time script-edited for one of the soapies until, finally, with her late twenties staring her in the face, she threw it all in to come travelling with Lucy and me. A wise move. She'd had shingles the year before and was overworked and overstressed. Things hadn't changed too much for her in London; she was still working in a high-powered environment. But the adventure of 'being away' usually carried us all through.

We'd all decided to go and see the world while we could still get British visas. Moni needed a straight entry visa and then found sponsorship via her work, while Lu and I had residency and nationality rights, via various familial loopholes. Even though it seemed like career madness to up sticks and leave Sydney there and then, we bought our tickets, sending boxes of creature comforts in advance of our arrival. We wanted to do more than live out of backpacks, work in a few pubs and leave.

'You know, I'm not just popping over and coming back, I don't think,' I confessed to Mum and Dad the night before we left. 'I might be away a year or three. And I plan never to set foot in Earl's Court.'

'I know you'll do well,' Mum replied, as she sewed a last-minute green and gold 'Australia' badge onto my backpack.

'Are you sure you have enough money, Cara?' Dad asked for the fiftieth time, pacing the living room, openly perturbed at losing his little girl to the northern hemisphere's bright lights and promise. 'London's a bloody expensive place. You'll pay $4 for a cup of coffee.'

Dad was right. England was expensive. Once we arrived, our initial plan had been to get straight into a quick Eurail tour, drinking beer in Hamburg, meeting Italians in Venice, romping through poppy fields in France, and so on, before settling in London. But

Moni was offered temporary freelance work in our first week here, and the house in Lavender Sweep came up in the second. We were told rather grimly that pretty – and affordable – four-bedroom houses like this one were 'rarer than white snot in London' so we canned the Eurail idea, took the house and never looked back.

I'd come here with the intention of either studying film or writing freelance and had done exactly that. I'd written for everything, from the underground to the achingly trendy, been published in the *Guardian* several times and even helped out on a weekend workshop course on freelance writing, which made me feel that I'd really arrived. I'd also managed to do a part-time diploma in film studies at London University, I'd fallen in and out of love with a north Londoner called Jonathan McCarthy, and was generally thinking that London had done its job and perhaps a return to Sydney was in order. Then I was offered the Gaelle Carrington-Keane job.

'So what else has everyone been up to?' I asked, turning my attention back to the chicken and almonds sizzling in the wok.

Lu raised her eyebrows. 'Well, Moni has a date with Rufus tonight.'

'Really?'

At the sink, Moni drained the rice. 'Oh, Lu. It's not a date. Some distant relative of his has just arrived from the States for a summer holiday here. She's an actress doing summer school at the Barbican. I'm going to meet them both for a drink.'

'A-ha. He didn't invite us, though.'

Moni tutted. 'He thinks I can help her with some TV contacts for set building work or something . . .'

'Oh, by the way,' Lucy piped up as I served dinner. 'Speaking of Rufus, he also left a message on the machine earlier saying something about his brother's housewarming party in Hampstead next Friday.'

'Sounds good to me,' I said, dropping hors d'oeuvre scraps of chicken into Mouser's food bowl.

'Brilliant,' Moni added.

I found English men so much better at being best mates than Aussie blokes. True, you often needed to have the I-don't-want-to-snog-you-but-I-really-like-you conversation, but once you'd circumnavigated that, and if you didn't actually fancy them, you could be friends. Rufus was a special favourite. He was a neighbour, a thoroughly and frightfully English Champagne Charlie, complete with signet ring, public school education, career in stockbroking and headed for a comfy middle-class life in either a ritzier part of London or the home counties. He was a drop of the Englishness we'd all expected to sup in this country. He liked us, too, because we cooked for him, let him tan his pasty midriff in our garden and because we made him laugh. He also told just about the filthiest jokes I'd ever heard, all with a booming cut-glass accent.

We'd been sitting down to dinner nibbling and chatting for about fifteen minutes when the phone rang.

'Cara. It's Caaaaaam,' Moni whispered, fluttering her eyelashes and waving her fork at me.

I took the receiver, midway through a mouthful of chicken. 'Hello, Cam?'

'Hi Cara.' His voice reminded me of how he looked. I remembered his delicious brown eyes and easy manner. 'Look, I hope you don't mind me calling you . . .' He trailed off in the polite way that Englishmen do.

'No, no, that's fine.'

'Gaelle wants to know if you're free tomorrow for another meeting?'

'Er, yes, I think so.'

'Good. She's keen to get on. She liked you.'

'Did she?'

'Yeah. So, ah, are you okay? I hope it wasn't too much of a baptism by fire?'

Baptism by fire was right. A hangover, a weird, large, blonde woman and that bizarre work space of hers, not to mention the sexiest man I'd met for some time. But I was calmer now and I wasn't 'sharing', as the Yanks would say. Instead, I sort of chuckled breathily, to show that I was all right.

'Sorry about all that stuff she said about you drinking and so on, too,' he added. 'She's quite a woman.'

'I can imagine. Look, it was no problem,' I replied. Did he also think she was a loony? I imagined he must. I was still a little unclear on where he fitted into the picture, though, and thought it best to keep my own counsel.

'She can be a little awesome when you first meet her.'

'Yeah, a little. Have you been working for her long, Cam?'

'No, just a couple of months.'

'Right.' Lucy had put down her knife and fork, and was flashing the *True Love* Nirvana Card at me. I threw a scrunched-up napkin at her. 'So, um, Cam, can I ask you how you met Gaelle?'

'Sure. I met her in Ireland.'

'And?'

'She offered to take me on as her assistant to get this book published. I accepted.'

'Right.'

'I suppose I thought a few months with her could be fun.'

'That's one word for it. I think the main problem for me with Gaelle today was that I wasn't thinking on my feet,' I admitted.

'Drinking too much will do that to you.' Was he serious?

'I'm joking,' he laughed. 'She did something similar to me when we first met. But she's pretty harmless most of the time.'

'Okay,' I said. 'And one last thing. I was wondering, do you think Gaelle will want a lot about her current life in the book, or will it all be old stuff?'

'Well, that's up to you and Gaelle, really. I think her present is as interesting as her past. She's been chased for a while to write this book. Finally she's doing it her way – write it first, sell it later when she thinks it's ready. She has a long-standing offer from a French publishing house on the table. I agree that if she's going to do the book, it should be warts and all.'

'Are there a lot of warts?'

'What I mean is Gaelle should spell out what she really believes, for better or worse. But if she refuses to talk about something there's actually not a lot we can do to force her. She's worried about being made to look a fool, which is understandable. The only thing I do know is that she's happy to talk about what she did when she disappeared from Australia.'

'I see.'

'The rest is up to you and me to extract.'

'Okay.'

'Anyway, Cara, she does want you to come back tomorrow. You're being paid by the day, aren't you, so does that suit you? She wants to show you some of her work.'

I'd seen her work room today. I could only imagine what went on inside it. But I was involved already, so I agreed.

'Great,' he said. 'Can you come around at 10.30?'

'Sure.'

'So don't get too trashed tonight, will you, Cara?'

'No, sir,' I replied. Was he flirting with me? Was I with him? He was very friendly, for a sex god.

'So, I'll see you tomorrow, yeah?'

'Okay, then.'

I said goodbye and put down the phone. I liked the sound of his voice. This was a good thing or a bad thing, depending on how I wanted to look at it. In any case, seeing Gaelle at work could be fascinating. At the very least, I was bound to get a good laugh.

47

DREAM DIARY
29 JUNE: A SEVERED HAND

I felt myself falling into a deep slumber. At the other end of this feeling was Gaelle, in all her glory. I was in a tubular black belt, a belt where you might see asteroids dancing. I saw Gaelle and she was smiling at me encouragingly.

'You're scared, aren't you?' she asked benevolently.

'Scared of what?' I asked her back.

'Don't be scared. Just come with me.'

She took me with her. I was light and I was flying through darkness. There were little flecks of white around me. We flew to a mountainside, somewhere far away where I'd never been.

'Look in there,' she said.

She motioned towards a hillside, covered with lush green grass. Set in this hillside was a cave. I flew towards the cave, no longer questioning if this was real or a dream. I was plain curious. I neared the cave and peered in. On the sandy floor was just one item. A severed hand, with a large silver and ruby ring on the ring finger.

5

the queen crystal

Cam was there to meet me when I arrived for my second meeting with Gaelle. Today he sported the same twinkly eyes, heavy navy cotton pants, an untucked shirt with pink and orange swirls on it and bare feet. He'd shown astonishing taste in clothes thus far. I was already feeling quite a strong urge to see what was underneath them.

Under his arm, he had a red folder with 'Triumvirate Account' marked on it, and what looked like invoices and bills falling out of it. He set that down on a grand chestnut sideboard as he led me through the living room to Gaelle's work room. She was sitting on the floor on a Persian rug with two women, one older, one younger, both dressed in white. The younger one I recognised as Amanda from the previous day. All three looked as though they were wearing karate suits, but when Gaelle referred to them, she called them their 'white clothes'. Gaelle wore the same get-up: a pair of loose-fitting white cotton trousers and a shapeless, V-necked top to match. She said wearing the colour white meant the energy around them would 'flow more smoothly'.

Gaelle and the two women were cross-legged in a triangle formation and there was some tinkling, Asian-sounding music playing quite loudly. Cam and I sat down against the wall at the back of the room. I certainly didn't mind being next to him, in the dim light of Gaelle's work room.

'Now we must prepare the final part of this ritual and wash the sacred crystals that we will use today,' she announced. Gaelle heaved herself up to standing position and I started to follow, but she raised her hand. 'No. Just Amanda, Nadine and I will do this. Please remain here.'

Once they'd left the room, Cam filled me in on the details. The two women, he said, were Gaelle's most devoted devotees. He told me that Amanda, who was studying business management at college, had latched onto Gaelle after they'd met at a spiritual development course Gaelle ran annually. The slim and elegant Nadine was a homoeopath who'd been working with Gaelle on and off for years.

'They adore her,' he said. 'So. Have you ever seen anything like this?' he asked.

'Once. I was sent to do a story about the opening of a "stargate", when I was back in Australia . . .'

He looked confused.

'You know, like on the TV show. A sort of wormhole type thing, a portal to another dimension.' I shrugged my shoulders. 'I had to go to a sacred site in the Blue Mountains, just near Sydney, where there were about twenty people all sitting cross-legged around a long, golden ream of fabric on the ground, chanting to open this stargate.'

'Did it work?' he asked, eyes twinkling.

I nearly snorted with derision. 'God, Cam. How would I know?

But it made a good story.' I smiled. 'They all placed their watches and rings and things on the material, so that when the stargate opened, they'd be invested with some kind of higher energy.'

'Sounds just like Gaelle's cup of tea.'

I didn't say it to Cam then, but a major difference between writing about the stargate and Gaelle's life was that, for the stargate piece, I was fully expected to have a good laugh at the expense of these hippies. As for Gaelle, I was expected to write about all this . . . stuff . . . sympathetically and seriously. 'Give some people enough rope and they'll hang themselves,' I concluded.

He raised his eyebrows. Disapprovingly? I couldn't be sure.

'Funnily enough, though, the bloke who ran the whole stargate show, Kai, told me that writing the story was a part of my "soul's path", and just "the first step". I put that in the article. He said eventually I'd write something much more far-reaching . . .'

'Maybe he was talking about Gaelle's book?'

I put a faux shocked look on my face for Cam's benefit. He laughed.

'To be honest, I told the stargate story like it was — which meant Kai and his hippy mates were happy, because I simply reported what went on, and the editors were happy because they thought that what went on sounded hilarious. Kai reckoned he communicated with advanced souls from outer dimensions. Is that what Gaelle says she does?'

'Not quite.'

'What then?'

'Gaelle says — and I'm more or less quoting — that she's an advanced soul herself. She says something called the Earth Secrets were passed on to her by some of the world's greatest prophets, many of whom materialised on earth during the sixties and seventies. She says these "entities" came "in" at that time because people's senses were left wide open, through their use of acid . . . LSD . . .'

I checked to see if he was straight-faced. He was.

'She also says that she's a walk-in, half a human and half a Greater Spirit who walked into her earthly body when Gaelle was twenty-three. She's about sixty now, I think. A walk-in happens when a higher being and a human agree that the higher power can walk in to the human's body and use it for work here on the Earth.'

'Hang on. I've heard about this from my flatmate's boyfriend. He went to see a movie about it. About a boy who has an alien in him or something . . .'

'*Powder?*'

'Yeah. He went to see it last night.' Doo doo doo doo, once more.

'Gaelle will tell you that her humanity and spirituality were "expertly and totally braided".'

'Hello?' I wanted to say. Instead, I asked Cam why he was telling me this. Did he want all this in the book? It would make Gaelle look a complete fool and, although I was doing this for the money and because it was a good story, I didn't like to make anyone look stupid in print.

'She'll put it in her own words,' he said.

'I see.' Uh huh. Right. This was going to be some autobiography. People would end up making fun of her, like I made fun of the hippies in the Blue Mountains. I could see the *Women's Weekly* headlines now: 'Deranged Debutante: Socialite Goes Mental'. Poor Gaelle. There was nothing like being ravaged by the media to plant your feet back on the ground.

Gaelle, Nadine and Amanda returned from their bathroom break, holding their crystals. Gaelle said they'd been up since five, meditating and performing physical and spiritual cleansings in preparation for the duties they were about to complete.

'We have a big job ahead of us,' she announced, settling back into her spot on the floor. 'But I am feeling up to the job. Nadine and Amanda are here because I need their Earthly support.

'Let me tell you an old Hindu story to illustrate. There was a devoted Nepalese Swami who was practising astral travel in his cave on a mountaintop. The Swami ascended into the next dimension through his meditation, leaving his body vulnerable in the cave. In his absence, a tiger came into the cave and mauled it. He ate much of it there and then dragged the remainder off to his den.

'Now, of course, when the Swami's spirit came back from his astral journey, he found his body was simply gone. He knew he had the right cave, but his body just wasn't there. In its place was nothing but a pool of blood, and his left hand, still bearing his sacred Swami ring.'

Cam sort of chuckled as Gaelle concluded her tale. Amanda went white; Nadine smirked, but held herself in check. I didn't move a muscle. It was the story that explained my dream of the previous night. How could this be so?

'So we don't want anything like that happening today, okay, girls?'

Amanda and Nadine shook their heads slowly.

Gaelle placed a large red velvet cushion between her back and the altar table, getting her rather bulky body comfortable. As she and Nadine settled into their places, Amanda shifted this way and that to make the third point on the equilateral triangle between the three of them, which Gaelle explained was 'vital to the proceedings'.

'Do you have the Queen crystal?' she asked the younger girl. Amanda nervously removed a large parcel from a midnight-blue velvet bag. A fist-sized rose quartz crystal was wrapped loosely in a green silk sash.

'Right. Are we ready?' Gaelle asked. 'As you know, Carlos, Keeper of the Infinite Flame, is going to be contacted today. I have had word that we are to be in touch with him. I would like to state my intention to you two girls. I will go into a meditation and leave my body, and travel to find him. Once I have done that, I will create a diversion and get his attention.'

I had no idea who Carlos, Keeper of the Infinite Flame, was, but said nothing.

'You two,' Gaelle continued, addressing her assistants, 'are here to ensure that nothing happens to my body while I am out of it.'

Gaelle seemed lost in her preparations and I half thought she'd forgotten about Cam and me. Suddenly she turned, swivelling her head and sending me a laser-like blue-eyed stare. 'Are you all right, Cara dear?' she asked.

'Yes, thanks, I'm fine,' I replied, sounding as relaxed as I could.

'Good. Make yourself comfortable. It's important that you see this.'

I hoped she wasn't about to do some weird *Exorcist*-type thing and swivel her head the full 360 degrees, projectile vomiting all the way.

'As Cam has told you, I am a walk-in, an expertly braided star seed, the living soul of a higher spirit who has walked into an earthly body by arrangement. I can prove this, you know,' she said, looking at me. 'While you and most of the rest of the Earth's inhabitants have twelve-strand DNA, I have fourteen. Because I am half human, half alien.'

I looked at her and nodded. Arguing the point could have taken millennia. A blood test, however, would clear up the matter in days.

Gaelle took the crystal from Amanda.

'I am using the rose quartz to symbolise and amplify the love that we know is needed now,' Gaelle said as she held the rock up towards the ceiling with both hands. 'Cara. You are a part of the Whole Woman, do you understand?'

Nope.

She didn't wait for an answer. Her voice grew louder. 'The Whole Woman resides in this quartz. Starved of the love so beautifully encrypted in the carbonated dimensions of this Earthly gem, the Earth would wither. The love we seek today will bring back to Earth what has been drained away. Before it is too late. The Whole Woman returns. And so it is!' Gaelle fairly shouted the last sentence with her eyes scrunched closed in concentration.

Cupping the crystal meaningfully, almost clinging to it, Gaelle took the first inhalation of what she said would be a twenty-six-breath meditation. It was a variation on the ancient MoKoBo technique, which Gaelle told us she preferred to use when astral travelling. Her breath started coming very thick and fast, like a kettle about to boil. Thankfully, her head stayed in the same swivel-free posture as her body started to sway in a circular motion. She looked like she was going into a trance. I could only see her in profile, but she looked seriously out of it and out there. The room seemed to get hotter – or was it me? I wondered if she was faking it. Nadine was watching her closely, leaning in towards Gaelle as if looking for signs of distress. Gaelle had mentioned that trancing could be taxing on the physical body.

'Om om shanti om . . .' Gaelle began moaning, sounding either like someone speaking very pissed Welsh or like a record being played backwards at half speed. 'Om om shanti om . . .' Her face began to contort. The colour was draining from it second by second, starting at her forehead and moving down towards her chin.

I glanced at Cam, who raised his eyebrows. He looked very much like he had a sudden urge to be known as The Employee Formerly Known As Gaelle's Assistant. I was still wondering how she'd recounted the story about the Swami from my dream so perfectly. Gaelle's body was now swaying like a leaf falling on a windless day. She was moaning, Nadine was staring and I was starting to feel slightly faint.

I could hear Gaelle's voice in my head, but the room had gone white. The next thing I knew, I was gone. Elsewhere. Somewhere. Nowhere. Out of it. When I came to, I saw four faces peering into mine. Something strange had definitely happened. I felt as if I'd lost time. Cam, Gaelle, Amanda and Nadine were above me in a circle. Cam was patting my cheek with his hand, apparently trying to bring me round. It seemed I'd fainted.

'Cara?'

All I remembered was a vague sense of exhaling a loud sigh as my body collapsed. I now found myself propped up against the wall, my legs akimbo beneath my skirt, my hair over my face like a curtain, cutting out what little light there was in the room.

'Cara, wake up,' I heard Cam through my dazed state. 'Wake up, Cara.'

My mind cleared slowly and I opened my eyes properly. Gaelle and her acolytes were still standing over me, peering intently. I felt a mixture of disorientation and embarrassment. I wished they'd disappear. I couldn't speak yet. What had happened? At exactly the same moment, they all took a step back from me, except for Gaelle who stayed peering from above, her stare intense.

'Cara,' she said in a low voice. She said my name as if testing that I could hear her.

'Mmm,' I replied. This was too damn weird.

'Cara? Can you hear me? I need to be sure you can hear me.'

I can hear you, I thought. What do you want?

'Cara, listen to me. You got caught up in my trance.'

I said nothing.

'Cara?'

'Yes,' I uttered, finally. My voice had returned.

'You got caught up in my trance. Can you hear me?'

'Yes, the first time.'

'Okay, repeat after me, "I am in touch with Mother Earth." '

What the – ?

' "I am a Whole Woman and I am in touch with Mother Earth." Go on, say it.'

Naff off.

'I am a Whole Woman and I am in touch with Mother Earth,' she repeated.

'I am a Whole Woman and I am in touch with Mother Earth,' I said. Gaelle sighed with what sounded like relief.

'Good. You're grounded. Your etheric body has returned.'

Excuse me? What was this? Why did my head hurt on the inside?

Gaelle and Cam helped me sit up more comfortably. Gaelle clicked on the stereo, and 'I Feel the Earth Move' by Carole King started to play softly.

'You got caught up in my trance,' Gaelle repeated, holding my hand. 'It does happen sometimes. You're very open to it, but you've got a lot of resistance, too. Have you done much psychic work, Cara?'

At that point, had it not been for the fact that I was still bursting with curiosity about what writing this book might bring, I'd have just walked out. This was getting way too bizarre. Gaelle was a loony and I wasn't happy about feeling so freaked out. The fact that I'd had a Shanti Deva-induced hallucination about the glorious Cam, before we'd even met, or that Gaelle had practically recounted my dream from last night no longer seemed so weird. Life is strange. But compared to what?

'Maybe we should go out and get some fresh air and daylight,' Cam said, reading my mind, as everyone seemed to be doing lately.

'Mmm, yeah, good idea,' I agreed. 'If I can stand up.'

Cam put his hands under my arms and slowly picked me up. His body felt strong, and I liked muscular. Despite that, I was pretty damned keen to get out of the house as fast as I could. I wobbled through Gaelle's living room and down the stairs to the street. She just let me go. I felt ridiculous, but I was spinning out.

As I left, she called out to me, 'Cara, you'll be fine. I want to meet your friend Lucy. Bring her here next time.'

Trying to ignore her, I kept walking, with Cam bringing up the rear.

'That's it,' I said to him, moving as quickly as I could along the footpath. The sky was blue, for once, and there was birdsong in Eaton Square. Amazing what money could buy.

I pelted along, panting as I spoke. 'I'm out of here. She is too weird. What the heck was all that about?'

'Are you okay?' he asked.

'No, not really, Cam. You may or may not be surprised to hear that I am feeling a little stressed out. Is this normal? Has she done this sort of thing with you in the room before? What's this Whole Woman stuff?'

'Er . . .'

'And why does she want to see Lucy?' I stopped in my tracks. 'You know, I'm pretty sure I must have better things to do than get involved with some lunatic sixty-year-old. What's she into? Mind control? Who are those two weirdo sidekicks of hers? Why are you putting up with this?'

I had probably gone too far. Cam said nothing. In the silence, my brain searched frantically for one logical explanation for what had just happened. I'd fainted, sure, but somehow it felt stranger than that. And what about that bizarre Swami tale of hers which seemed to match my own dream so perfectly? Maybe I was just being sucked in by a great show-woman, but, if that was the case, why was I feeling so edgy? All I could think of were about 20 000 reasons why I didn't want to get further involved.

Cam put his arm around my shoulder. 'Cara, I'm so sorry about all this. Come on, let's walk slowly. You'll feel better. You just fainted.' Once more, my body welcomed his. This was too much. I had to keep a rein on what could easily become a crush on this person. And that wouldn't do at all. Not at work . . .

We stopped at the first café we came to, where, thankfully, everything seemed relatively normal. There were waitresses pouring coffee amid a general clattering of china and crockery, and office workers having morning cigarette breaks and eating ham and cheese sandwiches. I wanted to hang on to the normality.

'So,' Cam said.

'So.'

'Are you okay?' he asked. His voice rubbed me up the right way. Despite his soothing qualities, I looked at him with what I hoped was a sarcastic stare.

'You're pretty shaken, aren't you?' he ploughed on.

'Yes, as it goes, I am. Aren't you? What on earth happened in there? One minute I was listening to her carrying on, and the next you were waking me up.' Didn't he think this was odd?

'She said you got caught up in her trance, something about your etheric or astral bodies merging. I have no idea. But she also said it was proof to her that you're absolutely the right person to research the book.'

'When did she say that?'

'When you were out of it.' His eyes were big and brown and luscious and I wanted to dive into them.

'Maybe I just didn't have enough air and I fainted,' I said, feeling mightily challenged in my desire to stay on top of things. 'Have you seen her do anything like this before?'

He didn't so much speak as clear his throat, as if there was something he didn't want to talk about.

'Yes?' I prompted. 'Don't tell me you think her etheric bodies story is on the money?'

'Look, I'm not the type to buy all this cosmic stuff, but . . .'

'Yes?'

'Well, she's a strange lady . . .'

'I know. Go on.'

'I really have no idea if she's a charlatan, a wonderful hypnotist or what, but –'

'Tell me!' I demanded, loudly enough to make him laugh. 'Tell me or I quit.'

'Okay. I told you I went to Ireland, and that's where I met her?'

'I remember. It struck me as a little odd, though.'

'Why?'

'You don't seem to be someone who usually hangs out with . . . mystics.'

'What kind of person does?' he asked.

'I don't know.'

'Actually, I'm a stockbroker by trade. Or I was.'

'In Ireland?'

'No. I met Gaelle when I went to Ireland to get away from the City.'

'As in the city of London, or the City financial district?'

'Both,' he said.

'So what does all this have to do with her being a charlatan?'

'About two weeks after we met, she told me stuff about my childhood that she had no way of knowing, as far as I could work out. Stuff like how I gashed my knee really badly climbing Brighton Pier on New Year's Eve when I was about fifteen, that kind of thing. I grew up in Brighton. My folks are still down there.'

He paused and I used my years of journalistic training to give me the strength to say nothing – say nothing and your interview subject will usually continue. Bingo.

'One night, while we were both still in Ireland, I went to sleep as usual, and I swear to God I dreamed Gaelle was with me and that she took me astral travelling, or whatever it's called.'

'Are you serious?'

'Totally. We sort of flew up over Ireland, through the skies and suddenly we were over London . . . then we went down towards the south . . . over the motorways . . . and I don't know, I was sort of flying over factories, villages, down to the coast.'

'You are kidding me.'

'No. She asked me if I wanted to see my family and of course I said I did. My dad was struggling with angina at the time. He's okay now, thank God, but I was missing him. I went to "see" them is the only way I can describe it. They were fine. I just saw my folks asleep in their bed, well and happy. After I don't know how long she asked me if I was ready to go back to Ireland. I said yes, and we followed these silver cords that came out of our bodies, and then suddenly I was back in my bunk on the yacht I was living on in Schull harbour.'

'What yacht?'

'I was living on a yacht in the fishing village where I was working.' He waited for a reaction, but I said nothing. For someone with as many questions as I had in my head at that moment, it was a tribute to my ability to shut up.

'The following day, Gaelle called in to see me. She asked if I'd had a "good night's sleep". I said I had, sort of warily. Then she told me that she knew I was feeling a little homesick and that she'd wanted to help me feel better. I said that she had, and she left. I didn't mention my dream to her after that. I guess I also felt it was too weird. I like to think it was all a bizarre series of coincidences.'

'What kind of coincidences?' I knew that people like Lucy, who believed in the power of mung beans and crystals, said there was 'no such thing as a coincidence' and that 'everything happens for a reason'.

'I don't know. Dream coincidences.'

'Right.' What else could I say?

'Meeting her was something new. I was so hacked off with my life, and she was a tonic.' He looked at me. 'So, do you want a sandwich or something?' A waitress hovered, pen in hand.

I grimaced. He just didn't get it. He was cute, but he wasn't getting it at all.

'Listen, Cam. I've just fainted, Gaelle says I've been caught up in a trance, you tell me she took you to Brighton on some mystic night flight and, if I remember rightly, the last thing she said to me as we left is that she wants to meet my flatmate Lucy. I mean, what the heck is going on?'

'Cara, relax. There's not really that much point in getting worked up, is there?'

'Why not?'

'Well, there's nothing to be scared of. We both have a job to do and either we do it or we don't.'

'I can't believe you're so into it.'

'It's better than the money markets.'

'Hmph.' We sat in silence for a moment, when I added, 'Speaking of jobs, don't forget, Cam, this is work for me, too, and I have to be honest about something. This business about you sitting in on the interviews really bothers me.'

'Why?'

'Look, no offence, but when a journalist sits down with a subject, he or she needs to create a sort of, I don't know, intimacy . . .'

'And?'

'And I don't think that Gaelle needs a protector, and the idea of you sitting in on the interviews, watching me while I work, well, it doesn't exactly appeal.'

'Okay, look, we're not going to be doing interviews for a while. Let's just see how it goes. Maybe you can do them alone, once she trusts you.'

'All right. Maybe it's none of my business, but there's something else I'd like to ask you, Cam. What do you personally think about all the stuff that she comes out with? All that astral travel stuff. I mean, do you subscribe to it all whole-heartedly?'

He grinned. 'I don't know. I guess I've never really thought that there was any such thing as mediums or psychics, particularly. But I'm still trying to figure her out. This is a finite project, I'm being paid well for it, and it's sort of interesting to sit back and watch it develop.' He raised an eyebrow. 'I mean, there's a huge possibility that Gaelle's just a rich woman wrapped up in some sixties time-warp kick. Maybe, very likely in fact, I just had a weird dream and got sucked in. That's fine. But for me, this job with her means a chance to follow something interesting before getting back into whatever I end up doing for some serious money. For you, obviously, it's a chance to work on a project that's bound to be high profile.'

What he said made sense, but didn't make me feel any better.

'So how did you come to do the Shanti Deva story?' he asked, changing the subject.

'In a roundabout way. A film publicist I know called to say one of his female clients was seeing Shanti Deva for lower back pain. He thought it would make a good story to publicise her latest film. You know, "Superstar Actress Visits Alternative Healer". They'll do anything for publicity, when they're in the mood. Anyway, when I looked into Shanti Deva I found he had scores of alleged celebrity clients, so the *Sunday News* commissioned me.'

'For better or worse?' He smiled.

'Exactly.'

'Listen. You know what you're doing. Chill out about Gaelle. I say we just hang in there. If you have any major worries, call me.' He scribbled his home number on a piece of paper. 'I usually screen my calls or Gaelle would be calling ten times a night, but you can get me on this number if you speak after the tone, and here's my mobile number.'

'Thanks, Cam.'

'If it really does get too weird for you, just tell me. Are you okay for now?'

'I really don't know.' I felt a bit stupid. 'I mean, I haven't fainted since I was about ten.'

The bottom line was that despite my initial fight or flight response, I was sitting on a great story and my curiosity was bigger than my desire never to see Gaelle again. As Cam and I bade each other farewell, I considered asking him if he thought I could at least get out of bringing Lucy to meet Gaelle. I knew Lu would jump at the chance – especially if I told her about what had happened today – but somehow it was all too scary, and I wanted to keep Gaelle in another compartment of my life. In the end, I said nothing, deciding instead to see what happened, which is always easier.

I didn't feel like going home, so I wandered away from Eaton Square towards the river. I thought a walk along Embankment, some fresh air and the sight of the Thames might help.

It was still only mid-afternoon and London had that quiet hum it gets, when the pressure eases and all is spinning along nicely. Traffic dotted with black cabs snaked along the river, racing VIPs to crucial appointments, couriers threaded in and out of the jams while tourists, mums with babies, students, old folk and fellow freelancers were out enjoying a stroll. I loved London on a clear, breezy day like this. It was cold but not (too) grey, nor raining. An overnight storm must have cleared the air, making it possible to breathe again. It was days like this I was very happy to be working freelance, jobs with freaky folk like Gaelle Carrington-Keane notwithstanding.

Over the years, working in newspapers and magazines, I'd been assigned various 'beats', from court reporting to the women's pages to features. I loved interviews with people who really had something to say. High achievers. Veteran actors and actresses. Experts in their field, be it medicine or sports or relationships. Writing the autobiography of a mystic guru was an interesting detour.

When I first arrived in London and started freelancing, I'd slave in the morning, then wander around London in the afternoons. One of my favourite areas had always been Embankment, along the north side of the Thames. It was a stone's throw to Chelsea, Fulham and other yuppie havens. These days it reminded me of Jonathan, my English ex. When we met, he was working as a freelance photographer at one of the women's magazines where I sometimes worked in-house. We did one job together – interviewing the man who invented the contraceptive pill – and it was lust at first sight.

After that first meeting, I often bumped into him, either in the magazine's photographic department, or at the coffee shop across the road from the office. One evening, as I was about to leave for the day, he cut me off casually at the lift and asked me if I wanted to go for a drink.

'Do you fancy a quick snifter?' were his exact words.

I said yes and we spent a very wonderful couple of hours drinking outside a pub just off Shaftesbury Avenue, near Chinatown. It was summer time and the days were long. We'd laughed almost too much that evening, the way you do when you're with someone you seriously fancy. I've often wondered if all that laughing is a lovers' mating call, a secret way of letting someone know that their presence makes you happy.

Afterwards, we'd walked slowly towards home, down from the West End to the river and along Embankment. We walked as far as Chelsea Bridge, then Jonathan went his way and I went mine. But not before we kissed. It was the start of a relationship that lasted eighteen months, until I arrived at his flat one night and found him sitting alone on the living-room sofa, his head hanging despondently. I went to massage his shoulders and felt him tense.

'What's up?' I asked him.

He passed me an envelope, already opened, addressed to him and with a US stamp on it.

'Cara, read this and tell me what you think,' he said.

I opened the envelope and found a letter, printed on golden letterhead, from a company called GrafAds. The address was in Manhattan, New York, New York.

'They're one of the top advertising agencies in the States,' he said, as I scanned it, quickly realising that GrafAds were offering Jonathan – my Jonathan – a job. In their New York office.

The possibility of my joining him there was never discussed in any depth. I didn't want to start all over again in Manhattan. Neither of us wanted a long-distance relationship.

In any case, I guess we'd kind of fallen out of love by the time the offer from GrafAds arrived. They say it happens after eighteen months – something about the chemicals in your body which make you feel 'in love' with someone 'running out' after a time. At that point, apparently, you decide if you still like the person enough to commit to them forever, and I guess Jonathan and I decided that it was great, thanks for all the hormones and memories, but it was over.

Even so, I took the split to heart. The fact that it had been so good to start with, and so dead-with-a-whimper when it ended, shook me up. I thought love lived, not died. Maybe it wasn't love. I had no idea. All I knew is that I was still single a year after our split and he wasn't. I didn't know the details but, according to friends of his who kept in touch with me, he was out and about in Noo Yawk and seeing an architect called Georgie. Georrrrrgie, with a US 'r'. I mean, really. Every now and then I got a letter, postcard or e-mail from him telling me his latest news.

Did I want a new boyfriend? I wasn't sure. According to Lucy – and probably Gaelle for that matter, as it seemed they went to the same School of Metaphysics – we get what we want by creating it with our thoughts. So, if deep down I wanted to be single, then I would be single. As long as I was still too scared to commit to a new relationship, a new relationship would be unlikely to present itself. There was a part of me still smarting over the end of the love affair with Jonathan, shocked at how it collapsed within weeks of the first signs of trouble. But I'd have liked to have met someone, to have had a partner in life's adventures. The only time I really thought about – or really minded – being single was sometimes as I got into bed alone at night, with no-one to snuggle up to. These days, like Moni, I lived my romantic life vicariously through Lucy, and contented myself with my good male friends, like Rufus.

Just as I was getting closer to Albert Bridge, a black cab slowed. The driver looked my way and I decided I'd had enough exercise for one day. I hailed him and hopped in. At home, I checked my e-mails and found twelve messages waiting. One was from Mum telling me that she was well, that Dad was looking forward to his impending retirement and that my younger sister, Bianca, had been acting very suspiciously of late.

Several others were from work contacts in Australia, offering commissions. A few were digests from the Lou Reed mailing list I'd subscribed to. Some were from friends, local and Australian, sending their news and gossip or asking me to call them. There were two chain letters, which I deleted without reading. One e-mail was from Bianca, explaining that she hadn't told Mum and Dad yet, as she didn't want them getting over-excited, but that she'd met a guy called Tim at a party and had fallen madly, passionately, wildly in love for the first time. This was a shock. Bianca was only . . . twenty-five. She was still practically in nappies, as far as I remembered. It seemed like only yesterday she'd been wearing Boy George hats and doing a Buffalo dance 'around the outside'. How was it that she was suddenly old enough to be in love with a man called Tim?

I replied to all, urging my sister to send me a picture of her new beloved, telling Mum not to worry about Bianca, turning down the work offers by mentioning my new project, and sending a new e-mail off to the Oz News library, back in Sydney. Gaelle had told me she was a deb and that I should read up on her history, so I was hoping for more info. I'd never heard of her, but that didn't mean she didn't have a past. I asked Oz News to send through all they could find on Gaelle.

Then I went to bed and slept for eighteen hours, dreaming about astral travelling over London by night with Cam.

The next morning, the doorbell rang while I was still in bed. I hastily jumped into a little floral dress which always looked decent, even over a sleep-creased body. I yelled out 'Hang on!', brushed my teeth in five seconds, splashed my face with cold water, spritzed Eau Dynamisante everywhere and raced downstairs to open the door, half expecting a courier. I peered through the peephole in the front door. It was Cam Street, his hair shining in the sun.

What was he doing here? I licked my fingers and double-wiped for any leftover mascara smudges.

'Hi, Cam,' I said as I opened the door.

'Hi,' he said, smiling a big smile which shocked me by making me feel warm all over.

'Hi,' I said again. I smiled back. We could stand here and say hello all day, if that's what he wanted. But I doubted that was his plan.

'You don't look surprised to see me,' he said.

'Uh, I'm not, really, I guess,' I said, suddenly feeling very girly. I could have drowned in his eyes.

He sort of swayed towards me, as if hinting that he wanted to come in. Was it the eighteen hours' sleep I'd just had or did he tower over me like an angel, even as he stood before me? Was it my imagination or did I want to press my palms against his white cotton shirt, to feel the shape of his chest underneath the thick fabric? Get a grip, girl.

I asked him in and we sat down in the living room. I had the feeling he had something important to tell me. I was about to offer him a cup of coffee when he reached out his hand to me and put it on my thigh.

As soon as his hand made contact, the weirdest thing happened. Weird even for this week.

Firstly, as the heat passed from his palm to my leg, I felt myself change, like my body was turning into glass or something equally brittle, and then it sort of came back to normal, but lighter, and then, while feeling the energy pulsing through his palm to my thigh, I felt this heat stirring between my legs. It was like a ball, a sphere of fire, but not burning, just hot and warming, and it started to splinter out from its core, my breath started getting heavy and I felt as if sparks were running through my body.

He increased the pressure on my thigh, the sparkling fragments

increased in speed and intensity and, before I knew it, I was struggling and stifling an orgasm. I didn't want to do this. My body was
shuddering in this delicious, irresistible cyclical motion, and I was
panting. I was delighted, but trying so hard not to let him see what
was happening. I had no chance of anything.

As I drew breath and shuddered, he moved towards me and
before I really had any idea of what was going on, he was kissing
me, his arms around me, pressing himself up against me. He
smelled delicious. Of course, I kissed him back. Had I been Queen
of England about to commit adultery surrounded by a bevy of Fleet
Street photographers, I'd have continued. I felt my body turn to
liquid bliss. I was sliding down the sofa, while he climbed on top of
me. I could feel his weight on me, and it felt just as it should. It was
as if his weight was always supposed to be there, and I had known
it, and welcomed its return. I pushed my body up against his, wanting to meld, like they do on 'Star Trek', wanting to feel his outline,
contours and shape against mine.

He held me gently, our bodies warmly pressing together. I kissed
him back some more. He was such a slow kisser. If I'd really had my
wits about me, I'd have wondered how he knew how to make me
come by placing his hand on me. I mean, I've heard of the electricity
of a new lover's touch, and I've heard of Tantric sex where you bonk
but don't necessarily have an orgasm, and I've heard of ridiculous,
but this took the cake.

Suddenly, he was inside me. I can't really remember how that
happened, whether he took our clothes off, or I took them off, or
we both did, or they just evaporated, but they were mostly off and
he was inside me.

'I want you,' he whispered into my ear. 'I want to be inside you
forever, through every pore. I have always been inside you, you
have always known I was there. You were just waiting for me to
return.' Speaking through increasingly urgent thrusts, he continued
in his deep voice. 'We belong together. We always have and always

will, throughout the centuries and across time. I always knew that wherever you went, I would find you.'

He lay on top of me, sliding to the back of the sofa, and started to kiss my face. For a moment, the spell was broken and I realised where I was and what I was doing. This was too much.

He seemed to grow distant. Further away from me. I could hear a purring. I opened my eyes to find Mouser brushing his wet nose against my cheek.

Shit.

I'd just had an erotic dream about Cam Street.

God. It was 11 a.m.

After fifteen minutes' recovery time spent staring at my ceiling in shock, wondering if I'd really had an orgasm, I staggered down to the kitchen in search of head-clearing coffee. A copy of the *Daily Mirror* was on the table, open at the horoscope page.

Pisces: A day of days! Salute the sun and celebrate your intuition. Pay special attention to your dreams; they are the key to your future.

Help. I've always been unnerved by moist dreams about men I know. I figure it's my subconscious trying to tell me something I don't want to know. The worst one I ever had was about a rather annoying, overweight bloke with a moustache at one of the newspapers I worked for. In the dream, we were on two trapezes — me on one, him on the other . . . naked . . . and with a raging hard-on which — forgive me — kept going in and out of me as he swung backwards and forwards. I didn't much like this guy before the dream; after it, I couldn't look him in the eye for weeks.

Down in the kitchen, I flicked on the kettle and looked for my cigarettes. Then I remembered. I gave up three months ago. I noticed a yellow Post-it note stuck to the telephone. It was written in Lu's scrawl: '*Cam called. Please call him at Gaelle's.*'

I resolutely allowed myself time. I drank my coffee slowly,

brushed my teeth at length, this time for real, and went back to the kitchen to make the phone call. Cam answered. Naturally.

'Hi, Cara,' he said, his voice infused with friendliness. 'Thanks for calling me back so quickly. You know what, I had an amazing dream about you last night.'

'Really? What happened?'

'Oh, you know, just sort of, I don't know, you, er, just sort of drifted in and out of my house, um, dream, you know . . .'

'Well,' I said, for want of anything more intelligent to say. Then I added, 'I had a dream about you, too. Spooky, eh?' Brilliant comeback. Not.

'I see.'

'Yeah.'

Yeah.

'So, anyway, Cara, I called you because Gaelle really wants you to come over again . . .' He trailed off, obviously realising that I might not be in too much of a hurry to schlep around to Eaton Square after yesterday's fainting fit.

'When?'

'Is the day after tomorrow too soon?'

'Ummm,' I stalled.

'Are you still there?' he asked, finally.

'Yes, sorry, Cam,' I said as I caught sight of my latest Mastercard bill on its spike near the phone. 'No, that's fine. The day after tomorrow is fine.' Sold to the woman with the blonde perm.

'And, ah, there's one other thing, Cara . . . Could you bring your flatmate Lucy with you?'

'Why?'

'I don't know. Gaelle just really wants to see her. She said she sensed she was sad and needed cheering up, or something. She said to me, and I quote, that if I asked you about it, you would tell me Lucy really wants to meet Gaelle.'

'Hmmm.'

'So, is that right?'

Gaelle was too darn clever. 'Yeah, she does want to meet Gaelle,' I admitted.

'Okay, so ask her if she's free.'

Whether or not her delicate psyche was ready for the likes of Ms Carrington-Keane was highly debatable. After her recent romantic traumas, Lu was a sitting duck for someone like Gaelle. Even so, I felt duty bound to extend the invitation. I did, however, have a strangely unsettling feeling that if and when Lucy accepted the invitation, there'd be repercussions. I just felt it in my bones.

DREAM DIARY

1 JULY: I SAW YOU STANDING THERE

It was a dream of Cam and me. We were in a large house, a huge old London home. It was the eighteenth century. We were married, bohemian and in love.

I saw myself sitting in a room panelled with dark wood and set on two levels. I was downstairs, sitting on a stool by a very large picture window. I was painting a picture in oils of the parkland I could see through the window beside me. Behind me, upstairs, was a mezzanine level, where I had an artist's studio. I stayed at home and painted while Cam worked, this much I knew. There were other parts to the house, but this was our favourite area.

Cam came home from his day at work, looking mighty fine in eighteenth-century straight black pants, a white shirt and a smart grey frock coat. I put down my paintbrush and greeted him, kissing him gently on the lips and neck before leading him upstairs. When I took off my clothes, I saw that I wore striped underwear, with stockings, garters and a bodice. He wore long johns, which for some reason I found very erotic. We made mad, passionate love.

This time, the dream didn't freak me out. This time, I just enjoyed it.

warrior spliffs

The details I'd requested about Gaelle's life came through via e-mail from Oz News the next day. I read that she was in fact the daughter of a now-dead, but once very high-profile, Australian businessman called Clive Reno. She'd been born and raised in Rose Bay, a member of Sydney's Eastern Suburbs elite, the guys and 'gels' who wear Alice bands and say 'yah', sail yachts in the harbour and, latterly, drive Mercedes SLKs in any colour, as long as it's silver. Gaelle's evidently robust financial situation today was obviously a legacy of this heritage. She must have inherited heaps.

Gaelle had made her debut at eighteen, and at a tender nineteen married a dashingly handsome thirty-two-year-old named Brian Carrington-Keane, a young buck lawyer with political aspirations and well-placed connections. News of their speedy engagement threw the Eastern Suburbs matrons and their single daughters into chaos. Another serious catch bites the dust, whisked from under their noses by a teenage whippet of a girl. Photos of their wedding made it into *Vogue*. As Brian Carrington-Keane's wife, Gaelle had been expected to beehive her hair, slip her feet into pumps, and smile as she stood by her man, helping and accessorising him on his journey to political power. However, Gaelle hadn't done that. Instead, according to the news clippings, four years into their marriage, she had simply disappeared from their Vaucluse home, from the social scene and from Sydney, leaving behind her husband, her family and her friends, not to mention the *Women's Weekly* readers who missed her smiling face on the social pages.

Initially, it was assumed and rumoured that Gaelle had been kidnapped, perhaps for political reasons or even a ransom. Then the discovery of a goodbye note she'd left for Brian was made public, and pretty soon all of Australia knew that the young society lady had left her husband *of her own free will*.

The news stories written immediately after her disappearance concentrated mainly on the ramifications of her departure on Brian's political career. Then there was a rash of reported sightings of La Gaelle, as the magazines called her, pointing to her being in India. On the strength of these, it was variously rumoured that she'd 'fallen in with a group of Kashmiri LSD users and was being systematically brainwashed' or that she'd had a 'very serious turn and was living in a Pushkar nudists' colony'. Yet another theory was that she'd poured her inherited millions into a Goan cult's operations and was living the high life on the Indian coast, smoking grass and dancing under full moons wearing white clothes and flower garlands in her hair.

Now, years later, Gaelle was in London, ready to go public with 'the real story'. And I was to be the messenger. I chewed over the facts. There seemed a lot to take in. Moni came home from work and found me at the kitchen table, poring over my notes and clippings. Her eyes were gleaming.

'Whatchyadoin', C?'

'Reading up on some stuff for work.'

'Work schmerk,' she said, emphasising the 'schmerk'. 'You're not going to believe what Dale the Dickhead has come up with now.' She dropped her black satchel to the floor and headed for the fridge.

'What?'

'It's his most twisted concept yet. Infiltrating an Internet swingers' club . . .'

'What?'

'A swingers' club – where you swap partners.' She uncorked a bottle of white wine and poured us each a glass.

'No way.'

'Mmmhmmm. Sex sells. They've come up with a concept that they want me to produce. It's going to be a one-off prime-time special.'

'That's an honour.'

'Not.'

'Why not?'

'They want me to do our own fly-on-the-wall docu-soap. Send one of my reporters – or an actress – off to join this club. But to do it in secret.'

'What? Get one of your reporters to join a wife-swapping club?'

'I beg your pardon?' Lucy demanded, walking into the room.

'Are you telling me that these things still exist?' Frankly, I thought they were as passé as the Bay City Rollers and Wagon Wheels, and far less likely to have a revival.

'Believe it or not, they do. The Internet's made it easier, I guess. This particular club organises "parties" all over the country every month. Dale wants me to turn it all into a special one-hour investigation for the show. They're opening the phone lines afterwards for the viewers to call in. It's supposed to be an exposé of modern marriage. A lot of the club's members are married, bored, with kids and a mortgage. They want some extra-marital sex, without having to leave their spouse. So they join up . . .'

'That's sick,' I said.

'That's your opinion. Husbands and wives can join together, but apparently it's also open to people who want to get away from their partner. So they all turn up at the appointed secret location, shag each other senseless and then go back to their everyday lives.'

'What's it called?'

'Discreet Duets.'

'Erk!'

'Exactly. I found out about it last week. Some woman called Naomi phoned me and told me she'd joined up herself, and left her husband for a bloke she met at a Discreet Duets party in Hertford-shire. Now he won't leave his wife, despite his passionate promises of a few months ago.' Moni shook her head. 'She says she feels morally punished by God for her fling and wants the whole thing exposed, so other people don't fall into the same trap.'

'Lord.'

'They run the agency via e-mail and a secret Internet website that you need a password to log on to. She said she'd give me the URL the next time she calls. Of course, the minute I told Dale about it, he started making plans. Naomi feels so ripped off by Discreet Duets, she's quite happy to appear on camera and to help us smuggle some-one in there . . . She's already wrecked her marriage.'

'Really?'

'Firstly, she'll help us with getting membership, so we can get onto the site with a false e-mail address. They're quite paranoid about vetting people, precisely so that people like me don't get in there and blow their cover.'

'It could be an interesting insight into modern marriages and sexual mores,' I suggested.

'Absolutely. It would be, if Dale didn't also want us to somehow film inside one of their parties with a hidden camera.'

'What?'

'Leaving some poor sods very . . . exposed . . .'

'. . . so to speak.'

'So a few consenting adults around Britain could have very red faces.'

'But hang on,' I asked. 'How are you going to get a hidden camera into a place like that?'

'Mostly the parties are held in private homes. Obviously there are some people there who like to express their weird dress-up fetishes . . .'

'Like . . . ?'

'Like wearing Superman outfits. Or nappies. Or nothing but a pair of high heels. They're going to get an actress trussed up in PVC, with a hidden camera and mike sewn in.'

'God.'

'Dale the Dickhead wants us to use Madonna-like pointy tits with the camera on the end. I think it's his own private perversion. He says the shots will be so blurry it'll be hard to recognise anyone, but I know what he's like. Once he's got the chance, he'll run with it for maximum sensation.'

Lucy and I stared at her, our mouths open.

'Nice, normal suburban people wife-swapping. It's your basic "Blimey Vicar" exposé.'

'But if people are mad enough to join these clubs,' said Lucy, 'they shouldn't be ashamed of their decision or embarrassed about it.'

'Yeah, but what if they think it's okay, and their ultra-Christian boss doesn't agree? Or if their mum and dad see it? Or their kids' friends see it and they become the local laughing stock? I don't see it's my job to expose them, just for a few rating points.'

'Mmmm. On the other hand,' I added, 'it's an amazing opportunity, to produce your own one-hour special.'

'Is it legal to film people like that?' Lucy asked.

'We're looking into how much we have to hide their identity.'

'"Discreet Duets – Nudes Uncovered" by Moni Chancellor. I

can see it now. A prime-time exposé around the world. You'll be set up for life,' I joked.

Moni made a face at me.

I left it as late as I could to ask Lucy if she'd like to come around to Gaelle's with me the following day, hoping that she might have booked something else.

I was unsure about the wisdom of getting Lu involved in Gaelle's weird and wonderful world. The fact was that even though she didn't show it so much any more, Lu was in many ways still in the middle of her own crisis. Dealing with Niall and his latest contraceptive tangents was a mere distraction. Lu was going through what she liked to call 'a spiritual crisis', and had probably never been closer to packing it all in and going back to the Land of Oz.

Her torment was spawned by her English ex-boyfriend, whom she'd ditched four months earlier. Lucy had been seeing Alan, a faux Hooray Henry who worked in real estate, for nearly eighteen months. He was big and bossy and I think he made her feel secure. Small and blonde, she was perfect arm candy for Alan. In their future, Lucy-lost-in-love had seen marriage, babies and a shared blissful eternity in a small, vine-covered cottage somewhere within commuting distance to London. Monique and I had gone along for the ride, wishing her very well.

Sadly, it didn't work out like that. In fact, while Lucy was fanta-sising about learning baby massage and reading up on how to make the homemade aromatherapy creams she planned to sell from said cottage, Alan, it turned out, was eyeing up his blonde Sloaney secretary, Madeleine, who, in turn, was eyeing Alan's pay packet.

Maybe it was pre-engagement nerves, or a final fling, or maybe he was just an arsehole and it wasn't the first time, but one drink too many at the pub after work one Friday night had been enough for Alan to forget Lucy for a moment and to move in on ninety-three-words-a-minute Madeleine, who was waiting for him, arms and legs open. A few weeks after that fateful night, Madeleine announced she was pregnant, Alan confessed all to Lucy, and Lucy pronounced herself heartbroken and single once more.

We'd cried with her and consoled her, but in my heart of hearts I was relieved, and Moni was, too. We'd never been able to put our finger on what was wrong with Alan, but he'd never seemed like Mr Right.

In her misery, and probably hoping to find an escape route back to inner calm, Lucy had taken to hanging around Neal's Yard, the heart of London's New Age commercialism and home to a truck-load of herbal remedies and aromatherapy cures, crystals and Make-Your-Own-Candles kits.

Lucy had always had a tendency towards New Age preventions and cures. Now, as part of her attempts to 'clear' Alan and all his bad infidelity vibes from her churned-up system, her generally 'herbal' approach to life had gone into overdrive. Our bathroom shelves quickly filled with bath oils promising 'release from negative thought patterns'; in our kitchen, a cacophony of tasteless teas vied for cupboard space and pledged soothing relaxation and a confident outlook, motivation and strength. Finally, in every room in the house, little dark-blue bottles of essential oils started to appear alongside equally new oil burners. Lucy said the oils would bring everything from insight and vision to courage. The way it looked to Moni and me, Lucy was fully transforming herself into the kind of New Age junkie they make fun of in the Sunday supplements these days.

And when the lotions, potions and magic candles didn't change Alan back into a nice guy, or make Madeleine un-pregnant, Lu started to attend Neal's Yard-based weekend workshops – seminars with titles such as 'Discovering the Feminine Goddess Within', 'The Healing Power of Crystals' and 'Why Are You Always Unhappy?'.

It was at one of these workshops – on crystal healing – that Lucy met Niall. They'd flirted over obsidians at the Friday night session, simpered over rose quartz on the Saturday and had their first kiss after a long stroll home from the Sunday class. Lu was bursting with the news of her first post-Alan snog, and the relationship had gone from strength to strength. Niall knew his crystals, he could divine water, and he knew what to do with an aurasoma bottle.

In the two months they'd been together, Niall, for all his nonsense, had managed to win over Moni and me, at least to an extent; we even felt cheerfully obliged to wear the unique crystal pendants he'd fashioned especially for us out of stones, leather thongs and silver wire (mostly we wore them when we knew he was coming over). Lucy, in turn, had taken to refusing to leave the house without at least one healing blue lace agate in her handbag. We were pleased Lucy had bagged herself a sexy-looking shag, at least for a while. To help her forget Alan, if nothing else.

Of course, Lu was very free to accept Gaelle's invitation to 16 Eaton Square.

Cam greeted us on arrival, looking delectable as usual. I choked slightly as my erotic dream about him came flooding back to me. I introduced him to Lucy and we all adjourned upstairs to Gaelle's living room. Gaelle was in 'pottering' mode, tending her dozens of pot plants, spraying them with mist from a plastic water pump, and chatting to them.

'Hello, hello, do sit down,' she said, smiling at us. Cam and Lu sat down at opposite ends of the burgundy sofa. When I went to seat myself on an adjacent Regency chair, Gaelle waved me onto the sofa, too. I sat down in the middle, feeling like one of three birds lined on a wire for target practice, obedient and expectant. Not to mention unfeasibly close to Cam.

'Now,' Gaelle began. 'First things first. Cara. You left rather suddenly the last time we met.'

Guilty as charged. Something to do with fainting and trances and freaking out. 'Yes, I'm very sorry about that, Gaelle,' I mumbled in a tone I hoped was sufficiently apologetic.

'It's okay, because you're here now. And you've brought Lucy. Lucy, darling,' she said, fixing her formidable gaze on my friend. 'It really is wonderful to meet you. Again.'

Again? Let it pass, Lucy, I thought, half glad that Gaelle had turned her attention away from me, half worried about what would happen next.

'Sorry? Have we met before?' asked Lu, walking straight into Gaelle's trap.

'Oh, yes, we have met – many, many times, dear,' said Gaelle, adopting Mystic Standard Position A, her hands on her hips, her gaze penetrating, her tone loving. 'We've met in previous incarnations. Past lives, dear.' As she spoke, Gaelle pulled what looked like a small yellow flower from a plant. And ate it. Good Lord, she was weird.

'Past lives?' Lucy repeated. Hook, line and sinker, down in one.

'Yes, dear.'

Her gardening over, Gaelle came and sat down on her armchair, directly in front of us. 'What are you doing work-wise right now, dear?'

Was she about to offer Lu a job, too? Heaven forbid.

'I'm a graphic designer and I'm working on designing a range of fortune-telling cards. Nirvana Cards, they're called.'

'And they're to be used for divination, are they?' She picked at a petal that had apparently lodged in her teeth.

'Yes.'

'Good. Meditate on the meaning of each card before you set to work on the drawings. I think you'll find it a most satisfactory way of channelling inspiration.'

'Okay,' Lu said obediently. 'Thank you.'

'Now. Why are we all here today?' Gaelle asked rhetorically. Answering her own question, she leaned forward and reached into a Chinese lacquered box on the coffee table. Blow me down if she didn't pull out a long, thin and expertly rolled joint.

'Now,' she said, holding the joint up in front of us all with a smirk. 'Warrior spliffs. A warrior spliff is a joint which by this name is transformed into transformer. It's a transformer and transporter. It is our modern-day peyote. They cannot take it away from us. Say "ho".' She was addressing us all.

I looked at Lu to see her reaction. She was looking at me with the same query on her face. It had taken me all of about three seconds to convince her to come here. I wondered how it would be for her.

'Say "ho",' Gaelle repeated. 'It's a Native American acknowledgement that you agree with what I've just said.'

I sighed inwardly. Lucy giggled. She wouldn't be nearly as freaked out by all this as I was — I hadn't told her about my little fainting fit in Gaelle's work room because I couldn't face her getting over-excited about it. She'd be well into this. When she was in the mood, Lu loved a good joint as much as she loved psychics and mystics.

'Say "ho",' Gaelle repeated.

'Ho,' I breathed. I heard Cam say it, too. I didn't look at him. Last night's dream was painted all over my face, I was convinced of it. I felt sure he'd know I fancied the pants off him.

'Ho,' Lu said finally.

Cam had really urged me to ask Lucy if she wanted to come and meet Gaelle today, telling me it wasn't fair for me to make up her mind for her, despite my misgivings about bringing anyone to this place. I really was slightly freaked at the prospect of it, but I'd agreed it was only fair to pass on Gaelle's invitation. And Lucy couldn't have been happier about it. So here I was about to spend my afternoon stoned, with Cam on my left, Gaelle the mad woman in front of me and my gullible flatmate to my right.

Gaelle lit the joint and inhaled deeply. It was amusing to see a sixty-year-old sucking — expertly — on a scoob.

'It's Peruvian grass,' she told us, as she half held her breath. 'It's grown in the forests near Machu Picchu. The crops are abundant, ripe and dripping with oil. They're grown with love in dense forests for use only by people like me. The authorities there understand the Earth's history and future, and turn a blind eye to crops of this strain. In Peru, it's accepted that this grass is more than just a drug. It's more than something to enjoy at the end of the day. Peruvian grass will transport you. To other dimensions.'

I reassured myself that it wasn't what she said, but the way that she said it. She just had a very dramatic delivery. Gaelle passed Cam the joint. Today, he wore a pair of white trousers and a white shirt, topped with a Panama hat. He reminded me of an eminently undressable cricket umpire. His hair was back in the little ponytail again. Still sex on legs. He had a dubious look on his face, though, as he sucked on the scoob. Like he wasn't so sure that this was a good idea. I was, once more, fully freaking. I mean, I love a joint, but I've smoked enough grass to know that really killer strong stuff can blow the mind and Gaelle had been blowing my mind while I was straight. I dreaded to think what she could do to me when I was stoned on this shit.

'The flower I ate a moment ago?' Gaelle went on. 'It's a Gold-Blyth flower. It heightens the effect of this grass. For me.'

After sucking on the spliff like a seasoned campaigner Cam passed it to me. I inhaled three times and then three times more, for the hell of it. As well as being damn nervous, I was also really curious about what might transpire. I couldn't help it. I passed the joint to Lucy and waited for Gaelle to say something else. I was very aware of Cam's proximity. As the grass coursed through my veins, I felt it more and more. But I didn't want to think about that right now . . . Cam had shown nooooo signs . . . at all . . . of returning the . . . favour . . . Although he had dreamt about me, too . . . My mind floated and I realised I was very . . . very . . . stoned.

'While most use dope to kill self-awareness and mind, marijuana is medicine in my hands. Especially combined with Gold-Blyth flowers.' Gaelle, mercifully, had taken up her story again. 'This grass glimmers in the sunlight as though woven with gold dust, the same dust that the Masters are able to pluck out of the ethers just by snapping their fingers and commanding it to manifest. If you don't believe me, go to India and see it done yourself. I spent seven years in the company of my guru, Guru Tarshneesh. He taught me to pluck out the gold dust. One day, I may show you. It's very draining, though. And we don't want you getting caught up in my trance again, do we, Cara?'

I shook my head, feeling nervous. I hoped I wouldn't become paranoid.

'As I told you, because I am a walk-in I have fourteen-strand DNA, which means my trances are powerful.'

'Have you ever had a blood test to prove this?' I interjected.

She ignored me. She had the joint again and was puffing away. She could hold her Peruvian grass, this old bird. 'Lucy, did Cara tell you what happened to her here the other day?'

Divide and conquer. Oldest trick in the book.

'No,' said Lucy, looking at me accusingly, a grimace of hurt on her face. 'What happened, C?'

So I told her the story about 'getting caught up in Gaelle's trance' and her eyes widened until I thought they were going to pop out of her head. Gaelle would be held in even higher estimation now – not only reportedly psychic but also able to take others spinning out with her in her trances. Lu was awestruck. I noticed the much-diminished spliff had moved from Lucy to Cam. Me next.

Gaelle retrained her focus back to me. 'Now, Cara, what are we going to do with you? You and your friend Lucy are very special girls. But you don't know it. Lucy has a small idea, but you have totally blocked out your knowledge of your powers. I think you're afraid of them. So, what are we going to do with you?'

I stared at her. I wasn't sure I wanted a Cosmic Consciousness Personality Breakdown.

'Gaelle,' I began very slowly, 'what was that you said about pulling gold out of the ethers? And why did you want me to bring Lucy here with me?'

Cam passed me the joint and I had a few more tokes.

'Well, child,' Gaelle replied, 'they are two very good questions. Unfortunately, I am not going to answer either of them right now. Please take another drag and pass the joint.'

I complied, inhaling deeply.

'We don't want to waste that joint,' she said, addressing me, 'because we have work to do. All three of us. I can't answer your questions right now as I don't want to waste the effects of the gold dust you're so curious about. We are going to explore another part of this dimension today. Carlos, Keeper of the Infinite Flame, will join us.'

Gaelle smiled very broadly, as if this was the most fun she'd had in centuries. I was regretting those last bullish drags on the spliff. I don't know what I'd been trying to prove, but I'd learnt that six drags on a Gaelle joint were enough to get one very elegantly wasted. My free-forming brain wandered back to Cam. I manoeuvred my gaze to my left again. Yep, he was still there. I returned my attention to Gaelle, only vaguely aware of the fact that Cam's right knee was now rubbing ever so lightly against my leg.

Gaelle stood up. 'I want you to come with me, all of you, to my work room. Cam and Cara, you're here for the book, and you, Lucy, because you and I have a connection which I'll tell you about later. That's why you wanted to meet me so much, isn't it? Because you feel our connection.'

Lu stubbed out the spliff, at long last, and she and Cam followed Gaelle. I dragged my feet, very reluctant to head back into that strange room.

'Okay. Cam, pass out the mats, please,' Gaelle directed, once she had us in her incense-steeped parlour. Cam passed me a blue and rubbery bit of foam. He was smiling, as if we were partners in a bizarre fantasy.

'Sit down. Sit down, all of you. Lucy, don't be nervous. This will do you a lot of good.'

Lucy hadn't said a word for what seemed like ages. I was positive she was stoned off her tits and I hoped she was all right. She must have been wondering what Gaelle meant about them having a connection, because I sure as hell was.

'Everything is possible! That's what I want you to remember,' said Gaelle.

She was off raving about what we were going to do, but my stoned thoughts were wandering down another, far more interesting track. The subject of me and men. I hadn't had a decent love affair for so long.

At school, I had a two-year romance with a boy called Sam. I lost my virginity to him on Manly Beach at 2 a.m. after the Year Ten formal, and very lovely it was, too. When I went to university and he started work in computers, I decided I was far too hip for him, and that his mature attitude to life just didn't fit in with my bohemian student lifestyle, so he got the chop.

After Sam came David. We met in the uni bar when he lit my cigarette, two weeks after he dropped out of his engineering course. He was planning on travelling around Australia and was farewelling some mates before departure. After we met, he decided to hang around a bit longer. It really was first love. It wasn't insecure or unhappy, as it sometimes was now. It was honest and sweet and enduring. He found work as a night porter in a Pitt Street hotel, while I ploughed through my studies. Our plan was that we would take his deferred trip around Australia after I graduated, but when the journalism work fell into my lap so easily post-uni I was reluctant to make the break. He accused me of throwing our dreams out the window, and I accused him of not understanding my need to grab the career opportunities in front of me.

Since I came to London, Jonathan had been my one and only real amour. Though Cam had certainly captured my imagination of late.

I was still in total shock after my dream about him. Those dreams are so . . . personal. And real. I still didn't want to think about it.

By now all four of us were sitting on our mats, me facing Cam, Lu opposite Gaelle.

'Are you all right?' Cam whispered to me, still looking like he was enjoying himself.

'Sure.'

'Just go with it. It's fine . . .'

'Cara, move closer to Cam there,' Gaelle commanded.

I sighed inwardly and did as I was told. I was sure Cam was inching away in the opposite direction.

'Okay, okay, sit still,' Gaelle announced now.

My attraction to Cam was making me buzz. Grass did that to me. If I fancied someone and sat too near to them when stoned, I could practically feel my attraction vibes and energy slurping over their way. I'm sure Gaelle – or indeed Lu – would have had a good explanation for this. Maybe it was my aura trying to connect with his, or something. I looked at him face-on. He didn't seem to have noticed anything unusual. He wasn't even looking my way, but at Gaelle.

Gaelle told us we were about to do an 'Eye-to-Eye Exercise'. It would align all our energies and settle any disturbances in our astral bodies.

'I want you to relax now. And just look into your partner's eyes. Lucy, you look at me, Cara and Cam at each other.'

I looked as directed. This was a mind twister. A joke. Just what I didn't want to do, after the weird dream. I was very confused. Why was I so reluctant to admit how I felt about him? Was it the work connection?

'Why are you resisting, Cara?' Gaelle asked loudly.

Did she have eyes in the back of her head?

'All right. Now just sit quietly and look into your partner's soul. And remember: only love is real.'

As I'd already noticed from a distance, Cam's eyes were brown.

Up close, they looked very kind. And sexy. Perhaps slightly naughty. Certainly like they were laughing. His pupils were large, too, which I had read was supposed to be a sign of attraction. We were, however, in a darkened room.

'This exercise is designed to have two people make the deepest contact, at the highest level of mutual recognition possible – to connect soul to soul. As you know, eyes are called windows to the soul, and through them we see the deepest part of one another, our magnificence and wholeness. The essence of the person. We connect with their Inner Being, we see through their veils and into their souls. What do you see, Cara? Cam?'

Silence.

'What do you see, Cara? Cam?' Gaelle repeated. 'Feel the soul ties. Feel them.'

I decided to go with the reverie. If Gaelle wanted weird she could have weird.

'I see Cam's eyes very large. They're very deep brown.' They looked like a velvety night sky.

'Do you recognise them from somewhere else?'

Huh? The thought did briefly occur to me that I was supposed to be getting info out of Gaelle, not playing silly buggers in her work room. But she was paying me, so I figured she could waste as much of my time as she liked. Frankly, I needed a rest and, although this was trippy, it wasn't exactly hard work, was it?

Omigod. Suddenly I *was* seeing Cam in a new way . . . as . . . a . . . he had short hair . . . he was wearing a cassock, he was . . . a monk . . . a Franciscan monk, in a very old French abbey. I was a nun . . . no . . . a novice. We were in the same abbey, a huge monolith, with ornate tiled floors, heavy wooden pews, enormous vases filled with white flowers, magnificent high ceilings. Cam and I sat in pews facing each other on either side of the aisle. We were religious choristers, part of a group of males and females gathered together to sing in this large abbey, to welcome a visiting dignitary. I caught his eye.

We were connected. We knew each other. I could see it in his eyes. We couldn't have each other. We were monastics. It was forbidden.

'Do you recognise them from somewhere else?'

'Er. No.' I wasn't going to make a total dick of myself.

'There is no such thing as chance. All the people we meet in this life, we meet because of a karmic connection. Either they owe us or we owe them. We have known them before.'

I felt a very strong urge now to lean across the foot of space that separated Cam and me now, and to kiss him, as I couldn't have done back in my seventeenth-century monk fantasy. He was so close, I could hear his breath. Amazing what a bit of grass and eye contact can do for a girl. I felt my body swaying gently, from side to side. I felt I could see through his clothes. I wanted to wish away his shirt and spread my palms over his strong shoulders, push him, slowly, to the ground, so that he was lying down, his muscles tense, holding his breath, not daring to exhale.

'Okay, now I want you to come back in time to today,' Gaelle said.

How did she know I'd been time travelling? I didn't believe she could read my mind. Not really. I looked back into Cam's eyes for a reality check.

'All right. Now, Lu, take my hands. Cam, take Cara's. Hold her hands, rub them, feel the connection. We all know each other from before. That's why we're all here today together.' I felt my loins warming as Cam held my hands in his. 'Our paths go back over the centuries, through time, back to the Egyptian schools, back to Atlantis, when you were my students then, just as you are here today. Remember it, Cara, remember it, Cam, remember it, Lucy. Do you remember?'

I broke away from Cam's gaze as I heard a soft whimpering coming from Lu's direction. I turned to look at her and, sure enough, she was crying. Well, sniffling, really. There were tears streaming down her face and she was almost silently sobbing. She was catching her breath as she cried, holding it in. Shit, I knew this would be too much for her.

'She's all right, Cara – aren't you, Lucy?' Gaelle said rather than asked.

Lu closed her eyes, the corners of her mouth turned down, and she nodded twice, slowly, sadly. I guessed she was thinking about Alan and the demise of her dreams, of a lost rural life in thatched cottages, with dogs, Agas and school runs. Bastard. She'd done well to recover this much so soon after Alan. I hoped Gaelle's weirdness wasn't setting her back. But knowing Lu, she would say she was 'clearing blockages'. That's what she always said after she'd been crying.

'Okay, so now, let go of your partner's hands,' Gaelle instructed.

I realised mine were still in Cam's. His felt strong and not nearly as sweaty as mine. His face seemed softer than I remembered. I reluctantly took my hands out of his. He sort of smiled at me.

I was desperate to know if the experience had been as intense for him as it had been for me, but I would never have dared ask him straight, let alone when I was still in the midst of that slightly isolated feeling which comes with smoking spliff. Great for imaginings, crap for communication.

And then as soon as it had begun, it was over.

'You may all go now,' Gaelle announced suddenly.

I was feeling truly spaced out and in no shape to go anywhere, although the idea of escape from this scene was appealing. What was all this stuff about being her students previously? I didn't know I was her student in this life, let alone in another one.

'You have all learned much more than you know,' she said, as three stoneheads and a guru wandered back into the daylight of the living room. 'Cam will call you girls a cab.'

Back at home, Lucy turned from upset to inconsolable. She was blubbering. It turned out that while I had been imagining my life as a sexually frustrated nun, she was off in her own dream worlds.

'What was all that stuff about Atlantis?' she spluttered, sipping a cup of calming chamomile tea and blotting her eyes with a mashed-up tissue. She sat curled up in a homemade patchwork quilt on our peachy-coloured living-room sofa. The room was 'as warm and welcoming as a bordello', or so Rufus was fond of saying. Right now, as unseasonal rain beat down outside, Lucy appeared to need all the warm and welcoming comfort she could find. Gaelle's little Eye-To-Eye Exercise had brought up all the dross she had in her soul about her ex, Alan.

'It was so weird, C,' she wailed. 'I, I, I sort of dreamed . . . that we were on a sinking ocean liner. Everyone was trying to get onto the lifeboats. It was crazy, there were hundreds of people milling around trying to get a seat so they wouldn't die. I was desperate. I had a small dog with me, I was clutching him, as frightened for his life as for my own . . .'

She started blubbing again. I passed her another tissue. Lightning and thunder cracked the skies.

'Gaelle was fantastic. It was as if she could feel what I was feeling. I was looking into her eyes and I saw so much . . . understanding . . . And then I saw there was a space for me on one of the lifeboats. I was being called. I turned to say goodbye to the friends I was with, when suddenly a man yelled, "Stand aside!" We all stood back and he leapt from behind and threw himself into the boat before me. It was Alan. He'd taken the last space, the space that was mine. He was leaving me to die and saving his own rotten skin.'

She broke down in floods of tears again. I put my arms around her and let her sob.

'That's the last time you have to go around there,' I said, trying to soothe her. 'I'm so sorry you had to go through that.'

What did Gaelle want? For the fiftieth time in two days, I considered turning the job over to someone else.

'No. No, it was wonderful. Gaelle was so . . . knowing,' Lu insisted. 'It made me realise so much – that Alan didn't care about me, that if the chips were down he'd save himself and not spare me a thought.' Lucy wept. Her eyes were so red. It was years since I'd seen her this upset. The last time she'd let go of her emotions like this in front of me was when her grandmother died. The fact that Lu had inherited $400 000 as a result hadn't dulled the pain at all for her. She was such a sweet soul.

'I realised that the fact he'd got Madeleine bloody, fucking pregnant was . . . fate . . . If it hadn't happened, maybe I would have ended up with him forever. And maybe he'd have kept on cheating on me. I'd have been stuck in some little cottage in the middle of nowhere, far away from everyone, from you and Moni, let alone from Mum and Dad, and would have had to put up with it for the sake of our kids or whatever. But it was so weird. It was so vivid. Did you feel anything?'

Call me yellow, but I couldn't bring myself to tell Lucy that I'd had a similarly startling, although less upsetting, experience there in Gaelle's work room. The strange thing was that while I had walked away from it more dubious than ever about Gaelle and my involvement with her, Lucy seemed to have decided Gaelle was the key to her recovery from Alan.

'I want to ask her what she thinks about Niall and me,' she said. 'I mean, I really like Niall, but do you think he's my destiny? We're so different. He's always going on about healing and stuff and, well, maybe I need someone who lives in the real world . . .'

'What? Like Alan?'

'Nooooo,' she said, dissolving once more.

Nice one, C, I chastised myself.

Mercifully, that night was the night of Rufus's brother's house-warming party. It was becoming ever clearer that Lu and I – if not Moni as well – needed a good old knees-up to take our minds off the strangeness around us. I felt it was nothing a bottle of tequila, a couple of gorgeous men and some good music couldn't sort out. Hopefully. Moni arrived home from the office, exhausted as usual, and full of her own personal dramas.

Moni's work was usually fairly routine, despite run-ins with her boss, the long hours and last-minute panics which often kept her desk-bound until far too late. But tonight she looked extra cream-crackered. Mascara applied at some ungodly hour this morning was now turning her panda-eyed. Her usually neat hair had skewed into an unintended lightning-bolt parting. Her once sharp white shirt was creased and hanging out over her fashionable power trousers. She'd looked better. Right now, though, Moni saw that she had a sad, needy and confused flatmate to consider. It was clearly an all-hands-on-deck situation.

We recounted Lu's tale – minus the Titanic-esque details – as Moni lit the tealight under Lucy's essential oil burner and then lit a Marlboro Light from its flame. Taking a long drag, her breath seemed to reach all the way down.

'Come on, Lu,' she said encouragingly. 'You'll be fine.' She got up and put on Lu's *Whale Sounds* album – her favourite CD for relaxing jangled nerves. We sat in silence for a moment while the whales did their thing. Then the doorbell rang. Moni ran a hand through her hair and leapt up to answer it.

'Hi, Alex, come in, come in,' we heard her saying. She returned to the living room followed by a waif-thin, ethereal-looking hippy-type chick with a loping walk and the clearest skin I'd seen in a long while.

'C, Lu, meet Alex Curtis, Rufus's cousin, all the way from America. Alex, these are my flatmates, Cara Kerr and Lucy Daye.'

Alex greeted us with a soft, southern lilt. She was an astonishing sight, with spiky orange hair, shredded Levis, a Bob Marley T-shirt and tartan Dr Martens boots. She dropped a yellow rucksack to the floor and pulled out a book.

'Moni, this is the book I said I'd love you to read, and this,' she said, grinning, as she drew a photograph out of the book's pages, 'is the picture I told you about, of me and Ru when we were kids.' Moni took the photo, laughed so hard that she snorted, then passed it to Lu and me to see. It was of two kiddies squatting down on grass looking up at the lens. One child, presumably Alex, was dressed in a lemon dress with daisies stitched around the hem and neckline; the other, unmistakably our friend Rufus, was dressed as a cowboy.

'We only knew each other for one summer, when my mum came to live in London for a while when I was seven. It's amazing to see him again after all these years.'

'Look at Rufus's freckles,' Moni laughed.

'How are you two related?'

'Well, we're something like second cousins twice removed.' Alex smiled. 'I can never work out all that stuff. But our mothers went to school together in Switzerland.'

'Good to meet you, Alex,' Lucy said politely from the sofa, her eyes still red around the edges.

'Alex is busy tonight, so she can't join us at the party. She just dropped by to give me these and to borrow a book I said I'd lend her,' said Moni. 'I'll just take her up to get it.' They disappeared for a good twenty minutes, while Lu and I raked over the Gaelle fallout coals once more. Finally, Moni bade Alex farewell and returned to the fold.

'She's great,' she announced.

'Fab photo of her and Rufus,' I said.

'We should put it in a frame on the mantelpiece and show it to his new girlfriends.'

We all chuckled at that one.

'So is anyone in the mood for a party?' I asked.

'I am,' Moni said brightly. Lu looked less convinced.

'Okay. Then I think we should all give ourselves a good shake, bathe and reconvene down here for some wine in an hour or so. This is going to be a great party. We've all had days from hell. Come on, pleeeeeease?'

'I guess so,' said Lucy, stoically.

'Too right,' said Moni.

And so we did.

cadillacs and cads

'Baaaaaaaaabes! My darlings, how are you? Lucy, you look so tasty I wish I could eat you. And Moni, you look divine. You've lost weight, haven't you? Have you fallen in love? You're glowing! Come on, girls, get your finery together and let's hit the north! Here, Lu, open this bubbly. It'll do us all some good. Yah, it's going to be a great night. God, where's Cara? Has she got herself a shag yet?'

I could hear Rufus's booming voice from upstairs where I was in the bathroom applying the bronze blusher that Moni had picked up from the make-up lady at work. It was supposed to make you look healthy, tanned and summery – the way the English summer went, you needed all the help you could get. Right now, though, it was streaking and I looked more like a reject from a seventies Tia Maria commercial. Bloody hell. I was still in my bra and undies.

Despite my 'let's get happy' cheerleading earlier, I was dragging my feet a little bit. The wine we'd shared had helped, but, to be honest, all I felt like doing was curling up in a little ball on the sofa and watching the box. If only it were Saturday night – I could have indulged in some 'Xena'.

'Cara Kerr!' Rufus barked up the stairs. 'Where are you and why are you not ready?'

'Hey, cowboy,' I called back. Having managed to wipe off most of the blusher, I was now hopping into a little ensemble from Jig-saw that Lu had bought last season. We shared clothes, perfume, stories – everything except men.

Despite my reservations I tried to look forward to tonight. Rufus only took us to the best dos. He was usually dating some skinny, long-legged model – a new one each week – whom he'd met at the 151 Club, so there was never any danger of one of us becoming involved with him. He found the parties and we happily escorted him to them, like harem girls with their sheik. He was full of crap half the time, the sort of bloke who liked to think he had street cred because he cut up his coke with a Gold Amex card. However, he never took himself too seriously, so we teased him endlessly about his expand-ing waistline, receding hairline and life as an ageing playboy – he was all of twenty-nine. He was also the guy I'd 'seen' Moni bonking in my dream that night. I'd never told her about that.

Finally, we piled into his car – a convertible Cadillac, no less, complete with a pristine red and white paint job, silver trimmings and black leather upholstery. The weather was clear, so the top was down. Not many people owned convertibles in London, as you could only take the top down about five days a year, but Rufus loved his 'baby', as he liked to call the 1965 special. Lucky for him he had the dosh to keep it maintained.

With Ru at the wheel, singing Guns N' Roses tunes at the top of his lungs, Moni and I were piled into the front seat, so we were three abreast. Lucy sat alone in the back, her wispy blonde hair being blown into a bird's nest as we sped through Chelsea. Niall hadn't been able to make the party tonight; he'd promised to babysit for his sister who was out on the town with her hubby celebrating their third wedding anniversary. Although we were all miserable, we pretended to be in high spirits, as much to cheer up each other as to fool ourselves.

'My little bro has promised a night of nights,' Rufus yelled as we passed through Camden, its streets heaving with crusties and trendies left over from an afternoon's shopping or preparing for a night spent sitting in dark pubs talking about Dostoyevsky over their pints. 'I'm hoping for a smorgasbord of gorgeous gels.'

Rufus was incorrigible with his talk of 'girls with legs up to their armpits'. And he wasn't the least bit ashamed of it.

'You know, last night I really did very well,' he shouted. 'I was at the 151 and I met the most beautiful woman – Imogen – gorgeous, dark, glossy hair, clear, luminous skin. Only trouble was, she wasn't having a bar of me. So, do you know what I did? I tried something my bro and I had talked about, and it worked. I told her I was struggling with my sexuality. That I wasn't sure if I was straight, bi or gay. We talked for hours at the bar and I managed to finally extricate her from there and take her for a late-night coffee in Soho. We talked more. She totally bought it.

'I asked her back to my house for a nightcap – luckily she lives nearby, so she said yes. Once we got there, I pounced. Totally. I told her she'd driven me wild and that I knew from this that I wasn't gay . . .

'I got her into my room and I have to say that things were going extremely well, when who should bloody well turn up but Karla, that volatile Portuguese physio I've been shagging. She was livid.'

'Hell hath no fury like a Latino woman scorned,' Lu said.

'Are Portuguese people Latinos?' Moni asked.

'Si, señora. Their blood is very hot,' Rufus said. 'Anyway, apparently Karla had gone to the 151 after I'd left and some divot had told her I'd left with a woman. She fucking well let herself in, came straight to my room, found me with Imogen and read me the riot act.'

'What happened next?' asked Moni, intrigued.

'Imogen realised she'd been duped – I'd told her I hadn't had sex for two years and here was this bird telling her that we'd shagged the night before – and she got dressed and left. Which left me with Karla to pacify. Which I did quite nicely, I must say . . .'

'And where's Karla tonight?'

'As far away as possible, I hope,' Rufus laughed, turning off Hampstead High Street into Heath Street and then up further into the little winding lanes of NW3. He parked the Caddy askew over his brother Seamus's driveway and leapt out of the car over the door. Moni, Lucy and I piled out in a more conventional fashion, laughing as we went, our spirits raised by Rufus's dreadful tale. He was great as a friend, but you wouldn't want to screw him. It was hard to imagine that Rufus would ever settle down. Many women had tried and failed to tame him. It would take an über-babe. Until then, he was going to enjoy his socks off. And get his gear off, as often as possible.

Four things hit me when we walked in the door. The first was that this was a majorly ritzy apartment. It was essentially an enormous studio, a converted room in a large old home, but what a studio! The walls were wood-panelled and you knew the wood was old. There was an enormous picture window overlooking a Hampstead park, the ceilings were more than high, they were frightening, and at the back of the room, way above our heads, was a mezzanine floor, where Seamus, owner of this bachelor pad extraordinaire, laid his head and other things every night.

The second thing that hit me was that this was the room I had dreamed of the other night, when Cam and I were married and living a life of domestic bliss in the eighteenth century. *Of course*, I thought, fear freezing like an iceblock in my stomach. I closed my eyes and felt my head spin.

The third thing I noticed was that Cam was there. I saw him just as he saw me.

And the fourth was that Alan, Lucy's ex, was also present. Shit. He looked as if he'd eaten one corporate raiding lunch too many. His skin was florid and his cheeks were so flabby it was a wonder they didn't have their own cellulite. Uggh.

'Oh, God,' was Lu's response.

Since their break-up, Lucy hadn't seen Alan at all. She'd absolutely refused to take his calls, let alone accept the increasingly urgent requests to meet up that he'd left on our answering machine. In the past four weeks, it seemed he'd given up trying. It was sad for him, but too tawdry to be heart-rending.

'I'm amazed at the speed you've moved forward post-Alan, Lu,' I encouraged her. I'd have been pining for three or four years after such a love drama, fully furnished with the double whammies of betrayal and pregnancy. How do you get over that kind of thing?

'It's behind me,' she said strongly. 'I really mean it when I say I'd prefer to know about it now rather then when it was too late.'

Tonight would test her resolve, especially as there was a redhead who appeared to be standing close to Alan in a territorial fashion. I wondered if Lu had noticed and could only assume that she had. Chicks don't often miss tricks like that.

And beside the redhead was Cam. What the heck was he doing here? For a city of ten million people, London can be alarmingly small when you're trying to hide. I gazed around the room once more. There was no doubt that, give or take eighty or so modern-day Londoners, this was the room, the apartment, I had dreamed of the other night. In that dream, we had access to the rest of the house. But it was this house.

'Hi there!' I heard Seamus's girlfriend, Eloise, braying a welcome and snapped back to reality. She was a management consultant who'd been seconded by Anita Roddick to help shape the image of her burgeoning company in the early nineties and she'd made a mint. 'How naice touu see the Orstraaaalian contingent could maaaaay-ke it,' she said. Her accent was more royal than Liz's.

'Hello, Eloise.' I smiled back. 'Yes, we thought we'd travel up to have a few deep breaths of the rarefied North London air.' I was the polite one. I spoke to her. Moni and Lu didn't even bother with that half the time. I'd heard a joke once that 'Australians are just Brits who've been left out in the sun for far too long', but sometimes it was hard to see the connection.

'Okay, okay, girls, form an orderly line.' It was Rufus, shunting us all aside. 'Now, where's the bathroom?'

'It's through there,' I said, pointing to the panelled wall.

'What? What do you mean it's through there?' asked Ru. 'That's a bloody wall.'

'No, it's not,' I said. 'It's a doorway.' I went to the wood panelling and pushed hard on one square of it. Sure enough, a door sprang open, revealing a bright, white, modern bathroom behind it.

'How on earth did you know that?' Ru asked. 'Seamus only moved in here two weeks ago and even I haven't been here.'

'I had a dream about this flat the other night,' I replied. It seemed easier to tell him the truth than make up some complicated story.

Lucy was staring at me agog, but Ru laughed and let it pass and, before Lu and I had time to panic further about the fact that the two men most on our minds were also at this party, he manoeuvred the three of us into the bathroom. The fact I had known it was there hidden behind the panels was strange. So were lots of things these days, I reminded myself, as if that made it okay. But why had Cam been in my dream? Had we lived in this house before? That sounded like something Gaelle would say and I didn't want to think about it.

Inside, under the fluorescent glow in the ultra-clean, tiled bathroom, good ol' Ru made a ceremony of whipping out a bag of coke which he cut up, as ever, with the Gold Amex card on the marble top of the bathroom basin.

'Hey, hey, hey,' said Moni, who loved a bit of coke.

'Excellent.'

'Yeah, thanks, Rufus.'

Drawing it quickly and expertly into four long lines, he took out his favourite coke scooper – a tiny, solid-silver, vacuum hose-shaped snorting device Moni had brought back from New York a few holidays ago. He presented the little snorter to her, for first go. Then to me, then to Lu, then he had a go. Then it was a case of grin, smile, rub hands together, sniff and out the door into the party.

'Fly babies, fly!' Ru cried as he charged into the party throng.

Out in the thick of it, Lu suddenly went into instant, non-stop talking paranoia mode.

'Oh, shit, C, I don't know if I should have taken that stuff. It makes me feel funny at the best of times, you know. Why is Alan here? Why have I created this? We all create our reality, you know, C. I mean, whatever happens to us, we create it. We do it to learn lessons. What lessons do I need to learn from this? Why has this happened today, when I had that weird experience about him earlier? And now this party and drugs and Alan . . .'

On and on she went. Edgy, edgy, edgy. Amusing, if a little worrying.

'My karma must be sorting itself out for this to be happening,' she said. 'Maybe it's because I've started seeing Niall so soon after Alan? Maybe I should have had some breathing space? Maybe I should be celibate for a while and figure out what it is in me that drives me to be with someone like Alan. But at least with Niall I am learning.'

'What?'

'About crystals and love and stuff.' She was rubbing her hands frantically up and down her arms, as if she felt cold, shifting her weight from one leg to the other, her darting eyes scanning right and left for Alan. I always forgot how insecure she could be on coke. She was going to lose it before the night was out. This was going to be a doozey if we didn't do something quickly.

'In fact, I so wish Niall had been able to come with us,' Lu continued. 'I can't believe he had to babysit for his sister. You know, she really uses him sometimes, because he's so accommodating. He worships her. But she just takes his help for granted . . .'

Clearly thinking along the same lines as I was, Moni changed the vibes and the subject as she deftly pulled a bottle of Stoli out of her bag. 'Hey, let's go up to the mezzanine floor,' she said, leading the way. She looked great this evening. She'd started blow-drying her hair really straight and it suited her. She always reminded me a bit of Jackie O with a Roman nose and freckles.

'Alex was saying that her grandmother used to own half of Hampstead,' Moni said as we headed upstairs. 'You really should get to know her. She's lovely. She said tonight she might help me out with the Discreet Duets story.'

'How?'

'We have to get an actress to join up and pretend to be a wife in search of an adulterous lover. Alex said she might do it, posing as someone married to a much older man who can't get it up any more. All we have to do is e-mail her photograph and details to the secret website address . . .'

Moni led the way up the winding dark-wood staircase. This flat was amazing. Upstairs, there was the usual gang of suspects you'd expect to find at a Hampstead do. Girls in long boots and pretty, slinky, flowery dresses, boys in slightly bohemian white shirt and strange trousers combos. It was more opulent than Notting Hill, more bourgeois than South London. Lu and I were in low-slung cut-off pants and teensy tops, while Moni was more elegant in linen pants and a new Anna Sui top. We got away with it.

Once I was up on the balcony, I felt a lot safer. Down there was Cam. And Alan. Right now, I was happy for us to be separated. I wasn't sure what I thought about seeing Cam in a social environment like this one. He was a funny character. Keeping him safely at fantasy arm's length at work was one thing. I just felt nervous about the prospect of things getting complicated between us. I wasn't sure I could trust myself around him. He caught my eye and I waved down at him. I couldn't bear speaking to him right now. My head was still messy about the dream and this afternoon's little eye-staring caper. At the same time, I longed to know him better. He waved back.

'Hey, girls!' It was Rufus, on the floor below. 'How're you doing?' He pelted up the staircase towards our posse overlooking the party.

'Oh, I see,' he said. 'Up here checking out the talent, are we?'

'Yeah, you can tell which of the men have bald patches,' Lucy said disconsolately.

'Ah, what's up, sweetie?' he asked. 'Missing Niall, are we?'

'No, Rufus. In case you haven't noticed, Alan is here.'

'Yah, right, I saw him. He's not looking too well, is he? Bit unhealthy, wouldn't you say? Have you spoken to him yet, Lucy? Is that redhead the little bitch he cheated on you with? The whole thing sickens me. I just thank God you found out what he was like before you married the guy . . .'

Rufus meant every word he said.

'You really are far too wonderful for him. In fact, I've been trying to make a move on you for years,' he added.

'Oh, Rufus, shut up!' Lu sounded pissed off, but she wasn't. She was joking. None of us had ever had a thing for Rufus, not that we'd talked about. He was like a brother or boy next door, at best. He and Moni had had a snog months ago at a party in Wimbledon, but they'd both admitted it was a totally pissed affair and neither had mentioned it much again. We'd kind of got the message not to tease them about it, either.

'And as for you, you little fox!' He turned to grab Moni by the waist. She squealed as he tried to tickle her. Hmmm. Maybe there really was potential? You never knew. She started giggling and snorting with delight. In the meantime, no-one really knew what was going on in my head as we stood atop the party there on the balcony. I hadn't made much of the fact that I was feeling disturbingly attracted to my new workmate. I didn't really want to go into it, either. I wasn't sure why.

While Moni and Ru were busy with what appeared to be some kind of weird pre-mating ritual, slapping each other on the back, calling each other names and generally flirting, Lu and I stood almost stock still on the balcony, she watching Alan's every move, and me trying not to catch Cam's eye.

'Do you feel okay?' I asked her.

'Yeah, I do. He looks like he's lost a bit of weight, doesn't he?'

'Alan?'

'Yeah.'

I surveyed the man in question. He did look a little less portly. Which wasn't saying much.

'I guess the break-up had some effect on him, after all,' Lu went on.

'Yeah.'

'Cam's still down there. Don't you think you should go and say hello?'

'In a minute.'

'You know, C, I look at Alan down there and I wonder how I can be so messed up.'

'Messed up about what?'

'About men. About my love life. I mean, what's there to be confused about? Why would I rather be with old fat-head Alan down there than with the gorgeous, kind and caring Niall?'

'Yeah, right,' I replied. 'Maybe because there's nowt so strange as wimmin folk?'

Just as I was wondering whether I should tell Lu about my Cam dilemma, Cam himself started heading up the stairs towards us. As he got closer, I got another glimpse of those brown, brown eyes. Was it possible that he grew more attractive each time I saw him?

Seeing him walk up the stairs was a trip. It reminded me of seeing him walk up the stairs in my dream.

'Hi, Cara,' he said, smiling wickedly at me as if we were sharing a private joke that I had forgotten. 'Hi, Lucy.'

'Hi yourself, Cam.'

'So, how do you come to be here tonight?' Lu asked the question for me, bless her.

'See that bloke down there,' he said, pointing to a guy chatting to Eloise. 'He lives upstairs from me and knows Seamus, from work. How about you?'

'My friend Rufus is the brother of the guy whose party it is,' I said.

'Rufus being your boyfriend?'

'No. Just a friend. Here, I'll introduce you.' I called Rufus and Moni over and more hellos were exchanged.

Rufus was muttering, 'Now, now, my little children, gather round . . .' Cam was watching; I was watching him watch.

'How's the coke, lads?' asked Ru.

Moni reported it had been good, but the effects were over.

'Want something else?'

'What are you? A medicine cabinet?'

God. Not in front of Cam.

'Let's just say I was given an unexpected bonus at work last week.'

'What you got, mate?' This was Lu. Like she really needed more.

'Okay, kiddies, line up.' Ru delved into his pocket and pulled out a handful of little white tablets.

'Es!' he announced. Ru popped one into Moni's mouth, who received it like Holy Communion from the Pope. The rest of us held our hands out. Rufus asked Cam if he was up for it. Cam grinned at me.

'Thanks, mate,' he said, sounding surprised.

'And ve vosh it down viz tequila,' said Rufus, ever the actor. 'See you,' he said, scooping Moni up in his arms and kissing her like a bloke doing a tango in an old movie.

'Woah,' she said, looking flushed as he turned and disappeared down the stairs.

'Gosh,' I said. 'Is there something you're not telling us, Moni?'

Moni grinned wickedly and told us not to be ridiculous. Lu was staring over the balcony. And staring.

'Cam,' she said, 'I think your friends are motioning to you down there.' He looked over the balcony.

'Alan's leaving too,' Lu said softly. I really felt for her. Cam, who obviously had no idea of the enormity of what was going on around him, was smiling down at his mates.

'Yeah. They're leaving. Back in a sec,' he said. He ran down the stairs and got into a discussion with one of them. We watched as he looked back up and pointed towards us.

'You can get a lift back to South London with Rufus if you want,' I called out, and instantly regretted it. What was I angling for? What if he wasn't in the least interested and realised that I was? I still had to work with him tomorrow and the day after that.

'Yeah, you can,' Lu yelled down, sealing my fate, still staring at Alan.

'Thanks,' Cam yelled back, finishing up his goodbyes.

'He's kind of cute,' Moni said finally. 'Sort of weird, though.'

'I know. I think he's divine,' I replied.

'Do you now?'

'Yes I do, as it happens.'

'So, what are you going to do about it?'

'Nothing. I work with him, remember.'

'So what?'

'So . . .' I was about to think of a reason why Cam and I couldn't get it together when out of the corner of my eye I saw Lucy dashing down the stairs. Moni and I watched agog as she cut a swathe through the crowd towards the departing Alan, and cut him off at the door. Moni and I looked at each other in horror and raced down after her.

By the time we reached her, Lu was in full flight. Within seconds, people were standing back and watching and listening.

'So, what are you doing, eh? Leaving, are you? Just leaving. Well, it was very good of you to come here tonight.' Lu's arms were flying in angry gestures. Alan was looking nervous, very nervous, while the redhead was hanging back, her weight on one hip, her toe tapping impatiently.

'Answer me, bugger you! What do you think you're doing here tonight? You know full bloody well that Seamus is *my* friend. You are not welcome here.'

Alan's flabby pink cheeks wobbled as he shook his head and held out his hand as if to make some sort of stop signal. 'Lu, Lu daaarling,' he mumbled in his ridiculous cut-glass accent. 'I think you might have had a bit too much to –'

'Don't give me that!' she yelled, cutting him off. 'What would you know? You drink yourself stupid half the time to avoid facing up to what a schmuck you really are. What are you doing here, anyway? Who is this girl?' She gesticulated at Miss Redhead.

'Who? Oh, that's Sandy, you don't need to worry about her . . .'

'Oh, that's Sandy, is it? And where's Madeleine? You know, Mads? The pregnant one?'

'Lu . . .' He was going red, his ruddy complexion looking like the inside of a molten volcano.

'And now you're just bloody leaving without even saying fucking hello or goodbye. Well, I hope your ears turn into arseholes and shit all over your shoulders!'

'Now, just calm down, young lady. Behave yourself. You're making a scene and making a fool of yourself.'

Q: How do you make an Englishman nervous?

A: Threaten to cause a scene.

'I hope your testicles drop out and the cat gets them . . .' she went on, now pummelling his chest with her fists, searching through her mental thesaurus for another insult. At that moment, Rufus rushed to the rescue. He came from behind, grabbing her, kissing her ear and neck repeatedly. His arms were encircling hers, so all she could do in protest was to kick him on the shins, which she did. As she turned to release his grip, her eyes caught mine and for a moment she looked shamefaced.

'Rufus to the rescue!' yelled Moni, giggling and snorting more than ever. The E must have been taking effect, for this was surely no laughing matter.

'Back off, Rufus!' Alan yelled. 'I can handle this.'

'No, you can't, you twat. You couldn't handle a doorknob,' Ru replied.

At this, Lu's body relaxed. She turned back to Alan, who seemed rooted to the spot like the trapped rat he was. Lu seemed suddenly serene. Rufus's arm loosened a little and she dropped her head against his chest, revived briefly to deliver one last parting evil look to her ex and then let Rufus scoop her up in one easy gesture like a little girl and carry her away.

Once we were back upstairs, I expected her to be in tears but – far from it – she was livid. As livid as you can be with an E in your blood. Mine was also starting to do its stuff.

'Oh, God!' she was saying, her face white, her body swaying. 'He's soooooooooo infuuuuuuuuriating. Gooooooood, to think I nearly maaaaaaaarried him. Moni, gimme that Stoli.'

'A-ha! Harmony once more!' said Rufus. 'I'm going off to find more booze.'

'I mean, can you believe the nerve of that guy, coming to this party, this *housewarming* being held by Rufus's brother, whom he only knows through me, to come here and to bring that, that, that girl with him.'

'Can't blame you for being angry,' I said.

'No way,' added Moni.

'No,' said Cam, joining us on the balcony. He'd undoubtedly watched the whole scene downstairs but still had no idea what was going on.

'Cam, you have no idea what's going on,' Lu said, breaking into giggles.

'I know,' he said, breaking down himself.

'And worse, I mean, so, so, so, so much worse is that he would leave without . . . even . . . saying . . . goodbye . . . to me. I told him he was a pile of crap. I told him I hoped his ears turned into arseholes and shat on his shoulders . . .'

'We heard that.'

'Go, girl!'

'I told him that if I ever saw him again it would be too soon and he could just L.E.A.V.E. Which, I guess, is exactly what he was doing. Oh, God!' At least she was laughing.

'Hey, Moni.' Once more, it was Rufus's voice. 'Darling Mon-niii.'

'Moni, you're being called.'

'Yes?' she asked, peering over the balcony like Rapunzel.

'Can't find any more to drink. Let down your Stoli!' Rufus commanded.

Giggling, Moni took the top off the vodka bottle and held it tilted over the balcony. Rufus threw his mouth open and his head back, as Moni slowly tipped the bottle further and further until a slow stream began trickling out of the bottle, down to Rufus below, splashing into his mouth and over his face as he swallowed furiously. Moni stopped for a moment, to give him a chance to catch his breath. Then he opened wide again, for more.

Lucy and I forgot about Alan for a moment. Moni and Rufus? In some ways, this was more predictable than a pimple before a hot date, but none of us had really discussed it. There was something about the high-powered Moni and the lusty Rufus that fitted together nicely. It felt right, somewhere in my subconscious. Mmm, this E was rather pleasant. I was feeling kind of floaty. While other people seemed to be gripped by the urge to dance like jerking maniacs when a bit of Ecstasy went through their system, I felt like doing a slow-motion Michael Jackson moonwalk, moontalk, moonthink, mooneverything.

'Are you all right, Lu?' I asked her softly.

'Yeah.'

'Really?'

'No, really. Look at those two.'

'Sometimes, when I look around a party like this, with all these upper-crust Bright Young Things, I just dream of being in Sydney and having a beer in somewhere banal like Newtown.'

'Yeah.'

'Or going down to Bondi for a bit of a perve . . .'

'Yeah. On all those semi-naked, deeply tanned, muscular men.'

'Yeah. When a man takes his clothes off in summer here, it's nothing to write home about – and even then it's usually in the park at lunch-time.'

'But at Bondi . . .'

'Yeah.' We mentally, patriotically drooled. I looked over at Cam, wondering if he'd heard this snippet of girls' talk, but he looked lost in thought as he stared at the party below.

'Maybe we should go back to Oz for a holiday.'

'Yeah.'

'Back to a place where there are no trick words.'

'Like Magdalen and Cholmondley . . .'

'. . . and Norwich and Althorp . . .'

'God. We've been here too long, haven't we? Like Gaelle said to me the first time we spoke, ultimately a foreigner is an alien . . .'

We stood in silent contemplation. So much for the drugs spicing up the night.

'Listen,' I said. 'Why don't we go home?'

'What? To Sydney? Now?'

'No, to Battersea. Moni and Rufus are obviously enjoying

each other's company. Rufus will have to leave his car here, so we could get a cab . . . Cam, you can get a lift, unless you want to stay . . .'

I held my breath as I listened for his answer.

'Yeah, I'll head south, too,' he said.

Right.

We told Moni our plan. She said she'd come with us, then went down to tell Ru.

'Moni! My love! You can't leave me,' Rufus complained. 'You can't pour Stoli down my throat from a great height and then go home.' He grabbed her around the waist. I'd never seen such flirting between them.

'Moni, why don't you stay?' said Lu, making it easier for her. 'Someone should look after this drunken lout.'

8

one argument, one grope and a romance

Lucy pushed the window of the black cab down, moved to the little pull-down seat behind the driver, and stuck her head out into the rush of summery night air. We headed down through Belsize Park, Camden, the West End and over Waterloo Bridge, where I checked out two of my favourite London-by-night sights – St Paul's Cathedral on the left and Big Ben on the right. I also checked the time – nearly 2.30 a.m.

As we neared home, Lucy did the drunken sista thing and invited Cam in for a nightcap on my behalf. He agreed. We paid and tipped the cabbie and stepped out into the night air. I looked along the row for our little terrace house, but couldn't see it. They all looked alike after a few drugs. There was a bloke standing outside someone's place, so I assumed it wasn't ours. But it was.

'Alan!' Lucy hissed.

'Hi, Lu,' he said, stepping out of the shadows. His clothes were dishevelled, as if he'd been asleep in the bushes. His hair was all mussed up. He looked slightly wild. He held his palms open to us, in a gesture of honesty, but I didn't trust him one bit. Neither did Mouser, who was at his feet, hissing, which really was most unlike him.

'Ssshhh, Mouser. Hello, Alan,' Lu said, trying to sound airy and unconcerned when she was obviously very flustered. I winced. None of us was in a state for this.

'What are you doing here?' Her voice was more high-pitched and girly than angry. As if she was pleased to see him. What? How? After the party? The thought of Niall briefly crossed my mind. I wondered if it crossed hers.

'Aw, Lu,' he said, positively grovelling. 'I'm so sorry about before. I had to see you. I don't know. I got home and was going to go back to the party . . .'

'Back up to Hampstead?'

'Yeah. Then I thought that was a bit stupid, so I thought I'd come here and wait for you.' He was as pissed as a newt.

'You could have been here for hours,' Lu said. 'You're lucky. We could have stayed all night or gone on into the West End . . . I'm so sorry for the way I behaved at the party, too.'

Oh, Lucy.

'I was just hoping you weren't going to come home with another guy,' Alan said. I thought of Niall again.

Lu was standing close to him and I knew the case was lost. She might as well have shagged him there and then. It was the first time I'd sensed happy vibes coming from her in what seemed like months. Had she had an E? I couldn't remember now. I hoped not.

She opened our front door and we all walked into the living room. I knew it was only a matter of time before she and Alan went off to be by themselves. Leaving me with Cam and off my tits.

'So,' I said brightly, once we were inside. 'Who wants what? Tea, coffee, wine, water, beer, whisky. Name it.'

'Yah. Tea for me. I need it,' said Alan.

Yeah, you need something, I thought. Like a kick in the stomach.

'Coffee for me,' Lu said.

'Can I have a beer?' asked Cam.

'Sure. Do you want to come with me while I make the tea and coffee?' Cam and I went into the kitchen, leaving Lu and Alan to sort themselves out.

'So, how're you feeling?' he asked me.

'Good, thanks. You?'

'Yeah, good.'

Pause.

'Nice place.'

'Thanks. Where do you live again?'

'Clapham South. Just off Balham Hill.'

'Right.'

'Yeah,' he said.

'This has been a full-on night,' I said, as I reached for the tea and coffee, and flicked on the kettle, eager for something to keep my hands and mind occupied. I jumped up onto the kitchen bench, propping my feet up on the cupboard door handles to minimise thigh splayage.

'Yeah . . .'

Silence. The only sound was the water in the kettle beginning to boil.

He looked at a picture of Jack Nicholson as the Joker from *Batman* that we had pinned up on a kitchen cabinet.

'I like that picture of Jack,' he said. 'I've got exactly the same one up in my kitchen.'

'Really?'

'Yeah. Strange, eh?'

'Yeah.' I wished I could get it together to say something sensible. I was feeling nervous.

'I was pretty surprised to see you at the party tonight,' Cam said, perhaps trying to keep the conversation lively.

'Did you realise the connection between Seamus and Rufus and me?'

'No.'

'Right.'

Silence.

My E was peaking. I love the rush, but always feel a bit sad, knowing it's all downhill afterwards. I thought about the universe, astral travelling with Gaelle, my life as a nun with Cam, and then I tried not to think about it any more.

'So, what were you doing in Ireland?' I asked eventually. 'I went there once, to do a story about Waterford crystal. For an Australian in-flight magazine. It was . . . beautiful . . .'

'It is. I just went there to get away. I was into sailing and I had work there in a pub . . .'

'I thought you were a stockbroker before you worked for Gaelle.'

'It's a long story.' He half smiled.

'Did you love it?'

'Ireland was amazing. You've got a whole new world. You'd never guess that it was so close to London. It's an endless round of ancient stone buildings, Guinness and talking to old folk . . .'

He talked and I relaxed a little. As I unwound, a wave of heat which I recognised as desire raced through me. It was like someone had turned on a switch. Woah. We didn't say anything for a moment. But we looked at each other and he smiled and stopped talking. I melted inside. The fact that I worked with him raced through my mind briefly. Our eyes met in one of those as-seen-on-TV moments. I smiled, too. I loved this feeling of connecting with someone. I guessed it was showing. I raised one eyebrow. He took that as a green light. He started to move towards me. I really wanted to kiss him . . . Had since the day we met . . . It was like moonwalk slow motion . . . His lips were closer . . . I could feel and hear his breath.

As our lips met, my blood raced, my hormones did their thang, my mind stopped and my body came alive. It felt very good. Gaelle had mentioned that Kundalini sexual energy was released by meditating. Perhaps this was an alternative method of setting it off. I had sexual energy to burn in that moment. It swirled through me. He was a fantastic kisser. Sometimes it feels like love, kissing after drugs. His lips were as soft as Turkish Delight and more delicious. And he kissed me slowly, just like in my dream.

After a few long, hot moments, we broke away and gasped for air. I let the feelings of lust run through me. I licked my lips. He started kissing me again, this time harder and heavier. The intensity took me by surprise, the dreams I'd had about him replaying in my mind with a kind of spooky lucidity. Kundalini energy was powerful. I was losing my breath again. He put both arms behind me and pulled me closer to him, so my legs were parted and wrapped around his body.

THUMP! We heard the almighty crash of a door being slammed upstairs. Lucy yelled out Alan's name.

Cam and I pulled back from each other. 'Hang on a minute. Hang on,' I said, listening, then jumping out of his arms and off the bench. We stood, caught up in the drugs, the low light in the kitchen, our eyes fixed on each other. For a moment, he looked exactly as he'd done in my dreams. I tried hard to remember what the guy in the dream had signified. When Cam and I had first met at Gaelle's, I'd been sure it was him. But then I'd changed my mind. Now I could hardly remember it at all. I could hear Lucy yelling.

'FUCK OFF AND DON'T COME BACK!'

'You bitch! Fuck off yourself. You'd shag anyone.' This was Alan. Charmed, I'm sure. I rushed to the corridor. Standing at the top of the stairs, naked except for a towel, was Lu. Alan was at the bottom, half-dressed and cowering.

'Just FUCK OFF!' Lu yelled again. She raised her arm and pelted something at him. It hurtled down the stairs, whizzing past his ear before smashing against the front door and dropping to the floor in pieces. It was her clock. One of its pointy legs was embedded in the front door.

'You're fucking mad! You're all fucking mad!' Alan said, escaping into the night, the door slamming behind him.

'Fuck him!' declared Lu, her hands on her hips, her face radiating fury down the stairs. For a moment Cam and I just waited. To see if anything else was going to happen.

'C?' Lu squeaked.

'Lu?' I called up the stairs.

Finally, Cam spoke. 'Um. Maybe tonight isn't a good night.' He peered out into the corridor from behind me.

'Yeah, maybe,' I agreed. At that point the night seemed over.

Lu started to cry.

'So, ah, unless you want me to hang around . . . ?' he bravely suggested.

'Thanks, Cam, it's fine.'

Without saying another word about the heat and hormones left hanging in the kitchen, Cam went home. Lucy and I repaired to the living room and sprawled on the sofas wordlessly. All I could think about was the feel of Cam's lips on mine. And the fact that he'd gone.

'Wanna joint?' I asked Lu after a few more moments of reveries, delving into Moni's spliff box.

'Yes, please.'

I couldn't bring myself to speak about what had happened in the kitchen. I was too much in shock. A spliff would obliterate that nicely. Lu asked me if it would be okay for us to talk about what had happened between her and Alan in the morning. It seemed a fair trade. I was knackered. We sat for about half an hour, smoked the joint, drank our beer and passed out where we lay.

Moni returned at 8 a.m., with Rufus in tow. By this time, Lu was shivering under a patchwork quilt on one sofa, while I was huddled still fully clothed on the other. I felt wretched. Lu's moans made it clear she felt the same. Moni, on the other hand, looked like the cat who'd swallowed the cream. I gazed up bleary-eyed as she stood in the middle of the living room, a bottle of vodka in one hand, a ciggie in the other. Even at this hour of the morning, after a night of partying, drinking, drug-taking and hanging out with a madman like Rufus, she managed to look relatively fresh and elegant. The girl had style. I wondered if it was Rufus's charms that had put the smile on her face.

Clearly, we'd had our scandal quota for one night, though. Rufus said his hello and goodbye at speed. He and Moni had a few private moments together in the hall, but what went on was anyone's guess. To be honest, by this stage of the proceedings I was happy to wait for details. Even hot news wasn't as important as sleep. I took a sip of the glass of water on the coffee table in front of me and collapsed back into the sofa's down-filled cushions.

Moni came back to the living room. 'We got a cab home.'

Neither Lu nor I responded.

'So. Anyone feel like a post-mortem?' she asked hopefully, throwing a spare quilt over me.

'Nup,' I said, sliding under. Did my eyelids have sand underneath them or did I just feel like shite?

'Hmmm?' Moni insisted, clearly still up and at 'em. 'Lu? Wanna hear about my night?'

'Maybe later, Moni.' Lucy's head lolled on the arm of the sofa and her eyes closed.

'Fine,' said Moni, sounding slightly miffed. 'Goodnight then.'

DREAM DIARY

3 JULY: JUST FINE, JUST FINE

I saw myself at home here in Battersea. I walked into the garden. Cam and Gaelle were there, standing together, like mother and son. I wondered what they wanted. They whispered to each other again and again.

'Don't worry. She'll be just fine. No need to worry. She'll be just fine.'

I picked one of Lucy's Nirvana Cards and got Trust. *Cam and Gaelle told me to trust that the universe would take care of me.*

I hoped they were right.

9

example of a bad time

When I finally woke up, my head was reeling. I instantly remembered I'd kissed Cam. After the party and before Lu's drama. The kiss was divine. What a shame I'd sent him home, although if I looked as bad as I felt this morning, it was best he wasn't here to see it. I stood on my toes and checked myself out in the large mirror above the fireplace. Yep. Just as well. At least last night's dream didn't seem too worrying.

Despite my pathetic state, I was nonetheless the least sorry of my sorry household and thus the first to surface. Mouser heard my stirring and romped in, jumping around on my groaning stomach and miaowing hungrily, reminding me that I had an E comedown to deal with, not to mention hours to ponder Cam's delicious kisses. At the least the day would offer respite, and I might get some info out of Moni about what had happened with her and Ru.

I heroically dragged myself from the living room and up to the bathroom where I ran a bath. The straight-backed chair in the corner creaked as I slumped on it, staring into the steam as the water rose, wondering how life sometimes managed to veer off at such unlikely tangents, all in one night.

I lazed in the bath and scrubbed myself with some Body Shop bath oil. I'd once written a story for an Australian magazine about Ecstasy and acid, and had been told by an old hippy during my research that to clear your system after taking drugs, you should drink lots of water and take a hot bath, fully loofah-ing your skin to get rid of the leftovers seeping through your pores. It sounded feasible, so I scrubbed until my skin was pink. Finally, dried and fresh, I hobbled downstairs for a morning water and coffee and to read the *Daily Mirror*. I flicked on the radio to hear 'Nessum Dorma' pelting out, but it was all too much for my brain. Pavarotti would reduce me to tears on a day like today.

I called Mouser back from his lair, fed him and went outside into the garden for fresh air. It was an overcast day, which would at least be gentle on overwrought senses. I slipped *Music To Watch Girls By* into the deck for further comfort. Then I spent a couple of hours sorting through the notes on Gaelle the Guru that Cam had couriered over to me, reading and rereading the handwritten messages he'd included in margins and on cover sheets for clues to his personality. Where was a graphologist when I needed one?

At midday, I was joined by Lucy, who emerged wearing baby doll pyjamas, her hair mussed, dark rings of mascara under her eyes and smelling like last night's party.

We gave each other smiles where you don't actually smile but just sort of pull the corners of your lips upwards.

'Hi,' I said, wondering if talking was safe.

'Hi yourself,' she replied, taking her rose-tinted sunglasses from the bowl of miscellaneous items on the kitchen table and putting them on. I made us both another coffee and wondered if I should try to gently coax out of her the details about what had happened last night. Better to wallow in her misery than my own, surely. We went out into the garden, now both wearing shades. Lu lit up one of Moni's fags and I reached over for the packet of Marlboro Lights and did the same.

'But you gave up,' she admonished.

'And you've never smoked.'

We stubbed out the ciggies and finally, her horror story emerged.

'When I saw Alan at the party, I couldn't believe my reaction. I must have been in total denial.'

'De-Niall,' I said. She grimaced.

'Don't. While you and Cam were in the kitchen, he took my hand and kissed it and I guess it was the E, but I just . . .'

'Melted?'

'Something like that. I didn't go upstairs with him for that reason, though,' she protested. 'It's just that I had some strong feelings going on and I thought we should talk. My room seemed like the best idea.' She paused. 'When we got up there, Alan saw that I still had Mr Ted on my bed.' Mr Ted was the floppy chocolate-brown teddy Alan had given her the previous Christmas. With a sentimental fault line bigger than San Andreas, Lu loved the bear and still slept with him.

'Alan leapt onto the bed next to Mr Ted and was sort of sprawled there. So, I sat down next to him, meaning to talk to him. Which we did for a moment.'

'What did he say?'

'Something like, "You look beautiful tonight."'

'A-ha. That'll get you every time.'

'So, then, we sort of . . . started kissing . . .'

'Mmmhmmm.'

'It felt fantastic, it really did. So good to be back, you know, cuddled up against him.'

'Right . . .'

'Yeah, a bit like smoking when you've given up. You know it's a dumb idea and bad for you, but it's sometimes irresistible after a few drugs or drinks.'

'Fair enough.'

'We were going for it . . .'

'A-ha.'

'When he suddenly asked me about Niall. He asked me if I was still seeing "the hippy". I told him I was. He asked me if it was good sex. I mean, this in the middle of us, you know . . .'

'Charming.'

'Exactly. So, I got pissed off and told him to mind his own business. He insisted that he wanted to know. He was being a total arsehole. Asking me if it was as good with Niall as it was with him. Was Niall's dick bigger than his? Did I come with him every time? Like he was getting off on asking lewd questions.' She clasped her hands over her sunnies. 'I told him I didn't want to talk about it. He kept on and on. Eventually I asked him if he was still shagging Madeleine and if he'd done the redhead from the party.'

'Oh, God.'

'Exactly. Basically, one thing led to another and before I knew it, I was throwing his clothes at him and telling him to get out. You saw the rest.'

'Yeah, me *and* Cam.'

'Right. You know, Alan has no spiritual connection. Sex with him is just two people creating friction. With Niall, it's transcendence.'

'I can't believe you even considered giving Alan another chance.'

'C, I was going to m-a-r-r-y him, remember.'

It was one of those strange situations where you want to tell a friend that her feelings are being wasted on a jerk, but aren't sure if she's ready to hear the truth just yet.

And what about Niall? I wanted to ask. But I didn't have the heart. She didn't need a lecture.

For some reason, I still couldn't bring myself to tell her about Cam. It all seemed too personal and weird for general consumption.

So we idled away the day in the garden, drinking water by the gallon and looking forward to evening, when we could retire to our beds.

Moni finally arose in time for an early dinner. She came down the stairs also in pyjamas – blue silky ones – and also sporting sunglasses.

'You look great,' Lu joked.

'I feel it.'

'And what about last night?'

'What about it?'

'You know, a big guy, slightly portly, given to dramatics and shenanigans. Goes by the name of –'

'Rufus?' I added.

Moni was silent for a moment. Then she said, 'There's nothing to tell.'

'Come on, Moni,' Lu goaded. It was getting later and cooler and I was starving. I watched and listened as Lu tried to extract gossip from Moni. I called for a pizza and then went to the fridge and pulled out the cask of white wine. Desperate times called for desperate measures.

'We're just friends, you know that,' Moni insisted. 'Nothing happened. He was drunk and so was I.'

'Sometimes the most interesting things happen when people are drunk,' I cajoled.

'Well, not last night.'

Lu poured white wine from the cask. Mouser leapt onto my lap as I sat at the kitchen table.

'You were pretty flirty with each other last night,' Lu added.

'That was last night. As you saw, this morning I was here at my house and he, I can only assume, went back to his. Or to find Imogen or whatever her name is.'

Miaow. Did I detect a hint of jealousy?

Moni and I got out paper napkins and plates for our pizzafest, while Lu downed some white and relived her night of pain once more for Moni's edification.

'So, you almost bonked him?'

'Sort of,' said Lu.

'Well, you either did or you didn't.'

'It's hard to explain. He was more into it than me, if you know what I mean . . .'

'We salute you,' Moni said, raising her glass.

'To think I nearly married him,' Lu said for the fifteenth time. 'I think I'll go and get a good massage and some acupuncture from Rosie.' Rosie was her Filipino masseuse and needler, visited mostly in times of crisis. I'd had a session with her once and when I got home I'd written the one and only poem I'd ever felt remotely pleased with.

The pizza finally arrived and we ate our dinner in relative silence, speaking only to pledge drug-free futures of pristine purity. With dinner done and bed calling, we adjourned to the living room for end-of-the-day telly.

'I'm going to have a look at my screenplay,' Moni said, hovering in the doorway. 'I promised I'd get it ready for Alex to read this week.'

'So how's it going?'

'It's going well. The last scene I wrote had the main character, Suzanne, overhearing her flatmate Nicole bitching about her to their mutual flatmate Daniel . . .'

We must have looked a little lost because she added, 'You know, Suzanne loves Daniel and Daniel loves Nicole . . .'

We nodded hung-over recognition.

She collapsed back onto the sofa, unable to get up steam to move upstairs. 'I think it's going to work . . . I only have two more scenes to write.'

Moni had started writing *Time of Gain* almost two years earlier, and still all I knew was its title and that it was about a love triangle.

She said it dealt with 'feminine wiles and jealousy, honesty, love and infatuation' and she planned to send it off to an agent as soon as it was finished. She had been writing it on my computer and I'd promised not to peek at it. Although the temptation was almost overwhelming, I'd kept my word.

'God, I wish I could quit TV and write my screenplay full time,' she announced.

'Careful what you wish for,' Lu admonished.

'I'm serious. I'd drop TV in a minute if I could. Perhaps I should just quit and hope for the best. Dale the Dickhead is driving me insane.'

With motivation obviously burning a hole in her Vitamin B deficiency, Moni finally traipsed upstairs, leaving Lucy and me staring at *Fatal Attraction* as Michael Douglas tried to drown Glenn Close in a bath of bloody water. She was struggling and gasping and I felt a bit like her. Lu was on the sofa, gripping her throat, pretending to drown, too.

When the ad break came on, I couldn't contain myself.

'So, Lu, do you want to hear my news?' I blurted.

'Yes,' she said, brightening.

'I kissed Cam last night.'

'Whaaat? You didn't say.'

'Well . . .'

The sound of the phone ringing braced us. Alan? Rufus? Cam? Lucy picked up the portable on the coffee table and answered. My heart jerked into my throat as she looked at me.

'C,' she said, winking and smiling broadly. 'It's your sister, Bianca.'

I felt simultaneously relieved and disappointed and took the phone into the kitchen. While my head pounded with last night's excesses, Bianca filled me in on some family news and I tried to keep up: Dad was planning a retirement party, Mum was sending him off to learn how to play bridge so he wouldn't be under her feet at home, the cat had had kittens and Bianca's love life was stupendously wonderful. Her new man, she said, was self-made and ran his own Internet design company, he sent her roses after their first date, thought the sun shone out of her every orifice, was clever enough to have impressed Mum and Dad on their first meeting and sexy enough to make Bianca swoon, simply by walking into the room.

She raved and I listened. Then she asked me about my love life. I told her a little about Cam and she whooped ecstatically. I told her I was also smitten. That I didn't want to get too excited yet, as I hadn't had more than a simple kiss and certainly no red roses, but, yes, he floated my boat.

Just as I was about to try to find the energy to regale her with the finer details of our snog-sesh in this very kitchen, the phone started bleeping at me. Call waiting.

'Take it, C,' she urged me. 'We can speak more later. Tim's coming around anyway, so I need to get ready.'

I smiled to myself and said goodbye, then picked up the next call.

'Hello?'

'Hi.'

My heart jumped. 'Hi, Cam, how are you?' Suddenly my headache was cured.

'Fine thanks, Cara. And you? How are you feeling after last night?'

'Oh, you know . . . a little worse for wear.' I hoped he wasn't ringing about work.

'Listen. I really wanted to apologise for what happened . . .'

'Oh. Er, right. Um. Don't worry about it.' Oh.

'No, I mean, seriously, I really am sorry. It should never have happened.'

'Look, it's okay,' I said, feeling slightly bilious.

'It's just that I shouldn't have let it get that far . . .'

'I see,' I replied. God, how seriously did he regret this?

'It's just that . . .'

'Mmmm?'

'It's just that I'm seeing someone.'

'Oh.'

'I've got a girlfriend . . . up in Birmingham.'

Shit. Fucking, fucking typical. 'I see. Listen, Cam, forget it.'

'I mean, she's up there and I'm down here and we've been having some problems. I haven't seen her for a few weeks . . .'

'Right.'

'I mean, like about four weeks.'

'Got it.'

'But that's no excuse and it shouldn't have happened.'

I rather enjoyed it.

'I don't know, maybe it was the drugs,' he ploughed on, bravely. Loser. 'But I sort of . . .'

This time I helped him out. 'Got carried away?'

'Yeah.'

'Me too.' Let him off easy, the insecure girl's policy which always fails. 'Listen, Cam, it's probably for the best.'

'Really?'

'Oh, God, yes, of course.'

'Why?'

'Because we work together. I've got too much invested in this job to screw it up . . .'

'I see.'

I hoped I sounded convincing.

'Well. Thanks for understanding,' he said, probably relieved.

'You're welcome.'

Bugger it. I'd had a sixth sense not to get involved. Why didn't I listen? Fucking bloody girlfriend. Great.

'Anyway.' He changed the subject while I caught my breath, as any man worth his testosterone would do. 'How's your flatmate?'

'Which one?' What did he want now? Idle chat?

'The one I last saw semi-naked standing at the top of your stairs yelling abuse at a guy ducking for cover at your front door.'

'Right. Lucy. She's fine. A small matter of an undigested ex-boyfriend she's trying to get out of her system.'

'Looked like it. Anyway, this is really just a call to let you know that Gaelle wants to do the first interviews this week. I won't be around until Tuesday or Wednesday. I have to go down to Brighton to see my folks for a few days.'

'Excellent. I mean, I don't mean excellent you're not going to be here, but excellent we can get on with some interviews.'

'Yeah.'

'Cool, then,' I said, wanting to keep it brief and light.

'Call me if you need me.'

'Sure.' Why would I need him?

I couldn't take any more. I popped my head into the living room where Lu was still watching TV and bade her goodnight.

'But you were going to tell me about the kiss.'

'Don't worry about it.'

'What happened?'

'Nothing. We kissed and I told him I didn't want to mix business with pleasure.'

'Oh. Is that what he was calling about?'

'Yeah,' I said. 'Goodnight.'

Up in my room, with the light on and the curtains closed, I disrobed, looking at myself naked in the large mirror of my wardrobe. I hated the way my flesh was so white over here. I never had a chance to sun myself. And my body was so . . . floppy. I hardly did any exercise. I put my hands to my breasts, watching my reflection. It had been a very long time since a man had touched my breasts. I ran my hands down to my stomach. Thank God it was still flat.

I sat down on the edge of my bed and put my head in my hands. I could feel raw sadness welling. Emotions I'd stifled for a long time were bubbling up. Why was I alone? What was wrong with me? Did I have such a dysfunctional personality and gargoyle-like appearance that I was doomed to be alone forever, with just a paltry and limited range of scrawny, toothless and smelly suitors to choose from?

Now and then I wondered if I'd done something horrendous in a previous life to deserve the constant screwy relationships I ended up with. Perhaps I'd been a serial misogynist polygamist. Whatever. I'd never 'settle' for anything less than something very good.

As the tears flowed, the sadness increased rather than dispersed. What really bugged me was that I hadn't embarked into full Fantasy Mode about Cam, I hadn't let my imagination run wild. I'd mostly stayed centred and grounded, but that didn't matter because the bottom line was that I had been rejected. Again. I was attracted to him. He had a girlfriend. I was alone.

Mouser slunk into my room via the door I'd left ajar. The ancient Egyptians, Lucy had told me, believed that cats were placed on Earth to absorb our troubles. Certainly my furry friend seemed to know where and when I needed comfort. He pushed his pointy little face into mine and purred like a machine as I stroked his silky back, berating myself for the tears of need that were streaming down my face, wetting his fur as they fell. As I whimpered, last night's dream came back to me. '*She'll be just fine,*' Gaelle and Cam had insisted repetitively. I didn't feel overly confident that they were right, but I would try to think positively.

Maybe now was the time to go back to Australia. To the familiar. To the old school friends I knew and loved. The beaches I had grown up on. The family who cared and were always there. My family home, my parents, their fridge full of home comforts, their lush tropical garden and sparkling swimming pool. The family home was eternally a safe house from the woes of the world. I could always escape there. No amount of London excitement could ever replace that.

As I stroked under Mouser's chin so that he almost smiled, my sobs must have become louder. Pretty soon, my door opened and Lu walked in, a look of deep concern on her face.

'Hi.' I blinked up at her, ashamed of my tear-stained face and red-rimmed eyes.

'What's up, C?' she asked. Like she didn't have enough problems of her own to think about.

'Nothing.' Mouser was licking the tears that had fallen onto my hands.

Lucy came and sat down beside me on the bed. She smelled sweet.

'Was it something Cam said?' she asked, also stroking Mouser.

'No,' I lied.

'Do you want to talk about it?'

The humiliation. How could I tell her? Well, Lu, the problem is I am so repulsive that I am feeling really upset about it.

'Do you want to talk more about Alan?' I countered.

'C, do you want to talk about you? Talking about me isn't going to help you stop crying.'

'I don't know if I can.'

'Why not?'

'Because I feel pathetic.'

'Tell me.'

The crying started again. I cried until my body was shaking, Mouser hanging on for dear life as I rocked back and froth.

'I'm just so sick of getting involved in screwed-up relationships that go nowhere. Like Jonathan bloody McCarthy. I don't know if I'm ever going to meet anyone again.'

Lucy waited for me to continue.

'Cam's got a girlfriend.'

Lu paused for thought. 'Do you like him?'

'Yes, I do,' I admitted at last.

'How much?'

'Well. Enough.' Clearly enough to be a sook about it. I knew I was being stupid. I hardly knew him. But I couldn't seem to help it.

'I told him that it was okay and that I wouldn't have wanted anything more to happen anyway,' I sobbed. 'At least I escaped with my dignity.'

'I know,' she said. And she did. 'What are we going to do about it?'

'You tell me.'

Mouser miaowed. Maybe he was trying to tell me the world's romance secrets. Shame I can't speak cat.

'How come other people manage to have it together as a couple, Lu? What's so wrong with me?'

'Nothing. You're beautiful, talented and loved by nearly everyone you meet. There's *so* nothing wrong with you,' she tried to console me.

'Well, sometimes I feel like there is.'

'You can cook, you have amazing green eyes, you've written for the *Independent* and you have naturally perfect eyebrows.'

I spluttered a laugh.

'I know,' she said. 'How about we feng shui your room? You know, put all the things in the right place so that you've got a better chance of good energy flowing through here.'

'Okay,' I said, weakly, clutching at feng shui straws. Was it the same as origami?

'We'll sort out your relationships corner. We'll put symbols in there that will expand your love life.'

'What's my relationships corner?'

'The top right of your room. It's where the energy to do with your love life gathers, so what you put in that area is symbolic of your love life. Where you've currently got a stack of boxes hoarded.'

'They're Gaelle's clippings and all my old story notes and ideas, and files and things,' I said.

'Right. Well, at the moment you've got junk in your relationships corner. Either that or you're having a relationship with your work. Or you're clinging to old stuff in relationships. The first thing you need to do is get rid of the clutter in your room.' Lu had obviously decided feng shui was my rescue remedy *du jour*.

After that, bolstered by apple juice and some Lou Reed, we spent hours stacking the piles of old books, magazines and newspapers on my bookshelves. We took all the clothes that were piled high on the large wicker armchair near the window and folded them or hung them up. We took three dirty coffee cups and a plastic bag full of rubbish out of my room.

'Clutter is feng shui's enemy,' she said solemnly, undoubtedly quoting from some weekend seminar. 'Clutter stops the free flow of energy. Energy gets stuck if you have junk all over the place.'

Once the room was pared down to the basics, and once everything was stacked, folded and shelved as it should have been, Lu told me it was time to consider my relationships corner. It was now 1 a.m. For a second, I considered telling Lu about the dreams I'd been having lately. I hesitated and she started talking again, so I dropped it.

'Okay, if you're standing in the doorway of your room, the relationships corner is the top right-hand side,' she said. 'We need to find images that represent love to you.'

'Huh?'

'You know, pictures of Paris, or a picture of a beautiful man. Flowers. Wind chimes are good to keep the energy flowing. And pairs of things. Two candles, two vases, you name it.'

She started to dig around in the files wedged in my relationships corner.

'What's this?' she asked, holding up a large folder file box.

'My old Jonathan stuff,' I said. It was a box filled with pictures of me and Jonathan 'in happier times', as they call it in magazine captions. After our break-up, I'd thrown all my Jonathan bits and pieces into this one box. Since then, if I'd received a letter or card or e-mail from him, it had gone in there, too.

'No, no, no,' Lu said. 'No wonder your love life hasn't moved on since Jonathan. For goodness' sake, all this stuff about him in your relationships corner is a recipe for disaster.'

'I wish I could rewrite my past as easily as Moni does with the characters in her screenplay.'

We worked out that I didn't have to throw my Jonathan file in the bin, but could put it in storage in my cupboard, which fell in my Inner Knowledge area. Lu put my twin candlesticks on a small table in the corner. We moved the wind chime we had on the porch downstairs to my relationships corner near enough to the window to catch the breeze. Then we made a collage.

'Creativity is good,' Lu said, as we leafed through my old magazines.

Glad to have something to do which would distract me from my hangover, I used an old piece of leopard-skin-print wrapping paper for a background and chose three images for the collage. One was of a young, sexy Calvin Klein couple snogging, to represent lust, another was of a middle-aged couple holding hands, to represent commitment, and the last was of an old couple smiling, to represent longevity. I pasted these down, cutting sharp corners, so that it looked rather professional. While Lu wasn't looking, I tore a strip of paper from the bottom of one of the notes Cam had sent me with Gaelle's clippings. It had his handwriting on it.

'What are you doing?'

'I, um . . .'

'What's that?'

'A piece of paper with Cam's handwriting on it,' I confessed.

She twisted her mouth in thought.

'I don't know if you should put that in there. Maybe you should be open to whoever the universe sends you. Feng shui works by asking you to focus your thoughts on a particular part of your life that needs work and attention. By fixing up this relationships corner, you're putting good vibes into your relationships. But you shouldn't "demand" –'

'Ah, Lu, just a little demand?' I knew I wanted Cam, even though I knew I shouldn't, since he was taken.

'No,' she said finally. 'Stay open. Trust the universe to send you the right man, be it Cam or someone else.'

'Okay.' I could always stick it on later, when she wasn't looking.

'Thanks, Lu,' I said, once my room was complete. I gave her a hug. She'd helped me a lot, just by giving me her time.

I crashed straight away. Sleeping was the only answer I could come up with that would help me avoid dwelling on the Cam situation. What I needed to do was start concentrating on the Gaelle job at hand. It was a major opportunity and I didn't want to blow it. If I could just sit her down for some solid interviews, we could be getting on with things. If only, only, only.

10

fuck right off, hippy

Sunday passed in a haze of afternoon sun, newspapers and about ten messages for Lu left by Alan on the answering machine. They ranged from a polite early morning 'Lucy, darling, please forgive me . . .' to 'Bloody hell, you stupid cow, can't you see what you're throwing away?' by late evening. I just hoped they made Lu surer than ever that getting rid of this fool should be her major life's mission of the moment.

When I awoke on Monday, I was mightily refreshed. It was lovely to wake up in my newly ordered room. It even made me feel marginally better about the week that lay ahead. I wandered into the living room to check out the 'Big Breakfast' and I was somewhat surprised to find Moni curled up in my usual spot – on the sofa. With Ru's cousin, Alex. It was slightly bizarre to see them asleep on the sofa together. Moni looked like Mummy bear, Alex like the baby.

They had their heads at opposite ends of the couch with their legs entangled. I could see Moni's famous screenplay had been one of the evening's topics of conversation because a rare print-out of the nearly completed manuscript was on the floor beside them.

I started to move out of the room, not wanting to wake them. Moni opened one bleary eye.

'Morning.'

Alex woke up to this. They smiled at each other. I couldn't help wondering what they'd been talking about so late into the night that they'd crashed on the sofa. Why hadn't Moni gone to her own bed?

'Sorry,' I said in a hushed whisper. And why wasn't Moni at work? I hobbled into the kitchen expecting to find Lu. Instead I found a note on the table: *'C, I've gone round to Gaelle's. Come when you're ready — Lucy.'*

I felt as if I'd missed something. Since when did Lucy go to Gaelle's without me? When had they arranged this? Wasn't I supposed to be the researcher? Why had Lu taken off without waking me?

I showered, dressed and breakfasted on a Portuguese salami sandwich. Moni zoomed in and out of the kitchen explaining she'd arranged to take the day off and that she and Alex were going sightseeing. Plus, as Moni's screenplay was set in North London, Moni thought it might be good grist for her last-minute writing mill.

They departed and I stared into space, noticing Lucy's omnipresent Nirvana Cards on the kitchen table. I cut the deck and turned the top card over. It was *Trust*. I slipped it back into the pack and made my way to Eaton Square, via two buses, in time for 10.30 a.m. When I agreed to work for Mistress Carrington-Keane, we hadn't exactly specified starting times and I was buggered if I was going to try for brownie points by reporting for early duty.

By the time I arrived, Lucy, Gaelle and Amanda were in situ. And blow me down if Niall wasn't there, too, in khaki army trousers, a multicoloured knitted vest over a white shirt, and matching crocheted beret. Such a fashion plate.

'Hi, everyone,' I said breezily as I entered.

Gaelle had shifted her lumpy load of a body into a regal-looking Victorian armchair, which placed her above Lu, Niall and Amanda, who were seated at her feet in a half-circle, armed with pen and paper. Gaelle was wearing her white clothes again, which I took as a bad sign.

'Ah, Cara. You've arrived,' she said.

I had the distinct impression they'd been waiting for me. Gaelle remained silent as I ambled over various bods to sit in the space next to Lucy. Amanda solemnly passed me a pen and piece of paper while Gaelle watched wordlessly. I tried to get comfortable, but her silence was making me awkward. I caught Lucy's eye, and she smiled weakly.

'Did you know, there is one thing that all people who are late have in common?' Gaelle said finally, in the tone I was starting to realise usually preceded A Great Pronouncement. 'People who are late like to be noticed. They walk in when everyone else is already there. Waiting. Everyone watches them as they come in, greets them and gives them their attention. It's a shame you couldn't be here on time, Cara.'

I'll say. Call it Mondayitis, but I didn't like the way things were going.

'Anyway. Today we are going to be doing some written work.' What was this? School? 'Firstly, please list your primal question.'

Pardon? I was still trying to figure out what Niall was doing here. He winked at me from across the floor. He looked at home. What was a primal question? I wondered.

'Cara, stay with us. Push yourself. Go with me. Take a chance.'

I nodded silently.

'Okay. I've asked everyone to think back to when they were six or seven. Close your eyes. See yourself then. What were you doing?

What were you thinking? What question was always on your mind?'

This wasn't too hard. I remembered being six, living in the same house my parents lived in now. Life seemed like an endless summer. I hardly remembered winter, apart from the fact we changed out of summer uniform at school. Until I was about ten, I thought the summer holidays lasted for twelve months and that we had a year off at Christmas. I spent most of my time then in our back garden, sitting under the lemon tree which grew in the pebble garden near the pool. When it was really sunny, the pebbles would warm up deliciously. The only thing you had to watch out for were the bees that liked the citrus smell of the tree.

'What questions did you ask yourself back then?'

I knew immediately my question: 'Why can't I talk to people?' At six, I was horrendously shy. I have umpteen photos of myself between the ages of three and seven hiding behind my mother's skirt. Well, hiding behind her legs, actually, because this was the seventies and she was a hip mum who wore miniskirts. They're kind of cute photos, but I was seriously timid, which wasn't so cute as I grew older. It was a shyness which lasted until my teens. I was once incapable of speaking to strangers. And yet I saw people all around me doing just that.

I studiously wrote down my 'primal question'.

'Next, list the five things that are most important to you.'

Double easy-peasy. True happiness, real love, robust health, flowing creativity, massive wealth, ginormous success. That was six, but it would have to do.

'And your life's purpose.'

Trickier. I was feeling open so I scrawled freely. To love and be loved and to live life to the fullest.

The process actually took at least an hour and we all scribbled away non-stop. I was quite into it. No subject could ever enthral me more than myself. That was why all this mystic self-help stuff was so tasty. Finally, it was time for everyone to reveal their innermost thoughts. But only if they wanted to.

At this point, we all squirmed uncomfortably at the thought of self-exposure. How very English of us, and Lu and I weren't even natives. It was amazing what a few years of living in a repressed society could do for a girl's inhibitions.

'Cara, what did you write for your first answer?'

She couldn't seriously be expecting me to read out what I'd written, could she? I thanked God Cam wasn't here.

'Cara?'

'Gaelle, do I have to answer?' I was meant to be her biographer, not another one of her acolytes.

'No, you don't have to answer. But you'll feel better if you do. You may find that the very same questions that plagued you when you were six plague you today.'

That was true enough. While these days I could blather with the best of them, my current main question was why couldn't I tell anyone about the weird shit that had been going down in my life of late? I was living my life through other people's dramas, never voicing my own.

'I think I'll pass,' I said stubbornly.

'It's about time you asked yourself the Big Questions,' Gaelle said, before looking away from me, not even trying to persuade me to play her game, which disappointed me slightly. Perhaps that was what I wanted. Someone to encourage me.

'Lucy?' she asked hopefully. I felt like the class reject as Lu took a deep breath. No wonder I wasn't evolved and had disastrous experiences like Friday night with Cam. I hadn't progressed a jot since the age of six. I still couldn't talk to people. Not properly. Not unless I was pissed. It all made sense now. What hope did I have of achieving the goals of happiness, love, health, creativity, wealth and success that I'd scrawled on my piece of paper if I still couldn't communicate?

Lu unscrunched her sheet of paper and read solemnly.

'My main question when I was six,' Lu began, 'was, "Why don't I have a swimming pool?" '

Amanda burst out laughing. Gaelle shot her a sinister look. Niall cocked his head understandingly. But this was nonsense. Lucy grew up in a huge Federation house on Bronte Beach, twenty minutes out of Sydney's CBD. She couldn't possibly have wanted a swimming pool. Her parents' large home was two minutes from the silky Bronte sands. And, apart from anything else, what kind of a 'primal question' was 'Why don't I have a swimming pool?'.

'I see,' said Gaelle, momentarily flummoxed by Lu's response. 'I see. And, er, let's see. How did that make you feel? How did you feel about not having a swimming pool?' Good recovery from the guru in the chair.

'Um, we lived at the beach, so I didn't really need a pool . . .' At least she was still lucid. 'But I guess it means that I was hankering after something I didn't need, when all that I did need was right under my nose?'

Gaelle nodded encouragingly, her chins flapping.

'Very good. All that you need is within you.' Lu beamed back under the rays of Gaelle's approval. It made me want to puke.

'Well done, Lucy. And you, Niall?'

Niall, the veteran of countless self-help seminars, cleared his throat. This was a piece of cake for him.

'The question that came to me, as I thought back to my childhood, is funny,' he said, still in lotus position with perfect posture. 'I spent those years wondering when I was going to grow up . . . and have a beard.'

Niall looked so perfectly at home in this environment that I wondered why it hadn't occurred to me earlier how right he and Gaelle would be for each other. They could chat for hours about vibrations and Martians, cosmic rays and chakras. I wondered about him. Maybe he was another fourteen-strand DNA half human, half

142

alien. I really wanted to get these two to pathology for tests.

'So you dreamed of being a man?' was Gaelle's interpretation of Niall's reply.

'Still do, teacher.' He grinned. He was in good form today. He obviously hadn't heard about the weekend's antics in Lu's bedroom.

'Very good. And Amanda?'

'I wondered what the point was,' she answered in a little voice.

'Good. And do you still wonder that, Amanda?'

'Well . . . not so much, not since my work with you began.'

Suck.

Next, they revealed their mission statements, aims, goals and life purposes.

Lucy's, incongruously, was dietary.

'I want to eat more sushi. I equate health with healthy eating and sushi is the most healthy food I can think of.'

Not in London. You could get mercury poisoning in a sliver of raw tuna around these parts, so I'd heard.

'Excellent. So, you want to be healthier and eating sushi is the first step. Is that right, Lucy?'

'Yes,' she replied earnestly.

Amanda reported her life's purpose was 'to explore further dimensions of her spirituality and to lose weight'.

And Niall?

'I want to make a difference to members of higher and lower socio-economic groups by providing free healing technology, through chakra work, via the healing centre I hope to open,' he said.

'Don't say "hope" say "intend",' Gaelle chided. 'When you use the word "hope", you open the door to failure.'

Niall nodded. He and Gaelle were made for each other. We were lucky he hadn't wished to be reborn into a poorer socio-economic group so he could sympathise more with those less fortunate than himself.

'Like, I really wish we could live in a society where money wasn't an issue,' he continued. 'If we could work in co-ops and pool resources, there'd be none of the greed we see today. Money is the devil, man.'

'That's ridiculous, Niall,' I said. I couldn't help myself. This hippy trip was going too far now.

'No way. If we could move back to a barter system, there'd be a lot more love in the world.'

'How?'

'Money wouldn't be an issue. Co-ops are the way forward.'

'And how would Lucy get her swimming pool? She's a graphic artist. She'd have to design a lot of book covers to barter her way to a swimming pool. Would the co-op pay for that?'

'Chill out, C,' he replied laconically.

But I didn't feel like chilling out. I was pissed off. Co-ops were a pile of crap. One person did all the hard work while the others told them to take it easy. That was obvious to anyone with half a brain.

'We don't need much,' he rambled. 'Just the beds we sleep in, the food on our tables, the shoes on our feet . . . If we just trust the Universe, it will provide us with all we need.'

'Yeah, right, Niall. And who's going to pay for Lucy's disposable contact lenses? Or my electricity bill?' I asked.

'Relax, man. You're so uptight today. Money is a system we've developed to create a ruling class where one man, or woman, has superiority over another.'

I rolled my eyes.

'The people in this ruling class receive access to better education and have increased expectations of a higher standard of living, all too often not as a reward for their hard work but as a result of their genes,' he concluded.

'Right.' Spare me the PC crap.

'In fact, even you are a product of that system, Cara. We are bound to money, although we know it serves no good.'

Oh, fuck right off, hippy.

'Well, I don't know which tent you live in,' I said, as I found myself suddenly standing up, hands on my hips. 'But I have ninety pounds a week in rent to pay. I need money.'

With that, I stormed out.

'Someone's been eating red meat,' I heard Niall drawl ridiculously as I exited.

Within seconds I was on the street alone, all wound up with nowhere to go. It occurred to me that I often felt like this as I left Gaelle's place. With Lu and Niall, of all people, still in there with Gaelle the bloody Guru, I was left cooling my heels on Eaton Square. That was the only part of me that remained cool, however. The rest of me was on fire.

11

a little guesthouse in knightsbridge

'Cheer up, love. It might never happen.'

I was standing on Chelsea Bridge, overlooking the swirly grey Thames, as a tramp wandered by with this bright message. I didn't think people ever said that in real life. Anyway, what did this old bloke know? That it might not happen was the problem.

I had stomped from Gaelle's house towards Chelsea, as ever seeking the scenic beauty of the Thames but not finding it. Growing up in Sydney, the water was never far away and even in London I sought it when troubled. At my parents' home in Clontarf, on Sydney's North Shore, I could see the harbour as I went to sleep at night, if I slept with my head at the foot of the bed. The water was so calming. I can't begin to count how many hours I spent staring out of that window, at the black sky, with its tiny stars, and at the murky black water below, reflecting the moon, its calm surface disturbed only by the occasional ferry, which I could glimpse but not hear.

Once I'd learned to drive, in high school, going to the water at night was my escape from all manner of teenage angst. My favourite spot was down by Luna Park, just near the North Sydney swimming pool, under the gigantic Art Deco pylons of the Harbour Bridge. I would stare for hours at the lights of the city reflected in the water.

Today, my melancholy had the better of me and seeing the Thames was only reminding me of how miserable and homesick I felt. London was a long way from Clontarf.

The truth was that sometimes I was über-confused about The Meaning of Life. I mean, to be fair, I hadn't really given it that much thought. All those questions Gaelle had thrown at us today had thrown me.

She had told me in her guru-like fashion that it was time I asked myself the Big Questions. But what were they? What did I want, beyond having a good time? I had a sneaking suspicion I was about to open a Pandora's box that would be much easier left closed.

I sighed as I stared out from the bridge. I knew I shouldn't have just walked out of Gaelle's again. I was messing up. But it was all getting far too hard and complicated, not to mention confusing. I didn't want to get fired, but I was getting close to the end of my tether and my hands were greasy.

My proximity to Sloane Square prompted thoughts of retail therapy. But the King's Road was a bit out of my league this week, so I decided to go to Oxford Street to check out Hennes and Top Shop. I looked in my wallet to see if I could afford a cab, and found a crumpled joint in my purse, a relic from Friday night's party. Should I? Why not. It was a brisk afternoon, just the right time for it. And God knew I didn't want to think too hard right now. Was it that drugs are for people who can't handle reality or is reality for people who can't handle drugs? The jury was still out on that one.

I did a police check left and right and the coast was clear, so I scrambled over the fencing barrier between the street and the banks of the river, treading carefully down to the grassy edge, where I knew there were wooden pylons by the water. It wasn't Sydney Harbour, but it would do. A few tug boats and ferries were meandering up and down the river in front of me.

I lit the joint and ruminated on the Gaelle job. Maybe it wasn't worth it. It had started out so auspiciously and had gone downhill from there. Too bad about the money. Gaelle freaked me out. I didn't like her and I didn't trust her. Maybe I didn't like her because I didn't trust her. I mean, how could you trust someone who said they were a half alien walk-in in a human body and who chanted and sucked you into their trances? I didn't mind the stuff she said about souls and love, but the rest of it? Please. Plus, I wasn't happy that Lu was so into her, or that she and Niall were around at Eaton Square right now revealing their souls. So much for my big break. I was fucking it up big time. And bloody Cam Street had a bloody girlfriend. Why wasn't I surprised? He'd be back soon and I'd have to face him.

The joint finished, I scrambled back up the embankment and over the fence to hail a cab on the main road.

'Hey, Cara!'

I looked around and my stomach flipped. It was James Duncan, a guy I'd met at a party a year or so ago and had had a short affair with. Bonked him, really. That was all. At the time, I was just keen to have sex and he was a presentable, clean male with a pulse. A good-looking male with a pulse. Turned out, though, that like Cam he also had a girlfriend, only his lived in Paris. Unfortunately, I didn't know about her and he didn't tell me. After we'd shagged about five times, I didn't hear from James and we lost touch. The whole thing had been so half-hearted that I didn't really bother trying too hard to find out what had happened. Three months later, my friend Sandra invited me to his going-away party.

'Where's he going?' I'd asked.

'To live in Paris, to be with his girlfriend,' she'd said. Suddenly I understood why he'd just disappeared after our encounters. And why he'd been so distant the whole time we were (sort of) seeing each other. Now here he was, in smart casual.

'Hi, James, how are you?'

I hadn't gone to his going-away party, so he didn't know I knew he'd gone to Paris, let alone that he'd been shagging me while WG (with girlfriend). Slimy, lowdown, cheating rat. He was pretty gorgeous, though. He looked like the Neanderthal-built weekend rugby player he was. He worked in property development, had sky-blue eyes and a wicked grin. Wicked grins did it for me every time. I guess because they were another way of saying 'I'm trouble', and God knows that for a very long time I'd been highly attracted to trouble.

'Cara Kerr, what are you doing here?' he asked, amazing me that he remembered my first name, let alone my surname.

With the joint now coursing through my veins, I decided to be blunt. 'I've had a rotten day, I hate all men, and most women, and I'm probably risking losing my job by being here and not at the home of a mad woman in Eaton Square. I've just had a joint and I'm about to go up to Oxford Street. How about you?'

He was nonplussed. 'Ah, I've moved to Paris, did you know? But at the moment I'm working on a project which means spending a few days a week in London.'

Takes you away from your precious girlfriend, I thought cattily.

'I see,' I replied instead.

'So, do you want to share a cab? I'm going towards Oxford Street myself.'

Hmmm. 'Sure.'

'I wish I could have shared some of that joint with you.'

No, you don't, I thought, not after what's happened the last couple of times I've mixed drugs and men.

We hailed a cab and set off. Inside, I was reminded of James's bulk. Lying in bed with him felt a bit like lying in bed with a car, he was so big. I glanced at him as he instructed the cabbie. Sadly, he wasn't so huge in all departments, if memory served.

'Cara, it's great to see you,' he said. 'Do you know, I was going to give you a call.'

'Really?' I asked, mentally tallying up the last time I'd heard from him – twelve months ago. Yeah, right.

'I found that book you lent me, *Perfume*, and read it. It was fantastic. I was going to call to let you know.'

Well, that sounded mildly plausible. He was looking good, wearing stone-coloured chinos, a white shirt and navy tie.

'Hey, listen,' he said. 'I'm only going to be at this appointment for half an hour or so. Do you want to meet up afterwards for a drink?'

No. Yes. Yes. No. Don't know. 'Ah, I guess so. Why not?'

'Great. How about the Little Titchfield Café? We can go downstairs for those hot peppers they have for free with the olives and things.'

How sweet. The one and only time we'd ever met up and had a proper date was when he'd had tickets to a play in Drury Lane. We'd been to the Little Titchfield for dinner. I'd liked the free chilli peppers and he remembered. Aw. Score one brownie point.

We got out of the cab at Oxford Circus, agreeing to meet in half an hour. He wandered towards Bond Street; I went straight to Top Shop.

I loved Oxford Street. I'd visited it as a child and I still loved the colourful, flat facades of the hundreds of shops which lined it, seemingly for miles, and the bustle of the people who jostled for space on the footpaths. I loved the red double-decker buses and black cabs which snaked up the long stretch between Marble Arch and Tottenham Court Road, stalled in traffic jams that eased up only at about 11 p.m. This part of town brought out the Australian in me. It was Tourist Central and represented everything I'd ever expected London to be, as seen on postcards and in the movies.

I took the long escalator down to Top Shop. Time for a bit of self-hatred while I tried on clothes that didn't fit and I couldn't afford at the moment, anyway. I tried on a longish, floaty skirt with a tiny floral print, which actually didn't look too bad with my semi-suntanned legs, and was even within the limit of available funds on my credit card, so I bought it. I changed out of my old jeans into my new purchase. No harm in sprucing myself up for this little encounter.

Feeling a whole lot better, I wandered back into the daylight, which had turned quite sunny. With five minutes up my sleeve, I started to weave, still slightly light-headed, through the lunch-time crowds, walking briskly, dodging little old ladies and mums with strollers, before turning into Little Titchfield Street. I could see the boxes of colourful flowers outside the café a block away. This was quite fun and sort of exciting.

James was already there, standing outside the restaurant. He extended his hand to greet me, before kissing me politely on the cheek. I wished I'd sprayed on some perfume from a tester somewhere.

'You've changed,' he said.

I smiled. 'So have you.'

'Have I?'

'No. I'm being smart. I just bought this skirt now.'

'It looks great. Shall we go downstairs?'

'Sure.' Downstairs at the Little Titchfield Café was a sight to behold: it was a windowless cavern with raw stone walls and floors, roughly hewn wooden furniture which never quite felt safe, and countless flickering candles. It was eerie, bohemian and a soothing, unexpected contrast to the brightness of London outside. I always half expected to see Marianne Faithfull sitting crooning in the corner.

We sat down at one of the rickety tables and were presented with the much-awaited chilli nibblies which I hoed into as we talked. We ordered wine from the waiter. A couple of glasses and a plate of vegetarian lasagne later, the conversation was flowing.

'So, James,' I said finally, after we'd chatted about his job and my job, the weather, Paris, London and why he'd never called. 'I hear you went to Paris to live with your girlfriend?'

He laughed nervously, as you would.

'Don't worry about it.' I smiled, knowing I had the moral high ground. 'What's her name?'

'Anne-Claire,' he said. 'Things haven't been going very well lately. I was quite glad to get away.'

'Where are you staying?'

'At a little guesthouse in Knightsbridge.'

'Of course you are.'

'Pardon?'

'As if you'd stay anywhere else apart from a little guesthouse in Knightsbridge.' I was feeling bitchy and I didn't care. My mind kept wandering back to the events at Gaelle's house and the bloody Big Questions I was supposed to be tackling.

'Do you want to come and see the guesthouse?' he asked incongruously. 'I have to go back there pretty soon anyway to make a quick call. I can run you back to your place afterwards – I've got a hire car.'

'Um . . .' Come back and see my guesthouse. That was a new one.

'Come on, you said you'd had a bad day,' he urged me, paying the bill for our lunch. He poured the last of the wine into my glass, I drank it and we left. I knew what I was doing: I was setting up an afternoon encounter. I wasn't sure if I should be doing it, but I didn't care. Opportunity only knocks every now and then and, quite frankly, after the last couple of days I needed a little bit of distracting intrigue.

The guesthouse was horrible. All pink, flowery wallpaper, Laura Ashley fabrics and reproduction furniture. It didn't surprise me that James thought this was fashionable and chose to stay here. He clearly had no taste.

He led me towards the lift, and then down a pale beige-coloured corridor, finally opening a door into his room, which housed a double bed, built-in mirrored wardrobes, a tiny desk and a door which must have led to a bathroom. There was not much space, as the bed was very large. There was nowhere for me to sit except on the bed, so I sat there. Gingerly. I hate it when you have to sit on the bed. It makes sex seem so predictable.

James went straight to the little desk and leafed through some papers.

'I just have to make one phone call,' he said, picking up the receiver.

I listened vaguely as he talked about prime localities and investment portfolios. I got off the bed and wandered to the window to pull back the dingy, white nylon net curtain to see what was outside. The guts of another guesthouse. In the meantime, James had finished his call, put down the phone and was now facing me, looking as though he'd just closed one deal and had another in mind.

He came straight for me, striding across the room confidently, his arms open. He reached me, grabbed me and started to kiss me. He obviously felt that my presence in his room meant I was up for this. I was acquiescent. His large fingers squeezed into my body, gripping a shoulder and a buttock. I could feel him getting harder. It felt good to be in someone's arms and it felt good to be horny. I knew I could do this with no regrets, apart from remorse about his girlfriend. Somehow she seemed unreal because we'd never met. Not that that was any kind of excuse.

What he said doesn't matter now, because they were just words to keep the momentum going. He flattered me, he told me he enjoyed my body, that he'd always hoped to see me again. I let him unbutton my shirt and raise my new skirt. He was still dressed, although I had undone the buttons on his shirt. Not waiting for me, he started to tackle his belt buckle. He shook off his shirt and slid down his chinos. This was all so easy for him. Why was I feeling like the victim? I tried to find some enthusiasm. This was sex and I wanted some. Just not today. Just not with him. Just not now, when I was too raw inside to know what was going on. His hairy chest felt good against my breasts and if I'd thought for one second that he had one ounce of respect or caring for me, maybe I would have gone through with it with enthusiasm. But there was nothing.

He was fumbling for a condom. He was still kissing me. He shoved himself inside me and I felt horrid, hot stinging tears gathering at the creases of my eyes. I squeezed them shut and a tear ran across my temple. His body was so big, it made me feel tiny. But he didn't look at me as we had sex. And sex without eye contact is as meaningless and unfulfilling as a sneeze. At least pretend, damn you! He was thrusting in and out, hard and rhythmically. Suddenly, I couldn't take it any more. He had a girlfriend, dammit, and I knew it and he knew it and someone here had to make a stand. I felt as if my whole body was crying. With one great shove, I pushed him out of me. My breath was choking. He made himself come quickly afterwards, confused, panting and huffing like an old engine. I felt sick. This was too horrendous for words. I was out of breath, my head back on the bed, my eyes staring at the ceiling, waiting for the moment to pass. As it would. I wanted to leave and forget this had ever happened.

so long, sucker

I took a black cab home around 7 p.m., feeling like shit. What a great solution I'd come up with; get over feeling pissed off about Cam by shagging one of the least desirable arseholes I'd ever had the displeasure to meet. Why did I even consider it?

Moni greeted me first. 'Hey, C, Alex liked *Time of Gain*. She read it the other night. The ending moved her to tears. I think I'm nearly ready to send it off to the agent.'

'Hmmm. Good, Moni,' I responded generously.

'It's funny her being here, isn't it?' she went on. 'We're the foreigners, but we're less foreign here than she is, somehow. We're like the locals entertaining a visitor.'

'Part of the furniture,' I agreed glumly.

'And there's news on the dating agency story at work,' she continued.

'What?'

'You know, that dating agency story – for married people . . . Discreet Duets.'

'Oh, yes . . . ?' I asked half-heartedly.

'Dale's decided we're going ahead with the initial meeting with Alex and this Jean-Luc guy. Look.' She reached under the coffee table to a manila folder and took a wedge of letters out of it, all of which had printed-out, computerised snapshots stapled to them. 'We signed up and posted Alex's picture on the Net. These are the guys who responded to her ad.'

I flicked through them. David from Hampstead, Mike from Hammersmith, Lawrence from Stoke Newington.

'You mean all these guys are swingers?'

'Mmmhmmm. London-based orgy lovers.'

'Gosh.'

I scanned their e-mailed letters, which universally complimented Alex on her photo, listed the men's interests and had phone numbers – mostly mobiles – asking Alex to put them on her dance card for the next party. Moni handed me another letter, this one from a man called Jean-Luc, a French guy living in Ealing.

'Alex has chosen Jean-Luc for the initial meeting because he looks the most harmless. And he says he's into American women, so she fits the bill. They'll meet up for a drink and if all goes well, she gets invited to the next party as his special date.'

The picture Jean-Luc had sent was a blurry long shot, but I could see enough to notice that he was dressed in a pair of jeans and a woolly jumper and looked like the kind of middle-aged guy you'd meet at work and chat with cosily over the photocopier, not the sort to 'swing'.

'But she's not going to sleep with him, is she?' I asked. 'I mean, I've heard of selling your soul for your work, but selling your body? Or your friend's body?'

'Don't be ridiculous. They're meeting tomorrow night. Just for a chat, no filming.'

'I hope she'll be okay.'

'Me, too. I'm still not sure about prying into these people's private lives. Can you imagine how you'd feel if you were a quiet secretary who let her hair down at swingers' parties on the weekends and suddenly found herself splashed all over the telly?'

'No.'

'Alex says she likes the idea of the PVC bodice or catsuit . . . She's going to give Rufus and me a fashion parade, as soon as it's made up.'

'Whatever turns you on, Moni.'

'The next step after that will be for Alex to actually go to a party. I told Dale I'll only do it if he guarantees me that he won't show anyone's face. He has to pixilate them.'

'Pixy-what them?'

'Digitise their faces so you can't recognise them. Or just show the back of their heads. And disguise their voices . . .'

'A-ha . . .'

'I refuse to ruin lives for the sake of the show's ratings.'

'Good on you.'

'I'm pretty sure Alex can pull it off. She'll be paid for it by "Matt and Melissa", and she won't be in London forever, so if anyone does actually figure out that they've been scammed there's not much chance of reprisals.'

'I thought you'd decided it was a shite story and you didn't want anything to do with it at all . . .'

'I did. But it's such a good opportunity. It's the first special I'll have produced here, and they reckon they'll sell it overseas.'

'Sex does sell,' was the best response I could muster.

'Are you all right, C?' she asked, finally sensing my black mood.

'Nup,' I said. 'I think I'm getting my period, I'm feeling so shit. I might go upstairs. Sorry . . .'

I took a beer from the fridge, started running a bath and adjourned to my sad little bedroom, now feng shuied to within an inch of its life to increase my romantic chances. I hoped that a one-afternoon stand with James Duncan was not the sum total of its effects. Staring at the ceiling, I wondered how long this depression would last. I felt like doing nothing at all. Not talking, not listening, not watching telly – nuthin'.

After my bath, I lay awake for hours, as my fugue continued through the night. When I did eventually sleep my dreams were fragmented, but included trips to the seaside where I saw Cam with his girl, James Duncan with his, Lu with Alan and Niall fighting over her.

In the morning, I felt a little brighter. I checked my e-mails. There was one from my mum joking about the fact that both her daughters were 'obviously about to be married off' and perhaps we could have a double wedding on the night of Dad's retirement party to save money. It seemed Bianca had relayed my excitement about Cam to Mum and now she had absolutely the wrong idea. Mum was like most mothers – all she ever wanted was for me to be happy, married and rich. Although she welcomed my career moves, I think she believed a ring on my finger would be more satisfying than any amount of successful job applications. I considered e-mailing her back with the horrid truth about Cam and his girlfriend, but reconsidered. She'd be on cloud nine with the idea of Cam and me and Bianca and Tim all happy. Let her enjoy it.

There was also an e-mail from my ex, Jonathan, announcing he had been offered an exhibition in Los Angeles and was leaving Noo Yawk in a fortnight. His career was booming. There was no mention of his latter-day architect girlfriend, Georrrrgie, so I was left to guess as to whether or not she was the latest abandoned victim of his ambition.

I answered a query from Oz News about my late account and then, in payment mode, dashed off a few cheques to pay various other outstanding bills. At least I had some available funds in my bank account from the Gaelle job now, even if it also meant I had a heavy heart.

Feeling like I'd e-mailed half the universe and sent out more than half my earnings, I adjourned downstairs to read the paper for a while, wallowing. Then the phone rang. It was Cam.

'Hi, Cara,' he began. 'Okay?'

'Of course, Cam.' If you mean am I okay that you have a girl-friend . . . sure, I'm fine. Walk all over me. The rest of the world does. I felt a sharp pang in my fanny, and it wasn't lust for Cam. Shit. I knew that feeling. Bloody cystitis. All I needed.

'Listen, Gaelle and I have spent the morning sorting through the ideas she has for the book, about how to combine her life story with the self-help psychic stuff.'

'Yes?'

'So, she wonders if you could come around within the next hour or two? For a light lunch and a chat.'

I figured anything was better than dwelling, so I agreed to be there and got off the phone as quickly as I could, repairing to the bathroom to pee. Nothing but razor blades. Dammit. Physical pain to add to the emotional trauma. One thing I was realising from the events of the past few days was that it was going to be a rough ride if I was going to look inside myself and start asking myself some hard questions.

In the hour I had to kill before going to Gaelle's, I spent forty-five minutes on the loo trying to wee, and the rest of my time drinking copious amounts of water and using up leftover packets of Ural from the bathroom cabinet. I couldn't believe it. Cystitis is the bloody honeymoon disease. You're supposed to get it after too much sex. I'd had one shag in the past three months and got it straight away.

On my way to Eaton Square I picked up a large bottle of cranberry juice to calm the fire in my innards. Then I braced myself, pre-Gaelle. I was slightly concerned she'd be angry with me after my recent storming-out scene. After all, she was paying me good money to research and write her book.

I got the apologies out of the way as soon as I arrived, mutter-ing my regrets about 'leaving so suddenly yesterday'.

'Resistance,' she said annoyingly. 'You're scared, Cara. You're at a crossroads. You can see the path ahead of you, but it's obscured by your fears. We will talk about it later. For the time being, forget it. It's all part of the journey.'

If she was happy to let it pass, so was I. For a change, she took me, not to her work room, but into her airy and bright country-style kitchen at the end of the apartment. You could see right across the top of London from the kitchen table, where she sat me down. It was very homey, with bare, polished floorboards, an olde-worlde kitchen unit with a large chopping bench in the centre, above which hung heavy cast-iron pots, pans and ladles, stirrers, beaters, spatulas and wooden spoons. There was a delicious, home-baked smell emanating from the oven. Acolyte Amanda – the chubby one – was present and correct, hovering as ever. Gaelle the Guru was apparently playing hostess, perhaps trying to curry favour with me after my little stunt the previous day.

The windows were open and the scent of jasmine wafted in. I almost felt relaxed, as long as I didn't think about my persistent urge to wee. Gaelle poured me tea like the Eaton Square hostess she was, and I helped myself to sugar and milk, enjoying being waited on for once. Outside the window was a windowbox flowering with red, orange, yellow, blue, indigo and violet flowers. Although I was trying to stay grumpy with her, I couldn't help commenting on how pretty they were.

'They represent the chakra colours, Cara,' Gaelle said as I stared at them. 'The foliage is the green, which is the heart chakra. *Your* heart chakra seems a little stuck today, dear.'

'What's a chakra, Gaelle?' I asked finally. Might as well take the bait and get ready for Mystic Lesson No. 447.

'I'm glad you asked.' She grinned broadly. 'A chakra, well, it's an energetic connection, a conductor between the physical body and the universe's energy. Chakras work well when you're healthy. If there are tensions in your mind, though, they are reflected in the chakras and ultimately in the human body. A chakra meditation will ease the tensions.'

Right. Cosmic nonsense, but at least it would be good material for the book.

'Are you going to meditate, Cara?' she asked me.

'Gaelle, my mind is so busy I don't think I could.'

'That's what they all say. Give it a try. Are you hungry, dear?'

'A bit,' I admitted. The aroma was tempting. 'Back to the chakras. Where are they? Can you see them?'

'Oh no,' she said, sounding very serious. 'Well, I can, but you probably can't. Not yet, at any rate.'

I performed my new 'Stay Silent' trick.

'Well, you see, Cara,' she went on, 'they are energy centres, so just as you can't see electricity, you can't normally see chakras. Unless you decided you wanted to, when you might be able to learn. They're on the meridians,' she added, sweeping her fingers down my arm, sending a shiver through it. 'Meridians are the lines used as guides in acupuncture.'

'I see.'

'Now, there are a few things I want you to do. Will you agree to do something for me?'

'Ummm.'

She handed me a book – *Miracle Meditation for Beginners*.

'You must surrender, Cara, if you are to evolve. And meditation will help you. It will also release Kundalini which will improve your sex life.'

Yeah, right.

'And if you are to write this book with me, you need to meditate. It will relax you. It's just a matter of sitting down, closing your eyes and breathing, but it's a proven de-stresser and I know you are stressed. It will also raise your vibrations, which is essential.'

'Why?'

'Because you are dealing with higher energies. Meditation releases serotonin, with which I am sure you are familiar?'

'I don't think so, Gaelle . . .'

'It's the feel-good chemical that the brain releases when you take that designer drug of the moment . . .'

'Ecstasy?'

'Exactly. And it releases melatonin, which fights ageing. If you knew how old I really am, you'd understand that better. And it integrates the left- and right-hand sides of the brain and . . .'

'Okay, Gaelle, I get the message.'

'And it increases your endorphin count by up to 300 per cent. In fact, if you took a blood test of a non-meditator and a meditator, you could tell which was which simply by the level of cortisol in the blood . . .'

'Pardon?'

'Cortisol, a blood-serum stress indicator. Meditation lowers it. That's how we know it de-stresses you. Have I made my case?'

'Yes, but do I have to sit cross-legged and chant strange words?'

'No, dear.'

'But meditators do seem a bit . . . well, like Niall . . .'

'When you meditate you find inner silence and in that silence, many people find God.'

'I suppose it won't hurt.' Anything that could de-stress me was welcome.

'Listen, Cara, I'm delighted you're hungry. I knew you would be. Amanda, have those pies heated up yet?'

'Yes, Gaelle. Ready when you are.'

'Wonderful. Get them out then.'

And so, as if we hadn't just been discussing vibrations, energies and Kundalini sexiness, Gaelle supervised Amanda as she removed a tray of puffy, golden brown pies from the oven, setting them on a china serving plate. She fetched a large bowl of salad from the fridge, a healthy combo of lettuce, rocket, what looked like roasted pumpkin, fresh asparagus, pine nuts, grilled red capsicum and other delights, doused in balsamic vinegar. Very nice. Then hot bread emerged from the oven, a variety of crackers, slabs and wheels of cheese, sliced tomatoes and mozzarella drizzled with olive oil and a little pot of mayo. This was a minor feast. I wondered if I was being led by my stomach.

And then the meat pies.

'Ah, the food of our nation, aren't they, Cara?' Gaelle said as she took the top off a bottle of tomato sauce and set it in front of me. I felt a bit like Snow White being presented with a poisoned apple. Why was she feeding me? Weren't gurus supposed to be vegetarians?

'So. About yesterday. You were extremely upset, Cara, weren't you?' she said finally, after I'd taken my first mouthful of pie. 'What was it that got you so upset? Do you want to talk about it?'

She had to be kidding. I was saying nothing around her today. Or tomorrow. From now on, it would be me asking the questions. I'd had this Silent Researcher lark. 'Can we give that a miss, Gaelle?'

'You exhibited a lot of indirect anger towards poor Niall, who never did anyone any harm. He's a sweet thing. Not right for Lucy in many ways, but he has an exceptional heart.'

Whatever.

'I just wondered if you wanted to talk about whatever's on your mind. There's no such thing as an "upset", you know. They're just "set-ups". We create set-ups to teach ourselves our life lessons. We are all mirrors for each other. Tell me about your life.'

What was it with her? Did she want some goss? Well, Gaelle, the problem is that I fancy your assistant, Cam, and he's seeing some-one else, and it's made me feel depressed, so yesterday I exhibited Class A Self-Destructive Behaviour and went out and shagged someone I didn't really know. Sure.

The cystitis was striking again and I had to excuse myself. I came back to the kitchen with a winced look on my face which I couldn't shift.

'Are you okay?' Gaelle asked, instantly on the case. 'Reach out to me.'

'I'm okay, Gaelle,' I said, not sounding very truthful.

'Are you really?'

I considered my position. 'As it goes, Gaelle, I am not okay. I think I'm getting a urinary tract infection, which is a drag, because I hate them.'

I waited for her reaction.

'Why have you got a urinary tract infection?' she asked gently. This question seemed a little left-field.

'Why have I got it? I'm sorry, I don't understand the question. I presume I've got it because some nasty amoebas and bacteria invaded me recently.'

'Do you want to know why you have a urinary tract infection?'

Absolutely. 'Why?' I asked, almost rudely. I couldn't help it. I knew I wasn't going to want to hear what she had to say.

'We call our ailments "diseases" because we mean "dis-eases". Illness so often reflects tensions and a lack of ease in the mind. Your cystitis refers to your sacral chakra. I would say that your sacral chakra – your sex and food chakra – is out of whack. What have you been doing in that department that you don't feel good about? I would say that your problem is related to sex, not food. That you're either frustrated about sex, or sleeping with someone you feel you shouldn't be sleeping with . . .'

How did she manage such unerring accuracy?

'As I said, physical illness is a manifestation of tensions on the consciousness,' she continued. 'If something's not good up here –' she tapped her forehead, '– then the rest of the body follows. In your case, cystitis is a reproductive chakra issue. What have you been up to? What happened, dear?' she asked. I wondered how long it was since she'd had sex. Decades, I guessed. Perhaps she got her thrills vicariously these days.

'It was with an old acquaintance of mine called James. I bumped into him and we just ended up in bed.'

Just as I finished this loaded sentence, Cam walked in the door, looking appropriately agog, as if he'd heard my last words. He said hello and went to Gaelle's filter for a glass of water.

'I see. And you don't care for this man?' The question hung in the air like a bad smell.

'No.'

'And now you have cystitis,' Gaelle concluded.

'Oh, just tell everyone!' I rolled my eyes. 'I'm sure Cam is desperate to know.'

'Cam understands, don't you, Cam?'

Cam looked unsure, but nodded. Apart from a strange-looking Indian cloth pillbox hat, he looked unusually close to normal today, in a Hawaiian shirt over combat trousers. I had to get out of there.

'You know what, Gaelle, I'm feeling really bad. Do you mind if I cry off this session? I really need to get to a chemist. Cystitis shouldn't be left untreated, should it?' I tried to present it as bluntly as I could, so she'd have less of a chance to refuse me. I was shaken by Cam's presence, not to mention that I was fairly sure he'd just heard the juicier part of my conversation with Gaelle.

'Orange chakra issues,' she warned. 'Eat carefully. Eat honey and ice cream and pasta . . .'

Together?

'. . . wear orange underpants, bathe in sunlight and burn some ylang-ylang essential oil. And meditate.'

I got up and started to put my coat on, but Gaelle went on. 'Will you read the book I gave you about meditation? You need it.'

Maybe now wouldn't be a bad time to have a flick through. I could do with some de-stressing. 'Um. Okay, Gaelle. Sure. But I think I'll go now, if you don't mind.' And I went, promising to call, my heart pounding. Seeing Cam had shaken me up. I was so pissed off with myself for having fancied him and for everything that had and hadn't happened with him. Why was I reacting so strongly? I hardly knew him. I blamed all the weird eye-staring games Gaelle had had us playing. And all this New Age mumbo jumbo. It was quite clearly doing my head in.

I caught a cab home, wincing all the while. Back in the safety of my living room I devised a plan. I would call Gaelle tomorrow morning and tell her that I had a fever from the cystitis and would need to see the doctor, buying myself at least two more days of sickies. I couldn't face her now.

Over the next few days, I would indulge myself. I would lie around in bed until ten or eleven with the papers and cups of tea and catch up on my e-mails. Indeed, I finally plucked up the courage to e-mail Mum and tell her not to start planning her mother-of-the-bride outfit just yet, as things with Cam were not nearly as rosy as Bianca might have indicated.

By the next afternoon, the cystitis had eased. I took my new-found freedom from the tyranny of the toilet and went to see my friend Anita, who had blue hair and a flat in Hoxton, the seedier end of London favoured by those who thought Islington passé. Anita had once saved me from Death By Boredom during the five days we worked together as office clerks during my first year in London. She had been funding herself through her first year out as a website designer, back when such things were considered avant garde. As for me, I was just short of cash. These days Anita ran her own agency. We met at her offices for a chat, where she produced some thick, murky Turkish coffee available only at some obscure but hip deli in Stoke Newington. I remained mindful of my sacral chakra and sipped a refreshing orange blossom tea.

Mercifully, when I called Gaelle to give her an update on my health, she gave me the rest of the week off. So I went into full self-indulgent, cocooning mode. I had a reflexology massage, lunched with my friend Toni, and went CD shopping in HMV.

I went for a walk around the Common with my neighbour Jem, who was having triangular love-life complications with her two male flatmates and was more than happy to chat about her dramas while I listened. And I drank enough cranberry juice and Ural to sink a battleship and totally beat the cystitis.

I also decided I'd teach myself to meditate, using Gaelle's *Miracle Meditation for Beginners*. It looked easy enough. I'd read the instructions forty thousand times. Clearly, the moment had come to give it a go.

I took myself to the privacy of my bedroom for the big moment. Step One was to make a pact with myself that I was going to dedicate the next twenty minutes to me. That meant if the phone rang, I was supposed to ignore it. I checked my watch. It was 3.05 p.m.

Step Two was to sit comfortably. This was considerably easier than it had been when I felt like my urinary tract had had an unfortunate encounter with a jar of chilli oil. I sat on my bed, leaning a pillow against the wall.

For Step Three, I clasped my hands together, relaxed with back straight. I closed my eyes and forgot about my woes and started to listen to myself breathing, remembering Gaelle's words: 'Meditating's like hearing yourself living.' She'd told me that my breath might become 'finer', and sure enough, as I listened, my breathing slowed. It was a modern miracle, all right.

Despite the stressful state I'd been in, my body was actually slowing down.

Once my breath was regular, I was to start to 'hear' my mantra. Gaelle had given me a word: 'Om'. Not very original, but apparently it was Sanskrit for 'peace'.

I said the word in my head. 'Ommmm.' With each out-breath, there it was again. 'Ommmm.' I felt my head getting lighter and my body getting heavier with each release of my breath. 'Ommmm.' I never thought I'd see the day when I'd be sitting cross-legged in my bedroom chanting 'Ommmm'.

The book said that if you had a thought, you should acknowledge it and let it float away. There was no such thing as a bad meditation. 'Ommmm.' As I ommmmed, my mind wandered to what we had in the fridge for dinner. Because I was quite peckish. 'Ommmm.' I could go a comfort-food delivery pizza with pepperoni topping for dinner. 'Ommmm.' With mushrooms. And garlic. 'Ommmm.' Ooops. And then back to my mantra. 'Ommmm.'

I floated. I thought. I ommmmed. It's possible that I actually meditated. There were a few moments of mental quiet when my body felt emptied of a lot of dross. Finally I looked at my watch. Exactly twenty minutes had passed. That was it. I was supposed to sit here quietly for two more minutes and unwind. Maybe say an affirmation.

'I will do more meditating,' I announced to the universe, as I opened my eyes, feeling remarkably refreshed.

A couple of days and a couple of meditations later, with the weekend ahead of me and Gaelle temporarily off my back, my old mate and one-afternoon-stand, James Duncan, called me up.

'I'm having to stay in London for a few more days before going home. I wanted to know if you'd like to see a band tomorrow night?'

Against my better judgement I said yes. It turned out it was John Martyn, at the Clapham Grand – always a good spot to listen to a powerful, macho Scotsman sing his pumped-up folky tunes. We had a joint before the concert and I sat through it enveloped in a mellow high, swaying in time with the music, watching the crowds, hearing such songs as 'Over the Hill' and 'Midnight at the Oasis'. Loved it. At one point, towards the end of the show, James started leaning his big body into mine, our beers knocking together, him smiling.

It felt good and I felt like going with the flow. But I didn't want casual sex with a bloke who had treated me badly. At the end of the night he drove me home, parking his car outside my flat and turning off the motor.

'So,' I said, turning to face him in the dark.

'So,' he replied. Smiling the cute smile, white teeth shining in the streetlight.

'Listen, James, I'm not going to ask you in.'

'Oh.'

'Is that okay?'

'I guess.' He sounded gratifyingly put out and surprised.

'Good,' I said.

'Um, why not?'

'Because you have a girlfriend. And because you didn't tell me.'

'Come on, Cara,' he said, putting his hand on my thigh in an awkward, last-ditch manoeuvre. 'I'm a long way from home and it's late. And you know you want to.'

Oh, I do, do I? I reached for the door handle. 'No,' I said, finally deciding that this just wasn't going to happen. 'I think I'm going to go to sleep,' I said. 'Thanks for a great night.'

Perhaps it was the meditation. Perhaps it was a sudden rush of maturity. Perhaps it was the fact that I wouldn't have shagged James again even if he was the last man on earth. But as I walked the short distance to my front door, I felt life was improving already.

13

an impromptu date-type thing

Just as I was about to open my front door, it opened by itself. Moni, Rufus and Alex were in the hallway, evidently about to leave.

'Hi, guys,' I said. 'Hi, Alex.' Last time I'd seen her, she was half-asleep on the sofa. She was becoming a regular around here.

'Hi, Cara.' Her voice sounded ethereal, almost see-through.

'How was your date?' asked Ru.

'Excellent, thanks. John Martyn was great and telling James he couldn't come in was even better.'

'Hurrah!' yelled Lucy, emerging from the kitchen. 'I heard that. Well done!'

'Thanks, Lu. So Alex, how are you liking London?' I asked, still on a high, as we stood in the corridor, variously about to go in and out.

'It's cool.'

'And I hear you liked Moni's screenplay? I've heard it's wonderful.'

'It is,' she agreed.

'So . . . we'll see you later,' said Moni. 'Alex wants to show me some stuff and Rufus is going to take us for a drive.'

Tonight Alex had co-ordinated her feral-style orange hair with a lime-green skinny-rib top, worn under a pair of khaki overalls, with 12-hole Dr Martens boots to match. It was at once easy and hard to imagine her as the daughter of an oil tycoon. She looked like a hard-line feminist, but she had the peaceful presence of an angel. Serene and calm.

'What are you going to show them?' I enquired of Alex.

'Oh you know, just stuff,' Moni replied on Alex's behalf.

'Right,' I said. Hush hush, obviously. What was the big secret? Pah. Moni could keep her intrigues. I had a book about a delusional hippy woman to write.

They left and Lu brought out a steaming kettle and a wicker basket of her various teas.

'Chamomile, vanilla, decaf or peppermint?' she asked me.

'Tetley's, please.'

'Do you know where Niall is tonight?'

'No, do you?'

'Yes. He's gone with Gaelle. Up to the back of beyond of Northampton, to walk up a hill where he, Gaelle, Amanda and Nadine are going to do a midnight meditation.'

'No.'

'I kid you not.' She dunked my teabag thoughtfully.

Gosh.

'Do you think that's weird?' Lu asked.

'Yes, a bit. But surely you don't?'

'Well, I mean, I love all that stuff about aliens and walk-ins and chakras and so on. But I think I take it with a much bigger grain of salt than Niall. I mean, there've been plenty of times in the past week already when one of us has walked out of Eaton Square in tears or close to it. Let's face it. It can't be good for us.'

She had a point. 'So what are Gaelle and Niall up to tonight?' I asked.

'It's some special alignment of the planets and Niall said it was a time for really strong energy vibes, so they were off up Salisbury Hill for a session.'

'Wow. He's totally into it, isn't he?'

'He really believes her talk about being half human, half alien. He was telling me about dimensions the other day, how we're in the Third Dimension and about to ascend to the Fifth or some such thing, and about how when you're in the Fourth everything that you think happens, so if you're scared of scorpions and you think about them, for example, you're done for.'

'Sounds mean,' I agreed, settling back into the sofa.

'Yep.' She sighed. 'And Alan's been calling me up and saying he's sorry about the other night.'

Apparently, it was revelation time.

She sighed again as she took the teabag from her cup. 'What am I going to do?'

'What do you want to do?' I asked, stalling. If she was thinking of getting back with him, this was a serious matter. I didn't want to respond any old how. 'Lu, all I can tell you is something La Gaelle said. If you always do what you've always done, you'll always get what you've always got.'

'Wow. That's a concept,' Lu said. 'The thing is, though, the real problem isn't that he had an affair with Madeleine. Lots of people do that.'

'Have affairs with Madeleine?'

'No, have affairs. One-offs or whatever.'

This was true. Cam nearly did it with me the other night. James did it. And he tried to do it again, too.

'The only reason it became such an insurmountable obstacle was because Madeleine fell pregnant. If that hadn't happened, we could all have forgotten about it. Do you see what I mean? I could have forgiven him, and we could have got on with things. Moved on.'

'I see.' This was slightly disconcerting logic.

'So I guess what I'm saying is that I'm thinking about taking him up on his invitation to meet for dinner, or something.'

'Right.' Things had moved on apace for her since the clock-throwing incident. If only my love life progressed so rapidly.

'So, what do you think about that?' she asked.

It sounded like it didn't matter too much what I thought. It seemed it was fairly settled, so I wished her luck.

'At least you're not telling me that I can't come running to you if it all goes horribly wrong.' She smiled. 'I know there's a good chance it will. I have to trust the universe.'

I raised an eyebrow and sighed. 'You do that, Lu.'

Lu and I crashed at midnight. Moni didn't come home that night. She rocked into the kitchen about 10 a.m. the next morning, just as I was debating whether to take a brisk walk around Clapham Common or have breakfast on Battersea Rise with the papers. I'd have to go back to work tomorrow or the next day, so I wanted to make the best of my time on this sunny day, especially as I was kitted out in the floaty Alannah Hill number my sister had sent me from Sydney. 'So where have you been, young Missie?' I asked Moni on her return.

Moni said that she, Alex and Ru had spent the previous night drinking at the Alvery. This didn't explain where she'd *slept* the previous night. I presumed it was chez Rufus.

'We're going to have breakfast at Charlie's now to eat our way out of our hangovers,' she declared.

Charlie's was a greasy spoon caff on Battersea Park Road, with a clientele made up of toothless old men, workmen with Visible Crack Line problems and anyone else who was demented. It cost about three quid for all the bacon, eggs and sausages you could eat and the tea was okay, if you didn't mind well brewed. It was an excellent place for a hangover cure, but way too unhealthy for the day I had planned.

She flicked through some unopened mail left lying on the kitchen table. 'Oh, shit,' she said, holding up three envelopes with 'Discreet Duets' emblazoned on them. 'They must have biked these over from the office.'

'A-ha. The dating agency story from hell. What's going on?' I asked.

'Don't ask.'

'What's happened now? I take it Alex's meeting with Jean-James from Kilburn didn't go as planned.'

'Jean-Luc from Ealing.' She smiled. 'No. It was fine. He was strangely charming. They went to a restaurant in Acton and I sat at the next table eavesdropping. He was medium height, a bit balding, sweet. It was so weird to think that this guy was out for free sex. He didn't look the type to join a swingers' club at all.'

'I'm sure they never do.'

'He said his wife went off sex after the birth of their second child three years ago and doesn't know a thing about his membership, but it's the only sex he gets.'

'Lord. Was he really French?'

'Totally.' She opened the envelopes. 'These are just more punters wanting to meet Alex.'

'So what's the next step?'

'To get Alex to go to a party with the hidden camera. But I just have such a bad feeling about doing this.'

'What exactly?'

'Well, is it really anyone's business that Jean-Luc has joined Discreet Duets? Is it my job to be exposing these people's private lives on national TV, all for my boss's ego and the so-called good of my career . . .'

'It's a common career-woman's dilemma –'

'No, it's not,' she snapped. 'Most women don't get themselves into such ridiculous careers in the first place. What am I going to do? I'm not going to do this sort of thing for the rest of my life.'

With that, she picked up her keys and left. I went up to my room to do my hopefully calm-and-health-inducing meditation, then decided to go for a stroll along the King's Road. It was exactly what I needed. Why else was I working for Gaelle if not for the pleasure of being able to wander around looking for things to buy? The excitement I'd originally felt about writing the book was being transformed into frustration. Getting through to Gaelle was proving harder than cracking a Brazil nut bare-fisted, and the Cam situation didn't bear thinking about. I was teetering between glee and relief at having had some time off and wallowing in self-indulgent misery.

I ate a salad at the Chelsea Flower Market and enjoyed a glass of white wine. Afterwards, I went to Habitat to ogle its stylish home-ware. Like shoes, homeware was miles better to buy than clothes, because it never made you feel fat. I was just wondering how Moni was enjoying her brunch with Rufus and Alex when I saw him.

Cam.

Shit.

I hid behind a mountain of deep-blue glass vases, wishing myself invisible as I pondered my next move. To say hello or not to say hello? I checked to see if anyone was with him – he didn't seem to be with his girlfriend, or anyone else for that matter.

I took a step backwards as I considered my tactics, collided with a sofa and fell down into a sitting position, just as he noticed me. I'm sure I was blushing as he wandered towards me.

'Hi, Cara, what are you up to?' His smiling eyes looked like chocolate ice cream, only more delicious.

'Not a lot,' I said cleverly. 'And you?' I was so nervous. How ridiculous.

'I was just shopping for a present for my sister's birthday.' He looked around the store. 'Seen anything she might like?'

'Um . . .' I cringed inwardly as I remembered our last encounter, with me blurting out the sordid details of my shagging session with James to Gaelle.

'Oh. I did see something nice over there.' I started to walk towards the china area and he followed. There was a display of espresso cups and saucers, cream-coloured with black squiggly bits. I'd have liked to receive them.

'Get her those,' I advised him. 'She'll love them.'

'Oh. Okay. Excellent,' he said. 'Nice design. I'll get them.'

He started loading his fingers up with cups while trying to squeeze the saucers under his arm. I offered to help and, between us, we picked up a set of eight.

'Listen, I was just thinking about getting a coffee,' he said as we headed towards the till. 'Will you join me?'

I watched the salesgirl flutter her eyelashes at him as he arranged to have the cups and saucers delivered to his home address.

'Sure,' I replied. God, I was so hard to get.

Outside, it was still a deliciously sunny day. London seemed to come alive in summer. We wandered along the King's Road to a café called The Nosebag, a vegetarian place with seats outside. London had finally embraced the on-the-footpath Euro-dining style her cross-channel neighbours had had down pat for centuries. I watched him order two coffees at the counter, looking as good as ever in baggy drawstrings and a strange pinkish, paisley patterned shirt. How he managed to look sexlicious in the face of such profound sartorial crimes was a tough one. He definitely stirred my hormones, although right now I was so numb in certain parts that I was relatively cool, given the circumstances. I did feel sure I'd turned a corner, since my little outburst the other day, though, which was progress.

'So, Cara,' he said, as he sat down.

'So.'

'So are you well?'

'Yep. Good, thanks . . . And you?'

'Not bad.'

A silence hung in the air. 'Listen Cam, did you hear what Gaelle was saying to me the other day . . . ?'

'What about?'

'About orange chakras . . . and cystitis . . . and stuff . . .'

'I did hear the tail end of her lecture,' he admitted, grinning.

Nothing like getting these things out in the open. 'I thought so. Look, it's none of anyone's business, but I guess I want you to know that I'm not in the habit of jumping into bed with every Tom, Dick and Harry . . .'

The waitress set down two cappuccinos in front of us.

'You don't have to explain.'

'It's just that life has been a bit confusing lately.'

'For me, too.'

'Really?'

'Mmmm.'

I stayed quiet.

'Listen, I'm sorry about all that stuff about me and my girlfriend.'

'It's okay.'

'Well, it wasn't really.'

'I know.'

'It can get a bit tricky, can't it?'

'What?'

'You know – things,' he said.

'Yep. Things can get a bit tricky.'

'Thanks for helping me with my sister's present.'

'No problem.'

'Listen,' he said slowly. 'There's an exhibition on at the Eisenfeldt gallery . . . I was going to go if I had time.' He looked at his watch. 'It's open for another couple of hours. If you're not doing anything else . . . It's called "Heroic Trash" . . . it sounds . . . interesting . . .'

I was going to take this carefully. 'Sure, sounds good,' I said.

'Shall we walk up then?' he asked.

'Why not?' It would do me good.

So, we drank our coffees then ambled up towards Sloane Street then to Hyde Park Corner via Knightsbridge. We took the leafy route from there, threading through Green Park, then St James's Park, to Trafalgar Square. The streets were busy, but once we were inside the gallery it was peaceful, quiet and almost empty. Cam kept up a constant chat about nothing in particular as we wandered around. He was very easy to be around. And he made me laugh. And he had a girlfriend.

The exhibition was mad. Some of my personal favourites were a fluoro-lit plexiglass box containing a slab of grilled sirloin, set on a pristine white plate edged with the words 'Ode to Denis Leary' piped in curly pink icing, a mounted close-up of what turned out to be Britney Spears's erect nipple and a shot of Damien Hirst's armpit.

'What do you think?' Cam asked as we passed a giant, gilt-framed fingerpainting created especially for the exhibition by Brooklyn 'Spice child' Beckham.

'Very modern,' I said.

'That's one word for it.'

'I used to dream of coming to London and saturating myself in the culture . . .'

'And?'

'I mainly saturate myself in beer . . .'

It was deliciously dusky outside when we left the gallery, the wind blowing as though a rain storm was on its way. I didn't feel very protected in my summery slip as we walked through Leicester Square, with its cinemas and buskers vying for our money and attention. We walked toward Piccadilly Circus and into the heart of Soho. I imagined we were heading for a Tube.

'What did you think of Tracey Emin's used Kleenex collection?'

I laughed. 'Almost as beautiful as Pamela Anderson's old silicone implants.'

'I quite liked the video loop of Liam raising his fingers to various members of the Press.'

'Yeah.'

'So are you hungry?'

'Ah . . .'

'I know a great sushi place.'

'Oh. Sure. Sounds great.' Lord, this was turning into an impromptu date-type thing. With the exhibition's images of Pat Rafter's greased physique, Courtney Love's mascara tips video and the 'Smelly Cat' recording still whirring through my mind, I felt like I was floating as we wandered. There was no one moment that I could look back on, to say when this had started. Something had clicked even the first time I'd laid eyes on Cam at Gaelle's place.

He led me along Brewer Street, until we came to a Japanese restaurant called Toriyoshi. We had to walk down a flight of steps to get in, finally passing through some cotton curtains with samurai prints. Cries of '*Irashaimase!*' came up as we headed to a table for two. Cam ordered two Sapporos.

We scanned our menus, chatted idly, and finally I cut to the chase. I wanted to get to know him better. I think I also wanted to know how he came to be working for La Gaelle. I asked him to tell me the full story.

'You really want to know?'

'I'm curious.'

'Okay.' He paused and then pulled his wallet out of his back pocket. From within, he fished out a folded-up photograph which he passed to me. It was of Cam, with much shorter hair, in a striped shirt, his tie loose.

'Was that when you worked as a stockbroker?'

'Yep.'

'God, you look so different.'

'I was. See the guy behind me, looking around from his desk?'

'Mmmhmmm.'

'That's Steve. We worked together at Briarleys Bank . . . After a particularly bad day on the market floor, he just keeled over right in front of me.'

'God.'

'He had colitis, a serious problem with his intestines that you really don't want to know the details of. He could hardly eat, he lost a couple of stone and was in constant pain. His doctor said it was stress-related.'

'Erk.'

'Around the same time, another broker friend developed stress-related hypertension, aged thirty-three. High blood pressure due to overwork, in other words. Another I knew told me he threw up with stress nearly every morning – but never on Saturdays or Sundays.'

'Did you get sick?'

'No, but when I started dreading going into work so much that I referred to it as "going to Hell", it wasn't too hard to work out that there was more to life than getting up at 5 a.m. to be at work in time for the Hong Kong exchange and staying for the close of Wall Street at eleven . . .'

'Sounds fair.'

The waitress – who spoke even less English than I spoke Japanese – took our order. I went for my classic sushi rolls and miso soup combo; Cam chose chicken teriyaki. So much for the food. What I was learning was far more interesting.

'How long did you do it?'

'A few years. I was getting up before sunrise and getting home after dark, to an empty flat and microwave dinners. The firm's offices were palatial, but I worked in the middle of a huge room about as far away from natural light as you could get. Lunch was a couple of sandwiches brought to my desk by my secretary. I almost always had to take work home with me. I'd get back to the flat, watch some TV and crash, knowing I had to do it all over again the next day.'

'Sounds like a nightmare price to pay for being a master of the universe . . .'

'Maybe it wasn't as bad as I'm making out, but it wasn't a job I wanted to do forever. Not even for a few more years. I was earning a lot – more than enough – but I had no time to spend it.'

He put the photo away. 'Like I told you, I grew up in Brighton and I sailed most of my teenage years. After Steve . . . fell ill . . . I found a classified ad in the *Observer* run by a bloke from the south coast. This bloke, Terry, was looking for someone to sail his yacht over to Ireland.'

'You called him?'

'On a complete whim. It turned out he was ideally looking for someone who could sail his yacht over, then stay a while, taking tourists around the south coast of Ireland. He had a broken leg and was out of action for the summer, but had regular business he didn't want to lose. I didn't need to think about it too long.'

'So you just quit?'

'Pretty much. Everyone except my dad thought I was completely mad. My mother wouldn't speak to me for a month. My bosses at Briarleys Bank thought it was a "phase", and offered me, no obligation, six months' leave-of-absence. Before I left England, I paid off as much of my mortgage as I could. I didn't want to be squandering all of my savings on Guinness. I got to Ireland and I loved it.'

'Where were you?'

'In a village called Schull, on the south coast. I got there and did the "take-the-tourists-out" bit for Terry, which was fantastic. I'd take them out along the south coast, around the Fastnet if they were game, wherever they felt like. When the sailing season finished, I was offered a bar job in the local pub, so I took that. I met Gaelle at the pub.'

'And the rest is history?'

'Sort of . . .'

'Spending time with her is a big leap from broking.'

'Tell me about it.' He laughed. 'She's tried to explain some of her ideas about reincarnation and dimensions and so on, but I find it all a bit hard to take in.'

'Does that make it harder to do your job?'

'No. But it annoys her. The other day we were washing a pile of crystals she brought out of storage and she was telling me about the negative energy that can get sucked up by them, if you don't wash them properly in salt water. I just wanted to laugh.'

'And did you?'

'Not then.' He laughed now, his eyes crinkling like there was a party gathering at their corners. 'But I try not to make fun of her. I told her I would stick with her for six months and, since she's given me some breathing space until I have to make some serious career decisions, I figure I owe her the loyalty of sticking to our agreement.'

'What do you do for her?'

'Everything that requires paperwork. She's got me onto her finances, organising her taxes, and dealing with her lawyer about her publishing contract . . .'

'The guru's personal organiser.'

'It's okay. It's like a working holiday in some ways. It feels right for now. And I'm big on following my gut instinct, because it's nearly always right. Speaking of which, Cara, there's something I want to tell you.'

'What's that?'

He paused. 'It's about my girlfriend . . .'

'Yes?'

'What do you think I'm going to tell you?'

'I have no idea,' I lied. Actually, I had a few.

'Well, we broke up.'

'Really?' I said evenly.

'Yeah. I wanted to tell you. You must have thought I was a bit of an arsehole the other night.'

'Um.'

'Well, it's no excuse, but we only met a few months ago, just before she got transferred up to Birmingham for work. She and I haven't seen much of each other lately.'

'A-ha.'

'It seemed like the best idea . . . I don't usually cheat . . .'

'How long were you together?'

'Only four months. She wants to study in New York. She thought I could try and get work there too, on Wall Street or something. Total fantasy. It showed me how little we know each other.'

'My ex went to New York . . .'

'I hope they meet and are very happy together.' He laughed.

Well, this was a turn-up for the books.

'Are you okay? I hate break-ups . . .'

'Sure. It's always a bit strange, although in our case we didn't live in the same city, so it's not going to make that much difference I guess . . . And I don't want to stand in the way of her going to New York. She's a great girl, if a little dramatic.'

'Right,' I said, by now pretty much lost for words.

'Anyway, I wanted to tell you.'

Dinner arrived and we turned the conversation to other matters while we ate. Before long we were out on Tottenham Court Road. It was getting dim, the sky a pale pinky blue above the West End. Summer's evenings here were great, even in the city.

I chatted away non-stop as we walked. There's no reason why I should have been nervous, but I liked him a lot and that made me jittery. The funny thing was, he seemed to quite like me, too. He seemed very friendly and relaxed, not to mention gorgeous. This was the closest I'd been to him, physically, since we'd kissed on E in the kitchen. I liked him. I liked his woody smell. I liked his aura. I liked his smile.

'So what about you? Did you always want to be a journalist?'

'More or less. There was a period when I wanted to be an actress or a ballerina, when I was about six. But I pretty much spent most of my childhood reading kids' magazines and trying to write my own little articles. When I was a teenager, I'd interview my family and write up the stories, paste pictures of them onto sheets of A4, and make my own version of a family newspaper . . .'

'You're lucky.'

'Why?'

'Most people never have any idea of what they want to do with their lives.'

'Did you?'

'None. It was only because I got an economics scholarship to university that I ended up in stockbroking.'

'What would you really like to do?'

'Gaelle keeps telling me to "follow my bliss" . . .'

'Sounds like good advice, even from her,' I admitted. 'What would your "bliss" be?'

'Being a beach attendant?' He laughed. 'And you?'

'Apart from writing?'

'Yeah.'

'Going to hot places, shopping, watching Arsenal win.'

'Don't tell me you support Arsenal . . .'

'What's it to you, buddy?' I could smell football rivalry in the air. He pulled his keys out of his pocket. There was a small blue Chelsea badge on the ring.

'Oh. Not a Chelsea supporter. They're rubbish!'

He took that on the chin. 'Have you ever been to a match?'

'I went to Highbury for the first time last season.'

'Next time Chelsea play The Scum, we should go together.'

'Yeah, right. With you in the Arsenal section.' I laughed again.

'No way. You can come in and feel what it's like to have a bit of blue around you,' he laughed back.

'You've got to be kidding.'

It was about time to head home, I decided. Everything had been so relaxed and fun that there was a part of me that wanted to get the hell out, before anything became awkward, or we changed the excellent vibes with questions about what Cam's new singleness might mean to me. If anything. We walked to Trafalgar Square and agreed to share a cab. Even though we'd sat together in darkened rooms at Gaelle's, and he'd held me after I'd fainted, I was very, very aware of his body next to mine in the back of the taxi. He was under my skin. It was as if there was heat between us.

When the cab arrived at my house, I went to give him a quick kiss goodbye on his cheek when he turned his lips to meet mine. It was only momentary, but I felt my veins zap with electricity. His hands went to my shoulders lightly as the kiss lingered. They pressed gently against me, as if he didn't want to break me, or force me. His breath was sweet and warm. Intoxicating. His skin was radiating heat. His lips were smooth and soft. As he took a breath, I felt my insides go into meltdown. I wanted him. This realisation shocked me. I hadn't been sure until this moment. Now I knew. As he pulled away, I wondered if he felt the same way. From the way he'd kissed me, it seemed likely. Possible, at the very least. I got out of the cab and we both waved as it pulled away from the curb.

I levitated along the garden path to my front door with a silly smile on my face. Inside I found Lucy in the kitchen, sitting at the table under a dimmed light, poring over her Nirvana Cards again. I was out there in a la la land of bliss after my kiss.

'Hi, Lu, whachyadoin'?' I asked.

'Just wondering about these cards. Here. Have a look at them.'

I sat down opposite and tried to concentrate. 'Okay,' she said very seriously. 'My job is to take the concepts in the cards and do the drawings for them. For example, remember how I got the same card twice when I tried them for the first time?'

'Yep.'

'It was *Letting Go*. Here it is.' She found the card. It showed a woman looking slightly Mary Poppins-esque, flying up in the air as if she was being lifted up by a strong wind, hanging on to a rope which anchored her to the ground. 'See how great it is?'

'Mmmm. Yeah. Sure. Have you got any ideas for the English version?'

'Some. I did as Gaelle suggested and thought about the cards' meanings and got a few ideas. I've started the sketches. Wanna take a card now?'

'First tell me what the *Trust* card means.'

She flicked through her book and read: '*Belief in the best. Confidence. Using the power of your mind for the best possible outcome for all concerned.*'

I could live with that.

'Another one?' she asked bright-eyed.

'Okay.'

She gathered the cards into a pack and shuffled them before spreading them out in front of me.

'So. First fix on the present,' she instructed. 'Ask yourself, "What's going on for me now?"'

I asked the question mentally. If these cards were worth their weight in paper, the answer should relate to Cam.

'No, C, ask your question out loud.'

I smiled and rolled my eyes. 'What's going on for me now, oh, Nirvana Cards? What's going on for me now?' I plucked a card and handed it to her.

'*Resistance,*' she announced.

'What?'

'It's the *Resistance* card. Hang on.' She reached for the interpretation book. '*Resistance. Insisting on being right. Resisting another. Refusing to move forward or expand your views. Demanding your own way.*'

'Crap.'

'Why?'

'Who am I resisting?' Not Cam, that's for sure.

'Gaelle.'

'What?'

'You are, you know you are. You call her Gaelle the Guru and make fun of everything she says.'

'No, I don't.'

'Yes, you do.'

'Well, I disagree.'

'All right, then take another one.'

'Later, Lu,' I said, slightly annoyed at being reminded of Gaelle at a moment in time when all I wanted to do was enjoy reliving Cam's kiss. 'Where's Moni?'

'She hasn't been home all day. And it's late now. And she hasn't called, either.'

'Well, she went to Charlie's for a late breakfast with Rufus and Alex. They're probably still together,' I said.

'I really think there's something going on between Moni and Rufus, you know.'

'Do you?'

'Don't you? She wasn't home last night, today she turns up with him and tonight she's not home, last seen going to have brekkie with him.'

'I guess when you stack up all the evidence . . .' It sounded feasible, but I'd been too lost in my own dramatic world to pay much attention to anyone else's intrigues. 'More importantly, did you call Alan?' For all I knew, he and Lu were re-engaged.

'Yes. I called him and we had dinner tonight. It was really nice. We went to La Grillade.'

'Very nice, indeed. And?'

'And I think I want to see him again. At the end of dinner, I told him I didn't want to take it any further just now. It turns out that Madeleine is having the baby. He's going to pay child support, although at the moment she's refusing his offer because she's pissed off that he doesn't want to marry her. Or so Alan says.'

'Right. What about Niall?' I didn't want to make her feel bad about Niall and he did seem to be turning out to be a pretty unsafe bet, as he got weirder and weirder. But I felt for him. He had little or no idea about Alan's dramatic re-entry into Lucy's stratosphere.

'I haven't spoken to him. There was a message on the answering machine saying that he'd had a great time during the meditation with Gaelle and that we'd catch up tomorrow night.'

'Are you going to tell him about Alan?'

'In due course.'

'Fair enough.'

'Are you sure you don't want to pick another Nirvana Card?'

'Nah.'

'Are you chicken?'

'No, I just don't need Nirvana Cards to tell me about my life.'

'Go on, C.'

'Hey, Lu,' I said, changing the subject. 'Why don't you make your drawing for the *Resistance* card look like a picture of me and Gaelle? You obviously think it's perfect.'

I said goodnight, found Mouser and adjourned to my boudoir. It had been a very interesting couple of days, and I was feeling marginally revived. Tomorrow, it would be back into the mystic battlefield that was Eaton Square.

bygones

I went around to Gaelle's the next day with a purpose. It was time for business. I had my tape recorder and fresh batteries, a large, hungry Spirex notebook and four black ink pens in my pockets. I wanted results. I also knew Cam wouldn't be there until early in the afternoon.

To my surprise, a very knackered-looking mystic guru opened the front door. She seemed to have aged 300 years since our last meeting. She said she had a sore throat and seemed very down.

'Come in, come in, Cara,' she said. 'I'm very glad to see you. My throat has been giving me terrible trouble this morning.'

I followed her as she walked wearily up the stairs to her front room.

'How was the Miracle Meditation with Niall last night?' I enquired.

'Oh, it was wonderful,' she said in a low voice. 'We connected with Pleiades.'

'Right. So, er, have you taken something for your throat?'

'Yes, dear.'

'Maybe you caught a chill meditating in the hills,' I twittered, setting my interview paraphernalia on the living-room coffee table.

'Oh, it's not that simple. I've gargled some salt water, but as I explained to you with your cystitis, illness on the physical level is a manifestation of tensions on the subconscious. My throat's sore because I'm not expressing myself,' she said, coughing now. 'I'm constricting the energy in my throat chakra. The prana – that's Sanskrit for life force – is stuck.'

'Well, maybe if we start to do some proper interviews you might find the prana flows more freely,' I replied unsympathetically. This was more like it. I would bully her for a change.

'I'm feeling quite down, actually,' she said, surprisingly, putting her hand to her chicken-skinned neck. 'I don't know if I'm up to reliving all those old memories.'

'Really?' I asked.

And then she burst into tears. Her face just crumpled, wrinkling, going red and blotchy. She covered her cheeks with her hands as the sobs racked her big, flabby body. I shocked myself by feeling sorry for her. The sight of the old biddy crying moved me, despite the fact that I'd seen her as my major tormentor of the past two weeks.

'Gaelle, what's wrong?'

It was so unusual to see this woman doing anything but bossing people around, let alone weeping. I wouldn't have thought she had it in her. Surely all she needed to do to ward off a bad case of the blues was lay a few relevant crystals in a circle and do a meditation or midnight jig inside them? Or sniff some incense and a sprig of rosemary? Or something?

'Gaelle?' I asked. For all my meanness, there was something

about Gaelle I liked. She was pushing all my buttons and for that reason she drove me mad. But she was making me aware of things I'd never thought about before. For one thing, I was starting to realise that perhaps there was something more to life than sex, drugs and rock 'n' roll. I felt more connected to myself and to other people these days. Since I'd started meditating, it was as if I had cloned myself and was getting to know myself in an almost detached way. And yet I clung to the old version of me, too. I was confused.

'Come on, Gaelle, tell me what's wrong.'

'Ooooh,' she wailed. 'Nothing's going right. Nothing at all. Lucy's getting back with Alan, Niall's distressed, you are struggling with your feelings. Everything's so difficult now.'

I wondered what my and my flatmate's love lives had to do with her plans. You never knew.

'What is it, Gaelle? Are you lonely?' Maybe Lu could come over and feng shui her relationships corner . . .

'Lonely? Lonely? Ha!' she cried. 'There are more people in this room right now than you and me, my dear. There are all sorts of entities around, most of them good and most of them my best friends. From other dimensions, dear. If you could see how many people there are in this room right now, you'd be amazed.'

I looked around her living room. All I could see was the usual debris – tables and bookshelves groaning with filed and unfiled newspaper clippings, sheets of A4 paper with writing and drawings on them, folders marked 'Mataka Meditation' and 'Soul Screaming'.

'The other entities here are helping me. They're my strength. Carlos, Keeper of the Infinite Flame, who I contact from time to time – who I contacted the day you got sucked into my trance – he's my true lover. But he's in the Fifth Dimension, two dimensions closer to God.' She started to sob again, but heaving this time. 'A lot of good he does me there,' she cried. 'I haven't been touched by a man for eons.'

Well, it was only twenty-five years ago that you were married to Brian Carrington-Keane, I wanted to remind her. He must have touched you. I told her this.

'Oh, Brian,' she replied, dismissively. 'He was just a fool on my journey. I was young, far, far too young to understand my destiny and role at that stage.'

'I see.' I felt an urge to switch on my tape recorder.

'Will Lucy be coming today?' she asked.

'Um, I don't think so. You'll just have to make do with me.'

'Oh, Cara, you have such a skewed notion about my feelings for you, don't you? I'm just trying to push you along the line to your destiny. Don't you feel it?'

'Not really, Gaelle, I don't. Mostly all I feel is confused.'

'I know, dear, I know. Don't you worry, it's going to work out fine. There's no need to worry. You'll be just fine.'

We gazed at each other for a moment while I tried not to think too much about the fact that she had just repeated a line from one of my dreams. Why wouldn't she? Of course she would. She was like that. I was starting to believe that if anyone could read minds, she could. In that second, as I let go of my panic about her abilities, I saw her frailty for the first time.

'What are you trying to achieve, Gaelle?'

'I don't know what you mean.'

'What are you trying to achieve? What do you want from me, Lu and Niall? What do you want to gain with your book? Maybe it's about time we got a few things sorted out.'

'Cara, I am paying you so that we have as much time as we need to sort things out. Now is not the time and I can't answer your questions.'

'Can you tell me about what made you leave Australia? What it was that made you leave your husband and go to India?'

She tilted her head to one side and sighed deeply.

'All right, I will tell you,' she said. 'Turn on your tape recorder. I only want to have to say all this once. Do you want a biscuit?' she asked, pointing to a large Scottish shortbread tin. 'They're hash cookies,' she said. 'Homemade.'

'No, thanks, Gaelle. I think I'll stay straight for this.'

'As you wish, dear. You won't mind if I do, though, will you?'

'Not at all.'

And so she began.

'I decided to leave Brian one night. He was away. At a conference . . .'

Gaelle spent the next three hours telling me her tales and eating ten hash cookies. She was blitzed, but still lucid. I managed to concentrate totally. What she told me was fascinating. She told me about her decision to leave Brian Carrington-Keane. At the time she was living in a glass-walled, *Vogue*-style, two-storey apartment overlooking Sydney Harbour.

'It reflected my fishbowl existence,' she said. 'It was a beautiful house, perfect for entertaining – and we did a lot of that in those days.'

One of those days, one Saturday afternoon, the woman who worked as Brian's assistant came to their house.

'Mandy Walton was her name. She was a law graduate. Very ambitious. Blonde, like me. Everyone who worked for Brian knew he was having an affair with her. And I knew, too – his dutiful wife, so often pictured on his arm smiling.

'The press made up so many stories about why I left Brian. But the truth was, my heart broke that night at the house in Vaucluse. When Mandy arrived wearing a lime-green minidress under an orange winter coat, I knew I was no match for her. I was an innocent.

'She came into the living room, sat down on one of our cream sofas, lit a long cigarette, accepted my offer of a vodka and tonic and told me she wanted Brian all to herself. She told me that if I didn't leave him, she would go to the papers and tell them everything. She reasoned this would be far worse publicity for Brian than me leaving him. She was deadly serious.

'I didn't have to do much soul searching. I see that night now as the first step on my path. It was the catalyst I needed. I wanted nothing more to do with Brian Carrington-Keane, his mistress or his political life. I was happy to have the perfect excuse to leave. Brian was interstate, at a business meeting on the Gold Coast, or maybe it was Melbourne, I don't remember. All I know is that, after Mandy left, I went straight to my room – we had separate bedrooms – and packed my bags. I slept my last night in that house, then went straight to the airport in the morning. I bought a ticket to Thailand. Everyone thinks I went to India, and I've let them think what they like. I did go to India, but that was years later. It was in Thailand that I found myself. This was years ago, before the first backpackers arrived, or as they arrived, I suppose, because, really, I was one of them. Have you been to Thailand, dear?'

So, Gaelle was one of those mythical people who went to Thailand in the seventies, when it was still a dream paradise stretch of lush coastline and white, sand-rimmed islands peopled with locals who baked grass cookies for you and charged you peanuts to stay in their handmade grass huts on the beach.

'No, I haven't been yet. We just stopped in Bangkok airport for a few hours on the way over here from Australia.'

'I went to Sunrise Beach, near Rai Lei. And I meditated, slept on the beach, made friends with the locals, until one of them helped me out with shelter. I stayed there for three months.'

'What happened?'

'I met up with Pravas.'

'Pravas?'

'Pravas Krisana was his name. He changed everything for me. He taught me how to meditate.' It was amazing to see the look in her eyes as she tripped down memory lane. Her face softened. She seemed almost mumsy and lovable. Why did I have such strong reactions against her? Maybe she wasn't the mean loony I'd painted in my mind; in fact, maybe I was just scared of her.

'We lived on the beach, in grass huts. There were only three where we were, and no more than ten or twenty travellers at any one time. They used to sell us ganga cookies, long before the Thai authorities realised the combination of the scenery and the grass and the time we had on our hands was pushing us towards enlightenment and were ordered to clamp down on us, by the Grey Men.'

'Who?'

'They're the world leaders, dear, who want to stop the evolution of man at any price. They're the men who took all the references to reincarnation out of the Christian Bible, who keep women in Italy barefoot and pregnant, who put fluoride in the water to make everyone stupid . . .'

'Gaelle, what are you on about?'

'Don't worry, find out more about all that for yourself. The point is that we lived on Sunrise Beach near the Princess Cave. You can still go there now. It's a cave just on the shore, where fishermen come to light candles. They thought – and still think – that they are lighting candles to the Goddess of Fertility, in the hope that she will make the seas pregnant with fish, so that they can make a good catch . . .'

'But in reality they are . . .'

'They're lighting the flame that will make women of the new millennium great. From Isis to Aphrodite to me and you and Lucy and Moni. The time of the Sacred Feminine is upon us. Male gurus divide. The Sacred Feminine, the Whole Woman, combines.'

'So what did you do on the beach?'

'We meditated, we lit candles, we prayed, we made love . . .'

'Did your husband never try to find you?'

'I have no idea what he did, dear. I cut all contact with him. I was hardly going to send him a postcard letting him know my whereabouts. Once, at Sunrise, in the lead-up to the annual fertility festival, Pravas and I took ourselves out to an island just off the coast, Ko Dang, and meditated for four weeks solid, never eating, never sleeping, just breathing.'

'But how could you do that?'

'Anything is possible, if you direct your mind. Once I literally just disappeared into thin air, after a month-long meditation with Pravas. He saw me one minute, and the next I had vaporised.'

'No.'

'Yes, Cara.'

'And after Thailand?'

'After Thailand came India. Yes, I was there. No, I wasn't dancing naked under the full moon. Well, not very often.'

'Did you know half of Australia was wondering where you were?'

'I didn't care. I had found my soul's path. I stayed in India for a decade, living a simple life, until I met John Lennon.'

'*The* John Lennon?'

'I met him in India. He was there for a weekend, long after the Beatles had split up. He was there with Yoko because he, too, was a devotee of Pravas Krisana.'

'How did you meet him?'

'I met him through Pravas and we clicked. When I came to London eventually, I got in touch. He was the final link in my trail.'

'John Lennon?'

'Yes, dear.'

'Can you tell me what you talked about?'

'This and that. Higher consciousness. Our missions. You know, that sort of thing.'

Before I could insist she put me out of my misery and elaborate, the telephone rang.

Gaelle reached over to answer it.

'Hello? Philippe!' she exclaimed almost girlishly. I could have sworn she was blushing. Who was Philippe? The plot was thickening – and I still didn't know the half of it.

Listening to her was so easy that I sometimes forgot the aim here was to write a book about her life. I would have to get her life story down in a coherent form eventually and yet I still knew almost nothing about her. I felt I hadn't even managed to lift a corner of the veil that covered her, let alone have a damned good look underneath. The more I got to know her, the more she annoyed me. And the more she scared me. All these dreams, the developments with Cam, her pronouncements. It was all starting to feel scarily real.

'*Oh, c'est super.*' Gaelle had lapsed into French and was sounding chipper. '*Oui, oui, bien sûr. Oui, c'est mieux, oui. Mes deux assistants. Oui. Demain. Bien sûr.*'

She prattled on a bit more in French and finally put the phone down with a '*je t'embrasse*'.

Gaelle looked mighty pleased with herself. Her eyes were twinkling with glee. I had that feeling I got when I knew she was about to make a huge pronouncement. And she did.

'We're in business,' she said. 'We've got a deal for the book. I'm going public. The only thing you need to do is go to Paris to sign the contract. With Cam.'

I gasped, froze, then began to frantically juggle thoughts of finally getting this book out of Gaelle's head and into print, mixed in with mild concern about what on earth I had in my wardrobe to wear in Paris in July. With Cam.

Gaelle, it seemed to me, just smiled knowingly.

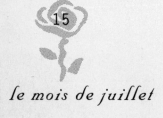

15

le mois de juillet

Cam and I caught the train to Paris together – if you can believe that. I could only just. I mean, all of a sudden Cam was (a) without girlfriend and (b) on his way to Paris with me. It was just too much. We manoeuvred our way through the impatient Franglo queues at Waterloo, into Carriage 16 for the 4 p.m. shuttle to Gare du Nord. Cam shoved our bags into the overhead compartment and I said he could have the window seat. He could have had anything. The idea of being alone with him for thirty-six hours, let alone in Paris, was sheer bliss.

There were half a dozen other passengers in our non-smoking carriage. Two French babes were seated at the table seats, their shiny brown hair in ponytails and both wearing slashes of what looked like exactly the same lipstick. I couldn't understand their conversation, but I caught snatches – the words Camden and

Portobello, Club Together, the Ministry of Sound and Roger kept cropping up. Clearly a post-weekend-in-London debriefing. In front of Cam and me was an old bloke in a blue-green tweed suit and a hat that had a small yellow feather in the band. My bet was that he was also French, although he stayed silent. Across the aisle was a middle-aged Italian woman, heavily made up and wearing a bold outfit of red and black, with her teenage son, whom she loudly called 'Paolo'. He sat quietly, looking earbashed, with a tiny brown terrier pup in a cage on his lap.

English sunshine lit the scene which sped past outside the window. The grey tower blocks of south-east London morphed at high speed into Kent's power stacks, then leafy dells and then Dover's seascape. We slid into the Tunnel with a whoosh, as if we were being sucked into a vacuum. The light outside turned to concrete darkness. Cam pressed his face against the glass and I strained to see the Tunnel walls through the reflection of the window. The Brits had clearly been in charge of decorating. The Tunnel was rusty, brown and unadorned, with not so much as a paint job. Perhaps the Tunnel's fate was to be a long tubular advertising space, like on the Metro. Mc-Mc-Mc-Mc-McDonald's, to read in time with the rumbling of the train.

Cam was wearing almost normal clothes again today. A huge, thick white cotton shirt with a retro Pirelli badge on it, worn untucked over frayed jeans and sneakers. I could feel his vibes. If you could see my aura, it would have been flashing pink and red – the colours of love and attraction, I understand – and pulsating in his direction like a laser. Oblivious to my internal ecstasies, he relaxed back against the window.

I thought about my situation. Me. Cam. Under the Channel.

What I really wanted to know, though, was what he was thinking as we chatted and I scanned the Chunnel magazine. Between ordering coffee from the trolley lady and double-checking our appointment time with Gaelle's publishers, Pigalle Press, scheduled for the next day, what else was on his mind? I was still curious about why he came to be so loyal to Gaelle. Was it nature or nurture?

'So, Cam,' I asked as I sipped my coffee, 'when you met Gaelle . . . You said you met when you were working at the pub in Ireland. You didn't say how you came to be her assistant . . .'

He looked at the scenery rushing past outside. 'Gaelle used to come into the pub quite a lot – she was staying alone in a local cottage and I think she wanted company.

'Sometimes the punters would stay up all night drinking until sunrise, especially if they'd just got back from a long fishing trip. Sometimes I was their lucky barman. One night like that, Gaelle walked into the pub for dinner, and we talked at the bar until dawn. When everyone finally left, I closed up and we walked down to the harbour together, where the boat was moored. I guess I thought she was amazing . . .'

'Why?'

'I was drawn to her. I wanted to hear what she had to say. I was going through a bit of an existential period. I'd been away from London for a long time and knew I didn't want to go back to the bank, but I didn't know how to make it official. She'd seen the boat and wanted a better look, so we got into the dinghy. On the yacht, she sat me down and did some kind of reading on me with crystals and Angel cards.

'Schull was almost surreal that morning, with its old stone buildings and the water and reflections . . . I've forgotten a lot of the details of her reading, but she told me what the cards and crystals I'd chosen meant – something about recuperation after too much hard work – and absolutely insisted that I go off alone for three days minimum, to relax. She showed me how to do her Miracle Meditation and said I needed to meditate and ask myself the Big Questions in life.'

'She said the same thing to me. So, did you do it?'

'I was planning a few days off anyway, so I told her I'd think about what she'd said.'

'And . . . ?'

'I took the boat down to Cape Clear, and moored off a little island, which was so small they didn't even have cars on it. I did what Gaelle suggested. I relaxed, walked, cooked my own meals or ate at the island's pub. I even meditated a few times, or at least I tried to. On about the third or fourth day, when I was meditating, I had this sort of flash. I don't know how else to describe it. I knew that I'd been in Ireland long enough, and I had this . . . vision . . . that I'd be working with Gaelle in London before long. She hadn't said anything about a job, but I had this strange feeling . . .'

'Intuition, my flatmate Lucy would call it.'

'Yeah. In(ner)tuition, Gaelle calls it. So, I went back to Schull, and within half an hour of our next meeting, Gaelle offered me the job as her assistant.'

I shook my head in awe. 'She seems so crazy. And yet she can be so on the money at times.'

'I know. I decided it was fate. I needed a reason to come back to London and she gave me one. I needed an income – and I didn't want to go back into Briarleys . . .'

'Too easy.'

'Sometimes I think I was mad to take this job on. She really does my head in sometimes, but I guess I feel I owe her something. She was there at just the right time. And I know the job doesn't have to last forever.'

'It's a living . . .'

'Yeah. To be honest, though, if I'd known her then as well as I know her now, I'd probably have steered well clear. Crystals and dimensions and in(ner)tuition . . .' He rolled his eyes. 'Sometimes it almost makes me nostalgic for stockbroking . . .'

'So she helped you through your dark night of the soul?'

He laughed, and I wanted to kiss him again very much.

Cam was so self-contained and confident as we rumbled towards France. I wondered if he felt any of the attraction I felt for him. The way he was sitting, his shoe kept knocking against my thigh as the train rocked along. I liked it. His gleaming brown eyes looked at me with happiness, brimming with energy. So desirable.

The train eventually pulled into Gare du Nord and we grabbed our gear. It was sobering to step out of the carriage into the terminal, with its enormously high ceilings and cold breeziness, and mazes of stairs and escalators to taxis and the Metro. We took the taxi option. It was 8 p.m. and rush hour and the Parisians had their yellow headlights on. The night was pink as the sun dipped. Our taxi driver was Hindu, going by the looks of the flowers and incense adorning his rear-view mirror. Which was fine, except it meant he didn't speak French and we didn't speak Hindi, or whatever his native tongue was.

Even so, with the help of the mini Metro map I'd picked up, we directed him, probably the long way, through Les Halles and via Le Marais, across the river to the Rue Saint Séverin in Saint Michel. At the reception desk of our hotel, Cam requested two single rooms and we took our bags up. Mine was a small *chambre*, with purple floral wallpaper, a tiny balcony over the street and a large white, tiled bathroom. After he'd dumped his bags in his room next door to mine, Cam came into my room. He pointed out a complimentary bottle of red wine on the dressing table, with two wine glasses, uncorked it with his Swiss Army knife and poured. We both stood in the middle of the bedroom and clinked glasses. I took three long gulps. If ever I needed alcohol, now was the time.

After we'd drained half our glasses, he reached out and entwined his hand in mine. As simple as that. My heart bounced. We put down the wine glasses and he drew me nearer until our faces touched. I breathed him in and smiled. There was something delicious about his whiskers against my cheeks. And then we kissed. The sweet sensation of pressing my mouth into his was familiar already. I felt my system going into bliss overload and let myself fall into the warm feeling of kissing him. My body melted into his. We both smiled. I managed to stop thinking for a few moments here and there, just enjoying the sensations I was feeling as I stared into his brown eyes, which were more luxurious than heated honey. I think it's called falling in love at third kiss. I blamed the upward curve of his lips. We kissed slowly. Long, deep kisses. It felt to me as if no-one had ever felt as turned on as Cam and I felt that evening in the small bedroom on Rue Saint Séverin. He pushed me back onto the bed and started to unbutton my shirt like we'd done this before. Omigod, the man was a gypsy Love God. He smiled right into my eyes. I felt myself drowning in them deliciously. He was the ocean and all I could breathe, and it was enough for me.

I was now encouraged to help him shed his gear. It was anticipation pay-off time. His body was long and smooth. I wanted to explore it. His skin was the colour of a light Bondi tan. I traced his body's dips, valleys, curves and protrusions. I went swimming in his flesh, diving in and out of the tendrils of his body hair, ducking under and into his armpits, breathing him, touching him. His thighs were strong, tanned and gripped me between them so I couldn't escape. Not that I tried. His arms were defined and rippled. The hair on his arms was coarse. His fingers were rough, yet gentle as they traced over me. I could hear his heart as I lay my head on his chest. His nipples were hard, his stomach taut, his toes tasty, his neck kissable, his forehead sweaty, his temples pounding, his hair damp, his eyes closed, his lips open, his veins bulging.

We rolled around on the thick white sheets of the hotel bed, getting tangled in the blankets, throwing ourselves over the bolster. He kissed me from my neck to my toes and I think I ran my lips and tongue over nearly his entire torso. I jabbed my fingernails into the flesh of his hard butt, rubbed myself up against his back and pressed myself into the roughness of his chest. I stroked the tanned flesh of his stomach with huge sighs. I listened to his rhythms. It became a blurry dream.

I was in shock, in love and in lust.

We finally spoke after what seemed like two hours.

'Cara?'

'Mmmm?'

'Did you think this was going to happen?'

'Mmmm. Maybe.' Even my eyes felt relaxed.

'You know the day we had to stare into each other's eyes?'

'Yeah?'

'Did anything weird happen to you?'

I asked him why.

'I had the strangest experience,' he said.

That jolted me. 'Me too. What happened to you?'

He was lying on his stomach, resting his head on his arms, looking at me. I could feel his warmth.

'Well, look, it's really weird. But I felt as if I knew you from before. It was ridiculous, but I saw you as a sort of religious person.'

'What do you mean?'

'I don't know. As a nun or a novice, in an old abbey. I was a monk, or a priest. You rejected me. We were lovers who could never be.'

'You're kidding?'

'No.'

'You are kidding me?'

'Why?'

'I had a similar, um . . .'

'Vision?'

'Yes.' I said. Doo doo doo doo doo doo doo doo. The truth is out there. Or is it in here?

'No way!'

I raised my eyebrows. 'I'd love to say I was joking, Cam, I honestly would, but I'm not.'

It was just too strange that we'd had the same vision during that eye-staring exercise at Gaelle's. It was bizarre, but also fantastic. But a part of me wanted to run away. I wanted to smoke fags and get drunk and not deal with the thousand terrors that were rising in my throat, even as we lay kissing.

'Do you smoke much dope?' I asked, apropos of paranoia.

'I used to. Not much any more, though. Gaelle really encouraged me to stop.'

'Do you see much of her? I mean, away from Eaton Square?'

'Not really. We used to go out for dinner occasionally to this little Thai place called Phuket's near her house. She said it reminded her of her time on Ko Dang with Pravas Krisana. And a couple of times I've gone around there to fix her taps or do other odd jobs, but she's pretty self-sufficient. Sometimes, I think she prefers to be alone.'

This felt so wonderful. But what if it was all just another of my realistic-feeling dreams? What if he got back with his girlfriend next week? What if he just wanted a quick shag in Paris and I was it? What would I do with all my emotions? Where had they come from and how could I send them back again?

The only answer was to spend a lot less time staring into his brown eyes and a lot more time being real and reminding myself that good men are hard to find and no man was a good man until proven thusly. I mustn't rush. And then he put his arms around me and we closed our eyes.

I couldn't sleep. I kept waking during the night and seeing him lying there, eyes closed, breathing deep and slow, at peace. I loved his face and savoured the chance to look at it so closely, without his knowing. It was softened and warmed with sleep. I wanted to kiss it. His skin was shiny and scented with musk. Our bodies were encircled. Unlike Jonathan, who would never hold me at night, Cam was the cuddling type. The realisation made me smile. I eventually dozed off with his hand around my waist.

At 4 a.m. I slipped out of his arms and out of bed, moving to the window overlooking the street. It was quiet out there. A few lone drunks wandered past under the glare of the streetlights; a girl with bleached blonde hair and a guitar on a string over her shoulder caught me staring at her as she rollerbladed home. She waved. A white guy with matted dreadlocks ambled past.

Cam slept on. Had it not been for Lucy warning me again and again that we create our own reality with our words, I'd have been tempted to describe the situation as too good to be true and maybe even as unbelievable. But it was true and I did believe it. I was happy. If this feeling could continue, I could be this happy for a very long time. Worries about missing Australia could be set aside for a bit while I revelled in this. Fears about whether or not Gaelle was a complete lunatic or just semi-deranged could be shelved, at least for the moment. I would finally get it together to ask some searching, searing and probing questions to get enough material out of her to write the book, the contract for which I would be signing the next day.

I got back into bed with Cam once more, aligning my body next to his, hoping not to wake him. He stirred a bit, then snuggled into me.

As I finally drifted off, I had the strangest thought. Gaelle would not only approve of what had happened here tonight at the Hotel Saint Séverin, she would be totally exhilarated. Relieved, even. I couldn't have told you why, but I knew this to be true. I saw her in my mind's eye, her blonde hair waving in a light breeze, a smile on her face and a twinkle in her eyes. I kept hearing her saying: 'Well done, Cara, well done, Cam. Well done, Cara, well done, Cam.'

At least everyone was happy.

16

wise men say

We woke up entangled. My body was alive again. My heart was congested with the intensity of my feelings, but I concentrated on relaxing and keeping them hidden, for fear of looking crazy. I let him love me.

At 9 a.m. there was a knock on the door. I watched Cam as he got out of bed to answer it. Fwoaaargh. It was room service with the breakfast we'd ordered last night: a large wooden tray covered with a thick linen cloth and carrying a length of warm baguette, two croissants, two large china bowls which served as cups, a large pot of coffee, butter and jam, knives and napkins. The aroma of the coffee filled the room as Cam placed the tray on the bed and we started tucking in. The taste of crusty baguette spread with cold butter and sweet raspberry jam always gives me an oral orgasm. The moment when Cam smeared the rest of the jam onto my right breast with his finger and then laughed as he playfully licked it all off with his coffee-hot tongue wasn't too bad either.

All I wanted to do was lie in bed all day, giggling and talking and kissing and reflecting on the delicious feelings coursing through my veins. But it was soon 11 a.m. and even I had to acknowledge it was time to get going for the meeting with the publishers. It was slightly depressing to remember why we were here – that we had a book deal to sign and that Cam and I were really workmates. It felt like a scene from someone else's new life.

While I lay back between the sheets feeling sated and delighted, Cam showered and got dressed. This time, in a suit. Until Paris, I'd only ever seen him looking like something the cat had dragged home from an eccentric's garage sale. Now he was a vision in a grey, slim-line, slightly shiny, fifties-style two-piecer. Just when I'd thought he couldn't get more gorgeous. Even his hair had been brushed.

Bad girl, stop it, a voice in my head chided me. Don't lose your heart. You'll only get hurt.

As soon as we were out of bed and starting to nudge our way back into real life, the alarm bells of caution known so well by single girls started going off in my head. Instantly, I became self-conscious and guarded. I showered and dressed away from him, standing in the windowless bathroom with the door shut. I applied too much brown eyeshadow and had to take it off and start again. My hair wouldn't sit right. This was a disaster.

As the panic rose, what I really, really wanted was to do one of Gaelle's Miracle Meditations. I could hardly believe I would ever want to do such a ridiculously lentil-eating thing. But I knew it would help. All I needed was fifteen minutes alone to gather my thoughts, take back my heart and start again. Cam would never need to know how loony I was.

Just then I heard his voice through the bathroom door.

'Cara, I'll be back soon. I just have to go downstairs. I'll be about half an hour . . . I'll meet you back here, okay?'

Thank you, God.

And so I did a meditation. The method Gaelle had taught me was said to be gazillions of years old and part of the Mastery of Life lessons handed down by Hindu gurus who lived in caves and approached Nirvana (without cards). However, it was also pretty easy, even for a Sydney girl in Paris, to understand and master. No great secret, as far as I could see. Before I started the meditation, I practised the little dedication trick Gaelle had taught me. You were allowed to dedicate your meditation to someone or something. I asked that I be given guidance about handling my situation with Cam. I surely needed it.

The eerie meditative depths greeted me. Only this session was different. Gaelle was at the end of the blackness to greet me. Why wasn't I surprised? Nothing about that old bat could surprise me. She had wheedled her way into my imagination and for all I knew was exercising some freaky, hypnotic sort of mind control over me.

'Love him. Live by your feelings and not by your fears,' came back the response. 'If you always give, you will always have. This is not the time to over-analyse.'

I scribbled these 'messages' down on the hotel notepad and went in again. Meditating deeply is like going down into a dark hole where there is nothing. Just blackness. No thoughts. No nothing. Only the odd 'om'. I half-expected to see Gaelle there again, smiling at me, or telling me off, or doing something, but apart from the initial 'message' about chilling out – which I believed came from inside me, not from some higher power – there was silence.

I came out of the meditation just as Cam returned. He found me still cross-legged on the floor, re-reading the notes I'd made. He'd had his hair trimmed.

'Wow,' I said.

'There was a barber shop downstairs. I thought it was about time.'

'In honour of Philippe?' I asked, absorbing and approving of the new look.

'Yup.' He smiled. He smelled of fresh air.

As we hurtled in a taxi towards the Champs Elysées offices of Pigalle Press, Cam brought me up to speed. 'Philippe Lopez is one of France's top publishers, according to Gaelle. They met twenty-five years ago, in Asia somewhere, and she says he's called her once a year ever since, asking her to get her autobiography written, so he can publish it. She's declined his offer every time, of course. Until this year. This time she told him she was ready.'

I didn't say much. My thoughts were too loud as it was. I was getting worried about this jolly book of hers. Exactly what did Gaelle expect? Would I live up to her expectations? If she'd been planning this book for this long, would I be able to rise to the occasion? I looked at Cam, who was staring out the window as we passed the fashionable shops of the premier arrondissement, his newly trimmed hair glistening in the sun. He felt me staring, turned towards me, looked into my eyes and smiled.

'Love him,' the voice in my head had said this morning. This seemed quite a tall order, given I'd only just bonked him. Was I cruising for a heart-shaped bruising?

Philippe Lopez's office was white. Very white. With high ceilings and lots of mirrors and altogether very eighteenth century. With Cam at my side, the memory of great sex coursing through my veins, and people all about me speaking French, my day was starting to feel surreal. I confess I didn't do much in that meeting with Philippe. I let Cam take the lead in discussing business. Cam impressed me by doing so in French, which only made him sexier. And as I didn't understand much beyond *s'il vous plaît*, *merci* and *très bizarre*, the time in Philippe Lopez's office afforded me the opportunity to daydream. My mind played over the events of the past few weeks. Starting with the first time I'd met Gaelle. And Cam. The time I fell into Gaelle's trance and Cam's sweet way of comforting me afterwards. The kiss. The news about his ex. All that stuff. It had been like a fast-paced dream. Now I was here with him.

I gazed out of the office's enormous picture window, which overlooked a perfectly manicured garden. Although it was summer, it was a chilly, blue-skied day. Nevertheless, Philippe had the window thrown open and cool, crisp air was streaming through. I loved Paris. I loved knowing that the Mona Lisa was somewhere nearby. That romance was in the air. That Gustave Eiffel had had enough vision to build his masterpiece.

'Cara,' I heard Cam through my reverie. 'Cara, here.' I looked around. With a smile on his face, Cam was offering me a rather beautiful, marbled fountain pen. Apparently it was time to sign the contract. *Mon Dieu.* Where had I been?

'What am I signing?' I asked him. 'Sorry, I sort of drifted off a bit.'

'This is the contract to say that you agree to write the book. That's all.' I looked over at Philippe Lopez. He was in his midfifties, chubby, rosy-cheeked, very bald and wearing an elegant brown suit that expanded to fit his gastronome's contours seamlessly. He suited his refined offices perfectly. However, despite the exquisite surroundings, he exuded a very benevolent air, which I found myself liking. So, I signed. As I did, I saw that the book was to be subtitled 'In Search of the Whole Woman'.

'Well, zat ees zat, zen,' Philippe said, clapping his small hands. 'Cara. You will receive copies of ze contract in ze mail. Same for you and Gaelle, Cam. I wish you a pleasant stay in Paris. How long do you 'ave here?'

'Just until this afternoon,' Cam said.

Dammit, Janet.

'Well, please enjoy your afternoon in my beautiful city.' The meeting was concluded and – having signed my life away and promised to write a book for which I still had only cursory preliminaries to go on – it was apparently time to depart.

'My driver will take you back to your hotel,' Philippe added.

Driver? Excellent. We were led by Philippe's blonde chignoned secretary to the front exit of the building where a white Rolls-Royce – no less – awaited us. Once again, speaking in French, Cam apparently told the driver where we were going, and we headed off.

'Where did you learn to speak French like that?' I asked.

'I did a year out here at university.'

'*Très* impressive. Philippe was a funny guy.'

'He's a multi-millionaire. One of the most influential men in French publishing. Well, in international publishing, really.'

'So, if I really am going to write this book, Gaelle had better start giving me some info, or there are going to be a lot of blank pages in it.'

'She will.'

'How can you be so sure? She's mucked me around so much already. I hardly have anything on her.'

'Trust her.'

'Hmmm.'

'Cara, there's something I have to tell you now.'

My mind boggled.

'What?'

'You won't believe it.'

'Oh, God. What are you going to tell me? I've signed the contract now. You might as well tell me the worst of it,' I said.

'Gaelle says she's about to leave.'

'The country?'

'The planet.'

'I beg your pardon? I'm sorry, I thought you said Gaelle reckons she's about to leave the planet.' I tried to laugh.

'She does.'

'Right. And where's she going to go?'

'Don't laugh. She's says she's going to ascend.'

'Ascend?'

'Ascend. Go up. To a higher dimension.'

'Right.' I looked out at the traffic speeding past us. I was in a white Rolls-Royce travelling through Paris with a man who (a) I really fancied, (b) I knew I could adore and (c) was telling me that our mutual employer was planning on ascending. To the Fifth Dimension. Hang on. He didn't say to which dimension. Why had I thought it was the Fifth?

'Um. So which dimension is Gaelle ascending to?' I asked.

'The Fifth,' he said. 'She says we're in the Third here and are going up to the Fifth, en masse, soon enough. We're all going to ascend. She's the advance party.'

Shit. 'What's the book title about? I saw it on the contract. Part of it says "In Search of the Whole Woman".'

'It's Gaelle's quest,' Cam said.

'What?'

'Gaelle's quest. She says that's where you come in.'

'What are you talking about now, Cam?' This was getting stranger by the minute. Just as Cam was about to explain this cosmic secret, the car pulled over. We were back in Saint Michel and had stopped outside Notre Dame cathedral. I wished I had a camera to take a quick snapshot of this extraordinary car and backdrop, but alas I was without. *Merde*. We scrambled out of the beast and onto the street.

'So, what were you saying about "A Whole Woman"?' I asked. Gaelle had mentioned this the first time we'd met, I was sure.

'Okay, think about it,' he said, taking my hand and heading towards the Ile de la Cité. 'Gaelle, in case you haven't noticed, has no sex life to speak of. She also has an unnatural fascination with you. And Lucy. And Moni.'

'She hasn't met Moni,' I said.

'I think you'll find that she has.'

'What? When?'

'Yesterday.'

'No.'

'*Oui, mon amie.*'

'Lord.'

'She says you, Lucy and Moni represent the three aspects of womanhood. Lucy is ultra-feminine, blonde and vulnerable. Moni is the other end of the spectrum, dark and masculine.'

'Moni isn't masculine!'

'Isn't she? Well, whatever you think about that, that's how Gaelle sees her.'

'And me?'

'You're the middle ground.'

'Cam, last night, after we finally, you know . . .'

'Yeah?'

'I had this very strange feeling that Gaelle would be pleased it had happened.'

'Yeah, me too.'

'Do you know a lot of stuff about her that I don't?'

'Not that I haven't told you.'

'When did she tell you about the Whole Woman stuff? About me and Lucy? And how do you know she saw Moni yesterday?'

'She told me, that's all.'

Majorly confused. This was the perfect description of my mental state now. Too confused. If Gaelle had these weird ideas about me, Lucy and, now, Moni, then a lot of things made sense. About why she'd been so keen for us all to get together, and so on. But why hadn't I seen it coming? How had she chosen us? What had we been chosen for? It was all so strange. The more I meditated, the more accepting I became of all this weirdness, but there were still limits.

'If Gaelle hadn't chosen me, Lucy and Moni for her great experiment, who would she have picked?'

'She said it had to be you.'

'Cam, do you believe her?'

'I don't know. I honestly don't.'

I'd have been happy to go back to the hotel room and bonk him all afternoon, but he took me instead to a small patisserie in one of the tiny back lanes on Ile de la Cité and we ate lemon tart and sipped English Breakfast tea – which seemed a bit silly as we were in Paris, but you can't beat Twinings. He told me more about himself and kissed me across the table twice. He told me about his family. His dad, Robert, a retired jewellery maker, and his mum, Maisie, and the cottage in Brighton he'd grown up in. He regaled me with tales about his sister, Robyn, who'd built a TV production company empire from scratch, his childhood dreams of becoming a sailor and about his cherished slop hound mongrel dog, Patch, whom he'd had since he was fourteen and who now lived with his parents. He was funny and happy and smiled a lot – and I liked him even more for it.

Finally we did go back to our hotel room. My body was transported by the feel of his skin on mine, by the look in his eye, by the sounds of his breath as he came. I was in lust. I knew love was around the corner, if I wasn't too scared. And I wasn't.

We took the train back to London that afternoon and went straight around to his place. His flat was impressive. Large, mostly orange in colour – as if he'd got a cheap deal on paint – and fairly tidy. I liked it mainly because it smelled of him.

Curious to know more, I looked around for and spied his bedroom through an open door. A large double bed covered with a surprisingly stylish ochre and cream duvet cover. It briefly occurred to me that this was the room he stood in each morning to concoct such design classics as baggy pants atop pink paisley shirt.

While I stared at the postcards and photographs pinned to his bedroom wall, he flicked on his answering machine and an electronic voice announced that there were ten new messages. As they played, it became evident that at least eight of them were from an increasingly desperate-sounding female. It wasn't hard to work out that the pleading voice belonged to his recently departed ex-girlfriend. Shit. It was one of those moments when Minties wouldn't even scratch the surface. He was as embarrassed as I was, and tried to flick off the machine, frantically pressing buttons. This was sort of funny in itself, as the tape wouldn't turn off and Cam ended up wrestling the machine until it fell off the small hall table and crashed to the floor, this bloody woman's voice still coming out of it.

'Cam! Pick up the phone! I know you're there! Answer me! How can you be so cold? I need to speak to you!' And so on. Hey, just what I'd always wanted: a deranged ex-girlfriend to contend with.

'Sorry about that,' Cam said sheepishly, once he'd pulled the answering machine plug from the wall socket and finally killed the drone of her voice.

'That's okay,' I said.

'It's Diane.'

'Your ex?'

'Yeah.'

'Thought so.'

We were still standing in the hallway. He came over to me, put his arms around me and we started to kiss. Eventually, he led me to his bedroom. It was late and turning quite chilly, so we threw off our clothes in a comedic fashion and launched ourselves under his duvet, hugging, just lying there in his bed, exhausted. As we warmed up and dozed, I wondered if he was going to see this ex of his again. To placate her. To argue with her. Perhaps to console her. I wondered if he still had feelings for her. And if so, where did I fit into the picture? How crazy was she? I didn't have to wait long for an answer. About fifteen minutes later, there was a knock on the door. It was late and I couldn't imagine who would be visiting Cam at this hour.

'I think I know who that is,' he said, his head still on the pillow. He wasn't moving. Then there was the sound of a key in the front door. It turned and before we knew it, there was a woman standing at his bedroom door. Screaming general obscenities like a woman on a roller-coaster ride. Except it wasn't a roller-coaster ride, it was her life. And mine. And Cam's. Tall, with long, mousy-brown hair and too many teeth, she launched herself at the bed. At us. Still squealing.

'Oh, God,' was all Cam said, before she fell on him.

'You've been here all along, haven't you?' she was yelling. 'Who is this?' That was referring to me. She dissolved into tears. And I have to admit I felt sorry for her. I mean, this was a classically nightmarish situation. She now had her hands on his cheeks and was trying to kiss him. It was at this point that I realised she stank of alcohol. I knew it was time for me to go. Naked, I slid out of the bed. She barely noticed. Cam was wrestling with her.

'Diane. Stop. Stop it. Please.'

'Who is this? Who is she?'

She turned to me. 'How long have you been seeing him?' she demanded. 'Is *she* the reason why you ended it with me?' Then she saw my backpack on the floor and leapt at that. I was by now less naked than I had been – I had managed to put my undies back on. I was trying to find where I'd tossed my bra with wild abandon. It was hanging off the wardrobe door, the black lacy strap caught around the handle. In the meantime, Diane was shaking my back-pack, grabbing at the Eurostar tag attached to its handle. Yelling.

'Eurostar. Paris! You've been to Paris together! Why? Cam?' As she shook the pack, a box of the condoms we'd bought in Paris fell out, its contents spilling everywhere. French french letters. Diane screamed and hurled my pack into the corner of the room.

At this point, I decided going out onto the main road in nothing but my undies would be preferable to hanging around in Cam's room. I lunged for my bra and grabbed my clothes off the floor. Quickly, I went into the hall, figured out where the bathroom was and shut myself in there, dressing as fast as I could. I looked at my reflection in the bathroom mirror. Under the harsh light, I looked less than glam. My face was red from recent kissing. My hair was a knotty mess. My feet were cold as I hadn't rescued my shoes and the floor was tiled. And I felt like shit. I needed to get out of here, but I didn't want to leave Cam with this woman. She might be mad, but there are plenty of men who love mad women. I was just getting to know him as I wanted to know him. I didn't want him running back to his ex just because she'd made a great show of passion. Dammit.

Holding my breath, I listened at the door for sounds. They had gone quiet. I hoped they weren't enjoying a blissful reunion that my presence had somehow been a catalyst for. Then I heard it: almost silent sobs from Diane. My heart bled for her. She was in trauma. She must have worked herself up about Cam's absence during the past thirty-six hours we'd been in *gai Paris*.

I let myself out of the bathroom and poked my head around his bedroom door. She was lying in his arms, weeping like a matinee movie star. He looked up helplessly at me. I spied my purse on the floor next to his bed and leant in to grab it.

'I think I'll go, Cam,' I whispered.

'Okay,' he replied.

Frankly, I could have done with a bit of begging and pleading with me to stay, but under the circumstances I made do. I went to collect my backpack from where Diane had flung it.

'Cara, it's okay — you can get your backpack later.'

'TAKE YOUR FUCKING BACKPACK WITH YOU. YOU'RE NOT COMING BACK HERE!' This, of course, was Diane.

'Don't worry about it. I'll get it back to you later,' Cam said again. 'Just go.'

So, I did. Outside, the evening was cool. I was still wearing just a summer dress, all sleeveless and sexy, but not very practical at midnight. My hair was unbrushed, my mascara was probably down around my cheekbones. And I'd left Cam in there with a drunk and emotional woman to whom he had made love countless times and perhaps would do so again in a fit of sympathy.

I chided myself as I jumped into the black cab which pulled over for me. How could I think that Cam would just end up in bed with Diane? But why wouldn't he? He had before. *Yes, but he's broken up with her now*, my internal commentator reminded me. Yeah, but only recently. *But he's met you now, you fool.* Yes, but who am I to enrapture someone? My head was spinning and I just wanted to go home and smoke copious amounts of Moni's grass to dull the pain. Paris had been such an amazing trip. Now this.

I let myself into the house and was gutted to find it quiet. Moni and Lu must have been asleep. I went first to the kitchen and put the kettle on. I needed some tea, just like Mum used to make for me when I was upset. Then I went to Moni's stash box in the living room. But I held back. Perhaps drugs weren't the perennial answer to blocking out reality. I felt like throwing myself down on the sofa, but I knew the kettle would be boiling soon, so I went back to the kitchen. I didn't want to feel upset. Mouser came in through his cat flap to greet me and I knew that even if I didn't want to feel upset, I just damn well did.

This was so bloody unfair. I'd finally met someone who rocked my socks and he had the mother of all ex-girlfriends on his tail. Our first night together at his place had ended up as a farce. He was probably stroking her long hair and comforting her right now, perhaps tracing a finger gently down her cheek, wiping away her tears, feeling amazed at the love he inspired in her. And maybe vice versa.

I felt sick. I made the tea and went back to the living room to veg. I toyed again with the idea of pillaging Moni's stash box. A quick spliff would do me good. But perhaps I should face life head-on for a change?

So.

No drugs.

No flatmates.

Just me and Mouser.

The Mouse curled up on my lap. I flicked the TV on with the remote control and there was Carole King on a retrospective of seventies' music. What was it with Carole King these days? Was she the only singer left on the planet? I could feel the emotion rising in my throat as Carole crooned 'Will You Love Me Tomorrow?' with a lusty, raw beauty.

Lucy had left the Nirvana Cards sitting on a pile of preliminary sketches for the new version on the coffee table. I picked up the pack, shuffled and drew one out, mentally asking about me and Cam.

'*Joy: Achieving your heart's desire. The triumph of goodness and love. Being connected to another. Channelling another's love.*'

Right. Tell me another one.

The sound of someone knocking at the door interrupted my pessimism. Obvious first thought from sad girl who'll believe anything at this point: could it be him?

I jumped up from the sofa, sliding Mouser unceremoniously to the floor, apologising to him as I flew into the hall. I flicked on the switch for the outside light and peered through the peephole.

Cam.

For about the first time in my life, I was so pleased I hadn't had a joint. I opened the door to let him in. He didn't even have my backpack with him, which I took as a good sign suggesting that he'd come to see me, not to say goodbye. I looked over his shoulder just to be sure. There was no sign of Diane out in the cool night air, just cars rushing up and down the dark street.

'Hi, there.' He seemed slightly hesitant. 'Are you angry?'

Was it possible that he didn't know how far gone up Cam Creek without a paddle I was? I wanted very much to hug him, but somehow, suddenly, I felt shy. So I smiled and shook my head to let him know I wasn't angry.

It was funny. We'd only spent a short amount of time together, especially intimately, but already I knew his delicious smell. He moved towards me and put his face against mine. I breathed him in as his whiskers grated against my chin. I thought I might make like a forties' movie star and swoon, but I managed to stay standing.

We hugged in the hallway. We talked, laughed and joked in the kitchen. He told me he'd placated Diane, made her tea, then called her a cab, so she could go and stay overnight with a friend. And then Cam and I climbed the stairs to my room together. *Joy* indeed.

impetus

The next morning I was woken by screaming. Sliding quietly away from the love god under my duvet, I poked my head into the corridor. Moni was on the landing, jumping up and down, shouting and waving a sheet of paper in her hand.

Wrapped in my fluffy towelling robe, I went out for a closer inspection of this Very Excited Flatmate who was blithering, 'Omigod! Omigod! Omigod!'

It was at about this point I noticed Rufus standing outside Moni's door — naked except for a skimpy yellow towel around his it-has-to-be-said slightly flabby, slightly pasty midriff. London was a figure killer for man, woman and beast alike. It was said they gave you a fat injection at Heathrow and I was inclined to believe it. Nevertheless, far more interesting than Rufus's flab was the fact that he was here at all. Outside Moni's room first thing in the morning. Apparently wearing no knickers. Very suspicious.

And then, as if things couldn't get any curiouser, popping her head out from behind Rufus, her shoulders bare, her hair all mussed up, was Alex. She also appeared to be naked. Everyone was naked. And halfway in or out of Moni's room.

'Moni? What's going on?' I asked.

At this point, Moni started to run across the landing in my direction, arms outstretched, heading right for me. I braced myself for impact, as she threw her arms around me and hugged me, jumping up and down, laughing. She seemed delirious.

'Moni? What is it? What's on the sheet of paper?' I enquired. I also wanted to ask her why Ru and Alex were leaning out of her bedroom apparently in the nuddy, but I figured that could wait.

'It's my screenplay,' she was squealing. 'They want to represent me! I've as good as sold it. Sooooooold it!' I sensed Cam behind me. He, too, was naked, behind my door, leaning his head out. He raised his eyebrows as if to ask what was going on. I made an 'I wouldn't have a clue' face.

'Moni, are you serious?'

She was. It transpired that Moni had sent her screenplay off to her number-one choice of agent, figuring she might as well reach for the stars.

'Alex liked it and that was good enough for me,' Moni raved. 'All I wanted was for it to be taken up by an agent – that shows it's good enough to be sold. That means there's life beyond the "Matt and Melissa Show".'

It was quite a morning heart-starter. However, I still had no idea what Rufus and Alex were doing in her room. I could smell sex in this house, and it wasn't just me.

'That's fantastic, Moni.' I hugged her.

'It's so amazing. I went to the ICA the other day to see the Claire Kellett exhibition and I met this woman who told me this would happen. She just came up and said something like, "You will have success in film and you will see your work on the screen." It was weird. And now it's true. Here,' she said, pushing me towards the bathroom. 'I want to brush my teeth.'

She sort of shoved me into the bathroom and closed the door conspiratorially. She had a very amused look in her bright eyes, like she had some juicy goss to share, and a wide smile to go with it. We brushed our teeth.

'C, is that Cam in your room?' she asked urgently, as she shakily applied Macleans to her brush.

'Mmmhmmm,' I said. 'Is that Rufus *and* Alex in yours?'

'Yes . . .'

'With no clothes on?'

'Yep.'

'Seriously?'

'C. They stayed the night,' she whispered, confirming my theory.

'As in, staaaaaayed the night?' I asked, perhaps slightly cryptically. Because what I really meant to ask was, '*Do you mean you shagged them . . . both?*'

'As in, staaaaaayed the night, C. Just like Cam probably staaaaaayed the night with you . . .' She was glowing.

'Typical Rufus,' I laughed.

'What do you mean?'

'Well, two girls and one Rufus. It's every man's dream.'

'Actually it was my idea . . .'

'Really?'

'I just thought, why not?'

'Go, girl.'

'So there you have it,' she said.

She kissed me on both cheeks dramatically, nearly knocking me sideways, and disappeared, apparently back to the *ménage à trois* going on in her room. I went back to Cam who was now reclining in my bed. I slithered back in next to him, and he gave me a big grin and moved towards me. I didn't even get a chance to tell him Moni's news.

After the amazing start to the day, Cam and I finally surfaced around midday for breakfast. I was prepared to offer the full disaster of bacon, eggs and trimmings in honour of his presence, but all he wanted was Weetabix. Ru, Moni and Lucy were in the garden sunning themselves and acted not the least surprised to see that Cam had been one of our many overnight guests. Alex had departed by the time I appeared, and Rufus was draining his last OJ before leaving.

Throughout the morning, Lu was very quiet and lost in thought. I wanted to ask her what was on her mind, but by the time Cam went back to his place, she'd gone for a walk by herself. So I decided to use the first free time I'd had in a while to collect myself. It's amazing how new love can send the brain into meltdown. It had only been two days since we left London for Paris and already Cam was in my system. I wandered up to the office on the top floor of the house, ostensibly to catch up with things, to see where I was and where I was going, and found a fax waiting for me on the machine.

It must have come overnight and was from my Aunt Martine, writing to tell me that she was vacating her beachside home in Byron Bay over the Australian summer – in other words, during the fast-approaching, evil English winter.

Your mother tells me that you've been commissioned to write a book. Well done! As I'll be away in India for at least six months from November, I'd like to let you know that, if you should so desire, you are more than welcome to come and stay in my house and write. It's fine for you to come alone or with a couple of friends, and you can use my fax for staying in touch with London if you need to. Though I suppose you're modern and have e-mail. The only thing I ask is that you water the plants and feed my cats, Claw and Dee.

Lord.

Martine was a wild brunette chanteuse approaching the end of her forties, though she wouldn't admit her age. In the mid-eighties, she'd had a one-hit wonder in the US with her debut album, which sold and sold and sold. Even today, annual royalty cheques – for airplay and sales – kept her sitting pretty. She bought Daybreak Cottage, right on the beach in Byron Bay, at the height of her success, just before the area became expensively fashionable. It was possible to walk from her living room to the sundeck and onto the sand in about ten long strides.

Being offered her Byron Bay place was a dream come true. I was overdue for a trip back to Oz, and this would be the perfect excuse. Once Gaelle and I had wrapped up all our business, done all the interviews, and I had a very clear idea of what was what, I would be able to sit down and start writing her book. I knew I needed time and space alone to do it in, so going to Byron Bay would be perfect for that.

Apart from leaving Cam, of course.

I took the fax downstairs to tell Moni. I made us a cuppa on my way through to the garden. After I sat down, I shoved the fax under her nose.

'Wow,' she said. 'Are you going to do it?'

I widened my eyes like a crazy thing. She was reading my mind, I knew it.

'I'd love to go . . .' I began. 'Who wouldn't?'

'But?'

'Well . . .'

'Let me guess. You don't want to leave Cam?'

'Aaaaaaargh! Yes, okay, I admit it, I am pathetic. It's true. I don't want to leave him right now.' This was indeed silly. How often does one get the chance to slither away to Byron Bay for a few months to write?

'Why do you think that's pathetic? It's fair enough,' Moni said. 'Understandable, even.'

'Really?'

'Think about it,' Moni advised. 'And while you're doing that, I'm going to break open the champagne to celebrate my success.'

'Absolutely,' I said, happy to change the subject. 'Your success is worth celebrating. Have you got any idea of how long it will take to find a buyer?'

'The agent said she would do her best to find someone in the States . . .'

'Yeah, go straight to Hollywood. It just makes you think, doesn't it,' I said. 'All those hours you spent slaving over it in your room.'

'Well, it does make it worthwhile,' Moni agreed.

'Well done. Now. On the subject of your recent successes, Moni . . .'

'Mmmm?'

'You, Ru and Alex made a very interesting sight this morning.' It really was none of my business, but I couldn't help wondering.

Moni giggled. 'We all got a bit pissed last night. Well, Rufus and I have sort of been together a bit lately – you might have guessed.'

'I did.'

'And last night things got a bit out of control.'

I wasn't sure which tidbit of information was more interesting. The fact that she'd found an agent for *Time of Gain*, that she and Rufus had been having it off as I suspected, or that she'd had a three-in-a-bed.

'But it's not going to happen again. Alex is leaving soon. She's going back to the States.'

We were silent for a moment. Then Moni jumped to her feet and announced she was off in search of champagne.

'Bugger Discreet bloody Duets, and bugger Dale the Dickhead!' I heard her yelling as she skipped to the kitchen.

We drank the afternoon away in a haze. It was sunny, I was in love and lust, a blissful state, Moni was about to marry Martin

Scorsese as far as we could see and at the very least was bonking Ru. Even Lu seemed teetering on okay, considering, by the time she returned from her stroll. She was still confused about Alan and Niall, but she entertained herself picking Nirvana Cards all afternoon, until she got the one called *Happiness*.

In the following weeks, life settled into something new. I wrote to my aunt and accepted her offer to stay at Daybreak Cottage. I secretly hoped Cam might come with me, too, but delayed mentioning anything to him. I'd dreamed of taking a lover there for years, and now I was finally going to have the chance to ask someone I adored to come with me. And if I knew Cam, he was mature enough to understand that asking him if he wanted to come to Byron with me wasn't tantamount to proposing marriage and babies. But I didn't quite feel the time was right to make the offer.

I wondered if Bianca would come and see me in Byron with her new man. She'd e-mailed me a shot of herself and lover boy on holiday in Vietnam. They looked happy and exhausted, soiled and in love. She'd captioned the pic 'Tim and I after a three-hour trek into the hills' and superimposed a big clip-art heart above their heads.

Around that time, one very big thing occurred. I stopped smoking so much spliff. Gaelle had said this would happen if I started to meditate, and perhaps it was brainwashing, but she was quite right. The more I did the meditation thang, the less I spliffed on. I felt a transformation was taking place.

Part of that transformation was my relationship with Cam. Getting to know him was an extraordinary adventure. Sometimes, I felt like I was peeling an onion that didn't make me cry. Layer after layer of person. I was constantly amazed that – aside from his slightly annoying stubborn streak – I liked each layer more than the one before. We spent a lot of time together, laughing, getting out and about, going to the movies, drinking warm beer at the Lord Alvery, and wandering around London, window shopping and searching for old vinyls. One afternoon, after we'd been let off work early at Eaton Square by Gaelle, I actually found the courage to tell him all about the incident with James Duncan which had led to the cystitis, and to my strange outburst in Gaelle's kitchen that afternoon.

'Do men ever have sex with someone like that and feel so wretched and so empty?' I asked.

He said that they did. Somehow, I'd never imagined that. We talked about the scene with his ex-girlfriend. She was back in Birmingham, reportedly dating wildly and preparing to leave for her studies in New York.

'Have you thought any more about those Big Questions that Gaelle mentioned?' he asked.

'Yes,' I said, despite not really wanting to go there.

'And?'

'And I think that I need to evolve. Mature. Grow. Or something.'

'Like everyone.'

I nodded.

'Anything else?'

'I want to be less critical of others and of myself.' Where did that one come from? 'And I think I should let go. And get more into my body and out of my head. I mean . . .'

He cracked up laughing.

I wasn't really sure where I was going with this ball. Part of me wanted to forget it all. There were questions bubbling up inside me. Like why did Cam mean so much to me? Was there a gap inside my soul that had to be filled by someone else? Did I need to love myself more before I could really love him? Sometimes I think life would have been so much simpler had I just got married at eighteen and moved to the suburbs.

'What are your strengths?' he asked me.

'I don't know.'

'Come on . . .'

'Well, Lucy says I have naturally perfectly shaped eyebrows . . .'

'Cara . . .' This was Cam's admonishing tone.

I stared blankly.

'Okay,' he prompted. 'Well, you like people. You like your friends. You have lots of people who love you,' he began.

'Mmmm.'

'And you're great when you get a strong idea in your head. You go for it.'

'And?' I fished.

'You're caring, loving.'

'Am I?'

'Sure.'

'Well, thanks.'

'So, how do you feel about me? What are the best and worst things?' he asked me, a glint in his eyes.

'Are you seriously expecting me to answer that?'

'I'm your lover. You can use me to work these things out.'

Was he mad? A closet pop psychologist? Or was this normal behaviour for men who worked with mystic gurus?

'Okay. The best thing is that I like your company. I like having you around to do things with, like hang out and chat. I like your spirit.'

'What else?'

'Um. I like lying in bed next to you while we read the papers and I like having breakfast with you, especially when you make fresh juice, and I like bonking you.'

'Excellent. Anything else?'

'I . . . um . . . I like connecting with you. I like it when we work together. Like yesterday, when we were discussing how the book should be planned out. I like your mind.'

'And the worst things?'

'Hang on. There's another thing. I like being close to you physically, not just during sex. I like your energy. You make me smile.'

He let that pass with another flash of his pearly whites. 'And the worst?' he persisted.

'Well, first, do you want to know what I think the worst thing about me is?' I asked.

'What?'

'Insecurities.'

'Like?'

'Sometimes I worry that I'm so unevolved it's not funny. That I can't see how anyone could ever fancy me, so how could you?'

'What?'

'What I said.'

He sighed loudly. 'Cara. I'm here because I want to be here with you. I think you're gorgeous. I adore you and I'm happy. Get that in your head and go from there. Okay?'

'Right.' I was still coming to terms with my own answers, so I didn't probe him with meaningful questions in return. I went inside to the kitchen and toasted us some crumpets instead.

At work, Gaelle was less and less on our case as we raked through the documents she'd provided for me to use as a basis for the questions I would ask her. I started outlining a structure for the book on my computer at home. I continued meditating regularly and kept struggling with my evolution. Cam kept coming around, despite my fears that he'd abscond to outer Siberia and I'd never see him again. I started to relax and really enjoy each day.

Lu, in the meantime, stayed single, seeing neither Niall nor Alan, and seemed a lot better for it. We started meditating together. We would go out into the garden at the end of the afternoon and sit and breathe. To start with, Lu would dedicate her meditations to either Alan or Niall. After a week or so, I noticed she started to dedicate them to herself, which I thought was a very good sign. Her Nirvana Cards were progressing well and she showed me the design she had for the *Resistance* card. Sure enough, it was a picture of two women, a tallish brunette who looked suspiciously like me, and a shorter, rounder blonde, who brought

Gaelle to mind. They were engaged in a tug of war, surrounded by drawings of broken hearts. Lord. Recorded for posterity.

'It's good, Lu,' I said truthfully. It was good, if a little scary. 'How did you do it?'

'I hand-drew it and manipulated it on the computer a bit. I'm quite pleased with it. But don't worry, I'm going to draw you on the *Joy* and maybe *Enlightenment* cards too,' she said. 'So you have nice pictures as well.'

'Thanks, Lu.'

'How is Gaelle, anyway?'

'Pretty incommunicado.'

'What do you mean?'

'She's hardly seeing me or Cam, or even Amanda or Nadine right now. She says she needs time alone "to process".'

'Well, at least you have a bit of a break from her.' Lu smiled.

'Mmmm.'

Moni's life, meanwhile, had taken a whole new course. I came home one afternoon to find her ripping up the Discreet Duets pictures of David from Hampstead, Alistair from Islington, Graeme from Purley. The shredded remains lay in a pile on the kitchen table.

'What on earth are you doing?' I asked.

'I'm destroying the last of the remaining evidence.'

'What's the problem? Aren't you going to do the story? I thought you said that Jean-Pierre was cool. For a wife swapper.'

'Jean-Luc,' she corrected me. 'And as far as wife swappers go, yes, he was okay. But, C, this whole situation is morally reprehensible.'

'Oh.'

'The idea of hidden cameras gives me the creeps. Dale knows Jean-Luc's story, he knows the man is married with kids, and guess what he wants me to do?'

'What?'

'Shoot a piece with Jean-Luc and then show the tape to the wife.'

'No way.'

'Yes. If the wife agrees, we'll speak to her about her reactions to finding out that her husband is a closet wife swapper, and interview her on air.'

'That's outrageous.'

'I know. I'm going to refuse.'

'Really?'

'Really. There's no way. This is not why I got into journalism or television.'

'It would be a sensational story . . .'

'I know.'

'An amazing documentary about modern life.'

'I know.'

'You could really make your name with it, if the right people saw it. It's got everything. Love, lust, infidelity, intrigue.'

'I know. But I'm not going to do it. If they don't like it, they can lump it. I'd rather do night shifts for the shopping channel than this crap.'

'Wow.'

'I'm serious. Alex agrees. It's getting out of hand. I'm telling Dale tomorrow.'

'Well, good for you, girl.'

'Thank you.' Moni looked a bit relieved, actually. 'Even TV producers have limits, you may or may not be surprised to hear . . .'

By early September, it was time for Alex to go home. Moni, Alex and Ru had remained friends throughout the summer, but Moni had intimated that a threesome wasn't necessarily an ongoing thing, although she and Rufus seemed extra fond of each other, so a twosome was a possibility. I sensed Moni didn't want to discuss her private life at that point and, anyway, we'd long ago gotten over teasing them about their night of passion *à trois*. We all accepted it like the Modern Folk we were. I think it might have happened once more after that, but this time I decided it was their business and didn't pry. In the end, Moni did indeed decide to back out of the Discreet Duets story, but she was saved the drama of telling her boss. The morning she announced to us that she'd finally plucked up the courage to break the news to Dale, she went into his office to find him in a blind fury. It transpired that Naomi, the woman who'd offered him the story in the first place, had gone cold on the whole thing, Jean-Luc's phone number and e-mail address were both suddenly disconnected and the URL for the Discreet Duets website had changed.

'They must have rumbled us.' She grinned. 'I can't say I'm sorry.'

We farewelled Alex with a dinner at The Ivy because she'd always wanted to go there. She even wore a dress for the occasion. For a present, Lu printed out an unapproved, but otherwise finished, pack of her Nirvana Cards, and I got them laminated. Lucy had done an immaculate job with them. Her cheeky pastel drawings seemed to perfectly interpret the cards' meanings, doing so with profound humour. I loved the drawings of me on the *Joy* and *Enlightenment* cards. Of course, Lu encouraged Alex to pick a Nirvana Card on the night of her farewell, for good luck. Alex closed her eyes and picked *Independence*, featuring a characterisation of Moni. It seemed very apt and we all cheered wildly.

Moni and Rufus got closer and closer after Alex left, and both Ru and Cam started to become regulars at the Lavender Sweep dinner table. I was still delaying telling Cam about Byron. I couldn't bring myself to do it. I didn't want to tell him I was going without him, but I didn't feel I could invite him, either. I didn't want to freak him out. I decided I would meditate on the best time to ask him. In the book Gaelle had given me, it said that if you asked yourself a question before your meditation, the answer that you knew to be right would bubble up from your subconscious. It was worth a try.

Although Gaelle seemed to have disappeared, I still saw Cam most days at Gaelle's or at nights at my place or his. The more we were together, and the more I saw that he thought I was okay, the more relaxed I became and the more I realised I *was* okay.

I liked the way he was cool even when I wasn't exactly on my best behaviour. And the way he understood when I went completely mental after a whole day's work got wiped from my computer due to a hard-drive crash. Even my crying tantrum didn't deter him. And he was okay even when he went away one weekend to see his mate John in Manchester and I worked myself into a state thinking he'd gone back to Diane. I then added to the mêlée by having a huge joint despite my resolution not to avoid reality with drugs, and ended up as wound up as a very, very wound-up thing. He called, found me like that, laughed and talked me through it, saying I should stop terrorising myself with my thoughts. Ha. He even made me speak to his friend John, which was mortifyingly embarrassing, but amusing in hindsight.

As the last days of summer sailed by, Gaelle remained infuriatingly secluded. Although she'd given me the very tasty starter of an interview pre-Paris, she was now quiet as a dead ant. She refused to expand on the John Lennon angle of her story, which frustrated me. She blanked me on the possibility of discussing The Whole Woman concept. She wouldn't even talk about the structure I'd mapped out for her book. Whenever I did happen to catch sight of her outside her blessed work room at Eaton Square, she'd scurry past me, saying she had a lot of thinking to do, now that she'd committed to going to press with her story.

Then she made her seclusion official. 'I need to meditate,' she announced, and took herself off to her work room for seven days straight. So, while she cogitated in there, doing God only knew what with pyramids and incense, I was treading water. The faded newspaper articles, magazine stories and old invitations were an interesting trip down seventies lane. She'd been quite the legendary icon of the day, at one point. But I needed more. The notes she'd scrawled for me about the book under such titles as 'Brian's Tragic Flaw', 'The Importance of Ascension' and 'The Whole Woman' were intriguing, but having transcribed them onto my computer and considered them from all angles, I was desperate to actually talk to her about them.

However, there was nothing I could do in the face of her refusals to see me – or anyone else. Whether I called her at home late at night in an effort to trick her into answering her phone, or left Post-it notes marked 'Urgent' on her work-room door or sent messages via Cam, Nadine and Amanda, she replied to nothing.

After I'd tried every last ruse I could think of to speak to her, I came up with a cunning plan; I would meditate my way into her thoughts. So I sat down in her living room – there was no-one else at Eaton Square and Gaelle was locked away in her work room – I closed my eyes and started the Miracle Meditation breathing that her book had taught me. I went into my meditation quite quickly. Usually there was just a feeling of peace, but this time it was like a trance. I saw Gaelle.

'Be patient, Cara,' was all she said to me. And just as soon as I had snapped into this light-headed state, I was out of it again. I was shaken.

In some ways, though, I didn't begrudge her this solitude.

'It's easy to forget what she turned her back on in order to become so weird,' I said to Cam, Moni and Lu one night over dinner. 'She must have had great mental fortitude. She could have lived a life of champagne and canapés in Sydney's luxurious Eastern Suburbs. Instead she left because she honestly believes what she's doing is right.'

The more I knew about her decision to seek spiritual enlightenment in the days when women were still mainly accessories, the more impressed I was. Plus, as much as I hated to admit it, the meditation she'd taught me really did seem to be doing the trick. I was certainly happier these days, although maybe that was due to other circumstances . . .

'Yeah. I wonder if I'd have had the spiritual wherewithal to just take off to Tibet or Nepal or wherever, if I had the calling,' Lu ruminated.

'The only problem is that now is the time when I need to speak to her most. I do think it's a bit rich to just come into our lives, twitter on about dimensions, instruct me to write her life story and then abandon us.'

'It's the worst possible time for me, too,' Lu agreed. 'I need to speak to her about Niall and Alan. I want some help. There's stuff going on for me that I haven't even told you guys about . . .'

'Like what?'

'Just stuff . . .'

'Are you okay, Lucy?' I asked.

'Sure. I will be. Honest. When I get some answers.'

'I know how you feel. I'd like to get some more info out of her about her life story.'

'And I want to know what's going to happen with my screen-play,' Moni added.

I had finally found the courage to ask Moni about the woman she'd met at the ICA who had predicted her screenplay would sell. Sure enough, she described the woman as having blonde hair, twinkly blue eyes, a big bottom and a hard-to-place accent. From this we were convinced it was Gaelle and, ever since, Moni had been desperate to meet her officially.

'Cam? What do you think about all this?' Moni asked.

He cleared his throat. 'She called me this morning,' he confessed.

'She called you?'

'At my house.'

'And?'

'She told me that she was very pleased with the way things are going, but that it was now time for everyone to stand on their own two feet.'

'And what did you say to her?'

'You know what she's like. There's not a lot you can say to her when she's made up her mind.'

'But that's crazy! Didn't you even try?'

'I said maybe she had a responsibility to stick with everyone, once she'd stirred things up so much. She just said there was "method in her madness".'

There was a collective sigh as we realised we were up against a woman who – when she wanted to be – was as immovable as a Giza pyramid.

'Cara, do you think Gaelle drives you crazier than she would if she was a bit more like you'd expect the average life-changing mystic healer woman to be?' asked Moni.

'What do you mean?'

'I mean that I think we expect our best spiritual teachers to wear white and float around talking about hearing the vibratory hum of the universe,' Moni went on. 'Gaelle's nothing like that. Perhaps that's why she's so hard to take seriously.'

'True,' Lucy agreed.

'I take her seriously,' I protested.

'You argue with her non-stop . . .'

'Yeah. And you got the *Resistance* Nirvana Card, too, C.'

'Give me a break.'

'But you have to admit that Gaelle isn't quite what you'd expect in a guru,' Moni went on. 'I mean, she's overweight, or at least she's let herself go to seed since her glory days as a socialite. She's single and apparently demented about some guy who lives in the Fifth Dimension. She smokes grass and can be quite abrasive . . .'

'It's all true,' I concurred. 'Maybe you've got a point. Maybe I need to look beyond her in-your-face exterior.'

Until now, the closest I'd come to New Agey types were Niall and Shanti Deva and, latterly, Lucy. While I had to admit they'd shown none of Gaelle's perspicacity or ability, they were at least all

238

well-versed in mystic lip service. 'Love yourself, open your heart', and so on, were their stock phrases. It was interesting to contemplate.

'Sometimes it's the people we least expect guidance from who turn out to be our guides,' Lu said knowingly.

'Mmmm.'

'Wanna pick a Nirvana Card?' she asked.

'No, thanks.' Despite the Gaelle dramas, I liked the way life was going and didn't want a pack of cards to tell me something I might not want to hear. I was happy, even though I had a funny feeling that life wasn't going to stay quite this simple.

DREAM DIARY
22 AUGUST: EPIPHANY

I was falling through the clouds, falling through the heavens. I was back in the ethers, where I had started that first night. I was between the heavens and above the Earth.

I saw the man with the beautiful eyes and this time I knew it was Cam.

I saw a green light pulsing in his chest, a round ball of energy that was emerald-coloured and shiny and hot. I saw this energy coming towards me, like a growing green rainbow moving through the air. It hung suspended between us before it reached me. I knew I had to generate the same phenomenon from my heart to his, to make our streams of love meet. I knew it was love and that love was tangible.

'Relax,' came Gaelle's voice.

I relaxed. I let my shoulders fall. I felt my heart opening and watched in awe as a stream of the most beautiful pinks and greens extended from my chest and melded with the colours coming from Cam.

'Epiphany,' Gaelle said as I slumbered.

I'm getting into this dreaming thing.

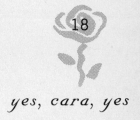

yes, cara, yes

Amid the mayhem and other-worldly madness of life with and without Gaelle, 3D-reality ticked on. The day of Moni's birthday arrived. It was the big 3-0 for her, and we'd planned a memorable dinner party to celebrate. Invitees on the night were to include me, Cam, Moni, Rufus, Lucy and Alan, as well as Rufus's brother Seamus and the dreadful Eloise, neither of whom I had seen since the eventful night of their party in Hampstead.

The day began lazily. Cam and I awoke at midday, long after Moni and Ru had gone out for a champagne breakfast at Bozo's Diner in Fulham. With Lu also nowhere to be seen, we had the house to ourselves, so we read the papers for a while, then made lunch from a collection of cheeses and cold meats in the fridge before settling, entwined, on the sofa to watch Woody Allen's *Sleeper* for the fourth time. I had it on video and Cam seemed obsessed by it.

'We're going to have to get up from here and go to the supermarket,' I said once the movie had finished. According to the duty roster we'd all agreed to, Moni and Rufus were to be the chefs for the night, Cam and I were charged with doing the Sainsbury's supermarket thing, while Lucy and Alan would be responsible for clearing up. Moni had left us a very specific shopping list pinned to the fridge door.

'Mmmm,' said Cam distractedly. 'You know, I was thinking about what Gaelle was saying about women, about you and Lu and Moni.'

'Oh, that.' He'd tried to allude to this before and I'd been evasive.

'Why don't you want to talk about it?'

'I don't know. It's "work", I guess. And to be honest I'm so unsure about how and what I feel about Gaelle right now.' I was also not really too enthusiastic about having more D&Ms about La Gaelle with Cam. If he was too into her, did that make him a loony?

'Okay. But listen just for a minute,' he said. 'The fact that Moni had that fling with Alex . . . It's the Gaelle thing. It's what she said about the Whole Woman.'

'What do you mean?' In Gaelle's notes for the book, there were indeed references to her Whole Woman concept, but none directly to me, Lucy or Moni.

'Okay. So, she hasn't put it in the notes in so many words, at least not in the notes that she's given you, but the Moni and Alex thing fits in with what she said about the male–female thing. About you representing the spectrum of femininity. You three girls.'

'What do you mean?' I gave him my full attention.

'Look. Lu is very feminine. Blonde. Gentle. And still confused about Alan and Niall, isn't she?'

'Yep. I don't think she's seeing Niall much at all now and, although she still hasn't quite detached herself from Alan, it's practically fallen apart, too. I think.'

'Right. She's very soft and sweet. She is the feminine extreme, if you like.'

'Mmmm?'

'Now. You and I are together. No great dramas.'

'No,' I said. In fact, only good dramas.

'And Moni, the masculine one – according to Gaelle – ends up having a thing with Alex. A bisexual thing.'

'She's also with Rufus,' I pointed out.

'Well, yes. She's not gay, but she might be bi. It's the masculine–feminine thing. Don't you see?'

'I guess so.'

'You're over Gaelle, aren't you?' he said.

'Just a bit.'

Since we'd been to Paris, Cam had taken up a lot of my head space. And it was a relief not to have to do constant Gaelle-inspired soul searching. I was fairly much over trying to figure out how she did the weird things she did with trances and meditations and dimensions and things.

'Why are you so tired of her all of a sudden?' Cam wanted to know. 'Aren't you excited about the book?'

'The book is one thing. I can detach myself from it and see it as work. The rest of it is so bizarre and scary, and I guess I'm happy with the way things are right now. I mean, I know I'm about to have to do a lot of hard yakka with the writing. The contract is signed. But there's a part of me that just wants to get on with it and do all the interviews and start getting it into the computer without any more weirdness. You know, just write it, watch it become a huge best-seller and then move on to the next project.'

'As if none of this had ever happened?'

'None of what?'

'The trance stuff, the Whole Woman stuff making sense the way it does. The fact that you and I are together and it almost feels like Gaelle had a hand in making that happen.'

'Do you believe she did?'

'I don't know yet. But you have to admit we've both at least felt it. That's weird enough for me to be getting on with.'

'Are you going all spooky on me?' I asked him.

It wasn't that I didn't so much *believe* any more. I just didn't want to. It was too complex. Just coping with daily life was enough for me, without thinking about entities and past lives and dimensions. He stopped talking and looked at me, raising his eyebrows. It was almost a challenge to dispute him. So he felt he'd been mystically guided to Gaelle the Guru because she did a strange crystal reading for him on a yacht in Ireland at a time when he needed some direction. He wanted to know more about her. Fine. Who was I to argue? Perhaps she did mystically suck him to her. Who knew? But her strange ways had also pervaded me – enough. And I didn't like it. I loved being a *Mirror*-reading, lager-drinking, telly-watching heathen. I didn't want to be converted to New Age Nice. Hell, no.

'Are you going esoteric?' I persisted, like I knew the answer but didn't want to hear it. 'Do you think that Gaelle planned it all? How could she? She's just a crazy old woman who knows how to shock, don't you think?'

'I honestly don't know,' said Cam. 'She is definitely odd. Yeah, she doesn't look like the average Saviour of the World, but we shouldn't let that influence us too much.

'You shouldn't be so hard on her, C. Why are you?'

I was going to tell him that she scared the living daylights out of me and that my first line of defence was attack, but instead I just shrugged and said, 'I don't know why. It's hard to believe her claims. If they're true, why doesn't she do something to prove that she is who she says she is? I mean, if it's true she's half alien and has fourteen-strand DNA, why not submit herself to a blood test and surprise us all?'

Before he could answer, Moni and Ru returned and Moni came

into the living room brandishing her shopping list, so there was no more canoodling or discussing to be done. Cam and I jumped into his beloved silver Peugeot and headed for Nine Elms.

I queued at the meat counter to buy the lamb for Moni's Middle Eastern feast, while Cam went off to find the right vegies. As I waited in line, staring out towards the enormous car park under grey skies, even the darkening London sky didn't seem as ominous as it used to. In fact, I was suddenly sure that this was the best summer we'd had for years. I was blown away by how much I was enjoying hanging out with Cam. He was divine. He made me happy. And I felt pretty confident he was happy, too. It had been such a long time since anyone had touched me emotionally.

Cam was grinning as he approached the checkout, wielding a giant zucchini like a sex toy. We had all we needed, checked it through and lugged eight shopping bags back to the car, driving home through Battersea. Maybe it was the meditating, or maybe it was the sight of the zucchini and the connotations it stirred in my subconscious, but like a bolt out of the blue I decided the time was right to mention Byron Bay to Cam. I couldn't put it off forever and, when you got down to it, I needed to go there and write, whether or not he wanted to come. The writing, I estimated, would need to start in about a month. Gaelle had told me she'd give me all the information I needed within the week. It was almost time to get started.

As we drove home, I knew I had to broach the subject. Inspiration struck as I pulled the big green zucchini out of the shopping bag and waved it at him.

'Hey, Cam,' I said, trying to sound breezy. 'Do you know what we call "courgettes" in Australia?'

He looked at me quizzically.

'Zu-keee-neez?' he said, in a fairly mediocre Australian accent.

' "Zucchinis". Yes. And, er, do you know what we call "mange-tout"?' I used my best French accent.

'No, Cara, what do you call mange-tout?'

'Snowpeas,' I announced. 'And we also call felt-tip pens "textas", duvets "doonas", tights "stockings" . . .'

'What do you call "stockings"?'

'Er. Stockings. I think. And we call off-licences "bottle shops" and –'

'– and you say "noy" instead of no, "parsta" instead of pasta and you can see the Southern Cross and we can't.'

'My point exactly.'

'What point?'

'We can see the Southern Cross in Australia.'

Cam was quiet for a moment, perhaps as dumbfounded as me at my babbling.

'Cam, what I'm leading up to is –'

'You're homesick?'

'Not exactly. But . . . my Aunt Martine has offered me her place in Byron Bay for a few months, if I want to go there and write Gaelle's book.' I looked sideways at him, wondering how he'd take it. He didn't flinch.

'Where's Byron Bay?' he asked.

'On the New South Wales coast, about twelve hours' drive north of Sydney. It's beautiful. It's a beach, though, not a bay.'

'I see.' He grinned as we swerved around into Lavender Sweep.

'She's going away and said I could go and hang out there for the summer . . .' I paused to let the news sink in. I had no idea what he'd say or think. We'd only been together for a few weeks, really. Perhaps he wouldn't miss me at all if I left for the other side of the world. Perhaps it was a one-sided affair of the heart.

'So, when are you going?' he asked as we cased Lavender Sweep for a parking spot.

'If I go, it will obviously have to be after I've done all the Gaelle interviews. So, in about a month or three.'

'Right.'

'So, ah, do you like swimming?'

'Love it.'

'In waves?'

'Yep.'

'With dolphins sometimes?'

'Sounds amazing.'

'You can do all that in Byron.'

'Cool.'

'So, er, what I'm trying to say is would you like to come with me?' I blurted, relieved by my own motor mouth. 'You could just come for a while, if you wanted, just to check it out.'

He smiled as he reverse-parked. I held my breath. He turned off the ignition and we got out of his car. Cam started hauling the plastic bags out of the back seat while I waited for an answer. Although he had a smile on his face, which seemed like a good sign, he was saying zero. We took the bags up the garden path and into the kitchen. Moni and Lu were out the back with Rufus, sipping Pimms. Lu walked in with the Nirvana Cards and offered Cam the outspread deck. Before I could intervene – lest he get the *Don't Go There!* card – he picked one and passed it back to Lu.

'*Impetus. Go forward. Be propelled into the future. Willingness to learn through inspiration will bring the right answers to you. The right answers will move you forward with energy.*'

'So?' I asked Cam once we were alone and unpacking groceries. 'What about Byron?' I grinned shakily. A simple yes or no would do. Even a positive-sounding maybe would suffice at this point.

He smiled back.

'Mmm?' said I.

'Yes, of course, Cara. Yes.'

'Really?'

'Yes. In theory, if it happens, yes, I'd love to come. I've got no plans after Gaelle yet. I've got some cash, about 10 000 books I want to read and I could do with another summer . . . this time on an Australian beach. I can rent my flat out, I suppose, if we go for more than a month. And I'd love to go with you.'

He stopped unpacking herbs and spices and his arms encircled me in a big hug. I looked deep into his eyes and very much liked what I saw. Once upon a time, sharing a tender moment like this, I would have been tempted to make cracks about the sharks that might devour him off the Aussie coast or some such thing, but I just stared.

'Hey, you two smoochers, what did you bring me?' This was Moni. I squeezed Cam again and pulled away.

'We got everything you asked for. And guess what?'

'What?'

'Cam's coming to Byron with me!'

'Hurrah! I told you he'd say yes.' This was Rufus, standing behind Moni.

'So, did everyone know about this trip except me?' Cam asked.

'I was a bit nervous about asking you.'

'Well, you didn't need to be. Come with me.' He took me by the hand and led me out of the kitchen and up the stairs to my room.

'Don't forget – you guys have to set the table!' Moni cried out behind us.

'We won't forget,' I promised, shutting my bedroom door.

19

a night of nights

So Cam was coming to Byron with me. There was a part of me that was slightly nervous, but I also knew it could be fantastic. Hanging out on the beach, maybe doing some writing, listening to music. I liked the idea of enjoying his company there, and of seeing him in a sarong under a blue Australian sky. Later in the afternoon I faxed Aunt Martine to tell her the news. Cam and I then set about performing our duties by transforming the dining room for Moni's birthday celebrations.

We vacuumed, dusted and threw open the windows for fresh air. Then we tackled the table, laying down a white damask tablecloth my mum had given me, overlaying that with a ream of blue Indonesian batik. We added Lucy's fine white china and silver cutlery, Moni's long-stemmed wine glasses and a dozen or so tea-light candles we'd bought at the supermarket. The final touches were white linen napkins and a bowl of flowers in the centre.

Moni had started cooking, and by early evening the aromas emanating from the kitchen were mouth-watering. As Cam and I twiddled and tweaked in the dining room, we caught glimpses and soundbites of Moni and Ru arguing non-stop about the best way to toss this and sauté that. They seemed to be having more fun than the average chef and had already opened a bottle of red. Lucy, meanwhile, was upstairs in the bathroom making herself beautiful. She'd seemed a little low earlier, so I went up to say hi.

'Greetings.' I popped my head around the bathroom door, expecting to see her applying eyeliner and lipgloss.

She turned to look at me with a start.

'Fancy a beer or a wodka?'

'Not right now, C.' She looked at me dolefully, then passed me a small cardboard box.

It was a pregnancy test kit.

'Oh God, Lucy.'

'Six days late.'

'You poor thing.'

'Come in,' she said.

I sat on the edge of the bath and her face dissolved into sadness.

'Lu, is this what you meant when you said there were things you weren't telling us . . . ?'

'Mmmhmmm.' She nodded, before bursting into more sobs. 'C, I don't even know if the father would be Niall or Alan.'

'Oh, God.'

'I can't have a baby, though, can I? I can barely look after myself.'

I was terrified that if I said anything, I might give her the wrong advice.

'You know, I once read that babies who end up being . . . terminated . . . are young souls who want to incarnate for just a few weeks. Who don't want the full human being incarnation experience . . .'

'I see.'

'Do you think it's true?' she asked me, blinking through wet eyelashes.

'I don't know Lu.' I hoped this pregnancy scare wasn't a result of astro moon-cycle contraception gone pear-shaped.

'C, I'm going to do the test sticks in here. Will you wait?' She went next door to the loo, I heard a flush and then she returned, setting the two plastic testers level on the shelf above the basin. She plucked a couple of fresh Kleenex and covered them up gently.

'I don't want to have to look at them,' she said, forcing a laugh as she sat down on the bathroom chair.

I took a long breath. 'I had no idea this was going on for you, Lu. I feel guilty. I've been so involved in my own happiness lately.' She must have been feeling very shaky. Firstly the Niall and Gaelle dilemmas, then Alan's reappearance, and the ensuing emotional mayhem. 'I haven't really been there for you very much.'

'C, you're so sweet. Don't be silly. You've been in lerrrrrrrve,' she said, smiling. She glanced at her watch.

'But you were so good to me when I was depressed recently.'

'Yes, but my dramas have been of my own making. For example, why did I invite Alan here for dinner tonight? He's probably expecting to stay over. I shouldn't even be seeing him.'

'You might be right.' Now was the time for honesty.

'It's about time I took responsibility for myself, I know that. Blaming Alan for making me unhappy is stupid. If he makes me unhappy and I stay with him anyway, it's my fault.'

'Did the Nirvana Cards tell you all this?'

'C. Honestly. Do you think I'm totally mad?'

'And Niall?'

'Our friendship is really strong, and we share the same ideals, but he knows Alan's back on the scene . . . and that hurts him. I'm so confused.'

Poor cherub. 'Maybe neither of them is the answer?' I ventured, radically. Without replying, she tapped her watch and stood up to look at the pregnancy tests.

'It's time, C. Will you look for me?'

'Are you sure?'

'Sure.' She passed me the empty packaging. 'There's a diagram on the side of the box. If there's a blue line, it's positive. If there's no blue line, it's negative.'

I carefully lifted the tissues.

I looked back at her, and smiled.

'You should see these for yourself, Lu.'

She jumped up, looked and squealed, 'Negative!' before bursting into more blubbering. This time, thankfully, she was also smiling through her tears.

By the time Seamus and Eloise arrived, just before sunset, I was showered, perfumed and ready for an aperitif. We assembled in the garden, Lu far more carefree than she'd been a few hours ago. We made ourselves comfy on an assortment of garden chairs and cushions, Rufus popped the champagne and proposed the toasts. We drank first to Moni's birthday, then to her success in probably selling her screenplay. Then we gave Moni her presents; Lu, Cam and I presented her with a day of health and beauty treatments at The Sanctuary, an antique bracelet Lu had found in a second-hand shop in Notting Hill, a few Johnny Loves Rosie hair accessories and a fifties-style scarf which was just perfect on her.

'Just right for your new screenwriter's image,' Lu noted.

Next Rufus presented Moni with tickets for two to Prague, a screenwriting computer program and a Polaroid camera, which must have been a private joke because her eyes flashed and she laughed uproariously when she unwrapped it.

As we watched the present-giving ceremony, Lucy eyed the hallway repeatedly. I assumed she was awaiting Alan, who'd phoned to say he was running late. When the doorbell finally rang, she sprang up to answer it.

Who should come through the door but Alex. All the way from America.

Moni and Alex both squealed and embraced each other. With green dungarees, an orange skinny-rib top and a pair of nine-hole Dr Martens, Alex looked her usual sartorially-sweet-yet-feral self.

'What are you doing here?' Moni asked as she ran her fingers affectionately through Alex's Number Two razor-cut mop, dyed the same burnt orange as her top. Or was it vice versa?

'I couldn't keep away,' she giggled into Moni's face. 'When you called about the agent and the screenplay and all, and you told me about your birthday, I couldn't not come. Mom bought me the ticket.'

'It's so good to see you again,' Moni said.

'And you, and you, Rufus, and you guys,' she said, smiling at Lu and me. 'I'm just here for three days. I've been asked to direct a play for the Venice Beach Fringe Festival in LA.'

As Rufus muscled in on the hugging and kissing, and Lu fetched Alex a glass of champagne, I snuck into the living room, to set her place at the table. I wondered how her presence would affect the dynamics of tonight's party.

Alan arrived half an hour later, dressed in his usual banker-wanker weekend uniform of chinos, striped shirt and brogues, clutching a bouquet of carnations for Moni. Forgive me, but every time I saw him, I was dumbstruck by what a Class A Prat he was. What on earth was Lu doing with him? Okay, so she was only half with him, but even that was way too much.

'Hi, Alan,' Lu said in greeting, as he stroked her hair. 'What kept you? Weekend work?'

'Oh, yah, I've been flat out. Helluva drive across town,' he said in his cut-glass whine. I hated the way he acted as if Battersea was the other end of the world, Holland Park snob that he was. 'I, ah, I brought some, er, vino, for you.' He said the word 'vino' as though it gave him street cred, which it didn't.

'Oh, thank you, Alan,' simpered Lucy, taking the bottle of red.

'It's rather a good drop,' he went on. 'Well, anything would be better than the Chateau Cardboard you girls keep in the fridge, eh?' He guffawed, his small head with its pink, puffy cheeks nodding at his own witticisms.

I was resisting the urge to slap him when Moni came in from the kitchen and announced that dinner was ready. We filed in from the garden. It was a warm, light summer's evening and I felt great. A few wines, some great people – with the exception of Alan – and a feast fit for Arabian royalty laid out before us: tabouleh, minty lamb, couscous with capsicum through it, felafels, fried haloumi cheese, all served with homemade mint tea.

Ru sat down flanked by Alex and Moni. I was impressed to see they looked like the happiest little trio in town, all three apparently more than delighted at this unexpected reunion. Moni giggled as Ru playfully plopped a blob of humus on her nose and made up jokes about chickpeas and yashmaks.

After we'd piled our plates, Rufus outdid himself with his birthday toast to Moni and her culinary skills. 'I never thought I'd go all gooey over anyone, let alone over an Aussie sheila, but thank you, Moni, for getting me in touch with my gooey side.' She blushed crimson as he laughed, then she playfully told him to naff off. Lu ran off a Polaroid to capture the moment.

It wasn't until Alan tasted the felafel that the shit hit the fan. Perhaps inevitably. He was already fired up after a G&T and three big glasses of red. He was becoming louder, more bumptious, arrogant, triple chinned and duller than usual. I happened to look at him as he shovelled the first mouthful of felafel into his mealy mouth, then spat the lot out onto his plate.

'Good Lord, what is this?' he asked, ever the diplomat. 'God, yuk.' He spat out more chewed-up remains. 'It tastes like chicken feed.'

'How would you know what chicken feed tastes like, Al?' I asked, showing equal diplomatic tendencies.

'Ugh,' he said, spitting tiny flecks now. Such breeding. 'For God's sake, Lu, what is it?'

'Oh dear,' whispered Eloise, clearly fearing a lapse of protocol.

'Moni made it. It's a felafel,' Lu said in a small voice.

'For goodness' sake, Alan. If you don't like it, don't eat it,' I added. That was telling him. Cam shot me a here-we-go glance.

'C, please don't get narky,' Lucy squealed. Unfortunately, she knew all too well that neither Moni nor I held Alan in high esteem. He'd messed her around one too many times for that.

'Felafels are Middle Eastern, Alan,' Moni said evenly. 'They're made of chickpeas.'

'Bloody vegetarians,' scoffed Alan, forcing an extra large forkful of lamb into his gob. My stomach turned and I looked away.

That could have been the end of that little incident. But Alex wasn't going to let it pass. 'Alan, what's wrong with vegetarianism?' she demanded. 'And how dare you speak to Moni like that!'

'I didn't say anything to her. I just don't like chickpeas, okay?' Alan whined.

'Well, learn some manners, you rude . . . git,' Alex shot back.

Alan looked aghast. The rest of us sat in stunned silence for a moment, our plates groaning with half-eaten delights. I caught Cam's eye. Thankfully, the awkwardness was relieved by the sound of the doorbell.

Rufus was nearest, so he leapt up to answer it. Cam leaned over to the stereo and turned down the music so we could hear who was there. I could hardly believe my ears. The voice that replied to Rufus's greeting was none other than Gaelle's high-pitched squawk.

I got up from my place to see what the heck was going on and there she was standing at the door under the yellow porch light. Gaelle looked as wild-eyed, powerful and brazen as if she were caught in the eye of a desert storm, not standing on the front doormat of a suburban London terrace on a summer's night. She wore baby-pink cord trousers and a textured cotton jumper knitted in multicoloured pastels. Around her neck was a stunning piece of jewellery I'd never seen on her before. A huge white quartz crystal hung off a silver setting on a chain, dangling in the area where I knew her heart chakra to be. She was carrying a rather large cardboard box, leaning back as it weighed her down. Lightning cracked behind her and I realised we were in for a storm.

When she saw me coming up behind Ru, she smiled broadly, as if glad to deal with someone who spoke her language. Rufus was looking slightly dumbstruck. God only knew what she'd said to him.

'C?' he said weakly, backing off.

'Hi, Gaelle. Rufus, this is Gaelle Carrington-Keane – I'm writing the book about her. Gaelle, this is my good friend, Rufus.'

'I know,' she said, beaming her wide eyes in my direction. 'Now, dear, are you going to ask me in?'

'Yes, of course, sorry, come on in, Gaelle. There are a few people you know here. Lucy and Cam, anyway.'

In a very funny way, I was glad to see her. Her seclusion had made me realise how I'd wasted my chance to get to know this woman. What she was doing here exactly now was anyone's guess, but my curiosity was piqued. Before stepping into our house, she turned and nodded at the two-tone Kombi parked outside the house. My heart sank as Niall got out of the bus. He might not want to be here tonight. He and Alan weren't exactly bosom buddies.

'Hi, Niall,' I stuttered, as he came up the path. Now it was my turn to sound weak. 'What's happening?'

Gaelle strode into the living room and stood in the centre. I could only wonder what Seamus and Eloise were thinking as they gazed at this uninvited guest as if they were watching a horror movie. Gaelle extended the cardboard box to me. Inside it were at least a dozen video tapes, marked with labels: *Gaelle 1*, *Gaelle 2*, *Gaelle 3*, and so on.

'These are my interviews, Cara,' she said. 'I've recorded interviews of everything I want to say for the book.'

What?

'That's it. I'm not going to say any more. You will have all the information you need to write my book as I want it to be written.'

'But . . .' I trailed off. Dammit. I wanted to interview her. I *needed* to interview her. I wanted some answers to some very specific questions. I had signed a contract. I didn't want to be put off with a bunch of pre-recorded VHSs.

'They are all I want to say,' she repeated.

So, Gaelle was throwing me yet another curveball. She liked me leaping and jumping to get them. This time there was nothing I could do.

'The really ironic thing, Gaelle,' I said, 'is that I've never been more curious to hear your side of the story than I am now.' I glanced at Cam. He nodded as if to say 'go on', which was at least supportive, if not terribly helpful.

'Listen, Gaelle, I need more than a few tapes. I have some big questions that need answering . . .'

Niall stood silently at her side like a powder-puff henchman.

'For the book,' I emphasised.

'It's all in there, dear,' she said, sounding reassuring. 'The marriage to Brian, why I left when I did, who I met. All about Thailand, even information about my years in India, as you wanted. All of it. Every last word. Trust me. And it's all you're getting, in any case.'

What could I say?

'I've even re-enacted one of the conversations I had with John Lennon. That should help you to sell your book, shouldn't it?' She sounded sarcastic. I felt as if she somehow knew I'd lost interest in her plans of late. Frankly, there was a big part of me that just wanted to finish it all off and yell, 'Neeeeeeeext . . .'

However.

'Hello, Lucy, dear,' she said over my shoulder. Lu waved mutely. 'And you must be Alan. Hello, there. And hello, Moni.'

'How does she know all our names?' Rufus asked me, as if I was the local Gaelle expert. I had no idea. He should ask Lu. Or Niall. While I'd spent my time trying to avoid her, trying to get a good story, then run off with Cam into the sunset, Lu and Niall had taken the chance to get to know her. I regretted not doing that now too, even as she stood before me and annoyed me. What had I missed out on learning?

'I don't know everyone's name, actually,' Gaelle said. 'I don't know these other three.' She gestured towards Seamus and Eloise and Alex. 'I'm Gaelle,' she said brightly.

'Hi, I'm Alex.'

'Lovely to meet you at last, dear.'

She looked at Seamus next. 'And you are . . . ?'

Seamus stiffly introduced himself and his blonde fiancée in the politest of English manners. Moni followed suit, introducing herself.

'But we've met, haven't we, Gaelle?'

'Yes, Moni,' Gaelle confirmed. 'At the Claire Kellett exhibition at the ICA. Did your screenplay get bought, as I said it would?'

Moni nodded slowly. I knew it. The woman who'd predicted her filmic success had been Gaelle. So, Cam was right. They had met.

'And I've been waiting to meet you, too, Alex. You've come over from the States, haven't you?'

'Dallas, Texas.'

'Wonderful. You mean a lot to Moni.'

Silence.

Gaelle turned to Moni. 'It was the story in your screenplay that touched Alex, you know,' Gaelle said to her. 'Isn't that right, Alex?'

Alex nodded. 'That was part of it.'

'And it's the first lesbian relationship for both of you, isn't it?' Gaelle went on, as if she was making coffee and asking, 'Sugar?'

Alex let out a stifled giggle. Moni's mouth was wide open. I felt a desperate urge to tell Moni that I'd said nothing to Gaelle about her and Alex. I had no clue how she knew about it. Any of it. I looked at Cam. Perhaps he was feeding her information? But he shrugged and looked as hesitant as the rest of us.

'Hello, Cam,' Gaelle said. 'I told you I might be here tonight, didn't I?'

'Yes, Gaelle,' he croaked.

What else hadn't he told me?

Before I had the chance to ask Cam when Gaelle had mentioned gatecrashing our little soirée, she continued speaking.

'So, you are probably wondering why I am here tonight at all.'

Too right, I thought.

'You must all come with me. Tonight is the night.' Everyone froze. Gaelle had a way of commanding attention.

'Do you know what night it is, Cara?' Always picking on me.

'Moni's birthday?' I ventured.

'Try again, dear.'

'I don't know, Gaelle.'

'Anybody?'

Everyone stared silently.

'It's the night of the equinox,' she said. 'Tonight is the night for transformation. You must all come with me.'

I waited to see if anyone else was going to say anything. Cam? Lu? Alan, even. But they all stayed quiet, the cowardly lot of them.

'Where do you want to take us?' Ru enquired finally, as Moni poured him a glass of champagne. The others just listened. It was a bizarre scene to be caught up in.

'Tintagel,' she said. 'We have to go to Tintagel.'

Of course. If Gaelle wanted us to go somewhere at this hour of the night, it would have to be Tintagel, a beach on the north coast of Cornwall. The area was said to be the hang of King Arthur and the Knights of the Round Table back when he and Merlin were doing their do.

'What? Now?' I asked.

'That's why I am here. I am leaving London soon. Leaving England. Cara has the tapes now, and I need you all to come with me.' She toyed with the large white quartz crystal around her neck. 'This is my ascension amulet,' she said as she held the jewellery up to the light. 'It's going to carry me through tonight.'

'Gaelle, do you seriously expect us to come to Tintagel with you tonight?' I protested. 'We're halfway through dinner!'

Suddenly her brave face dropped. She seemed so weak. Like she'd finally run out of steam. I almost felt sorry for her. Why was it so important that we went to Tintagel?

'I'll go,' Lucy piped up.

Really?

'Me, too,' said Moni. 'I want to go. I want to do something. I want to know more.' She had to be joking. I just wanted to go to bed. 'Dinner's gone cold and I don't like the vibes anyway,' she added.

'Why would you go, Moni?' I asked.

'I don't know. I really don't. Maybe because this is the woman who predicted correctly that I would have my screenplay accepted by the agent? I'm going.'

'I'm in, then,' said Rufus.

'Me, too,' said Alex. 'Where's Tintagel?'

Had Gaelle hypnotised them? Why were they agreeing?

'Okay, C?' Cam asked, as if it was obvious he was going, too. I squinted at him, as if to ask what the heck he was up to. He was just taking this on the chin. This whole thing.

'If you're going, I am, too,' Alan said to Lucy, putting his hand on her arm. Niall looked uncomfortable and Gaelle rested her own hand on his shoulder soothingly.

'You know that we all have to go, Niall, dear,' she said. He nodded and I could almost feel his pain. She turned to Alex. 'Tintagel is in Cornwall, dear.'

'Do you mind if we don't go?' Seamus stuttered in his Prince Charles-esque croaky voice. 'Eloise has an early business meeting tomorrow.'

'No, no, you two can go home,' said Gaelle. 'After you've taken a group shot of us all,' she said, pointing to Moni's new Polaroid on the dining-room table.

Thus at about midnight, Gaelle, Moni, Ru, Alex, Alan, Lu, Niall, Cam and I left the relative safety and comfort of our Lavender Sweep living room, piled down the driveway in what had become pouring summer rain and loaded ourselves into the large blue and white Kombi Gaelle had parked out the front. Niall took the wheel and started the drive to Tintagel. In the pit of my stomach, I had a funny feeling something bizarre was about to be revealed.

'Cam,' I hissed as we steered out of Battersea. 'You could have helped me to convince Gaelle to do some more interviews. This is a nightmare, just having tapes.'

'Sorry.'

'*Sorry*? How come you didn't help?'

'Cara, I couldn't. She spoke to me about it last week. She had made up her mind there were to be no more interviews. She was insistent. I tried to talk her out of it, but she wouldn't budge.'

'Why didn't you tell me?'

'She made me promise not to tell anyone that she was going away.'

'Where is she going?'

'Where she said.'

'Where?'

'To the Fifth Dimension, apparently.'

'How ridiculous.'

London was traffic-jam-free at this time of the night, so we sailed through Putney with the windscreen wipers going full pelt. Before we knew it, we were out of London and onto the motorway, going at high speed. Niall was in the front seat alone, bless.

The rest of us gathered in the back, the better to hear Gaelle's speeches. Moni, Rufus and Alex were sitting very close together, leaning against each other. Lu was next to Alan, but her body language wasn't looking good. I stayed warm against Cam the man.

'Tonight is all about Carlos,' Gaelle began quietly. 'Do you remember Carlos, Cara?'

'Who's Carlos?' bellowed Alan.

'Carlos, Keeper of the Infinite Flame?' I ventured. I had no idea who this bloke was, but remembered Gaelle mentioning him.

'He was with us the day I astral-travelled and you fainted, Cara,' Gaelle prompted me. 'The first day you saw me at work. Do you remember?'

I wasn't likely to forget. 'Didn't you also say something about him being your former lover?'

'He *is* my lover,' she said. 'Carlos is in the Fifth Dimension and I am going to join him.'

'Right,' I said.

'Yeah, right,' Alan added. 'If he's in the Fifth, where are we?'

'The Third Dimension; time is in the Fourth.'

'I feel like I've heard this theory before,' Moni said.

'You have, dear,' Gaelle replied. 'You heard this story before you came to Earth, when you were in the higher dimensions of the Fifth. But everyone is learning it now.'

Moni looked blank.

'Look around you, look at Discovery Channel on cable, look at the "X Files", "Charmed" and "Sliders", look at the stories of alien abduction, the mystical content of the Internet, "Deep Space Nine" and "Voyager" . . .'

'What about them?'

'It's not chance that these so-called "entertainments" are being released now. The time is ripe and the powers that be are releasing post-millennium information to us now.'

'Via "Deep Space Nine" and Scully and Mulder?'

'These shows help get humans used to the ideas they will need to work with after ascension. Look at what the Discovery Channel shows about the Great Pyramids of Giza. Their placement on Earth delineates the rising of the Sirius B star, which was so vital to ancient calendars. Look at the information about water erosion, which proves beyond doubt that the Sphinx is many thousands of years older than historians ever believed. They're loath to admit there was a technologically advanced civilisation on Earth long before the Egyptians.'

She turned her attention to me. 'Cara, I have something for you.' From her faux leather handbag she pulled a brown paper bag. 'I was going to save it for later, but you can have it now.'

Inside, there was a chain with a silver locket, which I opened. Inside was what looked like a lock of her permed blonde hair.

'You've been wanting me to have a blood test to prove that I have fourteen-strand walk-in DNA, haven't you?' she asked.

I looked accusingly at Cam. Had he been blabbing?

'Cam has said nothing,' she cautioned me, reading my thoughts as ever. 'You're a journalist. I know how cynical you people are. When I am gone, have the hair tested. You will see that this is so. Put it on now.'

'Oh, give me strength,' Alan burst out. What the heck was he doing here, anyway?

There was a silence as Cam helped me to fasten the locket around my neck.

'So, Gaelle, how are you going to go to the Fifth Dimension?' This was Lu, ever fascinated by Gaelle, life's vagaries notwithstanding.

'You will see, darling.'

She never called me darling. 'So who is Carlos?' I asked, just because I couldn't help myself.

'Whether you like it or not, you are all caught up in my plan, but as observers and participants. Carlos, Keeper of the Infinite Flame, is my only helper. Amanda and Nadine do their Earthly best, but Carlos loves and supports me across time. Time as Albert Einstein knew it. Non-linear. Everywhere. Amanda and Nadine are already in Tintagel waiting for us. Carlos waits for me just a little bit further away, if you know what I mean.' She winked at us girlishly. 'That's why I can leave tonight. Everything is ready. I knew tonight was the night.' She sat back with a big grin on her face.

'Have you been smoking, Gaelle?' I asked. I figured she was either stoned and hallucinating or on the verge of a nervous breakdown.

'Not tonight, dear,' she replied evenly. 'Now you, Cara, are here as a lynchpin. When we get to Tintagel Beach I want you to behave.' Cam nudged me and grinned. He knew I hated it when she gave me a hard time.

She glared at me. 'You are vital to the proceedings, Cara.'

'Mmmm,' I replied, sounding less concerned than I felt. I stared out the window at the fields speeding past. It was still black out there, but at the rate Niall was driving, there was a good chance we'd arrive before sunrise. I rested my head against Cam's shoulder.

'I'm going to sleep,' I announced.

'Cara,' Lu chided.

What? Was sleep now forbidden? Frankly, I didn't fancy hanging around to hear Gaelle's tales. I was worried my sanity might just up and walk away once and for all.

'Cara, listen to me,' Gaelle said. 'You are vital to tonight's proceedings. Because of your lineage. You are Cara Kerr. You are of the line.'

'What line?' I asked, curling my lip, my head lolling in time with the rhythm of the speeding Kombi.

'The Infinite Flame line, Cara. You and I are both from other worlds.'

'Which worlds?' What was she like, this woman?

'You are from the far-off star system Pleiades.'

'So, I am from Pleiades, am I? Does that make me an alien?' I felt Cam chuckling as I lay against him.

'You are. It's written in your initials. Cara Kerr. Your first name and surname. Put them together and they're the same as mine. Carrington-Keane. That's why I had to marry Brian. To buy my walk-in birth name with my body. Our initials are our stamp. You are an alien, although not high born. Carole King is, Calvin Klein, Caron Keating, Carlos, Keeper of the Infinite Flame, anyone with our initials. We are star seeds.'

'Carole King is an alien?' I asked. Talk about feeling the earth move under my feet. I could almost hear a chomping sound as Niall's and Lucy's brains devoured all this lovely New Age info. I looked to Cam for reassurance. He was just grinning. At least he was with me. If you believed Gaelle, he had always been with me. In a way, she might have been right. He was the perfect fit. I squeezed his hand.

'Tonight, our job is to return femininity to this planet, as a force for the new millennium. Remember the total eclipse of the Sun at the end of the last millennium. Mother Moon blocked out Father Sun. Femininity is rising like Venus the Morning Star. Femininity is a gentle power, but it is a power nonetheless. Tonight, you will find your power, Cara Kerr.'

As if on cue, Niall inserted a tape into the van's stereo. 'Tapestry', by that famous alien Carole King, poured through the Kombi. I didn't like the sound of any of this at all – apart from Carole, of course, who always sounded heavenly. Gaelle was on Mark 10 Warp Speed Fucking Full-On Turn-Up-The-Volume Freak mode. It sounded scary and I wanted nothing more to do with it, now that I had my interviews on tape. Cam slid his arm around me and I closed my eyes. I couldn't take any more in. I couldn't get out of the bus and I wasn't going to make an idiot of myself by asking, but I could sleep and ignore her. That's what I would do.

'There are ten million billion planets with humanoids on them. On this planet, our initials give away our secrets. John Lennon is from Gomeron in the Sixth Dimension, as are, of course, Jessica

Lange, Juliette Lewis and Jerry Lewis. Marilyn Monroe, Marcel Marceau and Mimi Macpherson are all from Cazelle. You get the picture. Some humans are from Sirius, some from Orion.'

She turned to the others.

'Look up at the stars one night and see which constellation most appeals to you, and you'll be seeing where you came from. But this isn't the point. Cara, you were sent to Paris with Cam for a reason. You had to do it. Just as Lucy had to leave Alan and Moni had to meet Alex. Come on, you must be able to see it. You wanted to be with Cam.'

I blinked at the lights of an oncoming car, momentarily blinded, as Alan mumbled something about rough patches.

'You chose Paris, Cara. You wanted it to happen. That was one part of your destiny that you weren't scared of. You wanted to open your heart chakra. I like to think of Paris as the heart chakra of the world, so where better to do it?'

She laughed again. Her mood seemed to have improved considerably now that she had a captive and Tintagel-bound audience. 'There is less fear there with you now, Cara,' she went on. 'But you chose your path and your connection with Cam. I facilitated.'

I shut my eyes tighter. I didn't want to know. Cam Street. Cameron Street. Go to Cameron Street. It was all coming back to me. Omigod. Cameron Street. When I had that weird dream after my session with Shanti Deva. The me on the ceiling said to the me in the bed, 'Go to Cameron Street.' Finally, it dawned on me. That was where I knew Cam's name from. Cameron Street wasn't a place, it was a person. I felt queasy. Perhaps it was me, not Gaelle, who was crazy.

'It's about time for you to progress, Cara,' she continued. 'Stop with the drinking and drugging. And before you say it, yes, I smoke, but I use it as a vehicle to mental flight.'

I groaned and refused to look at her.

'Gaelle, I think Cara's had enough for one night,' Moni said.

'What Cara is experiencing is resistance, pure and simple,' Gaelle replied. Next she'd be telling me resistance was futile. 'It's resistance and, of course, fear. She's angry with me, because she knows there's more than just a grain of truth in what I'm saying. She must admit there's more to life than meets the eye. Then my plan is complete.' Her high-pitched voice rang in my ears.

'Gaelle, look, may I ask you some questions?' Moni interjected before Gaelle could get going again.

'Yes, dear, ask away,' Gaelle replied patiently, mercifully shifting her gaze. 'That's what I'm here for. To answer your questions.'

'Okay, great. So, to start with, why were you at the ICA the night you came up and spoke to me, and how did you know that my screenplay would be accepted?'

'Hmmm. Let me see. I was at the ICA because I wanted to see the exhibition by Claire Kellett, one of my former students, another of the line. And I stayed because I knew you'd be there and I wanted to show you my abilities. If I hadn't seen you there and made the prediction about your screenplay, would you be here tonight?'

'I don't know,' Moni admitted.

'I saw your name on the guest list and decided the time was right to connect with you.'

Moni took this pronouncement in her stride like the slick professional chick she was. 'Okay. And so how did you know about the fact that we'd all been drinking at the Lord Alvery that very first night before Cara met you?'

'I focussed on your energies in my meditation. I told Cara that.'

'And?'

'And what?'

'Come on, Gaelle. There was more to it.'

'You're right. I confess I watched you through the living-room window. I listened in.'

'You sneaked outside our house?'

'No. I was so very sure that you, Lucy and Cara were the girls I had been searching for. But as a final check, before Cara and I met, I meditated and went to your home, astrally, to see you. I flew there in spirit. I felt your energies, then left. I hope you can forgive me for prying. I did have to be sure.'

She flew to our home astrally?

'You flew to our home astrally?' Moni repeated.

'Yes, dear.'

Rufus smirked.

'Right. Okay,' said Moni. 'Well, we'll let that pass. Shall we let that pass? Rufus? Yes? Okay. No problem.' She shook her head despairingly, her eyes glinting with amusement and fascination. 'So, answer me this if you will, Gaelle. Why us? Why not use some other people for whatever it is you're doing or planning? There are plenty of people out there with the initials CK. Why did you choose three Australian girls in London and not, say, three Andalusians in Auckland?'

'You are the ones. I knew it when I saw Cara's article in the *Sunday News*. But I am choosing you as much as you all chose me, before we incarnated. You three are the favoured ones, not just because of Cara, but because of your combined power and spirit which has meshed over lifetimes. I saw Cara's Shanti Deva article, and it resonated. When I saw the chemistry between Cara and Cam, I knew I was right. He is also destined to join us.'

What about Alan? I wondered. He and Lu were still showing bad body language behind me.

'We are the favoured ones for what?'

'To help me ascend. When Cara fainted in my work room that day, I knew it once and for all. She fainted through resistance, terror and recognition. That confirmed it for me, obviously.'

Obviously.

'Cara has been avoiding me for eons. Lifetimes. She is so afraid of knowing the truth about life beyond the Third Dimension. Moni, you're not scared, are you?'

'Not really.'

Gaelle brushed her hair out of her eyes with a world-weary sigh. 'You are more realised than you know, Monique. You just need to look into yourself a bit. But you will. And Lucy is semi-realised, although her head can be turned too easily. However, she's getting stronger. No. It's Cara who's still dragging her feet, and her spirit. We are not human beings, we are beings having a human experience. We have to go inside, to knock on our hearts and to see who answers.' While Niall drove stoically into the night, I played dead. I wanted to pummel Gaelle as she kept rambling on and on.

'We all have variously been teachers and students to each other over lifetimes. That's why we are at different stages of loving and trusting ourselves and each other. That's why some of us are more self-realised than others. It depends on how often we have allowed ourselves to take on the role of student.'

My realised and semi-realised flatmates gawked and lapped it all up, while I feigned sleep. I didn't want to know what she said I was supposed to be afraid of. I didn't want to be going to Tintagel, either. I wanted out of there. I wanted something comforting like tea, crumpets, raspberry jam, my mates, Cam and the Sunday papers, not midnight flits to moonlit beaches for interdimensional high jinks.

'If you can't accept what I tell you about the Fifth Dimension, believe in love,' she announced. 'Love is fleeting yet eternal. It's about connection. We are all connected to all life everywhere. Love is the Fifth Dimension. God, Buddha, Christ, the universe, call it what you want. It's about being as one with yourself, then letting that oneness extend to others. So, when we love we neither suffocate nor abandon, support nor drop. Lovers, true lovers, are timeless.'

I was going off the whole idea of Cam and me and past lives. Enjoying his company was one thing, but eternity was a scarily long time. What if I wanted to go and live in Australia and he didn't?

Gaelle made it sound as if she had planned everything that had happened in the past few months and there was a rather large control freak inside of me that refused to believe such stories. Yeah, right, I am from Pleiades and Carole King is an alien. Ha bloody ha.

The truth, though, was that I was terrified. Because deep down inside me, in that part of the unconscious where dreams come from, a little voice was reminding me: 'Think of the meditations, think of the strange dreams, think of the bigger picture.' Maybe the voice was right.

20

coming back to shore

As we drove into the small town of Tintagel with its winding, stony streets, I longed for a joint to see me through this mayhem and madness. Gaelle seemed quiet and calm now. She was 100 per cent right when she said I was fearful tonight, scared to examine what she'd told me about love. I'd been terrified of her since the first time we met. Since she told me I should drink and smoke less. Since everything.

I whispered to Cam, 'Just say that Gaelle does know what she's talking about. I mean, just say it's true that we're all spirits and connected and stuff . . .'

'Mmm?'

'If that's the case, what does it all mean?'

'Search me.' He laughed in a manner I'd have sworn was just a bit nervy. 'I guess we'll find out soon enough.'

'Trust me,' Gaelle said, as though she could hear what we were saying. 'Surrender and trust me.'

Right-o.

We drove through the town centre and out the other side. At Gaelle's direction, Niall took the first exit towards the coast. It was still as black as night as our little white bus turned off the bitumen, onto a bumpy lane. There were flat fields on either side of us and I could see the coast in the distance, under a full, luminous moon. Lucy was now fast asleep, curled against the window rather than into Alan. Moni and Alex were both resting their heads on Rufus's broad chest. It seemed their arrangement was quite cosy. Cam had his eyes closed. Gaelle, of course, was staring directly at me.

'What are you thinking, Cara?' she asked.

'What are *you* thinking, Gaelle?'

She pursed her lips as if considering whether or not she would deign to answer me. 'I'm thinking that perhaps you will rise to the occasion.'

'And do what?'

'You'll see.'

'Gaelle, don't you think now would be a really good time to tell me what is going on? Okay, let me admit it. You have got to me, you've touched me somehow, or moved me, and you've definitely shocked me. I'm even half inclined to think that you have, to some extent, in some really weird way, controlled me. I don't know. But I believe what you're saying.'

'At last, dear.'

'Well, I believe some of what you're saying. The Miracle Meditation works, absolutely, and . . . and I do believe in love.' Pause. Whirl of brain wheels almost audible. 'And I agree that our thoughts create our reality and affect what happens to us. I mean, even if you just look at it from the point of view of cognitive therapy and behavioural science, there's evidence that our belief systems shape our life experiences.'

'Cara, you're so left-brained,' she sighed. 'The right brain is for creativity, the left for logic. You work almost entirely from the left. The meditation will integrate both sides for you, but you must keep up the practice. However, you're right, too. Ask any psychiatrist. What you believe to be true is true, for you.'

I'll ask your bloody psychiatrist, I wanted to tell her. 'But, Gaelle, I just can't come to grips with the whole pyramids and eternal flames and dimensions and frequencies New Age thing. It just doesn't do it for me.'

'That's all right, dear,' she said. 'I realised the way to you was through meditation. You know, God, or the universe, or source, or whatever you want to call it, or him, or her, is just like a big chunk of mouldy cheese. His pungent smell drifts down the corridors of time and culture and eventually we all get a whiff. Some people smell him via confession and eating fish on Fridays, some by praying to Allah, some by interdimensional travels. It really doesn't matter, as long as you believe. In fact, go further. Look into your heart and know. Know. Believing assumes polarity between belief and disbelief. Knowing just is.'

Know what? I wanted to ask. Know that she was half an alien? Know she was right when she said we were all connected at a deep soul level? Know what? That 'life's an adventure and only love is real'?

'Know we are all one, that life's an adventure and only love is real,' she continued, not surprising me one iota by apparently reading my mind. Perhaps that was the breakthrough moment. If I truly believed (knew) she could read my mind, I'd believe (know) anything.

'We're all connected, Cara. That's how we can read minds, gauge feelings. But it's a matter of listening to your inner voice.' Suddenly, she looked away and out the window into the night. 'Niall, slow down and turn left into this paddock. Stop while I open the gate.' A shiver ran up my spine. We drove into the next field, up to the edge of the coastline, as far as we could.

The moon was so bright and high, it lit our way as we piled out of the van onto a steep gravel path which led us down to the coastline. There was a magnificent beach, now bathed in silver. Despite my mood, I was secretly delighted to finally see this part of the country. Up until that exact moment, no-one would have ever convinced me that England had a coastline to give Australia a run for its money, but this beach was crescent-shaped, set under awesome cliffs and surrounded by caves, nooks and crannies. Divine.

Cam gave my shoulder a squeeze as we began walking. Despite the brightness of the moonlight, I trod carefully, as if life was precarious, both physically and metaphorically. Gaelle led the way, Niall was next, followed by Cam, me, Lucy, Ru, Moni, Alex and Alan. No-one spoke, so all we could hear was the crunch underfoot as we approached the sand, then the sound of crashing waves.

Gaelle turned to Niall. 'Are you okay, dear?' she asked. 'I know this isn't going to be easy.' He nodded in the respectful manner he always had around her. I felt more shivers going through me as the hair on the very top of my head stood on end. The very top of my head, I had learned in the past few months, was where you find the crown chakra – which was about direction. Of course, I had no idea of which direction I was heading in as we descended. Other than south.

Gaelle took us onto the sands, exposing us to a rather unexpected sight. In the middle of the beach was a long table, covered with a white tablecloth billowing in the light breeze. It was surrounded by chairs and decorated with heavy gold candles, silver goblets and several carafes of what looked like red wine. At one end of the table were Nadine and Amanda, standing to attention in their usual white attire.

'Everyone, meet Nadine and Amanda,' announced Gaelle.

The girls waved meekly.

'Please, everyone, gather round and sit down,' Gaelle called.

As we took our places, Amanda and Nadine started to pour each of us a glass of wine.

'Drink,' Gaelle commanded.

The red liquid in the goblets tasted suspiciously like normal red wine and we all sipped it, except for Alan.

'I'm not drinking anything she offers me,' he said rudely, emptying his glass so that it left a red gash in the sand.

Lu looked at Gaelle, transfixed, Moni was dumbstruck, Alex alternated between terrified and giggly. Aside from this one little outburst, Alan was silent and had been since he got into the van. So that was all it took to shut him up – a meeting with a mystic guru. Cam had had the sense to put on a pair of cut-off black woollen gloves before we left home. Clever him – it was pre-dawn chilly. He peeled them off now and gave them to me. I put them on and thanked him. He took my hand. I couldn't speak.

Gaelle sat at the head of the table. 'So, back to my life story,' she said. She had no trouble getting my attention. After months of trying to see through her, around her, above and behind her, I wanted to hear what she had to say. It was all coming together.

'As you know, I was born into what our Hindu friends would call a high caste. The Eastern Suburbs of Sydney, where no sky is ever too blue, no crystal too fine, no laugh too social. They credit the New York social X-rays, but we invented the adage that "there is no such thing as too thin and too rich". And yes, I turned away from it. Everyone thought I was mad. Spitting out all those silver spoons. But when you've opened the Pandora's box of life beyond the Third Dimension, when you have glimpsed the Light and heard the celestial choirs, when you've spoken with your Guides and had your prayers answered, there is no going back. This dense Earth plane can only provide so much, and we must evolve.'

I felt like she was saying something I'd heard before, but I couldn't say where.

'So, as Cara knows, I travelled, lived, did the India and Thailand thing, and even took on a few students along the way. Now, I need to leave. Before I can, though, there is one last job I must perform.

I must help you three girls and some of you men. You represent my permission to leave this woman's body which I have inhabited over half this lifetime, walking in and out, filled with the power of Shiva, shooting arrows to show I care. Shiva's power was in the kindness on the painful tip of an arrow, sent flying, wounding and loving all at once, pressing and pushing people into progression. And I think I have done that with you three girls, have I not? Have I touched you? If so, I am karmically free. Have any of you learned anything? Wait before you answer.'

Lucy looked like she was about to cry.

Gaelle turned to face her. 'Lucy?'

'Yes, Gaelle?'

'Lucy, show me what you have learned. All of you, come walk with me.' She turned from the table and started to walk up the beach, towards a giant flat-faced rock which stood close to a cliff-face with an opening that looked like it could be a cave. I wondered how much of this Gaelle had planned, not to mention what she was going to do next.

With the rock behind her, she stood on the sand, her feet wide apart, looking as ever as if it took a wide stance to bear her weight. It was still so hard to reconcile her with the Gaelle Carrington-Keane I'd read about in the archives. Her face was unlined and glowing and clear most of the time and there was a brightness in her eyes, but when the light caught her at the wrong angle, as it did more and more often these days, she looked as tired as if she had indeed lived for thousands of years. Didn't she say I'd been avoiding her for eons? Well, there you have it. The old girl was exhausted. And it was my fault. The white quartz crystal amulet around her neck glinted in the moonlight. I touched my hand to the locket she'd given me.

'All I want is for you to know,' she said to us as a group. Then she went quiet and spent a bit of time positioning us in a circle, just as she wanted us.

'So. Cara. We will start with you.'

'Yes, Gaelle,' I said. I wanted to laugh.

'So, Cara. Tell me. Do you believe in past lives now?' she asked, as she set me in my position at three o'clock in the circle. I looked across at Cam and instantly felt it. It was too weird. I did feel a connection, it was true. There was a feeling that I knew him almost better than I could have done only a few months after our first meeting. I liked him in a way I had never experienced with my previous lovers. He was a man, not an object. He was real. There was an empathy and understanding that surprised me, and maybe him. Perhaps we were connected. And it wasn't just the dreams I'd had about him, either. It was our conversations, and the stuff we did.

'Cara, all I want is for you to know,' Gaelle said. 'Know that past lives are real, that meditation works and that everything is possible. We truly create it.'

The waves were crashing nearer my ankles. Nadine and Amanda seemed to be staring at me as if they were willing me to say something. Like what?

I thought about the weird ideas that had plagued me for the past few months. I thought about the strange way things were falling into place with Cam after years of rotten relationships. I thought about how Lu had been touched and helped by Gaelle. How the meditation techniques Gaelle had taught me had calmed me down. So, I relented for the second time.

'Okay, Gaelle,' I heard myself saying, 'I do know that there is more to this world than meets the eye. I believe we are mirrors for each other. Maybe we are all connected karmically, from past lives. No, I can't definitely buy that dolphins are aliens, not yet, anyway, and I'm not 100 per cent sure that rubbing my forehead stimulates my third eye, although I am open to the possibility that that's true. But, yes, meditation calms me down and sometimes when I look at my friends . . . or Cam . . . and when we do a Kundalini meditation . . . well, there's a funny thing that happens. A connection. And I do feel like I'm a part of something bigger. So, yes, perhaps we are all one. Part of a bigger spirit. I accept all that. I know it. Is that what you want to hear? I do accept it. Okay?'

'Okay.' She paused, but not for long. 'And?'

'And?'

'Anything else?'

'Um.'

'Love?'

Oh. That old chestnut. 'Okay. And I definitely think that, at the very least, we all should love.'

'Yes?'

'Life's an adventure and only love is real?' I ventured. Suddenly it seemed so obvious. Cam had shown me. Or had I shown myself, through Cam? My love for him had opened a new door in my heart. I felt like I was breathing the same air as everyone else, all of a sudden. 'Yes,' I said. 'The hippies were right. Love is good. Love works. I love love.'

'I see.'

'I am a Love-ist. All right, Gaelle?' I felt like doing a little jig down the beach, just to prove it. It was true. I felt lighter and brighter. I wanted to hug Cam for taking my hand and leading me to love. This was what it was all about. For me, at least.

'Good,' Gaelle said, probably reading my thoughts. 'And . . . do you love me, Cara?' Gaelle asked, her blonde hair curling in the morning dew. 'Do you love me?'

Hmmm. Very good question. I thought about it. I let the query run through my veins. I felt it.

'Of course,' I answered. It was so hard to 'live in the heart', as Gaelle, Lucy and their cronies constantly recommended. But I ploughed on. 'In a funny way, somewhere deep down, even though you drive me nuts, I do love you, Gaelle. Even if I never see you again after the book is written, I'll always remember you and love you. Well, I'll remember what went on between us when we weren't stoned, anyway.'

'Quite,' she said primly. 'But the important memories remain and the rest you have on tape.'

'True,' I agreed.

'And I will always love you.'

I felt so good. I wanted to relive the past few months, just to do it all better. I wanted to kiss everyone there, even Alan, and share my insights. I wanted to know more about Gaelle and how she had manifested all of this. But now it might be too late.

'Gaelle, are you planning on leaving now?' I asked. 'Is this really a farewell?' She had said she wanted to depart. 'Where are you going?'

'Cara, just as you love, I do, too. You have discovered what you needed to. Now, hug me,' she said. So, I hugged her. It felt incredible, being pressed into her large maternal bosom, her firm yet flabby body. I felt a most amazing rush of energy, and guess what? I really did feel I loved her. She was a dear old chook and, as far as I was concerned, I had no more proof that what she said wasn't true than I had that it was. That was enough for me.

'You helped me,' I admitted. 'Gaelle, you really helped me a lot.'

'I know. Evolve into the light. Write my book. And think good thoughts.' These were the last words she ever said directly to me. She let go and moved to her right. To Lucy.

She cleared her throat. 'Lucy. In a moment, I am going to ask you to make a decision. I want you to think carefully about it. It's a matter that you must resolve, and resolve now before anyone gets any more hurt.'

Lu looked nervous. I think she knew what was coming.

'Your decision will show your wisdom. Do you want to know what you have to do?'

Lucy nodded.

'You must choose between Alan and Niall. Now. Tonight. This has gone on long enough. Okay?'

'Maybe,' Lu whispered.

'No maybe. Why not, Lucy? Why not put Niall out of his misery, if you really want to be with Alan? Or if you don't want to be with Alan, but you want to be with Niall, let them know.'

Lu stared.

'Or perhaps you want neither?' Gaelle pressed.

Lu shifted her weight from one leg to the other, rubbed her arms up and down nervously, bit her lip. The rest of us stood with eyes and ears on stalks. Gaelle was perhaps a little out of order with this one, but Lucy seemed to be taking it well. How Niall and Alan felt was anyone's guess. Until . . .

'Now, just steady on for one bloody minute, you old bag.' It was Alan, of course. 'You bring us down here into the middle of bloody nowhere and stand us on this freezing beach and offer us God-knows-what to drink and then you put Lucy on the spot like that to make such a momentous decision? Imagine if she made the wrong choice just because you pressured her?'

'The third,' said Lucy once he'd finished. 'I want the third option.'

Go, grrrl.

'What?' Alan asked her brusquely, as if she were an annoying gnat getting in the way of his tirade.

'I want the third option, Gaelle. Sorry, Niall.' She was doing it. She was making her choice.

'And the third option is . . . ?' Gaelle asked.

'Neither.'

Yes.

'Correct,' said Gaelle. 'I said love was just around the corner for you, didn't I? I meant self-love, the greatest there is.'

'Mmmm. I understand, and I want to be with me for a while,' Lu said, stronger now. 'Sorry, Alan.' She turned to Niall. 'I am really sorry, Niall. You're a wonderful human being. I just want me by myself for a bit.'

'You're bloody joking, aren't you?' said Alan.

We all looked from Niall to Alan, like we were watching a

real-life break-up on 'Ricki Lake'. Niall stepped across the sand to Lu. His chiselled boyish face looked beautiful in the moonlight.

'It's okay, Lu,' Niall said, not touching her, but staring intently. 'I knew you were going to say that. Gaelle told me. You need some time alone.'

'Thank you.' She turned back to Alan, who jumped away.

'Don't touch me,' he snapped. 'I don't want to know. What's next, Mrs Carrington-bloody-Keane?' His voice resonated with anger. Apart from anything else, he was stuck with us, unless he fancied hitching a ride back to London. I felt so proud of Lu. That was a toughie. Niall seemed okay. He was pretty wise, under that hippy dippy exterior. Probably the wisest of the lot of us, give or take a few slightly dubious beliefs about topazes and quartz.

So, that was me and Lucy dealt with. Now Moni. What did Gaelle have in store for her? But before Gaelle turned to Moni, she addressed Alan.

'I give you one sharp Shiva arrow,' she said, her eyes bright. 'Alan, grow. Open, love and grow. Your life is on a collision course with disaster, but your heart is in there somewhere. Don't buy off the woman you made pregnant. Find unconditional love and you will find joy.'

Alan's response was a snort, signalling his disgust.

Finally, she addressed Moni. 'As you know, I needed all three of you together to make this journey. Your combined power makes you very strong. Moni, you know that you have learned as much, or even more, about life in the past few weeks as Lucy and Cara, don't you?'

'Um . . .'

'You have sold your screenplay, you have examined your sexuality and you have come to realise that true love is more important, and a lot more fun, than work.'

'I guess so.'

'And you felt good about your decision to back out of that unethical swingers story, didn't you?'

'How did you know about that?'

'I knew it was one of your lessons. That's all. Now, I need you to do something for me, Moni. I need your energy tonight to meld with the energy of Lucy and Cara. We've all been together before, and will be together again. I just needed to teach you, in return for the service you are doing for me and Carlos here tonight.' She paused and looked at Alan. 'Alan, if you want to, you can step out of the circle now. Or you can stay. As you wish. But make your choice now.'

Alan's face went white and his upper lip looked tremulous, as great, glistening tears formed in his eyes. He said nothing for a moment, then stood back from the circle and plonked himself and his fancy Harrods chinos on the sand. 'I'm staying to watch,' he said, like a petulant child refusing to go to his room.

'Fine,' said Gaelle, most uncharacteristically. She really didn't seem to care about him. Wasn't that my job? 'Now. Alex and Rufus?'

'Yes?' they said in unison.

'I want to thank you for the part you played in helping Moni find herself.'

They smiled and Rufus said, 'You're welcome,' with the kind of cordial tone he usually reserved for polite drinks parties with his parents' friends.

'Now would everyone please join hands.' Gaelle placed her own wrinkly hands against her cheeks, as if worried, before continuing. 'As I have already started to explain, the reason I met you was perhaps nothing to do with whatever you might have imagined. I met you because I wanted to help, and because I wanted Cara to tell my story and because, as a threesome, you girls provide me with the full energy of the female spirit. The feminine, the masculine and the middle ground. Together, you are whole.'

Gordy lordy. Cam's theory was right. Did he have inside info?

'Plus, and this might surprise you,' she went on, 'I met you all to meet Niall. Indeed, you, Cara, led me to Lucy, who in turn led me to Niall. Finding Cam was your karma. I needed you to be together, it's true, so that your energies were running freely as they can only do when your heart is open. You've been together through time and now your heart is open again.' This sounded true enough, whether I liked it or not. And I liked it more and more, these days, despite my recent equivocations. 'But,' she continued, 'I also needed Niall. I very much require him tonight. To enable me to leave. He completes the equation. Niall is a child of the Fifth Dimension.'

We all looked at Niall's handsome and lovable face set beneath spiky blond hair. Perhaps he did have a look of wisdom, if you squinted.

'Niall, you know your powers and your strengths will go on after I have left. You have the Fifth Dimension on your side and from today, all that you touch will turn to gold. Figuratively speaking, of course.'

Of course.

'You have been a great student, Niall, and you will make an even greater teacher. People will flock to you. You can help them set themselves free with your heart. You are clear and on your own path.'

I watched Lu watch Niall. What was she thinking?

'Niall, please take your place in the centre of the circle,' Gaelle instructed. 'Everyone else, keep holding hands.' So, like school-children playing ring-a-roses, Ru, Moni, Alex, Lu, Cam and I held hands while Niall stood in the centre like piggy in the middle. Gaelle stood outside the circle while Amanda and Nadine kept watch. She started speaking very loudly. 'Niall's masculine power will draw strength from the energy of the power of your feminine trio and help me ascend to the Fifth Dimension, two dimensions closer to God. You are all going there one day. The Fifth is just like Earth, but more beautiful, more serene, more of all the good things Mother Earth already is. The difference is that your heart is utterly open, your eyes see only beauty. But, before you pass into the Fifth Dimension, you must go through the Fourth, where everything must be love. Do you know why?'

No-one did, so no-one spoke.

'Because everything in the Fourth Dimension is instantly manifested by your thoughts. Here on Earth there is a time delay. You might think about wanting an orange in the morning, and not get one until the evening. In the Fourth Dimension, your every thought is instantly manifested. So, there can be no fear, only love, or we would be eliminated by our own thoughts. Try having a fear of spiders in the Fourth Dimension and you'll instantly be covered in the most venomous hairy-legged uglies on any planet.

'Once you pass through the Fourth, though – where time resides – and get to the Fifth, your struggle is over. There's no polarity in the Fifth, so where there is love there can be no fear. So unless you love spiders, there are no spiders.'

She paused to clear her throat while we considered her arachnid analogy.

'Real love can make miracles. Carlos has done his work. I leave the Earth tonight to be with him. I've managed to get you all here. Now it is only Carlos. I am going into the cave. Hold each other's hands, please. Niall, when you see the blue light pass around and around, come into the cave with me.'

She pulled a pocket torch from her coat and lit the way as she moved towards the wall of rock behind her. So, it was a cave, after all. All the better to do her spook business in. She stood outside the cave and called to Niall to catch the torch. As I watched its arc, I caught sight of the last remaining overnight stars above our heads against the ancient Cornish sky.

'Everyone, close your eyes and hum "Om",' Niall instructed us. Since when was he a mantra-giving mystic guru? Because there was no reason why not, we all closed our eyes and said, 'Om.' It was far too late to argue. As we started to hum, Alan jumped up from the sand and tried to pull Moni and Lucy's hands apart.

'I want to join in,' he blustered. 'Let me into the circle.'

Niall stepped back. For one moment, I thought he was going to tell Al to get lost, but the lovey dovey atmosphere of the dawn must have heightened his good nature.

'Okay, Alan, join the circle,' Niall said magnanimously. So, Alan joined us. I almost felt for him. I knew how it felt to miss out. I'd missed out on truckloads of Gaelle, and her teachings, because I didn't want to hear what she had to say. I hoped I remembered some of it. Things would be different from now on. I would convince her to do some interviews with me, once all this was over. The clippings and tapes weren't enough. I took it she wasn't planning on ascending to the Fifth Dimension right here and now, and that this was some kind of serious preparatory initiation. Surely.

Cam tugged at my hand and we exchanged glances. I felt no self-consciousness at all. Just connected, like Gaelle the Guru said.

As I looked away from Cam, the strangest thing caught my eye. A weird phosphorescent blue light was whizzing around the circle. Just a very faint light. I watched the buzzing, comet-shaped light going around us, through our arms, around our hands and around and around the circle at . . . the speed of light, apparently. I looked at Lu across from me and could see that she saw it, too. We all could.

'What's happening?' Alan yelled.

'Be careful,' Niall replied. But Alan ignored him and leant over Lucy to try to touch this weird blue light. It touched his hand and he was thrown back onto the sands with a scream, leaping as if he'd been electrocuted. Apparently, the vibes of the blue light didn't match Al's energies. He lay slumped on the sand, moaning.

Then Gaelle screamed from the cave.

'Caaaaaaaaaaaaarrrrrrrrrrrrrrrrrrllllllllllllllllllllooooooooooooos.' That'd be Carlos, Keeper of the Infinite Flame. Fifth Dimensional lover boy.

Niall broke away from the circle, flicked on the pocket torch and ran to the cave yelling, 'Gaaaaaaeeeeeeeeeeeeellllllllle', as if his soul were crying. We watched as he disappeared inside. The blue light that had been in our circle rose above our heads, exploded like methane and disappeared high into the sky with a whooshing sound. We waited in the silence. And then something happened. With a loud bang, there was a huge flash of blue and white light from the cave, followed by two screams. Niall's and Gaelle's.

Cam broke away from the circle to run and see what was happening, and the rest of us followed. Inside, the cave was lit up by the torch on the floor, shining at Niall who lay slumped on the dirty ground, his face and hair lightly singed. Burned. He looked like he'd just had a mini-keg of dynamite blow up in his face. His spiky blond hair was now brown on the ends and he was lying as if he was dead. But he wasn't. Alan picked up the torch and shone it directly into Niall's eyes. Niall raised his head to look at us.

'Where did she go?' He sounded groggy as he squinted from the torch's flare into the murkiness of the cave.

Damned good question. Where was Gaelle? There was nothing in the cave except Niall, flat on his back and looking mightily confused. Where was she? How had she got out? Then I noticed. The only other item in there was a large round crystal amulet. The one Gaelle had been wearing around her neck tonight. It was still rocking back and forth on its own silver setting, as if it had been thrown to the cave's floor with tremendous force.

There were no two ways about it. Gaelle, it seemed, was gone. Outta here and back to the Fifth Dimension, I guess. Two dimensions closer to God. Either that or she'd pulled off a fantastic party trick with a stick of gelignite and a trick door.

I couldn't help myself. Even after everything, I had to check once more. I grabbed the torch from Alan to investigate the cave walls. I felt ridiculous, but I had to make sure there was no escape hatch. My hand felt along the ridges and crannies. I knocked, pushed and pulled at the rock, but there were no secret exits to be found. Just a whole lot of cold, mouldy lichen.

I walked sheepishly back to Cam, who was shaking his head and grinning at me. He held out his arms to me, as though he'd forgive me anything right now. Gaelle had often said anything was possible. It seemed she was right. She'd vaporised. Dematerialised. Ascended to the Fifth Dimension. Apparently. Cam took my hand and squeezed it.

Ru hugged Moni and Alex to him. The silence of the early dawn was broken only by choking sobs and sniffs, as Lucy started to weep.

epilogue

Gaelle was . . . at the end of the day . . . she was . . . God, what was she?

I'd been staring blankly at my laptop screen for so long, the scrolling screensaver had come on. *Life's an adventure . . . Only love is real . . . Think good thoughts . . .* The silver words flashed across the blue background. They were some of Gaelle's last words to me.

I'm sitting overlooking Byron Bay. It's an azure blue-skied and sunny day, the air is fresh and salty with just enough breeze to keep me from overheating as I write. The white-capped waves are rolling in relentlessly, the sand looks shiny and hot and the dolphins are out there cruising — perhaps communing with aliens, for all I know.

Right now, Lucy's down on the beach chatting to a Russian back-packer called Jascha. I can see her from here, making wild arm movements on the shoreline as she tries to teach him the principles of body surfing. Though we've raked over and over the events of the past few months, she's never spoken one word of regret about the decisions she made back at Tintagel regarding Niall and Alan. I'd even go so far as to say she's happy. She's certainly glowing. It's amazing what a bit of sun can do for a girl's general vibe and complexion. Down with winters, I say.

We got a letter from Moni three days ago. She's living it up in LA with Alex for a few weeks, while she and her agent see people about *Time of Gain*. They've already had one firm offer, but Moni's agent is convinced they can do better, so they're holding out and doing more rounds. Moni's nervous about not saying yes to the first person to take the bait, but her agent's convinced her to hold out for that top-end five-figure sum so she can retire gracefully to London to work on her next masterpiece.

Alex will go home to Texas after the LA trip, and Moni will go back to Rufus and Mouser. Ru's back working hard on the markets, saving up for the house he and Moni are 'maybe going to buy together if things keep going as well as they have been', according to Moni.

Ru e-mailed us to say he had a beer with Niall the other night in Battersea — well, Ru had a beer and Niall drank OJ. It seems things have changed a lot for burgeoning guru Niall. He's now totally recovered from his cave explosion adventure and not only working on the idea of opening a healing centre, but actually in the process thereof. He found premises in Islington and is holding Tuesday and Wednesday night classes in what he calls Interdimensional Consciousness Healing. He's already built a following of Niallists who claim he's an extraordinary teacher and healer. According to Rufus, people are claiming to have been cured of minor ailments, from warts to headaches to backache, with his touch and techniques. He's even had some success with a woman with a club foot, so I'm told.

Niall's coming out here to see Lucy next month. She hasn't said too much about it, but I know she's been e-mailing him and they talk on the phone a lot. It seems Niall emerged from the whole Eaton Square experience sparkling. In his wildest dreams, he says, his plan is to start a world-wide chain of healing centres – supported by donations only from those who could afford to pay, of course. Apparently Niall devotes five minutes every morning to sending Lucy 'lots of love and healing vibes from across the planet' and is wetting himself about his trip Down Under.

Alan, meanwhile, wrote to Lu to say he'd quit his job in London and bought a home in the Cotswolds. Don't know quite what possessed him, but he's now working as a mortgage broker to the local Sloanes, and swears he's a changed man. Not changed enough for Lu, although she wishes him well.

As for Gaelle, she had indeed disappeared, apparently for good, that night in the cave. She said she was going to the Fifth Dimension and maybe she was telling the truth. I think of her at odd times – at sunset, when Lu, Cam and I roll one of our famous medicinal scoobs as a rare treat and go barefoot down to the sand to watch the sky turn pink and orange. Or when Cam and I do a Kundalini meditation together. Or when we're just sitting down for a meal and the local radio station plays a Carole King song. At the right moment, a good Carole track, like 'Way Over Yonder', can bring tears to my eyes.

I think of Gaelle a lot. Sometimes I even dream about her, when she's back as strong and powerful as ever, usually to harass me, if I haven't been doing my Miracle Meditations regularly enough for her liking, or if I haven't been eating properly, or if I've been smoking too much spliff. I usually take her advice. I figure it comes either from her in the Fifth Dimension, or from my deepest sub-conscious, which must know what's best for me. I'd probably freak if she turned up on our front porch tomorrow, but I do miss her.

Cam still swears she was for real. And I almost do, too. I mean, I had a physical manifestation of her beliefs. The woman disappeared into thin air, dammit. Almost before my very eyes. What she told me, about life, connections and the universe, is still with me and speaks to me about mortality and eternity. Day by day, I'm taking it in.

For all this, we know nothing about what really happened to the infamous Gaelle Carrington-Keane. The day after her mother-of-all-disappearing-acts from the cave, Niall, Cam and I went around to 16 Eaton Square, but the place had already been boarded up and was on the market. She'd apparently organised the sale before her 'flight'. This didn't surprise me at all. She was tricky to the last. Nadine and Amanda, of course, were no help – all they'd say was that she had 'left the planet', as she'd said she was going to. And all I had to show for my time with her was a Polaroid, a box of VHS tapes, a sheet of paper on which I had written my primal question that afternoon around at her house, and the book on Miracle Meditation she had given me. Of course, I also have the locket with her lock of hair in it. I might get around to testing it for the fourteen-strand DNA she claimed it would reveal, but somehow physical proof doesn't seem so important now. 'Knowing' the truth – not 'believing' it – was Gaelle's passion, and I like to think that I don't need proof any more.

When Niall looked into the documents Gaelle had given him for safekeeping the night we drove to Tintagel, he found her Will and a note making him her legal proxy. Most of her money was to go to the Miracle Meditation Foundation in Goa, India. She also left Niall a tidy sum, which he's using to lease the Islington rooms where he does his stuff.

So, Gaelle disappeared and she hasn't come back yet.

Rufus checked out Eaton Square for us as recently as two weeks ago and new owners, a smart City couple, had moved in. No-one knew where all Gaelle's stuff went, not even Amanda and Nadine. She's got disappearing down to a fine art, that woman.

A few weeks after the night of the dramatic events at Tintagel we all moved out of Lavender Sweep. It just seemed the right time. Lu,

Cam and I came back here to Australia, Lu armed with her ever-present trust fund and me with an advance payment from Pigalle Press. It felt kind of funny to be paid for personal development and finding a great lover. But I'm not complaining. I miss the Premier League, proximity to Paris and M&S undies, but I don't miss the cold and grey, the daily crush of humanity and being a foreigner. And I relish the Aussie sun and skies and beaches and eating big fat prawns without fear of mercury poisoning, and meeting people with such outrageously broad Aussie accents that I think they're faking it for the tourists. That makes me laugh.

Out on the sundeck Cam's hanging in the hammock, waiting for me to finish up on the laptop, so we can go for a swim. He's found work helping out a local surfwear manufacturer with their five-year business plan. It's not Wall Street, but he doesn't have to wear a suit and the money he's earning more than keeps us rolling in wine and sunscreen. I love the feeling of waking up next to him in the morning, knowing he's there at the start of my day, and will be back at the end of it. The boy rocks my socks, even when he forgets to take out the rubbish/that butter needs refrigerating in the Australian summer/that sand in the bedsheets is scratchy. And what he's done with my aunt's vegetable garden is worthy of 'Burke's Backyard'. He's happy to stay in Oz for the foreseeable future, which suits me fine. Very fine. Without going overboard, I could say that there are moments when I'm ecstatically happy. Is that too girly? Sometimes I look at him and wonder if we really have been together for eons, like Gaelle said. I don't know. But I truly love being with him now. In this lifetime, as Gaelle would remind me to say.

ALSO AVAILABLE FROM PENGUIN BOOKS

SHOE MONEY
Maggie Alderson

Have you ever wondered why . . .
- Even the truly stylish find it hard to do smart casual?
- All men look like James Bond in dinner jackets?
- All four-year-old girls are obsessed with pink?
- Fashionable people always wear black?
- Blondes have less fun?
- Some people will spend $6,000 on a handbag?

This book will explain all of these mysteries and many more.

And even if you've never pondered any of these issues, Maggie Alderson will amuse and entertain you with her finely tuned observations about everything from global style icons to when to wear that perfect red dress – with the leopardskin shoes, of course.

Australia's wittiest fashion and lifestyle commentator delivers a delightful bundle of wicked charm.

VISIBLE PANTY LINE
Gretel Killeen

Should we bring back the Visible Panty Line (because wearing a g-string is sexual harassment)?

Are you allergic to your friends?

What is the difference between having a child and passing a camel through the eye of a needle?

Why will no man ever appreciate anything a woman achieves academically unless she does it in the nude?

Some people have an extraordinary way of viewing the ordinary. This book is a collection of wit, poignancy and silliness from one such person.

RALPH'S PARTY
Lisa Jewell

Meet the residents of 31 Almanac Road in a romantic, engrossing novel that takes you up the garden path, through the front door and into the most intimate parts of other people's lives.

Ralph and Smith are best friends. Until they fall for Jemima, their new flatmate. Jem knows one of them's the man for her – but which one?

Karl and Siobhan live in the flat above. Happily unmarried for fifteen years, it looks as if nothing can spoil their domestic idyll.

Except maybe Cheri, the femme fatale in the top flat. She's got her eye on Karl and she isn't about to let his fat girlfriend stand in the way . . .